Praise for Ber
"THE REIGNING
HISTORICAL
and Her Novels

"Bertrice Small creates cover-to-cover passion, a keen sense of history, and suspense." —*Publishers Weekly*

"Ms. Small delights and thrills." —*Rendezvous*

"An insatiable delight for the senses. [Small's] amazing historical detail . . . will captivate the reader . . . potent sensuality." —*Romance Junkies

"[Her novels] tell an intriguing story, they are rich in detail, and they are all so very hard to put down." —The Best Reviews

"Sweeps the ages with skill and finesse." —*Affaire de Coeur*

"[A] captivating blend of sensuality and rich historical drama." —Rosemary Rogers

"Small is why I read historical romance. It doesn't get any better than this!" —*Romantic Times* (top pick)

"Small's boldly sensual love story is certain to please her many devoted readers." —*Booklist*

"[A] delight to all readers of historical fiction." —Fresh Fiction

"[A] style that garnered her legions of fans. . . . When she's at the top of her form, nobody does it quite like Bertrice Small." —The Romance Reader

"Small never ceases to bring us an amazing story of love and happiness." —Night Owl Romance

BOOKS BY
BERTRICE SMALL

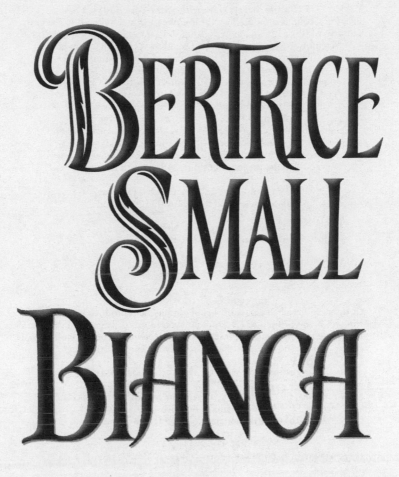

BERTRICE SMALL
BIANCA

The Silk Merchant's Daughters

 NEW AMERICAN LIBRARY

New American Library
Published by New American Library,
a division of Penguin Group (USA) Inc.,
375 Hudson Street, New York, New York 10014, USA
Penguin Group (Canada), 90 Eglinton Avenue East, Suite 700, Toronto,
Ontario M4P 2Y3, Canada (a division of Pearson Penguin Canada Inc.)
Penguin Books Ltd., 80 Strand, London WC2R 0RL, England
Penguin Ireland, 25 St. Stephen's Green, Dublin 2,
Ireland (a division of Penguin Books Ltd.)
Penguin Group (Australia), 250 Camberwell Road, Camberwell,
Victoria 3124, Australia (a division of Pearson Australia Group Pty. Ltd.)
Penguin Books India Pvt. Ltd., 11 Community Centre,
Panchsheel Park, New Delhi - 110 017, India
Penguin Group (NZ), 67 Apollo Drive, Rosedale, Auckland 0632,
New Zealand (a division of Pearson New Zealand Ltd.)
Penguin Books (South Africa) (Pty.) Ltd., 24 Sturdee Avenue,
Rosebank, Johannesburg 2196, South Africa

Penguin Books Ltd., Registered Offices:
80 Strand, London WC2R 0RL, England

First published by New American Library,
a division of Penguin Group (USA) Inc.

First Printing, October 2012
3 5 7 9 10 8 6 4 2

LIBRARY OF CONGRESS CATALOGING-IN-PUBLICATION DATA:
Small, Bertrice.
Bianca: the silk merchant's daughters/Bertrice Small.
p. cm.
ISBN 978-0-451-23795-8
1. Florence (Italy)—History—1421–1737—Fiction. I. Title.
PS3569.M28B53 2012
813'.54—dc23   2012021141

Set in Sabon
Designed by Spring Hoteling

Printed in the United States of America

PUBLISHER'S NOTE
This is a work of fiction. Names, characters, places, and incidents either are the prod-
uct of the author's imagination or are used fictitiously, and any resemblance to actual
persons, living or dead, business establishments, events, or locales is entirely coinci-
dental.
   The publisher does not have any control over and does not assume any responsibility
for author or third-party Web sites or their content.

BIANCA

Prologue

Florence, 1474

The beggar was an optimist but not a fool. He shrank deep into the shadows of the doorway as he heard the footsteps coming down the nearby alley. Two men, well muffled in dark cloaks, emerged from the narrow passage carrying a wrapped bundle between them. Making their way down a narrow flight of stone steps to the muddy shore, they put their burden into a small boat, climbed in, and rowed out into the middle of the river that ran through the city of Florence.

The night was very dark. The thin sliver of waning moon cast no light whatsoever. The fog was beginning to thicken as the wet mist touched everything. The beggar could not see the little boat and its inhabitants now, but he heard the distinct splash of something being dumped into the Arno. *A body, no doubt,* he thought, and he crossed himself. Then the small vessel became visible once more as it emerged from the water to be pulled back up onto the muddy shore. The two men got out and, making their way to what passed for a street again, disappeared into the darkened alley.

The beggar never moved as with unseeing eyes they passed by a second time without noticing him. He didn't even dare to breathe. He knew that if he was to see another day, no one must see him. The footsteps of the two men faded away. The beggar closed his eyes to doze, in relative safety for the moment.

Chapter 1

She was the fairest virgin in Florence. Or so it was said of Bianca Maria Rosa Pietro d'Angelo. High praise considering that red-gold or blond hair was considered the height of beauty, and Bianca had ebony tresses. She also had flawless features, an ivory complexion, a heart-shaped face, and eyes that were a startling shade of aquamarine blue. As she crossed the Piazza Santa Anna from her home with her mother more and more, gentlemen came to catch a glimpse of what they could of her features, which were carefully and modestly concealed by a bowed head and a light veiling. An audible sigh of regret arose as mother and daughter entered the church for morning Mass.

"They will be waiting when we come out," Bianca said to her mother.

"*Sempliciottos!* They are wasting their time," her parent replied. "I do not mean to waste my daughters on Florentine marriages. I was sacrificed by Venice to this dark city. I will not allow my girls to be. Only my love for your father has kept me here."

They found their way to the chairs set aside for their family and knelt in prayer on the embroidered red and gold kneelers. Mass began. They had music, which many smaller churches in the city did not—but Santa Anna Dolce was the family church of the Pietro d'Angelo family. It had been built by them a hundred years ago across from their large palazzo, which stood on the opposite side of the piazza. Upon its walls it had murals that depicted the life of Santa Anna, mother of the blessed Virgin. Besides the main altar, there were two other small altars. One to Santa Anna herself and the other to Santa Maria. The windows were stained glass. The floor, squares of black and white marble.

The Pietro d'Angelo wealth generously paid the livings of the three priests and the small choir that served it. The choir was a mixture of eunuchs and ungelded men with rich, deep voices. As long as they sang, they received a small stipend and were allowed to live in a dormitory attached to the church. The choir was a particularly excellent one, and much envied by its neighbors.

As their voices died, Orianna Pietro d'Angelo sighed softly with relief, Mass concluded. She had a busy day ahead of her and little patience for piety except where it benefited her. Father Bonamico was waiting for them at the door to the church. He was a chatty old man, and fond of the Pietro d'Angelo children. "Bianca's prospective suitors grow more each day," he noted, nodding approvingly. "Word of her beauty spreads."

"It is ridiculous," Orianna said irritably. "Have they nothing better to do than hang about like dogs after a young bitch? I must speak to Gio about seeing that the piazza is cleared when we cross to the church and back. Next they will be stomping and hooting at her. Her reputation will suffer then, though she be as innocent as a lamb."

"They have too much respect for your husband to do that," the priest responded.

"They are afraid of him, you mean," Orianna answered drily.

Father Bonamico chuckled. "Perhaps that too, gracious lady. Young men will be young men. The lady Bianca is quite lovely. You cannot blame them for looking."

A small smile touched the mother's lips. "Well," she allowed, "perhaps not." Then she gracefully descended the church steps, her daughter behind her. "Walk next to me, Bianca," Orianna instructed the girl as they reached the bottom of the stairs. She linked her arm with her daughter's, and the two moved back across the square together towards the palazzo. They had almost gained their destination when a young man sprang in front of them holding out a small beribboned nosegay to Bianca.

"For you, *madonna*!" he said eagerly, smiling, his brown eyes shining.

Bianca looked up, startled, but her mother slapped the flowers away.

"*Impudente! Buffone!*" she said, scolding him sternly. "Where are your manners? We have not been introduced, *but I know your mama*. She shall hear of this breach of etiquette on your part. She did not raise you to accost respectable maidens in the public square, or to offend their parents, as you have now done."

"Your pardon, *signora*, *madonna*," the young man said, bowing shamefacedly.

The two men who guarded the palazzo's main doors, finally remembering their duties, rushed forward and beat the young man away. He fled howling across the piazza while the others gathered and laughed at his retreat. Then they too began to disperse, hurrying after the daring one to learn what he had seen when Bianca briefly lifted her eyes to him.

"You should have come and escorted us from the church," Orianna told the two servingmen furiously. "You saw that crowd of ruffians leering at the lady Bianca. If you do not do better in the future, I shall tell your master that you are dilatory in your duties and have you both dismissed." She swept past, stopped, and then glared at them, waiting for the palazzo's main portal to be opened so she might enter her home.

Bianca gave the two men a sympathetic look and hurried after her mother.

"A sweet maid," one of the men said as he pulled the door closed behind his mistress and her daughter. "It will be a fortunate man who gains her to wife."

"And a rich one," the other man replied.

His companion shrugged, the motion conveying his thoughts as clearly as if he had spoken them. Of course the girl's bridegroom would be a wealthy man. Her father was a wealthy and important man. Master Pietro d'Angelo was not likely to give any of his four daughters in marriage to a man lacking in distinction. The one who had just passed by would surely be matched soon. She was just fourteen, the second-eldest of her parents' seven children. Her brother Marco had been born nine months to the day after their parents married. The lady Bianca had come thirteen months later, to be followed by

Georgio, Francesca, the twins, Luca and Luciana, and finally the little *bambina* Giulia, who would be four soon. The *signora* had produced no more children after that.

Like a good wife, the lady Orianna had given her husband seven healthy children. She was content with her privileged status as the wife of the man who ruled the Arte di Por Santa Maria, the city's silk merchants. Their guild was named for the street on which the city's many silk warehouses were located. The lady was aware, as all rich wives were, that her husband had a mistress he visited discreetly at a house he owned in a section near the river. It was the custom of important men to keep a mistress. One who did not was considered either parsimonious or less than a man. The master respected his wife publicly and, it was said, privately. He never flaunted his mistress, though her identity was known. He set an excellent example for his sons. Giovanni Pietro d'Angelo was a good master.

The servingman drew the great door closed once the women had hurried through. The city was becoming alive around them, although Piazza San Anna was a quiet enclave. The church and its musicians' dormitory took up a side and a half of the square. The family's palazzo took up another two sides. There was only one way both in and out of the piazza, which took up the remaining angle of the square. There was also a small park that was open to any whose behavior was respectable. The greensward had a beautiful white marble fountain with a naked marble naiad seated at its center. She was brushing her long hair. The water nymph was surrounded by fat, winged cupids, several of whom held porphyry vases from which water poured into the fountain. There were lime trees and terra-cotta pots of peach-colored roses that the family gardeners kept in bloom most of the year but for the winter months. There were three white marble benches for visitors to rest upon, and white crushed-marble paths for strolling.

From inside the palazzo, you could see the park only from the windows at the very top of the building, for the marble edifice had no windows on its lower floors. It was a Florentine belief that only a foolish man encouraged robbers by putting windows where someone could peer in from the outside and view your possessions, thus tempting theft. The Pietro d'Angelo palazzo was built around a large garden.

As in all families of wealth and importance, respectable adult women did not leave their homes except on rare occasions, such as attending Mass or going to their villas in the countryside outside of Florence. Privileged daughters might accompany their mothers to church, as Bianca did, but their only other foray outside of their father's homes would be when they were married or entered a convent. The garden served as a place for recreation and fresh air. It was there that Bianca now found her sister Francesca.

"Were there men again today waiting for you?" she eagerly asked. She was seated with her nursemaid, who was brushing her blond hair. Francesca's golden tresses were a source of great pride to her. They were washed weekly and rinsed with fresh-squeezed lemon juice and warm water. And she always dried her hair in the bright sunlight while her nursemaid slowly brushed the long locks so they might gain the full advantage of the sun.

"Yes," Bianca answered. "A larger crowd than before."

"I heard that one accosted you," Francesca said, her face turned to her sister's. "I don't know why our mother does not let me come to Mass with you."

"How do you learn such things and I am barely back in the house?" Bianca asked.

Francesca giggled. "Whenever they know you are returning from church, a bunch of the housemaids run to the top of the house and the windows overlooking the square to watch your passage back across the piazza. Ohh, I wish I could be with you. Did you keep your swain's bouquet? Let me see it!"

"I would not take any kind of gift from a stranger, or any man for that matter, but our father and brothers," Bianca replied primly. "Such a query tells me that you are far too young to be allowed out, Francesca. You have only just turned ten. I was not permitted to accompany our mother until I had celebrated my thirteenth birthday last year. Remember, you are the daughter of an important man of business from Florence and of a Venetian *principessa*, Francesca."

"Oh pooh," came the airy reply. "You have become so stuck-up of late. Well, you'll be gone soon enough, for our father is even now arranging a marriage for you. By summer you will be wed, and mistress of your own house. Then our mother will take me across the piazza to Mass with her."

"What do you mean our father negotiates a marriage for me? What have you heard, little *ficcanaso*?" She grasped a lock of her sister's hair and yanked it hard. "Tell me at once! Who is it? Do you know? Is he handsome? Has he come with his father to negotiate with our father? Speak, or I will snatch you bald!"

"Ouch!" Francesca protested, retrieving her hair from Bianca's grip. "I only overheard a little by chance. I was passing by our father's library yesterday when I heard voices coming from the chamber, and the doors were closed."

"You eavesdropped!"

"Of course I did," Francesca said. "How else would I learn anything that goes on in this house? I put my ear to the door and heard our papa say that our mama did not wish their daughters to marry within the Florentine community. That he agreed, and planned for our marriages to benefit the Pietro d'Angelo family to the maximum. Papa said he had all the influence he sought or needed in Florence.

"The man, his voice was hard, and he told Papa that a marriage to *him* would ensure the security of the Pietro d'Angelo family. He reminded our father that a debt was owed to him. It would be paid in full when his marriage to you was celebrated. Father asked that he request anything else of him but such a union. The man laughed. Oh, Bianca, I did not like his laugh. It was cruel." Francesca shivered with the memory.

"Madre di Dios," the older girl whispered almost to herself. Then she said, "What else, Francesca? What else did you hear?"

"Nothing. I heard someone coming. I didn't want anyone catching me. You know Papa would have whipped me for it. I didn't dare stay," was the regretful reply.

Bianca nodded. "I will speak with our mother," she told her sister.

"Ohh, please don't tell that I eavesdropped!" Francesca begged.

"I won't," Bianca promised. "I'll say I heard the servants gossiping. Mama will tell me if any such arrangements for my future have been made. She will know."

"I don't want you to marry and leave us," the younger girl admitted. "I didn't mean it when I said I'd be glad to have you gone."

"I know that, little *ficcanaso*," Bianca assured her sibling with a small smile. Then she went off to find their mother and learn the truth of what her sister had heard.

"Your mother is closeted with the master," Fabia, her mother's servingwoman, told Bianca. Then she lowered her voice to speak in a more confidential tone. "It is something serious, for I heard your mother raising her voice, which is most unlike her."

"I have heard rumors regarding a marriage for me," Bianca said softly.

Suddenly the door to her mother's privy chamber was flung open, and her father, his face dark with anger, strode out and past them, exiting Lady Orianna's apartments.

"I will never forgive you for this, Gio!" her mother shouted after him. *"Never!"* Then, seeing Bianca, she burst into tears, turned, and slammed the door shut behind her.

"I must go to her," Fabia said.

Bianca nodded, and left her mother's rooms. Her mother had shouted. Orianna never shouted. And she had looked positively distraught. Orianna Rafacla Maria Theresa Venier, a *principessa* of the great Venetian Republic, never raised her voice, never allowed her emotions to show, and yet she had done both within hearing of not only her eldest daughter but a servant as well. Whatever was happening was not a good thing.

Francesca awaited Bianca in her elder sister's bedchamber. "What did you learn?" she demanded.

Bianca told her of the scene that she and Fabia had just witnessed.

Francesca's blue-green eyes grew round. "Our mother never shouts like some common fishwife," she said. "And to tell our father she would never forgive him . . . what has he done to incur such wrath from her?"

"I do not know," Bianca said, "but I suspect if we are to learn, it will be sooner than later." A rap sounded on the closed bedchamber door. "Come!" Bianca called out.

The door opened to reveal their eldest brother, Marco. He stepped quickly into the room, closing the door behind him. "This is all my fault," he said, taking her two hands in his own. "I must beg your forgiveness, Bianca." He looked genuinely shamefaced and sorrowful at the same time.

Both of his sisters looked totally confused.

Finally Bianca said, "Why must you ask for my pardon, Marco? You have done nothing of which I am aware that would require it."

"Sit down," Marco invited. "Not you, Francesca. You must leave. What I have to say is for Bianca's ears only, not yours, *bambina*. Go now." He pointed to the door.

"I am not a baby. Giulia is the baby. I am ten going on eleven, Marco."

He smiled, and gently tugged on the thick golden braid into which her hair was now fashioned. "Don't listen at the door," he cautioned her with a mischievous grin.

"Oh! You!" Francesca huffed as she left the bedchamber.

Marco watched her go down the wide corridor and around the corner. She turned to stick her tongue out at him before she disappeared, which caused him to chuckle as he turned back to Bianca and shut the door to the room firmly. "Come," he said, taking her arm by the elbow. "By the window, where the little *ficcanaso* can't hear us when she sneaks back to listen, which she will." His face grew serious once again. He looked like a younger version of their father, with curly black hair and bright blue eyes.

Bianca smiled, amused. "Yes, she will." They moved to the window, and Bianca said, "What disturbs you, Marco?"

"My actions have put your future in jeopardy, I fear." Then he began to explain in low, measured tones. "I apologize for what I must tell you, for I know how sheltered you are, and a virgin of good family should not hear things like this, but I have no choice, Bianca. Several months ago my friend Stefano Rovere and I were visiting a certain lady known for her amorous skills, who willingly shares them with young men just beginning to explore such masculine delights," Marco explained. He actually blushed as he spoke, for he was fifteen and did not discuss such things with respectable women.

"You visited a courtesan," Bianca remarked calmly. "Our mother has mentioned such women to me. She and I pray for them. It is not an easy life, I am told."

"The woman died as Stefano vigorously rode her," Marco said bluntly, for he could not think of any way to put it more delicately.

"*Madre di Dios!*" Bianca exclaimed, crossing herself.

"It was then that Stefano and I did a foolish thing," Marco continued. "The woman's house was empty of servants the night we visited. I wanted to call the authorities and report the woman's death, but Stefano did not wish to do it. He feared the scandal, should we be accused of killing her. He feared his father's anger over such a disgraceful situation, that his father should be forced to pay a bribe to keep the watch silent. He feared that someone connected with the woman would know it was Stefano Rovere, son of Florence's most famed lawyer, and Marco Pietro d'Angelo, son of the head of the Arte di Por Santa Maria who had been the last to be with this courtesan."

"What *did* you do?" Bianca asked almost fearfully.

"We wrapped her naked body in a Turkish carpet, weighed it with several heavy stones, bound it, and then carried it to the river," Marco said. "We rowed the body into the center of the Arno near the Ponte Vecchio and dumped it into the water. The stones assured that it sank to the bottom."

"God have mercy on the poor woman's soul," Bianca murmured. She was pale with shock over her brother's confession. "But why should this unfortunate courtesan's death affect what will happen to me, Brother?"

"My tale is not yet completed," he responded. Then he continued. "Stefano then decided we should go to his father and tell him what had happened. He said his father was always accusing him of being an idiot. He wanted to show his father that he had been able to extricate himself from a nasty situation without his help. I did not think it wise. I thought, having disposed of the body, we should keep silent. No one would have known, as there were no witnesses to the deed."

"And was Master Rovere pleased with Stefano?" Bianca asked quietly. How did a father react to a son who had just disposed of the dead body of a courtesan in secret?

"Stefano's father is a hard man. He listened. Then he hit his son a blow that bloodied his nose and sent him to his knees. Master Rovere went on to explain in that cold, calm voice of his that the sudden disappearance of such a woman of certain reputation as well known as this one was would surely be questioned. He explained that it would now be necessary to fabricate a story to cover up what had happened, and protect our reputations. Then he sent me to fetch our father, Bianca.

"When Father came I stood and listened as Master Rovere explained to him what had happened with us earlier; that he had already sent his people to see that the house showed no signs of any sort of a disturbance. Several of the woman's gowns and other clothing, along with her jewelry box, were removed so that it appeared that she had gone on a sudden journey. When the courtesan's servants, such as they were, arrived in the morning, one of Master Rovere's own servants would be waiting to explain to them that their mistress had been called away suddenly and did not know when she would return. Her affairs in Florence were now in the hands of her lawyer. The servants would be paid off generously and the house shut up. Thus would the scandal be avoided.

"Our father thanked Master Rovere, who smiled at him and said that Father would now owe him a debt that must be repaid whenever Master Rovere required it of him. Father agreed, saying that the Pietro d'Angelo family always paid their debts, and returned a favor twofold. Whatever was required to eventually cancel out the debt would be done." Marco then grew silent, looking with pained eyes at his beautiful sister.

And then she knew. Bianca Pietro d'Angelo might be sheltered, but she was not unintelligent. "I am the payment Master Rovere has required of our father," she said quietly. "He is a widower and seeks another wife."

"I should rather see you in a cloistered convent, or even dead, than married to that man!" Marco burst out bitterly. "This is all my fault!"

Bianca was silent for several long minutes. Finally she spoke. "Papa has agreed? Of course he would have agreed, for our mother told him she would never forgive him. Why did he agree, Marco? Would Master Rovere take nothing else in payment? And several months after the fact, would the scandal be so great? His son was involved as well. After all, you did not kill the woman. She simply died while entertaining a pair of young men. Yes, it was wrong to dispose of her body in such a fashion, but you and Stefano are guilty of nothing more than being fools."

"Father offered him money, even a ten percent share of his warehouses, anything else, but Master Rovere was adamant. He will have you as his wife. Nothing else will satisfy the debt Father owes him. It has now become a matter of honor for our parent, Bianca," Marco explained to his sister. "Our father cannot be seen to eschew the debt simply because he now finds he does not like the payment asked of him. After all, he agreed to pay whatever the price, and did not question the cost at the time."

"Yes, I understand," his sister replied. "Has a date been set for my marriage?"

"Papa and Mama will tell you of your fate tonight. I don't know what they have decided. If I know our mother, she will attempt to delay the inevitable as long as she can."

"Yes," Bianca agreed, "she will."

"I had to tell you, Bianca," her older sibling said. "I know Papa will not tell you why you are to marry this man. It is too shameful that you must be sacrificed for my sins. I did not want it to come as a complete shock to you. You should have a French duke or a princeling of Venice for your husband, not this man! His reputation is vile, for all his skills in the courts."

Bianca was frightened and heartsore by what Marco had told her, but he was her beloved brother. She was closer to him by virtue of the thirteen months that separated them in birth order than to any of the others. She would do whatever her family requested of her to protect him, to protect their good name. "It will be all right, Marco," she assured him. "I must marry eventually, and I am of an age to do so now. Our mother has raised me to be a good wife and chatelaine. I will have children to comfort me, and he, like all wealthy and important men, will have a mistress to entertain him. When the novelty of having a young wife has worn off, he will leave me in peace. Yes, I had hoped to wed out of Florence, but if it is not to be, then it is not. There is no use weeping over what cannot be changed." She patted his velvet-clad arm. "Leave me to absorb this so I am able to behave with some decorum when our father speaks to me. I do not want our parents to be ashamed of their eldest daughter when I am informed of my fate. Nor do I wish to cause a further breach between them. Rather, by accepting what I must with obedience, I pray I will heal that chasm that has opened to separate them."

He nodded and kissing her on the forehead, left her bedchamber. In the corridor outside he found, as he had anticipated, Francesca lurking and eager to know what had transpired between her elders. "Nay, *ficcanaso*, you may not go in and badger Bianca. What we have spoken about will remain between us. She is resting now."

"Marco!" Francesca gave him her prettiest pout and a little smile.

"No," he said, taking her by the arm. "One of the house cats has just birthed a new litter of kittens," he said, cleverly distracting her. "I'm surprised you didn't know about it. It's the red, white, and black one we call Tre. Let's go and see what she has spawned."

"Aren't you too sophisticated to look at litters of kittens?" Francesca demanded.

"Not when it's with my little sister," Marco replied, taking her around the corner and off to the kitchens, where the cat was certain to be found. The cook loved cats, for they kept the rodent population down and her stores in the storeroom safe.

Bianca had heard Francesca's voice outside her chamber. She was grateful that Marco kept the younger girl from the room. She wanted to be alone to consider what was about to happen to her life. She had met Stefano Rovere several times, for he was Marco's best friend and was often invited to eat at their table. He was a serious boy. It would not be so bad if she were betrothed to him. At least he was young. But to marry his father? Bianca shuddered. And there was a younger brother. Could she tell her parents that she had heard a sudden calling from God and wanted to become a nun? It was doubtful they would believe her, even if she insisted it was true.

The morning ended and the afternoon passed slowly until it was time for the main meal of the day. Her parents were unusually quiet during the meal, although the younger children were so lively it was not likely that anyone noticed. The family and their servants crowded about the table in the *sala da pranzo* eating the pasta and meats the cook had prepared for them. There was a large bowl filled with grapes and oranges. Neither Bianca nor Marco could eat a great deal, something their mother noted to herself. Francesca had told Orianna that the two had been closeted for a brief time in late morning.

"Bianca." Their father spoke.

"How may I serve you, *signore*?" the girl replied.

"You will leave the table and go to my library. Your

mother and I would speak with you shortly," Giovanni Pietro d'Angelo said. Then he picked up his silver goblet and drank deeply. That he looked troubled was not reassuring.

"At once, *signore*," Bianca responded. She did not look at any of them about the table but rose and hurried from the room. Entering the library, she stood awaiting the arrival of her parents. They did not keep her long.

Her parents seated themselves in two high-backed chairs and beckoned Bianca to stand before them. Her father's face was serious and pained. Her mother looked as if she had been crying. There were actual tears in her eyes now.

"You are to be married," her father began. "Your bridegroom is a man of both wealth and importance here in Florence. You are a most fortunate girl, Bianca, to have attracted such a husband."

"May I know the name of this illustrious gentleman, *signore*?" Bianca asked in a quietly measured voice. She was amazed by her tone, for her legs were slightly shaking.

"He is Sebastiano Rovere, Stefano's sire," her father replied.

"Stefano is only older by several months than my brother Marco," Bianca heard herself saying. She had no choice in this matter, but suddenly she was angry at her father for not fighting harder to protect her; for the bitter and hopeless tears her mother had shed this day, and would continue to shed. "You are giving me in marriage to a man old enough to be my father? How could you, Papa? How could you?" She hadn't meant to lose her temper, but the situation facing her was intolerable.

"A young wife needs the firm hand of an older husband,"

her father answered sharply. Her words had stung him. "You must learn to curb your temper, Bianca."

"I am told this man's reputation is less than respectable," Bianca persisted. Did the gossips not hint that he had murdered his first two wives?

"Who has told you such things?" her father demanded angrily. "It is not your place, daughter, to speak disparagingly of a man you have not yet met. Sebastiano Rovere is the most skilled attorney in all of Florence. He is respected and he is rich. No maiden of good family could ask for more than that."

"The servants will gossip," Bianca responded pertly. "They say that while he is rich and clever at his craft, he is wicked and godless. And this is the man you have chosen for me, Papa? Have I been so wretched a daughter then that you are willing and eager to entertain the first offer for my hand that is brought to you?"

"You should not be listening to the idle chatter of menials," her father responded through gritted teeth. In his mind, she was correct, but it was not her place to criticize him. She did not know of the circumstances that had brought about this catastrophe. He had no other choice. Marco was his heir, and his reputation for honesty would surely suffer if the truth came out about that night. It was the sort of thing that was never forgotten, and it would reflect on the family's silk business. It could not be permitted to happen.

"Why must I marry this old man?" Bianca asked him. "Could you not have found me a younger husband? A noble husband?"

"How dare you question my decision, daughter? You have never before done so," her father replied, defending himself.

She was his daughter. It was her duty to obey his every wish whether she approved of it or not. "I have never before beaten you, but I will, Bianca, should you defy me in this matter. It is not your place to say whether you will or you won't wed the gentleman I have chosen for you. I have accepted Sebastiano Rovere's proposal of marriage in your name, and you will wed him as soon as the date is fixed. That is the end of the matter. Now there is another matter that must be settled. Your *fidanzato* has heard of the spectacle you have been causing in the piazza when you go to Mass with your mother each morning. He does not wish his future wife to be the center of such foolishness. You will again join your younger siblings when Father Aldo says Mass in the house chapel every day."

"But I am not responsible for the behavior of those young men," Bianca protested. "I like going to Mass with my mother. I like Father Bonamico."

"Your reputation must be preserved, Bianca. Sebastiano Rovere is the most sought-after and respected lawyer in all of Tuscany. His bride cannot be said to be anything less than pure and untouched. She cannot be like a common woman of the streets, whistled at and shouted after by strangers. The matter is settled."

Bianca opened her mouth to challenge her father again, but Orianna finally spoke.

"It is little enough to ask, Bianca," she said in her quiet voice. "Father Bonamico will come to the palazzo to hear your confession each week. You should find it flattering that your *fidanzato* is already jealous of you."

Bianca pressed her lips together and bowed her head in submission. "Yes, *Madre*," she said. "I hope I will have the time I feel I need to grow used to this marriage that you have planned for me."

"Of course, *cara mia*," her mother reassured her quietly. "It will not, cannot, be for several months at least. Your trousseau and your bridal gown must be made. This is not something that can be easily or properly done if it is done too quickly. Do not think about it, *cara*. Now run along and share this exciting news with your sisters and brothers."

Bianca curtsied to her parents and, turning, hurried from the library. She did not find the announcement that she was to marry exciting. She was horrified that her father could not have found another way to satisfy his debt to Sebastiano Rovere. How old was the man? Stefano was at least seventeen, and there was another, younger brother who might be the same age as her second brother, Georgio.

She shuddered. It was disgusting that an old man should want a young wife. She was hardly pleased that his hold over her had already been put in place, and she was now forbidden to cross the piazza with her mother so she might attend Mass. How dare this old man impugn her honor? Did he think she would encourage the men who waited to catch a glimpse of her? It was unbearable!

Entering the rooms she shared with her younger sisters, she found Francesca waiting for her. "Well, is it marriage?" the young girl wanted to know.

"Yes. To Stefano Rovere's father," Bianca said with a shudder.

"He is an old man!" Francesca exclaimed. "Why would Papa allow it? I did not think any of us would wed in Florence. Mama has never wanted it."

"I have no idea why this match has been made," Bianca

lied to her younger sibling. There was no need for the curious Francesca to learn of Marco's error in judgment that had led to this disaster for her. "However, I cannot disobey Papa, as much as I would like to do so. I do not go to this marriage joyous."

"Well, perhaps since he is so old he will die soon. Then you'll be a rich widow free to do as you wish. You can take a lover who will please you," Francesca said practically and sanguinely with typical ten-year-old logic. She tossed her blond hair. "I will marry a prince one day."

Bianca did not reprimand the girl for the thought. It actually gave her hope. But she did say, "You will wed whom Papa chooses, but I hope for your sake he is a prince."

"When's the wedding?" Francesca wanted to know. "I will need a beautiful new gown for it. Not as lovely as yours, of course, for it will be your day, but nonetheless I would show at my very best. Who knows who will see me."

"The date has not been set yet. I think our mother will protect me as long as she can," Bianca replied. "She made some remark about trousseau and gowns."

"Our mother is very clever," Francesca observed. "There are several proprieties that must be met. You will have to formally meet him. That must be done privately. Perhaps he will come and escort you to Mass one morning before the official proclamation. Your marriage to this man must then be announced with the proper ceremony, for both families are distinguished and you do not want unsavory gossip circulating regarding your association with him." Francesca was much like their mother in that she studied all the social customs associated with their world. "That should take at least a couple of months, perhaps even a year," the young girl said hopefully.

"Perhaps," Bianca replied, not telling her sister that she had been forbidden to go into public any longer. *Santa Anna!* If she could delay this union long enough, perhaps he would lose interest in her. Still, if Sebastiano Rovere did escort her across the piazza and people were made aware that she was his affianced, the crowd of eager young men might disperse for good. Then she would not be cloistered until she wed, after which she would be cloistered anyway. She would suggest it to her mother, who she knew enjoyed her company in church.

Orianna came, as was her custom, to bid her daughters good night. Having done so, she took Bianca aside in the girl's own bedchamber to speak with her. "Your poise in accepting your father's decision was pleasing to me at first. I am happy to know you can behave wisely. However, you should not have fought with him. He does not want this marriage any more than you or I do, but he has no choice in the matter."

"Marco has told me of the reasons for this marriage," Bianca said candidly. "Had he not, I should have collapsed with my fears. Is there no other way for my father to repay this debt to Master Rovere? Why is he so determined to have me for his next wife?"

"Your father has made every attempt to do so, as you already know," Orianna responded. "Rovere will have nothing less than you for his bride in order to settle the debt. I do not know if he has ever even seen you, Bianca. I believe he wants a blood tie in order to protect his own son, for if Marco were to go to the authorities first, it would be difficult to save Stefano from some punishment and would thereby tarnish Sebastiano Rovere's reputation. He is a powerful man, but when a man is that powerful he attracts enemies both openly and secretly. They will always be seeking for a way to bring him down. But a marriage between our houses gives him the security of blood between us. And, too, your reputation declares you to be young, fresh, virtuous, and very beautiful. An older man with a beautiful young wife is much envied. Rovere likes to be admired and envied by others. Having you for a wife will be a coup for him."

"I know he is old, but how old?" Bianca asked her mother, thinking as she spoke that without her brother's foolishness she would not be in this position.

"Your father tells me he has thirty-six years to his life so far," Orianna answered.

"Madre di Dios!" Bianca half whispered. "He is twenty-two years my senior!"

"Your father is older than I am," Orianna reminded her eldest daughter. "An older husband is not such a bad thing, my daughter."

"Papa had at least seen you. He told me he first saw you in a gondola with Grandfather passing him by on the Grand Canal. Although his suit was accepted by your family, despite the fact he was a foreigner to them, he was expected to court you, and you had the time to come to know him. When you wed you were familiar with the man you were marrying," Bianca pointed out.

"Sebastiano Rovere will come to meet you, Bianca. It will be several months before I allow this marriage to be celebrated," Orianna said. "Trust me to protect you, for I will not allow anyone to force this marriage any sooner than I must. But your father is frightened of this man, and I will not be able to hold him off forever."

"I understand, *Madre*," Bianca replied. "And you may trust me to do what I must to protect our family. However, I wonder if Signore Rovere were to escort us across the piazza to Mass once or twice, the young men who come to see me would understand the significance of his presence and depart, never to return. I must tell you that I am offended that my own honor would be questioned by a man who does not know me."

"A clever argument, Bianca," her mother said approvingly, "but first I shall attempt to convince Signore Rovere to change his mind by telling him it comforts me to have my eldest daughter by my side at Mass. If he forbids you, then he takes something away from me. We will see what that argument brings us. Certainly he would not deny a mother her daughter's company, especially as you will soon be gone from this house. It would not be wise, however, to reveal to him that you are a clever girl. He would be stricter with you then if he knew it."

Bianca smiled and bowed her head slightly in appreciation. "Thank you, *Madre*."

Orianna smiled back at her daughter. She was not happy about this union her eldest daughter was being forced to make. But she would keep Bianca from Sebastiano Rovere as long as she possibly could do so. She intended to see that every obscure custom was celebrated with regard to this coming marriage. And when her husband and Rovere complained, she would weep and sob that it was her eldest daughter being taken from her. The first of her children to get married. Would they spoil all her joy in such an occasion?

And, of course, a dressmaker must be brought from her own home in Venice to design and sew the trousseau that was to be made for Bianca. Venetian fashions were the finest, and she would sigh regrettably, more elegant and original than those in Florence. Of course, when word of that got out, there would be an uproar, but Orianna would hold firm. Her eldest daughter's wedding gown and trousseau must be designed and sewn by the Venetians who would come to do so.

Orianna smiled to herself. Oh yes, she could delay the inevitable for at least a few months' time. If only she didn't have to do so. If only Bianca could have a fine young man from Venice or a French duke for a husband instead of the most debauched man in all of Florence. She cursed her oldest son softly beneath her breath and then quickly took it back. Men could not help being the fools they were.

Chapter 2

The Moorish slave girl moaned as the thick leather strap descended upon her bared buttocks for a twentieth time. She silently and carefully counted the strokes her master laid upon her plump golden flesh. Two more and she would shriek piteously. Another and she would call for mercy. Usually he hit her twice more before he released her to fall to her hands and knees, buttocks raised. It was a routine she followed with him, and he never realized at all that it was she who controlled the situation.

After beating her twenty-five strokes he would mount her and relieve the lust that mistreating her had roused in him. Afterwards she would praise his prowess and beg him for more, curling into his lap as he fondled and squeezed her breasts. Sometimes he could comply, but more often he could not. He was a man who needed to inflict pain in order to perform as a normal man might. Now it was said he was taking a new bride. The Moorish slave girl felt pity for the poor girl, whoever she was. She shrieked. Another blow followed. "Please, master," she begged him. "I can bear no more!"

"You can, and you will, my barbaric little bitch," he growled at her. Two more blows followed. "Now on your knees, and service me!"

The Moorish slave girl fell upon her hands and knees. Her bottom was burning from the beating he had inflicted on her with his leather strap. She elevated her buttocks and waited for him to plunge himself into her. He did not disappoint, for once aroused he was a most satisfactory lover. The thick, lengthy peg of hot, smooth flesh probed deeply, and she enjoyed a surge of pleasure before remembering her duties. "Oh yes, master!" she cried to him. "Your weapon is mighty, mightier than any I have known before you. Do not send me away when you take your new bride. I live but to pleasure you, my lord!" She squeezed him with the well-trained muscles of her sheath.

His fingers dug into her scalp, and grasping a handful of her long hair he yanked her head back, demanding, "Who told you I was to wed, bitch?"

"The household is filled with gossip, my lord. If I spoke out of turn I beg your forgiveness," the Moorish slave girl whimpered.

Releasing his hold on her hair, his two hands gripped her hips. "I have no intention of sending you away, Nudara," he assured her. "You will soon have other duties, my pet. You will teach the little virgin I am marrying how to please me." Sebastiano Rovere laughed darkly. Then he concentrated on pleasuring himself with his slave girl, fucking her hard and deep until his lust exploded in an unusually fierce burst of excess that left him—as well as a surprised Nudara—extremely satisfied.

Afterwards, as the slave curled herself into her master's lap, Nudara spoke daringly. "It is said she is the most beautiful girl in all of Florence, my lord. Is she?"

"I have no idea," he responded. "I have never laid eyes on the wench. I want, I need, a blood tie with her family. Marriage is the most powerful bond I can make. The girl is ready for marriage. She has begun to walk out with her mother, and in the process has attracted a number of admirers. Before one of them soils her, I will have her."

"A virgin of unimpeachable lineage will be worthy of you, my lord," Nudara said.

"Aye, she will," he responded.

Nudara began to caress him, her skillful fingers slipping beneath his robe to stroke him. "Take me again, my lord. Think of the girl's beautiful, silken, smooth, ivory flesh beneath your hands; her hitherto untouched breasts, their little nipples puckering with your kisses; her plump thighs opening for you, and you alone," the slave girl purred in her master's ear. Then she licked it, blew softly, and feeling his new arousal beneath her buttocks, she quickly mounted him, her back to him, drawing his hands around to her large, full breasts.

He grasped them, half panting, half moaning in her ear as he began once more to piston her. The images she had raised in his mind with her words had surprisingly aroused him. Was it possible that a new young wife would restore his vigor? Untouched flesh. He licked his lips as he strongly fucked Nudara. The Pietro d'Angelos would have kept the girl pure. He would be the first man to touch her. He would be the only man to touch her. She would be fearful that first night, and he

31

would see she was. The thought of her fear was, in itself, arousing. He fucked Nudara harder, enjoying her moan of surprise at his renewed potency. He suddenly felt as if he could go on like this with her all night.

But of course he couldn't. He was expected shortly at the silk merchant's house to be formally introduced to his bride-to-be. He would want to bathe before he went, and dress in his finest robe so that the little virgin would be truly impressed by his magnificence. Let her begin to understand the honor being done to her, to her family. While the blood tie was a matter of safety for him, it was a great honor for the silk merchant and his kinsman to be allied with the Rovere family.

Releasing his lust a second time, he pushed Nudara from his lap. "Enough, you greedy little bitch," he grumbled at her. "I will be too weak to go to my appointment."

Turning, she smiled at him. "I have pleased you today, my lord, and I am glad."

He said nothing more to her but shouted for his body servant, Guido, to attend him. The man came quickly, not wanting to cause his master's good mood to fade.

"Your bath is ready, my lord," he said leading the way to the special chamber that was set aside for bathing in the Roveres' palazzo. Not all houses, not even those of wealthy and important men, had such places set aside for just washing. It was much like a Turk's home, but Sebastiano Rovere was a meticulous man in all his habits.

"What do you propose I wear to meet my *fidanzata* for the first time, Guido?" he asked his servant as the man took the garment he had been wearing and handed it to another servant for disposal.

"I would suggest that new, rich brown velvet robe you

recently ordered," Guido said. "It is trimmed with gold on the sleeves and neckline. The sleeves are also trimmed, as is the hem of the robe, in a pale, gold-brown fur. It is both elegant and impressive, master. An innocent maiden would be dazzled by a man who came before her thus garbed. Actually, any woman would be."

"Yesss," Sebastiano Rovere murmured slowly in reply, picturing the garment and then seeing himself in it. "An excellent suggestion, Guido. Go and get it out while I am bathed. It will also do honor to her family if I am so grandly dressed, which should please the silk merchant and his wife. I am told she is the daughter of Venetian nobility."

"So it is said, master," Guido agreed. Then bowing, he hurried off to prepare his master's garments for this evening's visit.

Sebastiano Rovere gave himself over to the ministrations of the servants whose duty it was to bathe him. His vanity assured they were female, three Greek slave girls who always admired his male form and made complimentary remarks about his body. He knew that, despite his thirty-six years, he was in excellent physical shape, for he was usually careful in his diet, unlike most Florentine men, and he exercised, working with his fencing master several times a week.

His new wife would have no complaints about marrying a paunchy old man. And if she were like most gently raised females, she would have been taught that fucking had but one purpose. Procreation. Since he wanted no more children, he would leave her mostly in peace after their wedding night. He had Nudara to serve his darker needs. And he had a beautiful and very expensive mistress who was paid lavishly to take no other lovers while she was under his protection. He was envied for his mistress, which pleased Sebastiano Rovere quite well. Now he would possess the most beautiful girl in all of Florence, and would be doubly envied.

Having Bianca Pietro d'Angelo for his wife would add to his status as an important man. Her father was head of his guild, and as such served in the government from time to time, like all important men. But Sebastiano Rovere wanted one day to attain the elected position of chancellor. Rovere might not know it yet, but Giovanni Pietro d'Angelo was going to help him gain that post eventually.

The slaves bathed him, washing his hair as well. They massaged his body with sandalwood oil. He left the bath, but not before pinching the buttocks and nipples of the slave girls, who giggled and made lascivious gestures at him, which caused him to laugh. His mood was buoyed even further when he saw himself in the fine new robe in which Guido dressed him. He was a handsome man, he had to admit to himself.

And even as Sebastiano Rovere prepared to meet Bianca Pietro d'Angelo, the girl was being dressed in a new gown of the finest rose-colored silk. The fabric molded itself to the line of her graceful young body before blossoming into a full skirt. The neckline was low-cut and square. The sleeves were full. The bodice of the gown was decorated with silver embroidery, and the sleeves edged in delicate silver lace. Her long dark hair was left loose but held back by a rose-and-silver-striped ribbon. Pale pink pearls set in silver hung from her ears. About her neck was a dainty rope of pink pearls from which hung a silver and gold crucifix.

"I've never had such a gown," Bianca marveled.

"The color suits you," Francesca said ruefully. "It wouldn't suit me at all."

"You are many years away from such a gown as this," their mother said. "Do not be in such a hurry to grow up, my daughter."

"But if I can grow up quickly," Francesca said, "I can marry that Venetian prince you were considering for Bianca before Signore Rovere asked for my sister. Our grandfather must be very disappointed to have that match stolen from beneath his very aristocratic nose."

Orianna sighed. "You are too outspoken, Francesca," she scolded. "And you must stop listening at doors. Do not deny it, for we both know it is the truth."

"But nobody ever tells me anything," Francesca complained.

"Much of what you learn is not your business, which is why you are not told," her mother replied sternly. Then Orianna turned back to Bianca. "I will call for you when it is time for us to introduce you to Signore Rovere. He is certain to want a bit of time alone with you. Say as little as possible to him, and be modest."

"Would he decide to change his mind if I forgot my manners, *Madre*? If that be the case then I shall do what I must to discourage him," Bianca replied.

"Regretfully, it will not change his mind, for he is determined to have the most beautiful maiden in Florence as his wife," her mother said. "Signore Rovere is a collector of fine and rare things, my daughter. You are one such thing, and as it is within his grasp to have you, he will."

Bianca shuddered and Orianna put a hand on her shoulder to reassure her.

A servant came to tell the mistress of the house that their guest was even now coming through the little park towards the palazzo door. Kissing Bianca upon the top of her dark head, Orianna hurried off to join her husband. Together they greeted Sebastiano Rovere, ushering him into their palazzo.

"You honor our house," the silk merchant said, welcoming their guest and bowing.

"'Tis I who am honored," Sebastiano Rovere replied, bowing in return.

"Allow me to present my wife, Orianna Venier, to you, *signore*."

Sebastiano Rovere bowed over Orianna's elegant little hand, kissing it. *"Signora,"* he murmured. "The legend of your beauty does not do you justice."

"I am flattered by your gracious words," Orianna answered him, wanting to yank her hand away from him, but with supreme self-control allowing him the time to release it.

"We will have wine in the gardens," Giovanni Pietro d'Angelo said.

"A charming idea," their guest agreed. "And I will be allowed at long last to meet your daughter, the lady Bianca, soon?"

"Of course," the silk merchant replied as he led them outside.

It was early evening and the sun had not yet set. They sat together upon two marble benches amid the greenery. A well-trained servant brought silver goblets of sweet wine for them. Sebastiano Rovere noted the goblets were decorated with small stones of black onyx amid pale gold scrollwork. They were exquisite, and for a brief moment he was jealous, for he did not believe he possessed any goblets as fine.

"Is the wine to your taste, Signore Rovere?" the silk merchant inquired politely.

"It is delicious," was the reply. "Will you not ask your

daughter to come and share it with us?" Rovere pressed Giovanni Pietro d'Angelo.

Orianna raised her hand, and a servant was immediately at her side. "Tell Fabia to fetch the lady Bianca to us," she said in her beautifully modulated voice. Then she turned to their guest. "It will be but a few moments, *signore*, but before my child joins us I have a boon to ask of you."

Sebastiano Rovere was surprised, but he was feeling extremely pleased with himself at this moment. "Please, *signora*, you have but to ask."

"You have requested that Bianca no longer attend Mass at Santa Anna Dolce with me. Please, *signore*, I beg that you rescind that order. I understand your concerns, and I share them with you. But soon Bianca will be gone from my side. I have gained such great pleasure these past months worshiping in my daughter's company. Perhaps if you would escort us to the church yourself several times, your august presence would discourage any bad behavior, along with the knowledge of your betrothal." Orianna reached out and put an elegant, beringed hand on his velvet-clad arm. "Please, *signore*, do not refuse a mother's plea." She gave him a small smile, astounded by the cold eyes that looked back at her.

He considered her words. It was hardly a request he could refuse without appearing mean-spirited. He forced a smile. "If it means so much to you, *signora*, then of course I will grant your boon." Then catching a movement out of the corner of his eye, he turned his head. His breath caught in his throat at the sight of the girl in her rose-pink gown. He came to his feet, pleased to see he towered over her. He felt his cock twitch beneath his elegant robe, pressing almost painfully against the fabric of his trunk hose.

"Thank you, *signore*," Orianna said, almost cringing at the lust that touched his face when he saw Bianca, though it disappeared as quickly as it had come.

"Come forward, Bianca," her father said, beckoning her.

She had gotten a quick look at him before he had seen her. He was a handsome man, Bianca thought. Perhaps it would not be so bad after all, even if he was twice her age. She glided forward, eyes lowered, her ebony lashes brushing her ivory cheekbones.

She curtsied perfectly without so much as a wobble.

Beauty and grace, Sebastiano Rovere thought, well pleased. For once the gossips had not lied. If truth be told, they had not praised her highly enough.

"Signore Rovere, may I present to you my eldest daughter, Bianca. If having seen her now she continues to please you, then she is yours to wife," Giovanni Pietro d'Angelo said, almost choking on the words as he said them. How could he do this? And yet if he did not, his eldest son—their family— would be ruined by this vile, powerful man.

"I am overwhelmed by the exquisite beauty and purity I see in your daughter's face. Her presence as my wife will bring great honor to my house, and I will gladly have her to wife," Sebastiano Rovere said. Then, suddenly reaching out, he took up the girl's small hand, kissed it almost reverently, asking her, "And will you have me for your husband, Bianca Pietro d'Angelo?"

No! No! No! she wanted to shriek, but she knew what was expected of her. "I am magnified that you would have me, *signore*."

He kissed her hand again, this time a bit more enthusiastically. "We will walk together in your father's garden," he said without even bothering to ask her parents for their permission.

Startled but not knowing what else to do, Bianca turned away with him. He led her from their sight deeper and deeper into the greenery and floral beds until finally they came to a single marble bench set amid some rosebushes. He drew her down, seating himself next to her. Bianca was a little frightened. She had never before been alone with a man. She wasn't very comfortable. "I think we should go back to my parents," she said nervously. Her heart was thundering.

He laughed softly and lowly, which frightened her further. "You have never been with a man before, have you? Of course you haven't," he said with a chuckle. "Do you realize that I am the only man you will ever be allowed to be alone with, Bianca? I am to be your lord and your master. You will obey my every wish."

She was silent but suddenly angry at his presumption.

"Look at me! I want to see your eyes, Bianca," he told her. His fingers grasped her small chin and almost forced her head up.

She was going to have to look directly at him. She felt brief nausea but swallowed it back. She could not, would not, be afraid of this man. Fear gave the instigator of that emotion power over his victim, and while she must wed him, she would not give him the privilege of controlling her heart, her mind, or her soul. Bianca raised her lashes and looked directly into the dark eyes of the man she was to marry. It was like looking into black ice. "The color of my eyes is said to be unique," she told him quietly.

Sebastiano Rovere stared, amazed by the beauty and clarity of the girl's eyes. He would find aquamarines to match their color and have a necklace and ear dangles made for her. He would have her wear them naked with her hair down. Blue, ivory, and ebony. The mental picture in his mind was almost too much to bear as he considered her spread upon his bed, ready for him. His male member ached painfully. "Will you give me a kiss, Bianca?" his voice rasped. *Slowly, slowly,* he cautioned himself. She was innocent.

Bianca was startled by the bold request. "*Signore*, I do not believe such a thing would be considered proper by my parents."

"The betrothal agreement has already been signed," he told her. "You are mine but for the wedding ceremony, Bianca. Your beauty, your manner have all pleased me."

He grasped her by her slender shoulders. "I *must* taste your lips!" And he put his lips on hers, his lust communicating itself quite clearly to the girl.

Bianca was horrified. The kiss. Her first kiss screamed with his need to possess her totally. She struggled against him, yanking her head away from the marauding mouth that assaulted her. "*Signore!*" she gasped, and then breaking away, she fled from him into the thick greenery of the gardens.

He immediately gave chase. He could not permit her to return in tears to her parents. He would look like a lustful fool. She had stopped in her flight, obviously listening to see if he was still behind her. "*Dolce* Bianca, I beg you to forgive my eagerness. I apologize for taking forcibly what you had not offered. Come out and we will return together to your parents."

Listening to his words, Bianca wondered how sincere they were. Not at all, she suspected, but he did not want to look a fool before her parents, and the truth was she did not want to put him in that position. As her husband he would have total control over her life, and could make it quite miserable. She needed to remain on his good side.

"You frightened me, *signore*," she told him.

"I know! I know! It was unforgivable of me, *dolce* Bianca," he agreed. "Your innocence is so very tempting to a man of my experience. I shall endeavor not to frighten you again. Forgive me!"

Bianca stepped out from behind a row of tall bushes. "I do, *signore*."

"Ahh, *cara mia*, you make me the happiest of men," he swore to her. Little bitch! He would soon show her the extent of his power over her. His cock twitched again.

Bianca tucked her hand into his arm. "Let us return to my parents," she said.

They walked back through the gardens as the evening deepened around them.

"When will you set our wedding day?" he inquired of her.

Her mother had advised her to expect such a question, and told her how she must answer it. "Oh, *signore*, first a new wardrobe must be made for me. And my wedding gown will take time. I must make a retreat with the nuns to ensure the success and happiness of our union. It will be at least several months before I am ready."

Sebastiano Rovere gritted his teeth at the thought of such a delay, but it was actually no more time than any respectable betrothal would take. "If I must wait," he told her, "then surely you will allow me the privilege of kisses and caresses in order to whet our appetite for the marriage bed. I will admit to being a man of great desires."

"I know naught of such things," Bianca said. "I will ask

my mother if such things are permitted, for I would not sully my family's name."

"Of course, of course, *dolce* Bianca," he agreed. "Remember, though, that the legalities have all been signed and sealed. As Florence's premier attorney, I drew them up myself and saw them properly executed. I would not bring shame on either you or your good family."

"If my mother says it is allowable, *signore*, then you shall have your kisses and your caresses, I promise you," Bianca told him. "Ah, here are my parents awaiting us."

He almost laughed aloud at the relief on the faces of his in-laws. Did they think he meant to ravish their little virgin in their gardens? Then he realized that had he been able to manage it, he probably would have. She was a most delicious tidbit, and ripe for his picking. "We have had a most delightful stroll," he told Giovanni Pietro d'Angelo. "I shall look forward to other such rambles while we await our wedding day." He smiled at Bianca, who was now standing next to her mother. Then he bowed to his hosts. "I shall not overstay my welcome this evening," he said.

"Allow me to escort you to the door," the silk merchant said, and the two men departed the garden, leaving Orianna and Bianca together.

"You look paler than usual," her mother noted once the men were out of sight and hearing. "Did he attempt to take liberties with you?"

"He kissed me," Bianca said hesitantly, not wanting to go into detail.

"That was to be expected," Orianna replied.

"You did not warn me, *Madre*, that he might do so."

"I had forgotten what inexperience was like," Orianna

admitted. "I had older sisters who advised me what a courtship would be like. You had only me. I'm sorry I failed you, and that you were startled, Bianca. What did you speak of?"

"The wedding day," the girl said.

"You told him it would be months away, didn't you?"

"I did, *Madre*, and it was then that he said if he had to be patient, I must allow him the privilege of kisses and caresses," Bianca told her mother. "I told him I must be certain such behavior was proper. Is it?"

Orianna sighed softly. "Yes, it is. He has signed the marriage agreement, and but for the Church's blessing, you are already his wife. You must allow him to have his way."

"*Oh,*" Bianca responded, not certain she liked the idea of caresses, and as for kisses . . . but there was no help for it. Her mother said it was allowed, and so she must bear it. And would probably get used to it in time. Her mother did not seem to mind her father's endearments.

The next morning, Sebastiano Rovere appeared to escort Bianca and her mother to Mass. Her first appearance in the doorway of her father's house brought a cheer from the young men gathered in the piazza. It died as Florence's most famed lawyer stepped out behind her and took her arm. Together they crossed the piazza with her mother and entered the church. When they exited an hour later, there was a larger crowd of young men, but they were silent. Then one caught sight of the large, deep red ruby betrothal ring Sebastiano had slipped on Bianca's finger when Mass had concluded. A hiss and a hum vibrated through the crowd, followed by a sound that resembled mourning.

The lawyer smiled, well pleased. While her family did not intend to make a formal announcement until a few evenings from now, it would be known throughout Florence by the noon hour that Sebastiano Rovere was to marry Bianca Pietro d'Angelo. He expected the crowds to lessen over the next few days, and they did, as Florence realized there was no hope. The most beautiful virgin in the city was to wed a powerful and important man, which, of course, was just as it should be.

Bianca could see the disappointment upon the faces of all the young men who had so faithfully paid her their court over the last few months. She felt sorry for them, and couldn't help but wonder if her fate would have been different if Sebastiano had not come into her life—if her brother Marco had not been such a fool. When Bianca put the whole situation into perspective, it was ridiculous. To think that the accidental death of an unknown courtesan had catapulted her into the arms of a man she did not want to wed.

He returned them from Mass but came back that evening to take Bianca deep into the gardens once more. "Did you speak with your mother?" he asked her, and she knew exactly what it was he sought to know.

Bianca nodded. "But, please, *signore*, I beg of you, do not hasten me."

"You belong to me now, *cara mia*," he purred at her. Then he stopped, and turned the girl to face him. "I am going to kiss you," he told her. "You will open your mouth, *cara*, and give me your tongue when I do."

It was a startling command, but before she had a moment to question it, he was kissing her. He held her tightly, her breasts pressing flat against the velvet of his robe. His tongue slid along her lips, encouraging her to obedience, and Bianca opened her mouth for him. Immediately his fleshy organ began stroking her tongue, exploring her mouth. She gagged with the shock of the invasion, but he did not release her. His kiss grew more lustful, deepening, as Bianca struggled for air, for it seemed he had sucked it all from her body. Her small palms pushed against his chest, and she grew faint, sagging in his arms. She gasped deeply, drawing several breaths into her lungs again, and to her shock his attentions continued.

Bending his head, he began pressing kisses on the swell of her small breasts as she attempted to recover herself. His wet mouth seemed everywhere, and then a hand pushed past the fabric of her neckline to pull one of her breasts free. He groaned as he stared at the small, perfectly round globe in his hand. Then his mouth closed over her helpless nipple, tugging fiercely. Her fragrance surrounded him and drove him wild with raging desire. He knew he had to stop soon or he would commit a forcible act. But she was so delicious. So ripe for his taking, and he wanted her.

"*Signore!* I beg you, cease!" Bianca cried as he sucked upon her innocent flesh, arousing emotions in her she had never known. "*Please! Please!* No more, I beg you!"

Reluctantly he raised his head from her snowy bosom. His eyes were glazed with his lust. He drew a ragged breath, but then covered the little breast. He knew his cock was surging so strongly in his need for her that he was surprised it didn't push through the fabric of his trunk hose. No woman, least of all his two previous wives, had brought him to such a state without a touch of the dog whip. He was both astounded and thrilled by the knowledge that this girl could have such an effect upon him. Particularly given his age.

"You are a temptress, *cara mia,*" he told her.

"I did not mean to entice you, *signore,*" she said lowly.

"Will you always kiss me with such fervor? Why did you suckle on me?"

"Didn't you like it when I caressed your sweet little breast?" he asked, not bothering to answer her questions.

"It was strange. I felt . . . I felt strange," she told him. "I thought only babes suckled from their mothers' breasts."

"I want no children of you, Bianca. I have two strong sons, one of whom will wed shortly before we do. I will not spoil what I suspect is a perfect body beneath your gown. That body now belongs to me, and you will reserve it for my pleasure alone, *cara mia*. Before we marry you will know much of what I require of you."

Bianca did not tell her mother of his words, or his actions as the next few months went by. She dreaded his visits, for she never knew what he would do. When the weather began to chill, they were given the privacy of a small salon, in which he slowly educated her to his taste. She almost fainted the first time she was given a view of his manhood. He made her kneel before him before he uncovered himself to her sight. Then he taught her how to handle his cock, delighting in her gentle, delicate touch, in her gasp of shock as he thickened and lengthened before her sight. When he was hard, Sebastiano instructed her to kiss the very tip. She did so, reluctantly.

Another time, when he was suitably firm, he explained to her how to lick him, starting with the satiny head of his cock, then slowly bathing the length with her tongue. He might have waited until Nudara could teach her these things. He had fully intended to do so, but he found he was gaining great pleasure in teaching her himself. Once a tiny pearl of his juices bedewed the tip, and he forced her to lick it up. "I sometimes enjoy being sucked dry, *cara mia*," he told her. "Best that you get used to the taste now."

Bianca was horrified by such a suggestion, but there was worse to come for her, she found. Her fifteenth birthday came in December, and after eight months of betrothal, her wedding date was set for the week after. Learning of it, Sebastiano Rovere became bolder in his tutoring of his bride-to-be. His hands began to roam beneath her skirts, stroking her silken thighs, rubbing her mons, and then one evening the curious finger of her *fidanzato* pushed between her nether lips. His lips and tongue engaged with hers as he began rubbing a tiny nub of flesh with that finger.

Bianca moaned as it caused that secret flesh to tingle. Stronger and stronger the sensation grew, until she could bear it no more. She wiggled against the finger until a lovely burst overcame her, and she sighed with open pleasure.

He laughed softly, darkly. "I am glad to see you can respond so naturally to my lovemaking," he said. Then his finger pushed into her up to the first joint.

"*Ohhh*." Bianca gasped.

"I just want to see how tightly your virginity is lodged, *cara mia*," he reassured her, and he moved his finger deeper into her sheath. She was very tight, her sheath narrow. Breaching her would be divine. She would feel pain, as the membrane blocking his finger's passage was strongly fixed. The very thought excited him. She whimpered, and he withdrew the finger. "There, there," he soothed her.

Was there any escape, Bianca wondered in the days that followed? No, there was none. She would belong to this man till she died, and she would have no children to comfort her, to distract her from him. She had never seen the palazzo in which she would reside after the wedding ceremony. She knew his younger son lived with him, but the boy had just been betrothed to Carolina di Medici, a distant relation of Cosimo.

Stefano, who had wed Violetta Orsini in October, had been given a charming little palazzo in which to live with his new wife by his in-laws. Stefano's father-in-law knew well the dark reputation of Sebastiano Rovere and did not want his daughter living in the man's home. A silk merchant himself, Signore Orsini wondered how Rovere had managed to gain the hand of the fair Bianca Pietro d'Angelo from her usually prudent father. He felt sorry for the poor girl.

Bianca knew she might ask to see her new home, but she did not. Seeing it would have made the reality of her life fact. But she did wonder if the gardens were as lovely as her father's, for like most respectable married women, she would not leave her home except on rare occasions. Her servants would do the marketing. Sebastiano Rovere was an extremely old-fashioned man and had told her quite frankly that a priest would come and say Mass when she wished it. There was no church on his piazza. Unless it was a wedding or a funeral, it was unlikely she would even see her sisters again, although she knew that her father, being less traditional, would allow her mother to visit her.

"You will come tomorrow," Bianca said to Orianna as she was being dressed for her wedding.

"Not tomorrow, but in a few days' time," Orianna promised her daughter, thinking as she did how beautiful Bianca looked in her wedding gown.

It was silk, of course. A very rare fabric, for it had not been imported from China, as all of the bolts in her husband's warehouses were. It had been spun from the thread of the silkworms Giovanni Pietro d'Angelo raised himself in a hidden garden of mulberry bushes outside of the city. There was enough silk this year for one gown, and no more. Pure white, the fitted bodice with its squared neckline was embroidered with pearls over lace. The sleeves were lace-edged silk, heavily embroidered with gold thread and pearls.

The full skirt was lace trimmed at its hem. Bianca's long dark hair was left loose, and she carried but a single white rose in her hand.

All of her siblings were to be allowed to attend the ceremony in Santa Anna Dolce, a rare privilege, but Giovanni Pietro d'Angelo was proud of his family. An occasion such as this one gave other important men and their wives the opportunity to see the strong, healthy children he and Orianna had produced. He would soon have to find a wife for Marco. Georgio would go to the Church next year. He was clever, and Giovanni had no doubt he would one day gain a cardinal's red cap. Having a cardinal in the family was a useful thing, as the Borgias in Rome were discovering.

But today was for Bianca and her marriage to Sebastiano Rovere. While his conscience still troubled him over the match, he had, as his daughter had, resigned himself to it. Nothing could be changed now.

Chapter 3

Because of the time of year, an awning had been run between the palazzo of the Pietro d'Angelo family, across the piazza, and up the steps of Santa Anna Dolce. A cold, light rain fell as the silk merchant brought his eldest daughter to her destiny. His wife and children had preceded them and now waited in the crowded church. Despite the fur-lined cloak that had been put over her shoulders to protect her, Bianca felt cold, and the garment was removed the moment they entered the building.

Her father led her up the long aisle of the church past nameless people she did not know. Some smiled at her. Others simply marveled at the girl's extraordinary beauty. Some whispered to their companions knowingly. Bianca was numb. She would shortly have the Church's blessing on her marriage. She didn't want it! She didn't want this union. She was terrified of Sebastiano Rovere, who now stood waiting for her at the end of the aisle, a toothy smile decorating his darkly handsome face, his lust barely concealed.

Her father put her hand into that of Rovere. Bianca remembered to acknowledge him with a small nod of her head. They knelt at Father Bonamico's instruction. She answered when required, but she didn't really hear the words being spoken. She just instinctively knew what was expected of her and performed her duty. That was all that would be needed of her from now on. That she do her duty.

And after the church had done what was expected of it, Bianca and her new husband led her family and the guests back across the square to the Pietro d'Angelo palazzo, where tables covered in the finest linen cloths and topped with golden candelabras had been set up in the formal *sala da pranzo*. Bianca had never had a meal in this dining room, with its mural-covered walls and coffered ceiling. Their family ate in a smaller and more intimate chamber. This was where her father entertained his guests. Tomorrow there would be another wedding feast given in her new home by her husband.

The menu was extensive, with several kinds of pasta, salads, and roasted meats and poultry. There were freshly baked breads and rich wines. Unlike many, Giovanni Pietro d'Angelo did not serve his best wines first and afterwards his worst, believing as so many did that no one would notice. He served only his best wines for the entire feast, which led the bridegroom to imbibe too much.

Sebastiano Rovere knew he was drinking too much, but tonight he could not seem to stop himself. Soon, soon Bianca would lie naked in his bed, at his mercy. The thought of her fear, of her screams as he took her virginity, excited him almost beyond bearing. And she was fearful of his attentions, he knew. She accepted his kisses easily enough now, but when his hands would roam over her nubile young body, a look would cross her face and she would struggle not to forbid him, although he knew she wanted to do so.

He turned his head to look at her now. The neckline of her wedding gown had been cut particularly low. Her full young breasts almost swelled over the lace edging, and he had seen many men in the room tonight admiring the view. *Little bitch,* he thought. *She will soon learn at my hand the consequences of her teasing.* His fourteen-year-old son, Alberto, could not take his eyes from Bianca's tempting cleavage. Alberto needed to have a wife. Stefano had told their father that the young devil could hardly keep his cock in his hose these days. Sebastiano chuckled. Alberto was like his father.

It was time to go home. They had remained long enough to satisfy custom, and he wanted to fuck Bianca now. He arose from his seat, reaching out to pull Bianca up too. "My friends," he said, his voice slurring, "it is time for me to take my bride to my bed. I thank you all for coming, and will look forward to your company at our own wedding banquet tomorrow."

Bianca looked like a young deer caught before a hunter. Orianna came quickly to her daughter's side. "I will see my daughter settled in her litter, *signore,*" she said and led Bianca from the *sala da pranzo.* "You know what is expected of you," Orianna said in a no-nonsense voice she hoped would calm Bianca. "I have carefully instructed you, daughter, and I know he has had his hands all over you these past few months. Whatever you do, show no fear. The deflowering is quickly over and done with, Bianca. Then all you need do is let him have his way with you. His condition is such that I doubt he will do much more tonight than what is required of him. And after the newness of you wears off for him, or you get yourself with child quickly, it is unlikely he will disturb you but for now and again."

Bianca nodded. It all seemed so simple to her mother, but it was not. "He wants no more children," she told her mother.

Orianna looked shocked. Then she said, "It is not up to him. It is up to God."

The litter was waiting outside the palazzo. Orianna helped her daughter into it, wrapping a wool and fur robe about her. "Agata is waiting for you," she said. "God bless you, my child. I will come in a few days to see you." Then Orianna signaled the litter bearers to be on their way. By the time her new son-in-law reached his house, Bianca would be waiting for him in their marriage bed.

It was almost an hour before Sebastiano Rovere came forth to mount his horse, and with his son, Alberto, and their armed escort, departed for his own house. Arriving, he found the palazzo quiet. A servant opened the door, greeting his master.

"Where is my bride?" he asked.

"She was brought to her apartments when she arrived, my lord. Her servingwoman is with her."

"Have her brought to my rooms immediately," Sebastiano ordered the man.

"At once, my lord," the servant said, hurrying off. Reaching the newly refurbished apartment of his master's bride, he knocked at the door and almost at once found himself facing a stern-faced servingwoman. "The master wishes his bride to join him in his chambers," he said to the woman.

"My young mistress is awaiting her bridegroom in her own bed."

"Mistress, in this house we never question the master's orders," the servingman said quietly. "Please, I beg of you, do not send me back to him with such a message. He can be particularly harsh when he is defied, or drunk. Tonight he is drunk."

"It is unorthodox, but wait while I see my little lady properly garbed, and then show us the way. My name is Agata."

"I am Antonio, and I will wait," the man said.

Agata went back through her mistress's new apartment to the bedchamber, where Bianca was waiting for her husband in her bed. She was naked. "Your bridegroom has sent a servant for you to attend him in his rooms," she said disapprovingly to the girl.

"Then I must go," Bianca responded, arising from the bed.

"Put this on," Agata told her mistress, handing her a long, plain, silk night garment. "The manservant is waiting. I will go with you, but mark the way well for you will have to return on your own. I will be here awaiting your return."

Bianca put on the nightgown Agata held out to her. Shouldn't he have come to her bedchamber on this their wedding night? But then she knew nothing of wedding nights. Barefooted, she followed Agata through her apartment and out into the corridor, where a manservant awaited them. To her relief, he kept his eyes politely lowered. The silk was very sheer. She watched carefully as they went. Her husband's rooms were not far from hers, much to her relief, and were at the end of a passageway.

The door opened. Another manservant stepped out. "If you will come with me, mistress, I will bring you to the master," he said politely. "I am called Guido, mistress."

"Go! Go!" Agata murmured. "God and his blessed Mother protect you."

Bianca followed Guido into Sebastiano Rovere's private rooms. They crossed a dayroom. The servant knocked upon the door of another chamber across from the first chamber. "Master, she is here." He opened the door, and after a moment's hesitation Bianca stepped inside. The door behind her closed with the finality of a prison door.

The room was dim, the only light coming from a large fireplace. "*Signore*, I have come at your request," Bianca said. Her eyes growing used to the dim light, she saw him sprawled upon a large canopied bed in his wedding robe, which was now stained with wine and food. "*Signore*," she murmured again, not certain if he was asleep.

"Take off that garment," he said. "I want to see you naked, *cara mia*."

She obeyed, already feeling shamed by his disrespect.

He stared at her and licked his lips as if he were anticipating a fine meal. "Come closer," he said.

She moved closer, although how she managed to work her legs Bianca was not certain. She was very frightened, and she could see he was indeed drunk with her father's good wine. She had drunk more than she was used to drinking, but she felt no effects from the wine at all.

"Turn around. Do it slowly," he said.

Bianca followed his instruction, rotating herself around a turn.

"Put your hands beneath your breasts and hold them up for me," he said. She was delicious. She was perfect. For months the very sight of her, the mere thought of her, had caused his male member to rage with lust. Tonight he felt nothing. *Nothing!* Sebastiano Rovere was suddenly angry.

She saw the anger staining his face. "Do I not please you, husband?" she asked him. Was he angry at her? What had she done? He reached for something upon the table next to the bed. Bianca saw it was a small dog whip. Her eyes widened with surprise as he arose, and turning her, pushed her face-down upon the bed. She felt the whip upon her buttocks and shrieked with both her surprise and her pain. But beating her did not help. He had not hit her hard enough to even break the skin, but she was sobbing piteously, and he found it annoying.

"What have you done to me, you little bitch, that I cannot perform as a man now?"

"I have done nothing, husband," she cried.

"You have!" he snarled. "I have lusted after you for weeks, but tonight my fire is dead. It would not be so had you not done something to me. Is it a spell you murmured, or something you slipped into my wine, Bianca? Answer me!"

"I have done nothing," she told him, sitting up to face him.

"You must be punished for this wickedness, *cara mia.* I can see you are fearful of losing your virginity. All brides are. If I cannot do what is necessary tonight, someone else shall. Then you will not be afraid, and my potency will be restored. Guido!"

The servant's head came round the bedchamber door. "Master?"

"Fetch my son, Alberto, and hurry!" Sebastiano Rovere shouted.

Guido disappeared, to return a few moments later with young Alberto. He had found the boy about to make use of Nudara's charms and wondered if the master knew.

He pushed Alberto into his father's bedchamber, and then, shutting the door, put his ear against it to listen. What was the master going to do?

"She has cast a spell on me in her fear," the senior Rovere told his son. "You will take my place and breach her. Have you ever taken a virgin, my son?"

"No, Father," the boy answered. His young cock was hard and raging for pleasure.

"Well, you will marry next year, and for your sake you should know what a real virgin is like to fuck for the first time," Sebastiano Rovere said.

"Father . . ." The young man hesitated. "This is your wedding night, and this is your bride. Would you not enjoy taking her first-night rights?" He could see his father was very drunk.

"Fuck the little bitch, or you are no son of mine," Sebastiano said. "Only when you have ploughed her well will this curse she put on me dissolve. I am certain of it!"

"If you do this incest, you commit a mortal sin," Bianca warned both men. She scrambled across the bed, seeking an escape, but there was none.

"Get on your hands and knees, you little bitch!" her new husband ordered her. His hand fastened into her long hair, forcing her back and into the required position.

Alberto hesitated as Bianca began to tremble. When she turned a tearstained face to him in a silent plea, he felt all of his desire drain suddenly away. Despite his young age, he was as lustful as his sire, but he simply could not do this thing that was being demanded of him. She was his new stepmother, and it was incest. Alberto feared the Church perhaps even more than he did his father. His cock withered away.

"I can't do this, *signore*. I just can't!" He fell back away from Bianca.

Sebastiano Rovere began to beat his younger son with his fists. "*Cordado,*" he snarled. "You would disobey me?" He pounded at the boy mercilessly.

Still shaking, Bianca turned over and managed to gain a half-seated position. "Sebastiano, I beg you to cease beating our son. He has only done what was right."

Her gentle words cut through his fury, which he now turned on her, slapping her face hard several times as Alberto took the opportunity to slide off the bed, and flee the chamber. "Bitch! You dare to instruct me?" Several more blows followed his query. "Did your mother not teach you to respect your husband, Bianca? You will now learn your place or, with God as my witness, I will kill you with my bare hands. You won't be the first disobedient woman with whom I have dealt." He yanked her over his lap and began to spank her tempting bottom until it was bright red and she was sobbing uncontrollably with the stinging pain and burning he was inflicting on her helpless flesh.

"Sebastiano, Sebastiano, you are hurting me," Bianca cried out. "Stop—I beg of you! Please stop!" She wiggled her body in an attempt to escape his punishment.

"Bitch!" he hissed at her. "I will tell you when it is time to stop," he said fiercely, but as he did he realized that his cock was suddenly as hard as iron. Quickly rolling her off his thigh and onto her back, he mounted his bride.

She moaned as he drove into her and started moving rhythmically inside her. She shrieked as he forced himself through her maidenhead, the numbing pain engulfing her briefly, and then thankfully receding. Bianca's face was wet with her tears. Her eyes were closed tightly. She was tighter than any woman he had ever known. The walls of her sheath almost strangled him. It felt wonderful, and he found himself now unable to cease fucking her. "Open your eyes," he commanded her. "I want you to see me as I use you. You are delicious, *cara mia*!"

Bianca lay silent now beneath him, her eyes still shut.

"Disobey me," he said in a pleasant tone, "and I have ways to punish you that you will not like, *cara mia*. Now open your eyes for me, Bianca, and afterwards I shall give you your wedding gift as a reward."

She didn't want him to beat her again. Bianca opened her eyes and looked up at him. She struggled to keep her gaze neutral so he would not see the dislike she felt for him now. She would never like this man. Indeed she already hated him. He had forced her into a mortal sin. How could she confess such a thing to a priest? She would never forgive him or herself for yielding to his depraved nature. Better she had died.

"You have the most beautiful eyes in the world," he told her. "Never have I seen such a color before, *cara mia*." He continued to fuck her as he spoke. "There was obviously a Northman in your family, Bianca. Do you think your ancestress was violated by one, or was she wed to him? Do you know, *cara mia*? Is there some tale about it in your family's history?" The thought of it excited him, but then suddenly his crisis overcame him. His juices flooded her, and he fell away from her, groaning. "Sleep now," he told her. "We will make love again when I have recovered my strength."

Make love? Was that what he called what had just transpired? Moving away from him, she curled herself into a fetal position and slept to block out her shame and her disappointment. But twice again in the night, Bianca was awakened by her husband so he might satisfy his lust for her. After the third time, he told her to go back to her own rooms. Grateful, the girl covered herself with her silk night robe, and creeping from the bedchamber, made her way back to her own quarters, where Agata was awaiting her.

Seeing her young mistress's face, Agata said nothing. Instead, she led Bianca to the bathing room, bathed her, and then bringing her back to her own rooms, fed her a goblet of wine with a sleeping potion. Sleep would restore the girl's spirits, which Agata could see had been badly broken, but it was only temporary. Bianca was a Pietro d'Angelo, and she would not crumble.

Bianca slept well into the next afternoon. She awakened to have to dress in a sapphire blue velvet gown embroidered in gold and crystals, for their guests were shortly due. Her husband came into her apartment unannounced, bringing with him a dark red leather case. He smiled at her and nodded his approval of her garments.

"I have brought you your wedding gift," he said. "You will wear them tonight when we entertain." Opening the case, he displayed for her its contents. Nestled on the ivory satin lining of the case was a magnificent necklace of blue aquamarines set in gold. The stones were large, almost vulgar in their size, but the color was pure.

"The first time I saw your eyes I determined you must have a necklace like this," he told her as he affixed the jewelry about her throat. "Later when we are alone, you will wear them for me naked with your hair loose." He kissed the side of her neck.

"If it pleases you, Sebastiano," Bianca said quietly, restraining a shudder, and using his name for the first time. Could he hear the venom in her tone?

"I like the sound of my name on your lips," he told her. He set the matching ear bobs in her ears. "And yes, it would please me very much." Now he kissed her lips.

Madre di Dios! Was this how it was going to be? Bianca wondered. He had no idea of her distaste. The necklace seemed to burn her skin. Or was it his kiss?

"Our guests will be arriving. Let us go and greet them together," he said, taking her arm and leading her from the apartment.

It was her first real party, and oddly it was the company that caused Bianca to enjoy it. They were honored by the presence of Lorenzo di Medici, current head of the great House of Medici, who had inherited the position from his late father, known as Piero the Gouty, the son of Cosimo. Though he was considered ugly by the standards of his day, with his dark, bushy eyebrows, long, flat nose, and large jaw that jutted forward, his dark eyes were intelligent, and his long, thick, straight black hair, which he wore at shoulder length and parted in the middle, was admired. He was known for his kindness, his athletic prowess, and his intellect. The House of Medici had never had such a head. The Medicis' wealth, banking skills, and wise counsel made them the most influential family in Florence.

He was kind and mannerly. Knowing it was Bianca's first real adult party, he had insisted on being seated at her right hand rather than at her husband's. "Why would I want to sit next to you, Sebastiano, when there is such a beautiful young woman at the other end of the table?" While disappointed, Sebastiano Rovere was pleased the Medici had taken notice of his new bride. She was already bringing stature to his house.

"My lord, you are very gracious," Bianca said to him.

Lorenzo di Medici's dark eyes twinkled. "While I am with you, *signora*, no other man in this room will flirt with you, thereby angering your husband. This should be a happy time for you. You are outrageously beautiful, you know. How on earth did Rovere gain such a treasure as you, *cara*? I had heard your proud mother wished to wed you into Venice and that your princely grandfather was already considering certain families."

"My father owed my husband a great debt, my lord," Bianca admitted. "I should not tell that to anyone, but for some reason I trust you. You have a kind face."

"Your secrets are safe with me, *cara*," he replied with a chuckle. "So you think my face kind, eh? Neither my brother nor I is considered handsome. Now, my children are thought to be quite handsome, especially by their mother. They have not my face."

"I would not know that, my lord," Bianca admitted. "I have lived a most sheltered life until yesterday. My husband says I will be well cloistered for my own safety, for the city can be a rough place."

"I cannot blame Rovere for keeping you close, *cara*. He is right. Florence is a beautiful but dangerous city, but I suspect the world will come to you." Reaching out, he fingered her necklace. "I collect rare and beautiful things, *cara*. Your necklace is quite spectacular. A gift?"

"A wedding gift from my husband," Bianca admitted.

"The stones match your eyes perfectly. It is amazing that he was able to find such perfect gems," the Medici said. "I might have had them cut a bit more delicately, but it is a striking piece, and you wear it well."

"It is vulgar," Bianca heard herself say.

Lorenzo di Medici laughed. "It is, indeed, but you must never tell him that. I am certain he went to great difficulty to find the stones, *cara*."

After their guests had left, her husband came to her apartment to tell Bianca how pleased he had been with the excellent impression she had made on his guests, particularly the Medici. "They are envied, but they will always hold the power in this city as long as they wish to, wife. Remember it. Having the friendship of the Medici is no small thing."

"I am glad to have pleased you, Sebastiano," Bianca told him.

"You will come to my bedchamber in an hour," he said, and then left her.

"*Madre di Dios!* I had hoped to be spared tonight," Bianca said when he had left.

"You were with him almost all of your wedding night," Agata noted. "Did you not enjoy his passion?"

"He is a monster," Bianca replied. "Do you think my mother will come tomorrow? I very much need to speak with her."

"Perhaps," Agata said, and she gave her mistress a small goblet of wine to calm her nerves. Taking a man for the first time was always difficult and especially for a girl who had been as sheltered as the Pietro d'Angelo daughters. In time, Bianca would get used to her husband's attentions. She might even come to enjoy them. Many women did.

When the hour struck, she escorted her mistress to her husband's apartment, where Guido awaited to take his new mistress to the bedchamber.

Entering, Bianca was shocked to see a naked woman in

her husband's bed. Was this his mistress? She turned to leave, but his sharp voice stopped her.

"Remove your robe, and come here to me," he said. He was standing naked by the blazing fireplace.

Bianca shrugged the garment off and walked over to him. "Who is that woman, Sebastiano?" she asked him.

"Her name is Nudara, and she is my slave," he said.

"I did not know you kept slaves in this house, Sebastiano. My family does not keep slaves. It is a cruel practice," Bianca responded.

"Slaves are a necessary part of my household," he answered her. "It is not your duty to criticize how I manage it. Nudara pleases me well."

"I had been told that you keep a mistress, Sabina Cadenza. Have you disposed of her for this slave girl?" Bianca inquired, unable to keep the scorn from her voice.

He heard it, and slapped her lightly on her cheek. "Be careful, *cara mia*," he warned her. "I would hardly dispose of a woman who brings me public prestige among my peers. I have married you to burnish my reputation even further, but my appetites are large and varied. They must be serviced in private. Those appetites are in Nudara's keeping. She is most diligent in her duties," he said with a chuckle. "Now get into bed with her, Bianca. I will bring us all some wine and join you."

"She wants to disobey you, my lord," Nudara said in her smoky voice. "Do you not want to come and lie with me, pretty mistress? I will make you as happy as I do my master. We only need to learn what pleases you." Her tone was sweet, but Bianca heard the poison beneath the dulcet murmur.

Before Bianca might even think what to answer this creature, she felt the sting of her husband's dog whip on her buttocks, and cried out in protest.

"Get into the bed," he snarled, pushing her over to it.

She fell helplessly back upon it.

Nudara giggled and pulled at Bianca so that her whole body was now upon the bed. "Let me suck her breasts, master," the slave girl begged her master.

"You are so greedy," Rovere laughed. "Yes, yes! Go ahead and pleasure yourself. You will soon have to pleasure me."

"No!" Bianca cried, pushing the woman away from her and struggling to sit up.

Nudara pouted, disappointed. "She needs to be strapped, master. She will not play with me. Will you let her defy your orders?"

Sebastiano Rovere came to the bed with a large goblet of wine. He drank deeply, then set the goblet aside as he climbed into the bed to join the two women. "She is inexperienced, Nudara. We must take our time in educating her." He made himself comfortable, well-stuffed pillows behind his back as he gained a seated position. Legs spread, he dragged Bianca so that she sat with her back against him. His hands reached around to grasp her two round breasts. "You will do as I tell you, Bianca, or you will be beaten. First with a leather strap that will make your bottom blaze, and if you have still not learned your lesson, I will apply the dog whip hard enough to break your skin. The results will be very painful, I assure you." His fingers pinched her nipples in warning.

Bianca winced with the pain.

"Do you understand me, *cara mia*? Obey, or I will beat you," he murmured in her ear. "Did you know the sweet conjunction of your buttocks with my cock is warming it?" He dropped a kiss upon her bare shoulder. Then his gaze turned to Nudara. "Lick her and get her ready to be fucked. My member is beginning to stir vigorously. Spread your legs wide, Bianca." His thumbs began to rub her nipples.

Bianca was ashamed to find herself very fearful. It was disconcerting to learn she was not a brave girl. She believed him when he said he would beat her, and make her punishment painful. She didn't want to be beaten. She opened her legs, and was horrified to see Nudara crawl between them. It was worse, and she could not help the little cry that escaped her when Nudara's tongue began licking at her most private place.

Her husband began to whisper in her ear. "I know how skillful her tongue can be. The flat of it will caress the insides of your nether lips, *cara mia*. The pointed little tip of it will tease your love bud to passion. And when your juices begin to flow, and they will, I shall put my cock deep into you, and fuck you until you are screaming with your pleasure. You will give me that pleasure, Bianca *dolce*, whether you wish to or not. You cannot withhold it from me. *I will not be denied!*"

But she did deny him. Her juices flowed, which the teasing Nudara's tongue forced from her, but Bianca lay as cold as ice in his arms. She felt nothing but revulsion. His cock withered at her lack of response. He screamed his outrage, but Nudara quickly took that shrunken bit of flesh between her lips, and sucked him hard. Shoving her away, he then climbed atop Bianca, fucking her until she fainted from the excess. He next proceeded to use Nudara, but after a satisfactory period of fucking, she forced his juices from him, screaming her delight, praising his prowess and his skilled manhood.

When Bianca finally came to herself again, she saw her

husband and Nudara drinking wine. Nudara's sharp eyes saw that her mistress had regained a conscious state. They forced a small goblet of wine upon Bianca, and Nudara smiled wickedly as they did.

"It has stimulants in it to make you eager to be fucked," the slave told Bianca. "You disappointed the master greatly with your icy hauteur, but soon you will beg for him to fuck you. First, however, you must be strapped for your disobedience, mistress." And she laughed, quite pleased with herself for having engineered this scenario with Rovere while poor Bianca lay helpless and semiconscious.

"Kill me!" Bianca said to her husband. "I should rather be dead than suffer this abuse from you and your whore."

"Ahh, *cara mia*, does Nudara distress you that much? Then she shall go," her husband said in a kindly voice. "Get out, wench. I can see you have been having too much fun, which does not please me." He pushed the slave from the bed.

Scrambling to her feet, Nudara protested. "But, my lord, I sought only to please you. We have all drunk the spiced wine now, and I am eager for your love!"

"Find my son, and let him satisfy your itch," Sebastiano Rovere said caustically. "Did you think I did not know, Nudara? You are like an alley cat. Now leave me with my beautiful bride." He laughed cruelly as the girl skulked from his bedchamber. Then he turned back to Bianca. "I would never kill you, *cara mia*," he said, bending to kiss her cold lips. "The spices will help your blood to warm for me. In my eagerness, I have treated you roughly. I realize now you are a creature that needs to be cosseted."

Bianca lay silent. She could think of nothing to say at this moment. She did not resist when he began to stroke her body.

To her shame, the wine was beginning to have the desired effect, but she kept her lips pressed tightly together, making no sound whatsoever. She would not give him the satisfaction of knowing. If he believed the wine with its special mix of spices had not aroused her, he would, she prayed, not use them again on her.

It was difficult, however, to maintain her attitude of detachment. Her body was suddenly burning with a need she neither understood nor desired. She could feel the secret place first growing moist, and then distinctly wet with that odd need. He seemed to be kissing, stroking, and caressing every inch of her body. She bit the inside of her lip to prevent a scream from escaping her when he mounted her and pushed into her tight sheath.

"Ah, *cara mia*," he groaned, "how perfect you are!" Then he fucked her until his lusts exploded. Afterwards he remarked, "Your juices were copious, *cara mia*. Now you see how pleasurable such activity can be when you are eager for your husband."

With each passing day, she grew to hate him more. Her mother did not come, and she learned from Agata, who had learned it from Antonio, that Orianna Pietro d'Angelo had been forbidden entry to Sebastiano Rovere's palazzo each time she had come to see her daughter. Bianca was furious, but she knew her anger meant nothing to her husband.

He had a right to do whatever he pleased, and he knew the law well. Her rights were few.

Bianca knew she needed to please her husband in some special way so he would grant her approval to see her mother. And she knew exactly what would please him more than anything else.

He made a point of reminding her daily that she belonged to him, that it was he who controlled her fate. But the one thing he had never been able to gain from her in their six months of marriage was her cries of pleasure. Bianca knew her husband well by now. If she gave him that, he was certain to reward her, and she would ask to see her mother. It was the only thing she had with which to bargain.

That night when he called her to his bed, she went to him, her long dark hair and her body perfumed with the scent of the exotic moonflower. She dropped the pale pink silk robe she wore and slipped into his bed without protest. He was surprised, raising an eyebrow questioningly. Bianca shrugged casually. "Suddenly something is different for me, Sebastiano," she said softly, and took the goblet of spiced wine from his hand, sipping it slowly until she felt the aphrodisiacs beginning to surge through her body.

He grinned knowingly. "You want something of me," he said candidly.

"I do," she admitted truthfully.

"What?" he asked her.

"If I please you tonight, you will give me whatever it is I desire," Bianca said.

His dark eyes narrowed, but then, amused by her attempt to manipulate him, he agreed. What could she want? Jewelry? A new gown? She was a simple girl for all of her great beauty. "Very well," he nodded. "Please me, and I will give you whatever it is you want, *dolce* Bianca." Then he began to kiss her, and to his great surprise she melted into his embrace, which increased his ardor a hundredfold. He had never known her to be so willing. His hand went to her breast and she made a murmur of pleasure.

Sebastiano Rovere could hardly believe what was happening. For the past six months of their marriage, she had resisted him. He had taken her body a thousand times over, and yet he had received nothing in return but coldness. There had been times when he had felt as if she were not there at all, even after he had ceased letting Nudara join them to please her. Now she lay pliant in his arms, almost purring as he kissed and caressed her. What could she possibly want that had brought her to this point?

It took every ounce of her self-control not to shrink from his touch this night.

Bianca hated the hands that stroked her, the fingers that pinched her nipples and probed her body, her husband's superior air of possession. He revolted her to the point where she actually had to secretly swallow back the bile that rose in her throat. Instead, she concentrated on gaining what she wanted; he had promised her anything if she pleased him. "Oh, Sebastiano!" she murmured as his mouth closed over a nipple.

This was surely how a whore must feel, Bianca thought sadly. But then she reached down to cup his balls in her little palm. How she wanted to crush the very life from them as his lips and tongue slobbered over her breasts and belly. Instead, she squeezed him gently, tenderly, teasing his sac with her fingers. Then she released him to stroke his cock, which was already burgeoning with his need for her.

He groaned. "Ahh, *dolce* Bianca, *cara mia*, I have waited for this night!" Then flinging himself over her, he drove himself into the tight, wet heat and began to piston her vigorously. "I adore you, *cara*! You are mine and mine alone!" He had to control himself, for he did not want to release his juices too quickly. He slowed his pace.

Chapter 4

*B*ianca released the iron self-control over her body that she usually employed when in her husband's bed. She let the aphrodisiacs he had fed her take over, and shuddered as her natural desires exploded within her. She was astounded by the emotions assaulting her, and thought that if she could love this man, how wonderful that would be for her. But she didn't love him. She hated him. But it didn't matter how she felt. He must be satisfied with her performance tonight. He must believe that he had finally overcome her resistance.

"Oh, *caro mio*," she whispered with hot breath in his ear. "Fuck me! Do not stop! What a fool I have been to resist you, my Sebastiano! Ahh yes! Yes! Yes!"

How long had he waited to master this proud beauty, and now she was begging him. He would have laughed aloud had his lust for her not been so great. For the first time, he felt her sheath contract with strong shudders about his hard cock. He groaned and forced her legs up and over her own shoulders so he might plunge deeper and deeper into her heat. She began to scream, and he howled with his victory over her. Never had he known such pleasure with a woman as he knew this night with Bianca.

She fainted as he poured himself into her womb. There would be no child from this travesty, she knew, for Agata fed her a noxious potion each morning to prevent it. She came back to herself quickly, her hands caressing him over and over again as she praised his passion. She managed to rise from his bed to bring him more spiced wine. Then she bathed him and herself because she knew he would want even more now.

"Have I pleased you, Sebastiano, *mio amore*?" she purred as she pulled herself next to him on the bed and began to stroke his broad chest.

"You will need to do more before I give you your way, *dolce* Bianca," he growled. His head was still spinning.

Bianca giggled girlishly. "You are a magnificent lover, *caro mio*, and I know that once is never enough for you." Then, giving him a quick kiss, she slid between his legs and, grasping his cock, began to suck upon it most vigorously. *Madre di Dios!* She had become such a whore for him tonight. She would never get the stink of him off her skin. He began to swell in her mouth, and she teased his balls, letting her fingernails run gently over them.

He moaned and his hand wrapped itself into her ebony hair. "Little sorceress," he said accusingly. "I cannot believe you have brought me to a stand so quickly."

"You are ready?" she inquired of him.

"I am," he told her.

Bianca pushed herself up and onto her knees, presenting her round bottom to him.

He was quickly on her, and driving into her sheath eagerly. "Ah yes, *cara mia*!" he murmured into her ear. "I love how tight you are for me. That is why I ordered that your servant bathe this bit of you with alum and water each day. So you will remain tight for me, *dolce* Bianca. Only for me! Only me! No other man will ever fuck you."

"Only you, *caro mio* Sebastiano!" she cried out to him. "Oh! Oh! It is too perfect! Do not stop! Do not!"

He couldn't stop with her that night. He had her five times, and yet was not content. He allowed her to sleep in his bed, keeping her there for the next two days while he fucked her until finally she collapsed with his lust, even as he admitted his satisfaction. Having Bianca yield so completely was something he had not expected. If truth be known, he was beginning to become bored with her constant resistance. Only the fact that she charmed his business associates, especially the Medici, had saved her, for he had been contemplating her death. He had gained the envy of all of Florence in marrying her, but she had proved nothing more than a great beauty until last night. But now her capitulation to his amorous nature had changed all that. He might keep her for a while longer until she bored him a final time.

He had her carried to her apartments and heard the cries of the servingwoman, who had come with her from her father's house, when she saw her mistress's condition.

For several days he heard nothing, and then his own servant, Guido, told him that the mistress's servingwoman had sent word that the lady Bianca would speak with her husband. He brought a bouquet of roses from the gardens when he came to her rooms. "*Cara mia*," he said in greeting, bending to kiss her lips as he handed her the flowers.

Agata took them immediately.

"Sebastiano," Bianca said in dulcet tones, "your strength has quite exhausted me, but not so much that I would forget to ask you for my reward." She gave him a small smile as she spoke, her hand upon his arm as he sat at her bedside.

"You were superb, *cara mia*, and are deserving of whatever you desire of me," he told her in sincere tones. "What would you have? A new gown? A ring?"

"I want my mother," she answered him simply. "I am told you have forbidden her my company since our marriage. I am certain I have been misinformed and some foolish servant has acted on his own. I ask nothing more of you than to see my mother, *caro mio*. It is a little boon, is it not? And far less trouble and expense than a new gown or a jewel would be." She gave him another smile.

"When will you come to me again, *dolce* Bianca?" he said. "Come to my bed and give yourself as you did a few nights ago?"

"I will come whenever it pleases you," Bianca lied. "When will you allow me to send for my mother so she may visit?"

"In a few days' time," he promised.

"And I shall join you tonight if it pleases you," Bianca promised him.

"It pleases me well!" he said eagerly. "Send to your mother to come in three days' time, *cara mia*. As long as you continue to please me, how can I refuse you?" He smiled his toothy smile at her. "I will leave you now to rest, for you should know my vigor is fully restored," he said, leering at her. Then, kissing her hand, he left her.

"What have you done to him that his mood is so changed?" Agata demanded.

"I have played the whore," Bianca said bluntly. "Now fetch my writing desk and the vellum so I may write to my mother." She wrote the invitation, and it was, to her relief, quickly dispatched. Antonio took it himself and promised to return with an answer before the day was over.

That night, Bianca went to her husband's bedchamber to find the slave girl, Nudara, waiting with him. *"Caro mio?"* Her tone was questioning.

"We must have a little variety in our passion, *dolce* Bianca. Now that you have accepted your duties in my bed I thought I should bring Nudara for our amusement. I will even allow you to beat her, for she is a very naughty wench, aren't you, Nudara?" He chuckled darkly, and held out his hand to Bianca.

It had been difficult—nay, near impossible—to play his willing lover when they had been alone. Now she would have to do it with the slave girl present, and a part of his passion. She saw the girl looking at her slyly as if she knew exactly what Bianca had done, was doing. "I should like to beat her, Sebastiano," she heard herself saying. "I do not like the way she looks at me. She is too pert for a slave."

Sebastiano Rovere chuckled. He was very much enjoying the woman his beautiful wife was becoming. "What will you have? The strap or the dog whip?" he asked her, curious as to which she would choose.

"The dog whip," Bianca said sweetly.

"My lord, you cannot allow this!" Nudara protested.

"How dare you question your master, girl!" Bianca snapped at her. She took the little whip her husband handed her. "Lie upon the bed with your bottom raised for me."

"My lord!" Nudara threw herself at Sebastiano Rovere's feet.

With a wicked smile he dragged the girl up and flung her facedown upon the bed, smacking her buttocks as he did so. "Up! Up, wench. Your mistress will now attend your punishment and I believe she is right. You are much too pert."

She couldn't do it. She just couldn't do it, Bianca thought. But then she saw the avid and eager look in her husband's eye. Joining him in his depravity would bind him closer to her, and she had not yet seen her mother. The whip descended upon the hapless Nudara's bared flesh several times. She was careful not to break the girl's skin, but her blows were hard enough to give pain and caused the girl to shriek loudly.

Sebastiano was practically drooling with his excitement. His cock had risen quickly with each blow, and the slave's cries. When Bianca ceased after several blows, he moved behind the slave, grasping her hips and began to thrust into her. It was not her sheath, however, that took his cock. Unable to help herself, Bianca cried out, "What are you doing, Sebastiano?"

"There are several ways to fuck a woman, *cara mia*," he told her. "We shall do this eventually together. Give yourself to me, Nudara," he groaned as he pushed himself into her. "Give yourself!"

"Ohhh yes, master! I love it when you put yourself there!" Nudara cried out, and her pretty face was filled with dark lust. "Do it! Do it!" she begged him.

Madre di Dios! Bianca thought. What more is there to this horror?

"Tickle his balls, mistress," Nudara called out to her. "It will increase his pleasure tenfold."

"Take her instruction, *cara mia*," her husband commanded Bianca.

I am his whore. I must obey, and pretend I am enjoying it. Her fingers began stroking the hairy, pendulous sac that hung free and ready for her touch. "Is this pleasing, *caro mio*?" she asked him. "Am I giving you pleasure?"

And so the depravity and lust continued throughout the night, and for the next two nights. There was nothing that Sebastiano Rovere proposed in the privacy of his bedchamber that Bianca did not comply with until she thought she would go mad. But her mother was coming! She had sent back a verbal message with Antonio that she would come, and that was all that mattered to Bianca. Her mother would know how to help her escape this hell on earth that she had been forced into. And if she could not escape, Bianca planned on taking her own life, for she did not know how much longer she could keep up this charade with her husband and his slave girl. Last night he had taken pleasure in watching the two women, instructing them to kiss, and suck, lick, and rub each other's bodies. And when he had sated himself he told them of a man who raised miniature donkeys that were trained to mount women and service them. He was thinking of buying one.

Nudara, of course, had clapped her hands at his suggestion, asking him if had seen the size of a little donkey cock, and curious if it was big. Sebastiano Rovere had laughed knowingly, and assured her the donkey's cock was big enough to satisfy even her greedy maw. Then he made the slave girl don a false manhood made of leather, and watched while Nudara fucked Bianca with it. Bianca disappointed her husband when she could not seem to gain any pleasure from it, but she quickly redeemed herself by saying that only his magnificent cock was capable of giving her pleasure. He had then delivered what she claimed to desire, her apparently genuine cries delighting him.

Bianca shuddered with the memory of it. She bathed, and dressed, and had Agata dress her dark hair simply. Then she sent her servingwoman to await her mother's arrival. Her husband had gone off to the courts this morning, preparing to argue an important case. He was in an excellent mood, and fully prepared to win. She would be free of his interference. Agata returned, bringing Orianna Pietro d'Angelo with her. The two women fell into each other's arms.

Orianna was shocked by her eldest daughter's appearance. She was unnaturally pale. There were dark circles beneath her eyes. Her ebony hair, while beautifully dressed, looked faded, and she had lost weight. "What has happened to you, Bianca?" she cried.

At the sound of her mother's familiar voice, Bianca burst into tears. "*Madre! Madre!* You must take me from this house before he kills me with his excesses! I can bear no more! I have tried for my father's sake, for my brother's sake, but I will die if I cannot escape this man. You must help me! *You must!*" And she pressed herself into her mother's arms, continuing to weep.

Orianna turned to Agata. "What has happened to my daughter?" she asked the servingwoman.

"Mistress, I do not know," Agata said. "She will not speak on it, but I believe she is being cruelly abused by her husband when in his bed. There is a sly Moorish slave girl in the house, and Antonio has told me he brings her into the marital bedchamber. And *he* never comes to my young mistress's apartment. She is always sent for to go to him."

"Bianca," Orianna said gently, "you must tell me everything that has happened. I cannot help you if you do not. Do you understand me?" She tilted her daughter's tearstained face up so their eyes might meet. *"Everything."*

"I am so ashamed," Bianca whispered. "I did not know that people could do such things to each other, *Madre*. He has not even allowed me a priest so I might make my confession and at least relieve myself of this guilt. Oh, *Madre*! I do not believe you have ever known of the things he has done to me. It began on our wedding night." And then the younger woman explained to her mother in careful detail everything that had happened in the dark bedchamber of Sebastiano Rovere.

Both Orianna and Agata listened, each with a growing degree of horror as Bianca spoke. The mother pressed her lips together to contain her cries at the evil suffered by her child. The servingwoman wept silently, wishing Bianca had confided in her so she might have informed the Pietro d'Angelos of the wicked abuse being suffered by her young mistress. After an hour had passed, Bianca finally stopped speaking.

"Fetch my daughter's cloak," Orianna said sharply.

Agata jumped up to quickly obey, bringing the required item and wrapping it about Bianca's thin shoulders. Then she looked to Orianna. "Where are we going, mistress?" she asked the older woman.

"From this house," Orianna said. "You will never return to that man, Bianca. I swear it! I shall not let him ever touch you again."

"My father . . ." Bianca said softly.

"I am hiding you in the convent of Santa Maria del Fiore, just outside the city's walls," Orianna said. "Your father shall not know where you are until I can make him see reason, my child. You will have sanctuary and the protection of the

Mother Superior, who is my distant kinswoman. Come now!"
She took Bianca's arm.

"I am his wife," Bianca said despairingly. "His possession.
He can do what he wants with me, *Madre*. He has told me a
thousand times since our wedding day. If he finds me, he will
surely kill me."

"He will not find you," Orianna assured her child. "Now
let us hurry. Agata, come, for you must be hidden too."

The three women left Bianca's apartment and hurried to
escape the house. Antonio was keeping the door that afternoon. Seeing the trio, he opened the portal of the palazzo and
then turned his head the other way. The trio exited, but Orianna said to the servingman, "Leave this place with us. I will
take you into my personal employ."

"*Grazie*, gracious lady," Antonio replied, closing the door
behind them and following them out into the street. He helped
the lady and his young mistress into the waiting Pietro
d'Angelo litter. Then, walking beside Agata, the servants followed along.

The litter made its way to a busy market square, where it
was set down.

"There are litters for hire here," Orianna said softly to
Agata. "Find a bearer called Ilario and tell him Signora Pietro
d'Angelo is in need of his services."

"At once, *signora*," the servingwoman responded and hurried off. She returned a few minutes later with two litter bearers carrying a single chair litter.

The grizzled older man in front was smiling from ear to
ear. "*Signora!*" he greeted Orianna. "It has been a long time.
How may I serve you today?"

Orianna stepped from her family litter. "You may take me

home," she instructed him. "Antonio, you will attend me, please. Agata, get in with your mistress." Then she murmured lowly to her head litter bearer. "Take my daughter and her servant to Santa Maria del Fiore. Tell them she is a kinswoman to the Reverend Mother Baptista, and seeks both shelter and sanctuary. Say I will come to speak with the Reverend Mother myself tomorrow."

The Pietro d'Angelos' head litter bearer nodded silently. Orianna climbed into her hired transport. With Antonio by its side, it was borne from the busy market piazza while her family's vehicle took off in another direction, the four bearers moving quickly through the noisy, narrow streets towards one of the city's gates. Seeing the city for the first time, Bianca was fascinated in spite of herself. The noise was incredible, the smells many and varied. Some pleasant, and some not so. Vendors hawked their wares. Children played in the puddles, and on the cobbles. Dogs, some mongrels, some with expensive collars, roamed freely. Her bearers never broke stride but moved swiftly along through one of the city's gates. Down the highway and around a curve, they then stopped before a walled enclosure. The litter was set down, and the head litter bearer rapped on a small, almost invisible portal.

A tiny grille opened in the door. "Yes?" a voice inquired.

"I come from Signora Pietro d'Angelo, who is kin to the Reverend Mother Baptista. She wishes the lady I bring to you, and her servant, to have sanctuary. She will come herself tomorrow and speak with the Reverend Mother."

"Wait!" the voice commanded.

Several long minutes passed, and then the small portal opened and a tall, austere nun stepped forth. She went to the litter, drew the curtains aside, and asked, "Who are you, my child?"

"I am Bianca Pietro d'Angelo, Reverend Mother," Bianca replied.

"You are Orianna's eldest daughter?"

"Yes, Reverend Mother."

"The wife of Sebastiano Rovere?"

"Yes, Reverend Mother."

"You wish sanctuary for yourself and your serving-woman?"

"Oh yes, please, Reverend Mother!" Bianca's voice shook.

"Come in, then, my child, and your woman too," the nun responded.

"Oh, thank you!" Bianca cried. "Thank you!"

Agata climbed from the litter and helped her mistress out, and together the three women entered through the gate into the convent proper.

"Tell your mistress," Reverend Mother Baptista said to the head litter bearer, "that I shall very much look forward to her visit. And certainly you and your fellows know not to tell anyone where you have been."

"We have served our master and mistress for over twenty years, Reverend Mother," he told her. "We understand what is expected of us."

"God and his blessed Mother be with you, then," the nun said, blessing them.

Then she turned back, going through the small door in the convent wall. It closed behind her. She now turned to her waiting guests. "I will take you to the guesthouse that is reserved for ladies remaining with us for a time, as I expect you will be here a while. The convent grounds within these walls are safe for you to walk. Meals will be brought to you. You are expected to join us for the morning Mass and for Vespers in the evening. Are you skilled in sewing or embroidery, my child?"

"Both, Reverend Mother," Bianca answered. "And my Agata too."

"Good," the nun said. "You may help us with certain pieces that our convent is commissioned to do by wealthy families and churches. Or if you are able, you are invited to join those of this flock who garden, but neither you nor your servant will be permitted to be idle while you are here. Too much slothfulness will not help you to grow strong again, and if you are your mother's daughter, you are a strong woman beneath that aura of frailty and fear now surrounding you."

Bianca was rather startled by the nun's practical and candid speech. She had not thought that a woman from a convent far removed from the world would be so. She had always believed they spent their days in nothing more than prayer and fasting. She was quickly disabused of these notions in the days that followed.

The guesthouse to which she and Agata were shown was comfortable without being ostentatious. The furniture was sturdy and sensible. There were two bedchambers, a small dining room, and a salon. The bed in her bedchamber was hung with simple blue linen curtains. It had a trundle for Agata. There were two casement windows looking out upon an herb garden and a tiled fireplace. The floor was wood and had a woven rush rug.

On one of the whitewashed walls was a beautifully carved wooden crucifix. It was a simple but comfortable chamber.

The lack of bedding was solved in the early evening when

her mother's own servant, Fabia, arrived, bringing with her a feather bed, linen bedding that was fragrant with the scent of roses, a coverlet, and a small wooden trunk filled with fresh, clean garments, most of which Bianca recognized as her own, left behind for her wedding finery months before. There was even a hairbrush of smooth pear wood studded with boar's bristles and a matching comb. Fabia hugged Bianca with the familiarity of an old family retainer, and greeted the younger Agata, who was her niece.

The bell for Vespers chimed, and Bianca hurried off to join the nuns in their chapel for the evening service. She knew she might have been excused this first night, but she was so relieved at having been rescued so swiftly that she felt a strong need to go and give thanks. She had also not been allowed the comfort of any religious service since her marriage, as her husband did not want her speaking with any priest, even though Sebastian Rovere knew the seal of the confessional could not be broken. There were ways of getting around any law. Even Church law, and no one knew that better than the best lawyer in all of Florence.

Left behind, the two servingwomen spent their time making the room comfortable for Bianca. Fabia had even brought a small glass vase and a few roses from the Pietro d'Angelos' gardens. When the bed and the trundle had been made, the plain linen curtains hung on the window, the little wooden trunk set at the foot of the bed, and the few garments hung in the small wooden wardrobe, the two women talked.

"Did the lady tell you?" Agata asked.

Fabia nodded. "Although how much of it, I do not know," she answered.

Agata quickly recited what she knew, her brown eyes filling with tears as she spoke to her aunt. "She never confided in me, *Zia*. She told her mother she was too ashamed, as if she were to blame for what happened to her, as if it were her fault."

Fabia made the sign of the evil eye. "A curse on Sebastiano Rovere, although I am certain it is not the first plague sworn against his house. My mistress told the master after the meal, and the uproar has been considerable. He shouted that she would bring about the destruction of their house. She shouted that if Master Marco had used the intelligence God blessed him with, her daughter would not have been sacrificed to the devil."

"Rovere did not come?" Agata said, surprised.

"There was a messenger just before I left," Fabia replied. "My mistress will not tell the master where the lady Bianca is hidden. He will shout and fume, but eventually she will get him to see her way in the matter."

But it was late into the evening before Giovanni Pietro d'Angelo was able to fully absorb what his wife had told him and agree with what she had done. Sebastiano Rovere had sent an angry message to the silk merchant, threatening him with dire consequences if his young wife was not immediately returned to his palazzo. He sent Rovere's messenger back with a brief message telling him he had no idea where Bianca was, but invited his son-in-law to come in the morning and discuss the matter. Then he went to bed.

In the very early morning, before the silk merchant was even awake, his wife slipped out of the house. It was still dark, and the summer air was heavy and still. Careful to be sure that her son-in-law had not yet put a watch on her home, she crossed the piazza and sought Father Bonamico at Santa Anna

Dolce. The priest was already at his morning prayers. She knelt and waited for him to recognize her.

Finally, the white-haired priest rose. Turning, he smiled. "Good morning, my daughter," he greeted her. "You are up early, so I must assume there is a purpose to your visit. Come, and we will talk privily."

She followed him from the church and into a small study, where she knew he met those who sought his advice. Sitting in the straight-backed chair he offered her, Orianna Pietro d'Angelo told him everything that Bianca had told her the day before. She held back nothing. The priest had to understand the seriousness of the situation if he was to help them. Several times, she halted as her voice caught in her throat. She wept without even realizing it, slow tears slipping down her beautiful face.

Father Bonamico listened. His face, which had been serious before, grew shocked, horrified, and then angry by turns. He was more than aware of the evil man could do, having listened to many a confession over his forty years as a priest. Several times he murmured a soft imprecation and then crossed himself. He had been frankly surprised when he had learned of Bianca Pietro d'Angelo's betrothal to Sebastiano Rovere, for the man's reputation for depravity was hardly a secret, although rarely discussed publicly. Now Orianna told him of the reason Bianca had been sacrificed.

"I know," she said, "that my husband did what he did to save Marco, to protect the family name. I did not want such a marriage for Bianca. My father had already begun discreet inquiries among the important families in Venice for a suitable husband for his eldest granddaughter. But then Giovanni made this decision. He was certain that despite Sebastiano

Rovere's reputation he would treat our daughter with respect, for aside from the faint rumors of murder when his previous two wives had died, he had treated them properly. At least in public.

"I worried when he would not let me see Bianca these past months, but Giovanni said it was because she was young and beautiful that he did not wish to share her with anyone, especially her family. My husband believed that awful man had fallen in love with our child. And Bianca! Ah, my poor daughter! When she learned that I had been forbidden her company by her husband, what she did to gain his permission to see me!"

Orianna continued on in her tale.

"And as soon as you learned the abuse she was suffering you removed her from her husband's house?" Father Bonamico asked.

"I did! I could not leave her there, good priest. I could not!"

"Where is she?" he wanted to know.

"At Santa Maria del Fiore," Orianna replied. "Even my husband does not know. The Reverend Mother Baptista is a kinswoman of mine."

"Good! Good!" the priest told her. "She has sanctuary there, and even if Rovere should learn her whereabouts, he would not dare break the laws of sanctuary."

"I think he would dare anything," Orianna said. "I would go to her now before Rovere puts a watch on the palazzo. Then I shall be back in time for his visit. He will not delay in coming, I am certain."

"How will you get to the convent?" The priest's face showed his concern for her.

"I know a litter bearer in the nearby market square. I once saved his wife and child from illness. He has been devoted to me ever since," Orianna replied. "If you will permit me to slip through the church's back garden, no one will see me."

"Come back through the church when you return," Father Bonamico advised. "You must take no chances, my daughter, that anyone believes you were anywhere but here, praying and attending Mass. Kneel now, and I will bless you and your endeavors. You must tell Bianca you have spoken with me, and that I will come to hear her confession later today. After that, we dare not attempt to see her. Rovere is a determined man. He will want her back, and will turn the city upside down to find her. We must be cleverer and quicker than he is."

Orianna knelt to receive his blessing. Before she rose to her feet again, she took the priest's two hands in hers and kissed them. "Thank you," she said simply.

"For your peace of mind, my daughter, know that these conversations you and I have had, and will have, are under the seal of the confessional," he told her.

Orianna left the church then to slip through its garden and out a little gate at the garden's rear. Pulling the hood of her cloak up over her light auburn hair, she hurried through the narrow, winding streets to the nearby market square, where she found Ilario and his litter already waiting for business. She climbed into the single-chair vehicle and instructed him, "Santa Maria del Fiore."

Ilario recognized her, but said nothing. He and his helper picked up the litter and began the journey. As the streets were not yet crowded, they made excellent time. When they had exited through the city gates and reached the convent Ilario said, "You will want us to wait, *signora*?"

She nodded wordlessly, and then hurried through the small gate that opened to her knock. Less than an hour later, she exited, reentered the litter, and softly directed him back to the market square, where she paid him double the fee and hurried off. Coming forth from the church several minutes later, the hood no longer shielding her face, she walked slowly across the piazza to enter her house.

Fabia greeted her. "You made good time, *signora*," she said lowly. "The beast has not arrived yet, and the master is just now getting up."

Orianna nodded. "Is he aware I have been gone?" she asked.

"I believe so, for you slept in his bed last night," Fabia responded, and then she chuckled. "His servingman said he awoke smiling and in good humor."

"Tell the servants to feed him well, for he will want a full belly when he has to deal with that monster. Then come and help me change my gown."

"Yes, *signora*," Fabia said. "The young mistress was all right this morning?"

"She says she slept well for the first time in months, knowing she was safe," Orianna said. Then she hurried off to her apartments. Seeing Francesca skulking about, she called to her second daughter and the girl came to her. "You will remain in the nursery rooms with your sisters and little brothers until I tell you that you may come out. I will warn the servants to watch for you. If you are seen outside your apartments, Francesca, I will personally whip you. Not your father, who is too softhearted, but I will myself wield the switch. Do you understand, my daughter?" The mother looked sternly at her young daughter.

"Is it about Bianca?" Francesca asked.

"Do you understand me?" Orianna repeated quietly.

"Yes, *Madre*," came the reluctant reply.

"I will walk with you to your quarters." And taking Francesca's hand, the mother led the daughter to where she needed to be. Stepping into the nursery of her house, she instructed the three nursemaids as to her wishes, with a special admonishment to Francesca's servant. "If she is caught outside of this room, you will receive a whipping too," she warned the woman, who adored and indulged her charge.

"Yes, *signora*," the woman said, "but sometimes the child can be so persuasive."

"When you feel yourself yielding," Orianna said with a small amused smile touching her lips, "consider the cut of the switch on your plump bottom."

"Yes, *signora*!"

"Good! It is important that the household remain silent," she said, giving them her final word. Then she left the nursery quarters of her home to go to her own apartments, where Fabia was already awaiting her.

The servingwoman had laid out three gowns for her mistress's approval.

"The black makes me look sallow and weak," Orianna remarked. "The burgundy is too festive for this occasion. I like the medium blue, but it is too beautifully adorned. Find me a simple gown that is elegant but will not imply that his visit to my house is an honor."

"You have a dark brown velvet that is plain. The embroidery along the neckline is black," Fabia said. "It makes you appear stern, and perhaps even a bit older than you are. With the gold crucifix your father sent you last year to commemorate your natal day, it will give you an imposing appearance."

"Yes, that will do," Orianna agreed.

When Fabia finished dressing her mistress and arranging her auburn hair into an elegant chignon, she helped her lady fasten the crucifix about her neck. Then stepping back, she nodded. "It is perfect, *signora*."

A rap sounded at the bedchamber door, and Giovanni Pietro d'Angelo stepped into the room. He was garbed as soberly as his wife, but in black. He nodded, pleased by her appearance. Then he held out his hand to her. "Come, *cara mia*. He is here and awaits us in my library."

She took his hand and together they went to meet Sebastiano Rovere.

Chapter 5

When they entered the room where he was standing, he could see they were dressed for battle. *Well,* Sebastiano Rovere thought, *the law is on my side. I will have their daughter back in my house by noon today. I will beat her well for this breach of wifely trust. Then she will take my cock before she takes that of my little donkey. Nudara says the creature is quite proficient and as skilled as any man.* He glared at the Pietro d'Angelos. "Where is my wife?" he demanded.

"I have absolutely no idea," the silk merchant said quietly.

Rovere's face turned red with his anger. "I doubt your duplicitous wife can claim the same ignorance." He turned to Orianna. "Where is my wife, you Venetian harridan?"

"Safe," Orianna replied. "Safe, where you can no longer harm her with your disgusting perversions and bad breath."

"I have the law behind my request," he told her through gritted teeth.

"Then use the law to gain what you want," Orianna said. "But if you do, be certain that the Church will be told of your outrageous depravity; of what you did to my innocent child on her wedding night. I doubt even the law will condone your behavior when they learn how low you have sunk in your immorality to put your younger son to my daughter as if you were breeding a pair of animals," she warned him.

"Do not threaten me with the Church, *signora*," he said. "Need I remind you that my kinsman is Cardinal Rovere? I will deny before him everything your daughter has said of me. The Church will not believe the hysterical ravings of a young woman over a man of my reputation. Women are known to lie more times than not."

"If a man's word is so sacrosanct," Orianna said, "why did you permit your son to dispose of a dead courtesan rather than simply leaving her to be found in her bed? If your son told you the truth, *signore*, and the woman simply expired of excess, there would have been no marks of violence on her body to say otherwise. Once Stefano and our Marco came to you and told you what had happened, you became as complicit in their actions as if you had been involved personally. I do not believe that is proper behavior for a man of the court, is it?"

"Is it your habit to let a woman speak for you, Pietro d'Angelo?" Rovere demanded angrily. The bitch was far too clever.

Giovanni Pietro d'Angelo almost felt sorry for his son-in-law. He knew better than most that if her sex had not relegated her to the role of wife and mother, Orianna could have ruled Venice and Florence both. "I am a man of few words, Rovere," he said drily. "My wife, however, makes an interesting point."

"You will give Bianca an annulment," Orianna told their guest.

"On what grounds?" Rovere demanded angrily. "I have used your daughter well these past months. And you cannot claim I am at fault! I am known for my passion, and for my prowess. There isn't a courtesan in Florence who would say otherwise," he bragged with a smug smirk.

"Is the world privy to your marriage bed?" Orianna wanted to know. "You will say that Bianca has denied your husband's rights. That she has said she will give you no children. The Church will be satisfied, and our generous gifts will grease the way. There need be no shame upon you, *signore*. You do not love Bianca, and certainly she holds no love for you. You have had what you wanted of her. Now let her go."

"She will wed again, have children, and give lie to such charges," Rovere said. "It is then that people will talk, and I shall be made to look the fool."

"You have spoiled my daughter for marriage," Orianna said. "It is unlikely she will wed again but for love, and if she did it would not be in Florence. When the annulment is granted, she will go to live with one of my sisters. She will be gone from this city, and its excesses."

"You have figured this all out to suit your purposes, *signora*, but Bianca is *mine*. I will not let her go. You will return her to me, and she will live in my palazzo until she dies there," Rovere snarled at Orianna.

It was then that Giovanni Pietro d'Angelo spoke in a quiet but commanding voice. "My eldest daughter will never be returned to you, Rovere. If you would now accuse my son, Marco, of that courtesan's death, know that I will accuse Stefano. Your eldest son is now married into a good family. I am told his wife is expecting her first child. Will you expose a foolish and youthful indiscretion for the sole purpose of forcing an unwilling woman back into your bed?

"I must take a certain amount of blame for this travesty, for I should not have allowed the marriage between you and my daughter to take place at all. My wife begged me to reconsider, but I was not thinking clearly, and could only see misfortune if I did not acquiesce to your demand. I was wrong, and Bianca has paid for my error in judgment. I will not allow her to be further abused. Grant her an annulment, and let us be done."

"*Never!*" Sebastiano Rovere spat. "I will find her! It matters not where you have hidden her. I will find her! You cannot keep her from me. She is my wife. *Mine!* I will be certain she pays for her duplicity towards me. Her punishment will be slow, and it will be painful. I will break her proud spirit, and she will never again defy me."

The more he spoke, the darker his face became with his rage. There was spittle at the corners of his lips as his voice rose until he was shouting at them.

"You are a fool, *signore*," Giovanni Pietro d'Angelo said. Then he called for his servants to remove the furious man from his home. "Put him out in the street where he belongs. He is not to be admitted to this house ever again."

Two strong servingmen literally dragged Sebastiano Rovere from the palazzo. Having lost all sense of dignity in his outrage, the man struggled and cursed at them. They in turn were not inclined to treat him gently or with respect. One of the men in fact put a boot to Rovere's behind, giving him a final hard shove out the front door of the palazzo, where Rovere sprawled facedown on the cobbles.

He scrambled up quickly, shouting and shaking a fist. "You will regret this, Pietro d'Angelo! I will have my revenge on you and your family! See if I don't!"

They did not hear him inside the palazzo, for the walls of the building were several feet thick. After Rovere had been dragged shouting from the chamber where they had all been, Orianna collapsed into a chair, her face in her hands. Her husband heard a sob, but only one, and after a moment or two she uncovered her beautiful face. Her look was determined. Giovanni had seen that look several times over the course of their marriage. It meant she was ready to do battle, and she would not lose.

"He is a mad dog," Orianna said quietly. "He should be put out of his misery, as a mad dog would."

"Under the circumstances, the crime would be laid at our door," her husband told her in practical tones. "There is another way, I am certain, and we will find it, *cara mia*."

"He has no trade to ruin," Orianna replied. "Every judge and lawyer in Florence accepts bribes. It is considered commonplace to keep the business of the law efficient. It is the worst of his vices that we need to expose to the light of day."

"There are plenty of rumors," Giovanni remarked, "but he has been reasonably discreet. So much so that even the Church looks the other way."

"We cannot allow him to regain custody of Bianca," Orianna said. "And now with his intransigence, none from this household may go to her, for he will already have put a watch on our house."

"Did you not go early this morning?" her husband asked, smiling.

"Gio! How could you know that?"

"Because, *cara*, I know you. And did you really think that after the wonderful night we spent together I would not miss you the moment you left my bed?"

She laughed. "I went to an early Mass, and afterwards spoke with Father Bonamico. He suggested I use the church's little back garden gate as my means of coming and going," Orianna explained to Giovanni.

"You cannot go again," he said. "The danger is too great for Bianca."

"I know," she agreed, "and so I told Bianca. I have spoken with Reverend Mother Baptista. Bianca will be kept within the convent walls. Even if Rovere eventually learns where she is, he will not break the laws of sanctuary."

Giovanni nodded. "I concur," he replied to his wife. "We must find another place for her, far from the city, *cara*. For now, however, she must remain where she is. Our opportunity will come if we are patient."

The Pietro d'Angelos shortly afterwards departed Florence for their villa in the Tuscan countryside. It was cooler, and the children had more space to run free in the long, sunny days. They knew that Sebastiano Rovere had set a watch on their summer home. Marco, who remained behind to oversee his father's warehouses, sent them any news of their son-in-law. His guilt had been great upon learning of his sister's trials.

In the early autumn, the family returned to the city just as a great scandal involving Rovere broke open, giving them the opportunity to move Bianca from Santa Maria del Fiore to a new hiding place many miles from Florence. The lawyer had given a large party for a number of the city's prominent men. There had been rumors for weeks about some new perversion Rovere had found, and the guests came eager to partake of whatever it might be, for the lawyer was known for his originality.

No one was aware that the lawyer's bride had fled his house. As highborn Florentine ladies were rarely observed outside their homes, Bianca's flight had not become public knowledge; and she would certainly not be present, or even seen by her husband's guests, at such a gathering as they were planning to attend.

The night after what could only be called an orgy of spectacular proportions, the lawyer was arrested on a complaint brought against him by the head of the Arte dei Medici, Speziali e Merciai. His sixteen-year-old niece had been kidnapped the previous afternoon as she left his apothecary shop to bring a headache powder to her widowed mother, who lived in the house next to the shop. The distance was not more than half a dozen steps, but two villains had grabbed the girl and made off with her. She had been found battered, bruised, and barely conscious on the banks of the River Arno early the following morning by a fisherman. With great effort, the girl had cried out for her uncle.

Wrapping the naked girl in a blanket, the fisherman carried her to the apothecary, where, after drinking some wine with strengthening herbs, she told him her story.

The two men who had taken her had covered her head with a cloth so she could not see and brought her to a house. She was then taken away by a beautiful olive-skinned woman to be bathed and perfumed. They fed her wine, which made her feel strange. The woman was kind to her, and let the girl pat her pet, a tiny gray donkey. But then the woman brought her into a large chamber filled with men in fine robes, most with goblets in their hands, some already half drunk.

They howled with delight to see the naked girl. When they had finished with her, she was dragged from the chamber, taken from the house, and dumped on the riverbank, where she had been found.

Because she had heard his name and had seen his face, the unfortunate girl was able to identify her kidnapper. They carried her to his palazzo, and she identified it as the house from which she was taken after her shame. They brought five men before her, and she pointed to Sebastiano Rovere. He was immediately arrested and jailed, along with the two servingmen who had taken the girl and had been the first to rape her. The city was abuzz with the shameful scandal of an innocent maiden being so abused.

"This is our opportunity to get Bianca to safety," Giovanni told his wife.

"He will buy his way out of this difficulty," Orianna replied.

"Aye, he will," her husband agreed, "but not easily, or too soon, which is why we must act quickly, *cara*."

"What of those watching the house?" she wanted to know.

"They have hardly been discreet. I know where they are, and they shall be removed so we have time to do what must be done," he answered her. "I will send Georgio to Santa Maria del Fiore to tell Reverend Mother Baptista to see that Agata and Bianca are ready to leave in another day." Georgio was the Pietro d'Angelos' second son.

"So soon?" Orianna asked.

"The sooner the better, *cara*. She will be safe at Villa Luce Stellare," Giovanni replied. "Very few people know of its existence. It was part of my mother's dower, but she rarely left Florence, and she preferred the countryside to the seaside.

These past weeks I have had it opened up and cleaned so Bianca might be comfortable. I have employed local folk to serve her, and they but await her arrival," he told his wife. Then he called a servant and said, "Find Georgio, and say to him that his father says it is time."

"Yes, master," the woman said, hurrying off.

Two days later, word spread across the city that the victim of Sebastiano Rovere's perversion had died from the excesses that had been forced upon her. The imprisoned lawyer demanded his release, as there was no longer a witness against him. He was supported by the members of his own guild, the Arte dei Giudici e Notai. But the Arte dei Medici, Speziali e Merciai, the apothecaries and doctors, stood with their leader and his family. The girl's testimony had already been taken by the Church and recorded. They wanted murder added to the charges of kidnapping and rape.

Rovere testified that he had sent his men to find him a willing whore who would be paid for her services. His two servants, however, eager to avoid further torture, said he had told them to find a young maid, a virgin if they could. He had promised them they would get to have the girl's virginity so that when she entertained his guests, she would be free of any impediment to their pleasure. The men knew the apothecary had a niece upon whom he doted. She was sure to be a virgin, and she had been.

Rovere said the girl had no value to her family. They would be fortunate to find a husband for her, as she had little to recommend her. Highly insulted, the apothecary declared his niece was prettier than most, and he had already had several inquiries from fathers looking for a good wife for their sons. He said he had been training her, as she was a naturally skilled herbalist. She also cared for her widowed, ailing mother. Her family had loved her. Had it not been for Sebastiano Rovere's debauchery, the girl would have lived a good life. The apothecary, his guild standing behind him, wanted justice.

The day before Rovere's victim died, and while he lingered in prison, Bianca was moved from Santa Maria del Fiore many miles from the city of Florence to a small coastal villa with the silly yet charming name of Luce Stellare, which simply meant "Starry." Her parents came to bid her farewell, but they did not go with her. Even though Rovere was imprisoned for the moment, and Giovanni had removed the minions he had sent to watch their palazzo, the Pietro d'Angelos would draw no attention to themselves by leaving the city. Bianca traveled by horseback with Agata, surrounded by a group of men-at-arms sent by her grandfather in Venice. There was no one to return to Florence and gossip. Every precaution had been taken to keep her safe.

She wept, knowing she would not see her family for some time. "Will you ever be able to come to me, *Madre*?" she asked Orianna.

"Not until Rovere either grants you an annulment, or is dead" was the reply. "We can take no chances in him finding you, my daughter. Every day he does not have you in his clutches, his anger and need for revenge against you grow."

Bianca nodded. "I understand," she said sadly, and she did. She had convinced her husband that she was finally becoming his willing whore. Now he knew she had done it to gain a victory and escape him. He would not be merciful. "I would kill myself before I allowed him possession of me again," she told her parents.

"It should not come to that," her father told her. "No one

knows of my mother's villa, not even your brothers. You will live peacefully, and be safe there."

It had been so difficult to see them go. Ever cautious, they had come and departed under the cover of darkness in the hours before the dawn. She and Agata had left immediately afterwards, bidding Reverend Mother Baptista farewell, giving her their thanks for tendering them her protection.

"I will pray for you each day, Bianca, my child," the nun said. "The blessed Mother will protect you, I know."

Then they were absorbed into the middle of an armed and mounted troop of horsemen to begin the journey to the coast. The silk merchant had instructed the captain of the guard not to allow Bianca to be seen if he could avoid it. They were not to stop in any public place. Consequently, a small pavilion was set up for the two women when they stopped for the night. The captain himself brought them supper and made certain that the charcoal brazier that heated the tent was properly lit.

"We should reach the seacoast by tomorrow, *madonna*," he told Bianca. "There will be no need for you to spend another night in the wild. Your grandfather would not be pleased with these arrangements at all."

Bianca could not help but smile at the remark. She had met her grandfather only twice, but she understood exactly what the soldier was saying. "Please tell the *principe* that I am very grateful for his help," she responded.

"He wishes you had come to Venice, *madonna*," the captain said. "He would have protected you."

"But then the matter with my husband would have become public knowledge," Bianca said. "My father did not wish that. Perhaps one day I shall come to Venice."

"That would please the *principe*, *madonna*," was the

reply. Then the captain politely withdrew, leaving the two women alone.

"I miss the bells," Bianca said to Agata. "And the incredible quiet of the convent. I felt at peace there, although I have no wish to become a nun. It is strange being free and out in the world again."

"We are not so much out in the world as we might be," Agata said. "The villa will be a quiet place too." She helped her mistress from her garments and brought her a small basin of water in which to wash.

"There will be new sounds," Bianca noted. "The sea, the wind, birds, and farm creatures." She quickly washed her face and hands, drying them on a linen cloth that Agata handed her. Then she lay down upon the small camp bed that had been provided for her as Agata drew up the silk quilt.

"I hope we can sleep on these things," she said as she took her place on the second narrow camp bed and drew up the coverlet. "They have not built them for comfort."

But sleep the two women did. It had been a long day, their journey beginning before dawn and not ending until sunset. Agata awakened before the dawn, hearing the encampment stirring about them. She arose and quickly dressed, going outside to hail the captain. "Shall I wake my mistress?" she asked him.

He nodded. "If we leave before first light we shall reach our destination in early afternoon. Go and get something to eat."

Agata followed his instruction, fetching bread, fruit, and cheese for herself and for Bianca. Then she returned to the pavilion to awaken the younger woman. Like her mistress, she had lived in Florence her entire life, and other than trips to the

Pietro d'Angelos' villa in the countryside, she had never left it until now. She was curious to see the sea.

They reached Villa Luce Stellare, as the captain had promised, in midafternoon. Their party came down the hillside road they had been traveling to find the blue waters of the Ligurian Sea spread out before and below them. They had passed through no villages that day. Now they turned off onto a narrow dirt path that went down a rocky slope. At the bottom of the path lay a small villa that was painted yellow. They stopped.

The captain hurried to help the two women from their horses. "Here we are, *madonna*. This will be your refuge." He walked to the large oak door and banged on it.

Bianca looked around her. It was certainly isolated, and the little villa could not be seen from the road. *Perhaps,* she thought, a tiny tendril of hope curling in her, *perhaps I will be safe here from Sebastiano. I can make a life for myself at last.*

"Here is the mistress of the house," she heard the captain say.

Bianca turned her eyes to the door of the villa.

A small, plump woman stood there, smiling broadly. "Welcome to Luce Stellare, *signora*. Your father sent us word to expect you. Come in! Come in!"

Bianca turned to the Venetian captain. "You will remain the night?" she asked.

"Nay, *signora*. We were instructed to deliver you safely, but then be on our way immediately in order not to attract any unwanted attention to your arrival. The *principe* and your father were most firm in their instructions. We will begin our return today and follow the road above along the coast into Modena. Its *duca* has given your grandfather permission for us to travel through his domain into Venetian territory. I thank you for the offer of hospitality. I will tell your grandfather of your kindness, *signora*."

"*Mille grazie,*" Bianca said. "Please tell the *principe* that I am grateful for his protection, Captain."

He bowed smartly, and then mounting his horse, led his men back up the path to the coastal road they would travel.

Bianca stood a moment and looked about her. It was quiet, and the air was so sweet. There was a beach below the house. It was a narrow sandy strip that ran into a narrower span of small rocks. She would ask the servants if it could be walked, and how to get down to the beach. She turned and saw that the front door of the villa was flanked by a large, glazed blue pot on either side. The pots were planted with white roses, her favorites. She was certain her father had seen to that.

Giovanni Pietro d'Angelo could be a sentimental man. The roses, she suspected, were a peace offering. He had apologized to her for having insisted upon her marriage instead of seeking another solution to Sebastiano Rovere's blackmail. She had forgiven him easily, for he could not have known how brutal Rovere would be to a wife. The silk merchant was more than aware of the reputation for debauchery that his son-in-law possessed, but he had assumed that Rovere would not visit his vices upon his bride, an innocent girl of good family. That he had would trouble him for the rest of his life.

Bianca stopped to smell one of the beautiful roses. Its almost exotic fragrance was intoxicating. "Have it cut and brought to my bedchamber," she said to the patient servingwoman, who was still waiting for her to enter the villa.

"*Si, signora,*" the servant said. "You enjoy the flowers?"

"I do," Bianca told her. "Very much."

"I am Filomena, *signora*. It is my duty to oversee your servants. All, of course, but your own personal servingwoman," she amended carefully. "Come in now. Come in! They are all awaiting you. It is a small staff, for the *signore*, your father, said you would prefer your privacy and are little trouble."

Bianca chuckled at this observation. "My father knows me well," she agreed.

The servants had all lined up in the beautiful entry of the house to meet her.

There was Gemma, the cook, and two young maid-servants—one to help Filomena and the other to help the cook. Along with Agata, they constituted the household staff. There would be no men in the house, and again Bianca saw her father's hand in this arrangement. The outside staff consisted only of two brothers of indeterminate age, Primo and Ugo. They would care for the gardens and the animals.

"We grow much of our food," Filomena explained. "When your father came to open the villa after so many years, the old gardens were still visible among the weeds. The brothers have reclaimed much of it in the past few months, and will regain all of it by next year. There is a small grove of olive trees, and another of lemons. Primo says it may be possible to put in a little vineyard high up on the hillside. He says there was one there once, long ago. Some of the vines still survive. He brought some of the grapes for you this morning."

Bianca turned and smiled at Primo. "Thank you," she said.

Filomena nodded for the little group of servants to go about their business. "I will show you your new home," she said. "I imagine it is smaller than what you are used to, *signora*, but you will be comfortable. Your esteemed father has told me that you have been ill, and that life in the city is no longer for you. Is your husband dead?"

"No," Bianca said. *But I wish he were,* she thought silently. "I am seeking an annulment, Filomena. It was only discovered what an evil man my husband was after the marriage had taken place. He is now in prison awaiting his fate."

"Perhaps they will execute him, and then you will not have to bother with an annulment," Filomena said cheerfully. She was a country woman, and for her, simple solutions were always the best resolutions to any problem.

Bianca burst out laughing. "Yes, that would be a good result, but it is unlikely to happen. My husband is a wealthy and powerful man in Florence. He will escape his just due, but I will eventually get my annulment. For now, I hope I am well hidden."

"We will protect you, *signora*," Filomena said. Then she showed Bianca her new home, and was content to see that her *signora* was very pleased.

The entry to the villa was open and spacious. It had a center staircase leading up to its second floor. The main level of the house consisted of two small salons that were furnished with upholstered wooden chairs and tables. There was a little library with a long table and a straight-backed chair, as well as a dining room that held a table for six, and chairs to match. All of the rooms had doors leading outside into the gardens. The walls were paneled in light-colored fruitwood, and the floors were tiled in squares of pale beige. The dining room walls, however, were painted in a mural depicting a stag hunt. The library walls were built-in bookcases. Its ceiling was coffered.

Bianca followed Filomena up the wide staircase to the second level. There were three bedchambers, each with a tiled fireplace. Two of the bedchambers had alcoves to house a servant. But the chamber that was Bianca's had a small separate windowed room for Agata. Bianca's canopied bed was hung with pale pink silk brocade. Her windows overlooked the gardens and the sea. There was a tall painted armoire on one wall, and a matching chest at the foot of the bed.

"I hope this chamber will be suitable, *signora*," the housekeeper said.

Bianca looked around the chamber. The tiles surrounding her fireplace were painted with a vine that had magenta flowers. The vine with its flora twined from tile to tile, giving the impression of a living plant. "It's lovely!" she said, smiling.

"I will leave you then to settle yourself, *signora*. Agata will be with you shortly." Then Filomena hurried off.

Bianca quickly realized that the windows overlooking the sea were actually doors that opened onto a balcony with a decorative black iron railing. Opening the doors, she stepped out and looked about her. To her left, she could see nothing but the steep, rocky green hills, but to her right and perhaps a mile in the distance there was another villa. She wondered if it was occupied.

Agata bustled into the bedchamber, calling her inside. "It is not your father's palazzo in Florence, but it is charming, mistress. Can you be happy here?" She looked anxiously at Bianca, her warm brown eyes filled with concern.

"Yes," Bianca said, "I can be happy here. I could be happy in a peasant's hut as long as I do not have to put up with Sebastiano Rovere, Agata."

"May he burn in hell, and soon!" Agata said, making the sign of the evil eye.

Bianca settled easily into country life at Luce Stellare. She actually had more freedom in her life than she had ever had. She spent time exploring the gardens that Primo and Ugo were restoring. Unlike her father's palazzo, which had its kitchens on the lowest level of the house, the villa's kitchens were in the rear of the main floor. Outside its door was a thriving herb garden with both sweet and savory herbs. There was a small kitchen garden of vegetables, but there was also a large vegetable garden in another area that had two apricot trees as well.

The flower gardens were a delight not only to the eyes but also to the nose.

As autumn progressed, of course, the gardens died back, but the roses would continue to bloom until a frost signaled to them that it was time to rest. Frosts were light here on the coast, as the sea warmed the air. In Florence, it would grow wet and chilly, but here at Luce Stellare the weather would be mild.

The beach was safe to walk, Filomena told Bianca. She might even ride her horse, but the truth was Bianca enjoyed walking along the water. To Agata's relief, she wanted no companion with her. The servingwoman liked the gardens, but now having seen the sea, she was wary of it. She was content helping with the poultry, and she much enjoyed herding the goats. It was a calling she would have never suspected she possessed.

"There is a country woman in you somewhere," Filomena teased her.

"Bah! Even my old grandmother was born in Florence," Agata said.

Her first night at the villa, Bianca stood on the balcony of her bedchamber gazing up at the quarter moon. The clear black sky was so full of stars she quickly realized why Luce Stellare had gained its name. A faint warm breeze brought the scent of the roses in the garden. She closed her eyes and inhaled deeply. Then, remembering the distant villa, she turned her head and saw that it had lights. Someone was obviously in residence.

Bianca's curiosity was aroused. Who, she wondered, was her neighbor? Was it an old gentleman or lady living out his or her final days? Or perhaps a family? Since she was not going to socialize, it was unlikely she would ever know. But the following morning, she queried Filomena about the other villa. Her housekeeper would know, Bianca was certain.

"Who lives in that villa on the hillside?" she asked. "Do you know?"

"I do not know for certain," Filomena said, "but I am told it is some foreign prince. He comes and goes, for he does business in the city. They say he stands high in the Medicis' favor." She shrugged. "I have never seen him."

"I have." The little housemaid Rufina spoke up.

"You have?" Filomena glared at the girl. "And just where were you that you saw this man?" she demanded to know.

"On the hillside," Rufina said. "He is very tall with dark hair. He was walking the beach like our *signora* does. He didn't see me, Filomena. He seemed to be in thought."

"I do not recall my father speaking of a foreign prince who carries on business in the city. He is not a cloth merchant of any kind, for if he were, my father would know him, particularly if he carried on his trade with the Medici family. He cannot be anyone of great importance," Bianca said.

"He keeps to himself," Filomena remarked. "When we began work to restore Luce Stellare, he exhibited no curiosity, nor did he send his servants snooping to see what we were about. This is a good thing for you, *signora*. Particularly if he goes back and forth to the city. You don't want him gossiping about the lone female who is his new neighbor."

"Heaven forbid!" Bianca exclaimed. Filomena was right. She didn't need a nosy neighbor or his wife, for he certainly had a wife if he was a respectable man, someone who would attempt to make friends with her or wonder why she was at the villa without a man to watch over her. No. Her curiosity was satisfied, and it would be best if she and her neighbor kept to themselves.

The days fell into a comfortable pattern of meals, naps, and outdoor pursuits.

The servants were pleasant and easy to manage. Bianca found she had no complaints. It was peaceful, and they saw no one. As the days passed, she realized that she was actually beginning to feel safe again for the first time in almost two years.

Chapter 6

The winter passed without incident. Bianca had no visitors, nor did she receive any communication from her family. The narrow road above the villa remained empty of both man and beast. There was the sound of the sea, and now and again the wind or the screeching of a gull, but other than that, all was silent. Especially the nights. In the city, the nights had been noisy until the late hours, the sounds penetrating through the thick walls of her father's house. But here in her little villa, the winter nights were quiet. It was as if she were living in another world. She celebrated her sixteenth birthday with her female servants and forgot the anniversary of the wedding that had brought her such misery.

And then one spring afternoon, as she walked the beach, she saw a man striding in her direction. Bianca quickly turned about and hurried back down the beach, gaining the steep path to the villa. Once on it, she looked down. The man was still walking but showed absolutely no sign that he had seen her, or cared to talk with her. She found herself filled with a mixture of relief and disappointment.

The next day, the man was walking once again at the same time as Bianca. Her first instinct was to flee, but then she decided she would not. She had absolutely no reason to avoid her neighbor. He had shown no hostile intent, and running away like a frightened animal looked foolish and would arouse suspicion. She drew the hood of her cape a bit tighter and walked on, the pebbled beach beneath her boots crunching slightly as she did. There was a slight wind at her back.

He came closer and closer, walking with a purposeful stride. From the description Rufina had given her, it certainly had to be her neighbor. He did not look particularly foreign, Bianca thought as he drew closer. She was able to see his face from beneath her lowered lashes. It would be rude to stare at him or to meet his gaze, despite her curiosity. Only a common woman of the streets would do that.

He was very tall and sturdily built. His legs seemed quite long to her. He did not have the soft look of a merchant, but rather that of a soldier. He was fair-skinned with an oval face that seemed all angles and planes. His nose was long and aristocratic in appearance, his mouth big, with narrow lips. She could not see the color of his eyes, but the thick brows above them were as black as night.

He moved with a sure and steady gait, never pausing as if to observe her as they passed each other. He was dressed in a beautiful dark blue and gold brocade robe that blew ever so slightly around him, but whether from his own strong forward motion or the light breeze, Bianca couldn't tell.

He was well aware of her polite scrutiny of his person, but

showed no indication of any kind that he even saw her as he strode by. However, he found himself amused by her concentration not to appear inquisitive. Like any woman, she was curious, of course, but she seemed to labor hard to cultivate a disinterested attitude.

So this was his neighbor, Prince Amir ibn Jem thought. Who was she? All that his own servants had been able to learn was that she was a lady of a distinguished family. The little he had been able to glimpse of her revealed to his eyes a beautiful woman. What was a beautiful woman doing living alone in an isolated villa by the sea? Had she caused some unforgivable scandal and been exiled here?

She had fled his approach previously, but today she had kept walking. What had made her change her mind and see him as nonthreatening? He was a straightforward man, and usually mysteries didn't interest him. He had spent too much of his young life surrounded by them. When he finally turned about to walk back to his own villa, she was gone from the beach. Had she remained today merely to satisfy her own curiosity?

And what of his own curiosity? He would query his servants again. Servants always knew everything. But to Amir's surprise, they could tell him nothing more about the inhabitants of the nearby villa. Their brief contact had been with two gardeners before the lady's arrival. The men had told his men that they were expecting a lady, a relation of the villa's owner. The prince's servants did know that the villa was called Luce Stellare.

"Have them find out who is living there, or at least who owns the villa," he told his personal body slave, Krikor.

"Yes, my prince," Krikor said drily with the assurance of

a longtime servant. "I will do the impossible for you, as always." He was a short man, plump with good living, and he had been with the prince since his youth. "Why are you so interested in the inhabitants of that little villa? Ah! You have seen the lady! Is she beautiful, my lord?"

"I saw little," the prince replied, teasing his servant. "She was well cloaked, as a proper woman out in public should be."

"Is she young? Old?" Krikor persisted, knowing well there was more.

"Young, I think," the prince answered. "She kept her head down and her eyes lowered, but she was not bent, and her step was sure. She is a mystery, Krikor, and you know how I dislike mysteries. I must have them solved."

"Mystery and intrigue," Krikor said. "It is what comes of having been raised in a harem until you were seven. If only your mother had lived longer. She was wise beyond her years, my lord."

"My father's harem was hardly lively," Amir said. "The rebellious prince who sired me was a great disappointment to the few women he kept. He had too little time for them or me; quarreling with my uncle Bayezit over who will inherit Sultan Mohammed's throne is of more import to him. I will always believe my mother died of sheer boredom, Krikor, for she was an intelligent woman surrounded by half a dozen vapid beauties whose only interest was in attracting their lord and master."

"Yet you have managed to retain your grandfather's favor in spite of your father's bad behavior, my lord."

Amir laughed. "I have no desire to rule an empire, or to lead armies as my father does. My uncle will eventually win the struggle, for he is more determined and far more clever.

The Janissaries are favorable to Bayezit. He does not lead armies, but rather finds the best men to do so for him, thus guaranteeing him victories. The men of my family may be martial in attitude, but I always keep in mind my relations' penchant for disposing of troublesome male heirs," Amir said, chuckling ruefully, and Krikor nodded, grinning.

"As a merchant in Florence, I am hardly a threat to the empire builders to whom I am related. The information I send to the Ottoman regarding the affairs of the Florentines and their neighbors helps him in his decisions on how to deal with these Italian states. I have proven my value to the sultan in this capacity. My grandfather does not need another warrior. I know my uncle Bayezit, while wary of any of Jem's sons, will not move against me as long as I continue peacefully in my pursuits as a dealer in antiquities and fine carpets for the wealthy. Remember, Krikor, that my mother's people were merchants; that is how she ended up in a harem."

"It has made you wealthy," Krikor noted. "But do you not miss Constantinople? And what of your two lovely wives, my lord?"

"Aye, sometimes I miss that golden city," Amir admitted. "But remember, my home now is on the Black Sea away from the city in my little palace. As for the lady Shahdi and the lady Maysun, I took them as wives at the sultan's request, for he wished to honor their families. They are sweet women, but I hold no passion for them, else I should have brought them with me. The courtesans of Florence keep me well entertained."

"And yet the woman on the beach draws your curiosity, my lord," Krikor observed shrewdly.

"She does, and because she does you will find out who she is for me," the prince said. "I must know!"

"I will do my best, my lord," his servant promised.

The next day, Bianca walked earlier so as to avoid her neighbor. "I can take no chances of him learning who I am. He might be one of those men who attend those dreadful orgies my husband gives."

"Few know what that devil's young wife looks like, for he rarely allowed you to show yourself after the Medici showed an interest in you. Your husband is a jealous man. As if you would be unfaithful!" Agata said indignantly.

"Lorenzo di Medici could have been my brother. He was my friend, and nothing more," Bianca said. "I valued his friendship. But I never knew most of the men who attended those dinners. At least they were the more respectable of Sebastiano's acquaintances. This man who passed me on the beach does not look debauched, nor did he stare at me rudely, as a lewd man might."

"He didn't speak at all?" Agata asked.

"Nay, he simply went by, never breaking stride. I was very relieved, I must tell you," Bianca admitted. "An acquaintance would have required us to exchange names. Even if no one is aware that I have left my husband and seek an annulment, anyone learning my name might ask questions in the city. My husband would surely hear of it, and be upon me before I could escape him. I can't go back, Agata! I can't!"

"You will not have to, mistress," Agata assured the young woman. *Though how she bears this lonely life, I do not know,* she thought. She was lonely too, but at least she had the company of Filomena and the other women in the house for companionship. Bianca had no one really of her own age and station with whom to converse. And when were the Pietro d'Angelos going to communicate with them?

On her next walk, Bianca was suddenly accosted by a beautiful, long-haired hound. He was golden in color and unlike any she had ever seen before. He bounded up to her, wagging his featherlike tail, and immediately stuck his long wet nose into her hand. Bianca laughed and patted the dog's elegant, aristocratic head. His fur was soft, although his coat was heavy; even his legs were covered in the long, feathery fur.

"Where have you come from, you lovely fellow?" Bianca asked aloud, as if expecting the exotic creature to answer. Much to her surprise, the dog fell into step with her as she continued on her trek. She found she was actually enjoying the animal's company. Then she saw the beast had a narrow gold color about its slender neck. Bianca stopped and knelt, looking closely at the collar. It was engraved with the following words: *My name is Darius and my master is Prince Amir.* Could this be the prince who was her neighbor? Then she heard someone calling for the dog. Standing quickly, she saw a short man hurrying towards them.

Breathless, he bowed low to her. "I pray Darius has not offended you, *madonna*," the man said in accented Italian. "He does not usually run off as he did today."

"No," Bianca replied. "I quite enjoyed his company, but I am glad you have found him, and relieved to know he has a home. He is a beautiful animal."

"My name is Krikor, *madonna*. I am the slave of Prince Amir, who is your neighbor," he replied, bowing again.

Bianca acknowledged his courtesy with a tiny movement of her head, but then she turned away. "I must go," she said.

"The prince will want to know who to thank for finding his dog. He is quite fond of Darius," Krikor said.

"No thanks are necessary," Bianca assured him, and hurried away.

The prince laughed when his servant told him of the encounter he had with Bianca. "The lady wishes to remain anonymous," he said, "which but increases my curiosity. Are there any visitors to Luce Stellare, Krikor? Perhaps the lady has an important lover she does not wish to expose."

Krikor shook his head. "To the best of my knowledge, my lord, she lives alone with a small staff of servants. I have never seen anyone on the road stop at her home, but I do not sit and watch day and night. My instincts tell me she is afraid of something, which is why she maintains her privacy so zealously."

"Let Darius loose each day when she walks," Amir instructed. "He will come home without you fetching him. I see I must be patient in order to unravel this puzzle of my beautiful neighbor, but I will decipher it."

Bianca was surprised to find Darius coming to meet her the next afternoon when she reached the beach. He gladly accepted her pats and then trotted along as she walked. Bianca was no fool. After a few days, she realized Darius's appearance was not a coincidence. Certainly the dog had not gotten loose on his own again. He had been released to join her. Her neighbor was curious, which presented a problem.

"Walking upon the beach is one of my few pleasures," she said to Agata. "Eventually this prince will follow his animal. He will ask questions I do not wish to answer. What if he recognizes me? I cannot walk on the road. He is spoiling it for me." She was becoming agitated just thinking about it.

"Put a note beneath the dog's collar telling its master that you wish to maintain your privacy," Agata suggested. "If he is a gentleman, he will comply with your wishes." The servingwoman slowly and steadily pulled a hairbrush through her mistress's long ebony hair in an effort to soothe her. She knew Bianca enjoyed the dog's company. They must find her a pet or two to keep her distracted from her situation. Filomena would know how to accomplish such a task. She should have thought of it before.

"If only my mother would write to me," Bianca fretted. "We are so isolated."

"When there is something to communicate, your mother will write," Agata told the young woman. "Better she is careful than bring your husband down on us."

Bianca took Agata's suggestion, and the next day when she returned home from her walk she first stopped to carefully push the note she had written beneath Darius's gold collar. "Go home now," she told the dog, stepping onto the path leading up to her villa. She stopped briefly part of the way up to watch as the dog loped down the beach towards his own home.

The prince always knew the approximate time his hound returned and waited for him. Seeing his master, Darius trotted over to him, pushing his long nose into the man's hand. "Well, well, back from your walk already," Amir noted. "Did she ask after me? Is she as lovely as I think she is, or is it my imagination?" Then he saw the small parchment tucked beneath the dog's collar. "Ahh, she has sent me a love note," he chuckled and drew the parchment from the collar, opening it carefully.

Signore, it began. *While I certainly enjoy your dog's company, I hope you will not consider it an excuse to intrude further upon my privacy.* It was signed *The Lady from Luce Stellare*. Amir laughed ruefully. Did his neighbor not consider that her demand but whetted his appetite further to know who she was?

The next afternoon, Bianca found a new note beneath Darius's collar. Unable to restrain her curiosity, she pulled it out and opened it. *Who are you?* the note read. She crushed the parchment and stuffed it into the pocket of her cape. The afternoon after that there was another message attached to the dog. *Tell me your name,* it begged. She smiled, unable to help herself.

"He is flirting with you," Agata said, chuckling.

"He shouldn't be. Until I am told otherwise, I am a married woman," Bianca said.

"But he doesn't know that, and perhaps it doesn't matter to him. Men are like that, mistress," Agata responded.

"He cannot know who I am," Bianca replied. "Must I cease walking upon my own beach because this man is harassing me?"

"You can walk," Agata told her. "He will grow bored with this game if you do not play with him. Men can be such children."

So Bianca walked, and each day Darius would join her, but there were no more notes beneath his collar. Then one afternoon the dog appeared before her carrying a small covered basket in his mouth. He stopped, placing it before her on the pebbled sand, and sat down, looking up at Bianca anxiously. She heard a distressed sound from the willow container and lifted the lid. There, within, was a small, very furry white kitten.

"*Oh!*" Bianca exclaimed, unable to help herself from lifting the kitten from the basket. "Aren't you a darling!"

The small creature trembled and meowed piteously at her.

Bianca cuddled it close, making little soothing noises in hopes of comforting it. It was the most beautiful beast she had ever seen. On closer inspection she saw it had a gilt leather collar studded with tiny seed pearls. She kissed the kitten's head and seeing a note within the basket took it up with her free hand to read: *My name is Jamila. Please give me a home, gracious lady of Luce Stellare.* Bianca laughed softly. What was she to do? She could hardly refuse such a charming request.

Jamila managed to escape the confines of her hand and crawl up to her shoulder. Once there, she snuggled into the crook of Bianca's neck and began to purr. With that perfect feline maneuver, Bianca was lost. "You are a wicked little thing," she scolded the kitten softly. Then plucking it from its perch and tucking it back in the basket, she began to walk home again while Jamila complained and cried to be picked up and cuddled. The household of women fell in love with the kitten immediately.

"How could I refuse to take her?" Bianca asked them helplessly, and they all agreed that she couldn't, even Agata. Jamila quickly established herself as queen of the household, and Bianca was happier for her presence. She tucked a note beneath Darius's collar the next day, thanking her neighbor for the kitten.

The summer came, and still she heard no word from her family. Bianca could only surmise that Sebastiano Rovere was refusing to allow an annulment. The fact that he still had the power of life and death over her was unnerving. Nevertheless, she took comfort in the fact that he didn't know where she was; if he did, he would have come for her. The thought of going back to his large, dark palazzo with all its secrets frightened her. She avoided thinking about it, instead reveling in the warmth and sunshine of the summer months.

One afternoon as she walked her beach, she saw her neighbor standing on the heights above. He waved, and before she could stop herself Bianca waved back. Then she chided herself for her foolishness, but he had not taken the casual waggle of her hand as an invitation to join her, for which she was relieved. He was not there again for several days, but the second time he waved at her she was bound by her first actions to answer him back. Then she turned and walked quickly back towards Luce Stellare.

Bianca had to admit that she was as curious about her neighbor as he seemed to be about her. Who was he really, this man they called *the prince*? Was he really a prince? *A foreigner*, Filomena and Gemma said dourly. A foreigner—and foreigners were dangerous. He was a prince, little Rufina assured her mistress. She had spoken with a servant from the neighboring villa who was her male cousin. The prince, Rufina said, came and went back and forth to Florence.

Fascinated in spite of herself, Bianca asked the girl, "What does he do in the city?"

"Luigi says he is a merchant of carpets and rare things," Rufina told her. "The great Medici himself patronizes this prince's undertaking."

What would Lorenzo di Medici buy from this prince? Bianca wondered. But then she recalled that Lorenzo had a passion for antiquities and rare things, as well as for beautiful women. If this foreign prince catered to the di Medici tastes, then he would, if he had not already, make his fortune, for the di Medici did not quibble over the price of any item they desired. Their various homes were filled with beautiful paintings, sculptures, and other items of great value. And the rest of the wealthy in the city would follow the di Medici and buy from this merchant prince as well.

Bianca considered that her neighbor might be as interesting as the elderly silk merchant whom her father used to bring home for a meal now and again before the old man died. In his youth and middle years, this man had traveled to China, bringing back bolts of fabric greatly prized by the wealthy of Florence. He told wonderful stories of his adventures, which she and Marco were allowed to sit and hear.

It was the first glimpse of the world outside of her father's house that Bianca had ever had. She had once even told her parents she wished she might travel, but they had laughed and said her future was a wonderful marriage and a family of her own. Well, Bianca thought, that had not turned out quite as her parents had planned. She would have been better off traveling to faraway places. Perhaps this prince had marvelous stories to tell, but then, she wasn't a child any longer. She was a woman in hiding from a brutal and dangerous husband who would probably kill her if he could find her.

Still, Bianca reasoned with herself, she hadn't spoken to another human except Agata and the house servants in months. She had never heard of this foreign prince until she discovered him to be her neighbor. Certainly she would have known something of him if he had been known to her family or to her husband. And like her villa, his was always quiet and peaceful, with no guests or other visitors. Perhaps, just perhaps, she might allow him to speak to her. Perhaps she would even speak with him.

But how was she to open a dialogue with him after rebuffing him so strongly? Of course! What an *idiota* she was! She would write to him and have Darius deliver her note. The next day she tucked a scrap of parchment beneath the hound's collar when she was ready to send him home to his master. Bianca could have sworn the animal was smiling, his mouth open, his tongue lolling, as he loped off.

Amir smiled. When taking the note, he read: *Are you really a prince?*

The next day Bianca opened his reply. *I am Amir ibn Jem, the sultan's grandson*, it read. *Yes, I am really a prince.*

A daily correspondence began to go back and forth between them.

Is it true you sell antiquities to Lorenzo di Medici?

A Florentine who is not a merchant enjoys no esteem whatsoever, he replied, quoting the famed saying among the Florentines.

Bianca smiled as she read his answer and responded, *But you are a foreigner. You were not born in Florence.*

I am a Florentine by choice, my lady.

I thought all Turks were warriors.

When you are the sultan's grandson it is better to be a merchant.

Why? Was your father a merchant?

My father is a warrior. He quarrels constantly with his brother over who shall inherit my grandfather's throne one day. Eventually my uncle will kill my father, for he is more determined to be sultan and better suited to it. Royal Turks kill anyone, including family, that they consider rivals to their personal ambition.

If you do not want to be sultan one day, then I understand your desire for anonymity and privacy.

Could you not tell me your name?

It was such a simple request, and he had told her his name. She didn't have to tell him her whole name. She could tell him her first name. Bianca was not an unusual name. *I am called Bianca*, she wrote.

Now that we are friends, Bianca, and I hope you will consider me as such, may we meet one afternoon upon our beach and talk face-to-face?

I am a respectable woman, Prince Amir. If you understand that, if you understand that I am not seeking an adventure, then perhaps I could agree to your suggestion, Bianca wrote him back.

Bring a servingwoman with you if you fear for your good name, Bianca. I will not be offended. I would have you at ease with me, and not fearful that I will set upon you in some shameful manner.

"Well, well," said Agata, who was privy to her mistress's correspondence with the prince, "he is thoughtful of you. If you were a maid, of course, you should have to refuse, but you are not. You have been very lonely, I know. As long as the behavior you and this man exhibit is proper, and I am there to assure it, I see no reason you should not talk with him, mistress. Perhaps he may even have word of what is happening in the city since your mother has not felt secure enough to write to you."

Tomorrow, he read later that day when he opened the little piece of parchment he found beneath Darius's collar. Amir smiled to himself. He had not been so intrigued with a woman in a long time, but like the skilled hunter he was, he had let her come to him on her own terms. He was not surprised to see her coming towards him the following afternoon in the company of another woman. Perhaps she really was a respectable woman, but how respectable remained to be seen. He considered now that she was a wealthy and powerful man's discarded mistress, given a villa and sent away because she had become an inconvenience for whatever reason. Certainly the woman of a good house would not be alone, as she was.

He wore white trousers and a white tunic that extended to just below his knees as he walked towards her, his dark boots crunching the pebbles beneath into the sand. The white suited his sun-bronzed complexion and dark, wavy hair. The dog was by his side.

"Now he looks like a Turk," Agata said softly. "And he is very handsome."

She is beautiful, Amir thought as they approached, *and young too. What fool of a smug Florentine has tossed her away so casually?* She wore a silk gown, lavender in color. The puffed sleeves were plain and the dress had no train. It was a simple garment, but the fabric was of the best quality, he could see. Of medium height, she carried herself well. The aristocratic little face was not one of a peasant. Her hair was ebony. It wasn't dyed to suit the Florentine fashion of blond or red. Her skin was clear and very pale. Her eyes were light, although at the moment he could not tell what color, for she had them lowered politely. Yes, whoever she was, she was of high station and had manners.

"Your eyes are blue!" she exclaimed, surprised as they came close enough to truly see each other. "I did not know that Turks had blue eyes."

"My mother was English," he said. Then he bowed politely to her, and taking up her small hand in his, he kissed it. "Your presence honors me, *madonna*."

An odd thought struck Bianca as he released her hand.

His kiss had seemed like a brand upon her flesh. She felt her cheeks growing warm with color.

"Your eyes are like aquamarines," he said, "but then I am certain many have told you that before. I apologize I cannot be more original for you, Bianca."

"I am told the color of my eyes comes from a northern ancestor, *signore*," she responded.

"Let us walk," he invited her. "Darius and your servant will act as our chaperones."

It was mid-September. The warm air held a faint hint of autumn today. The turquoise sea was calm, its waves small and delicate, barely making a ripple upon the water as they fell with a gentle sigh upon the sand of the shore. Above them the ever-present gulls soared, complaining to one another in the light breeze. Bianca and the prince walked in silence for a time and then Bianca spoke.

"Why do you live here instead of Florence?"

"I do not like your city of Florence," he admitted. "I don't even keep a palazzo there. When I am forced to remain overnight, I sleep in a small apartment above my warehouse, but few know that. It gives me an excuse to avoid entertaining. My tastes are simple, and I have little patience with ostentation. I leave that to others who seem to need the acclaim such excess brings them."

"Do you belong to a guild?" she asked him.

"Not really, although the Arte di Calimala have said they consider me one of their own, despite my foreign origins," Amir told her with an amused smile.

"The cloth merchants are very important," Bianca said, "and your carpets are fashioned of wool and some of silk," she pointed out.

She was educated enough to know this, and he was more curious than ever. "Who are you?" he asked her.

Bianca stopped a moment before moving on again. "I cannot tell you that, *signore*, and I beg that you do not press me further. I will tell you that it became necessary for me to flee the city. My very life is at risk, even now. The villa in which I reside belongs to my family. I am a respectable woman, not a courtesan, but if I am to remain safe I must remain unknown to you."

"I will respect your wishes, Bianca, if you will agree to continue to walk with me," he said with a smile.

"I will agree, for I find your company pleasant, *signore*."

For several weeks, Agata accompanied her mistress each day as she walked with the prince. Then there came a day when Agata was sniffling, sneezing, and snuffling.

Bianca bade her remain at home, for it was a windy day. "I can go without you. I believe you will agree that Prince Amir has proven himself now."

Agata was feeling poorly enough that she didn't even suggest that Bianca let one of the housemaids chaperone her. She just waved her mistress off.

He asked after her about it, of course. "Where is your dragon?" he teased her.

"Ill, but not seriously," Bianca said. She bent and patted Darius. "His coat is so beautiful. How do you keep him that way?"

"Krikor brushes him daily," the prince answered and took Bianca's hand in his for the very first time. Though she was startled by the warm fingers suddenly curling about hers, she decided she liked it and said nothing. Agata did not come with them again, and each day Amir took Bianca's hand in his as they walked. But soon the weather would grow rainy and chilly with the late autumn. They would not be able to walk together, and the thought of it made Bianca very sad. It had been just over a year now since she had escaped her husband and come to Luce Stellare. She had grown to enjoy the prince's company.

Then one day a sudden rainstorm swept in on them from the sea as they walked. They were too far from either villa. Amir quickly led them into the mouth of one of the caves that edged the beach beneath the low cliffs. They stood watching the rain pour down in a silver sheet. It had been chilly before. Now the rain made it seem colder.

Bianca pulled her cloak tightly about her, but she was unable to contain her shivering. He put an arm about her, drawing her close against him, and then he spoke, breaking the deep silence that hung between them. "Tell me why you fled Florence."

And to her great surprise, Bianca found herself explaining to him her brother's foolish actions that had caused Sebastiano Rovere to literally blackmail her father into giving her to the dissolute lawyer as his third wife. "When my mother was finally allowed to see me many months after the wedding, I told her of what I had suffered with Sebastiano. She immediately removed me from his house. My family hid me in Santa Maria del Fiore convent until they were able to spirit me to Luce Stellare, which had belonged to my paternal grandmother's family. I have lived here for the past year while they have attempted to gain an annulment for me. My family warned me that they would not communicate with me until they had good news, for Rovere had put a watch on our palazzo in the city," Bianca explained. "I have heard nothing, and so I must assume that so far their efforts have come to nothing. I am certain he has used his kinsman Cardinal Rovere to block their efforts, but my mother's family is not without influence with the Church. I know that my grandfather in Venice will be working to free me. Now you understand why I have been so cautious, Amir."

"You have trusted me enough to tell me this," he said softly, suddenly happy. He knew of Sebastiano Rovere by reputation. He was of unsavory renown. To think this exquisite girl had suffered at the hands of such a man was unbearable, and he now understood much more than he had previously.

"You have given me no reason not to trust you," Bianca said. "But now that I have, my very life is in your hands. If you expose me, Sebastiano will surely kill me. He could hide my absence for a few months, but eventually it would have become public knowledge that I have left him and am seeking an annulment. And if he finds me, I will suffer greatly at his hands before the relief and release of death. He is an evil man."

"I do not know him," Amir told her, "but his character is that of ill repute, according to the gossip. He was jailed recently for a despicable act, but his victim died before she might testify in court against him. His cronies eventually saw to his release, as there was no witness remaining except those men themselves who, it is said, were all involved in the crime. The girl's family was of a lesser guild."

"I suspect I was gone from the city by then," Bianca said. "What did he do?"

"It is not something that should be discussed with a decent woman," the prince told her. "I will say the victim was an innocent virgin of a respectable family, kidnapped, and brought to your husband's palazzo, where she was raped many times by his guests and others. There was talk of something else but it is not for your ears."

"The little donkey," Bianca whispered fearfully in spite of herself.

"Yes," the prince said. "How do you know of such a thing? By Allah! He did not commit such a monstrous and savage act on you, did he?"

"He was considering it, but I escaped him just before the creature came into the house. He has a Moorish slave girl who is quite dissolute. Even more so than my husband. I am certain she was involved," Bianca told Amir.

His arm tightened about her. No wonder she lived in terror of Sebastiano Rovere. He was a monster and did not deserve to live. Nor did he deserve Bianca. She, however, was bound by her Christian church's law to the brute until she could obtain an annulment—or one of them was dead. The lawyer, however, was a slippery fellow. He could and would probably delay any bill of divorcement of his marriage until he could revenge himself on her. The rain continued to pour down.

Whom had Rovere married? She had told him all but her family's name. He cudgeled his brain to remember. *The most beautiful girl in Florence,* it had been said at the time. Who was she? Who was . . . The silk merchant's daughter! Of course! Bianca was the daughter of Giovanni Pietro d'Angelo. The family was a large one and beyond respectable. No wonder the man had panicked and sacrificed his eldest daughter to protect his own wife and other children. He would make it a point to learn more about the family when he went into the city next.

There was a rumble of thunder, and Darius whined.

"I know who you are now, Bianca. I will not betray you," the prince told her.

She looked up at him, and he wanted to drown himself in her aquamarine eyes.

"Thank you," she said softly.

Unable to help himself, he brushed her lips with his own, but when he sought to deepen the kiss she put two fingers over his mouth. "No, *signore*," she chided him, her beautiful eyes meeting his. "Remember that I am a respectable woman. While I seek to free myself from Sebastiano Rovere, I am still, unfortunately, his wife. I will not add adultery to my sins."

"You have no sins!" he declared passionately, catching her hand up and kissing it.

Bianca smiled.

"The rain is stopping," she told him. "I must go now." She gently removed the protective arm he had about her shoulders and felt a sudden loss. She had been so safe with that arm about her. Safer than she had believed in over a year. She gave Darius a pat, slipping from the cave's mouth to hurry down the beach and up the path that led to her villa.

He stood watching her go, the taste of her still on his lips. He had two wives back in Turkey. Women taken at his grandfather's request, but he had never been in love. He had no harem to satisfy his desires. It startled him to realize that he had fallen in love with the silk merchant's beautiful daughter. He realized she was not a woman to fling herself into an affair, no matter how lonely or unhappy she was. She would never have him while Rovere remained her husband. Something had to be done about that.

One day, when she was free, he intended to take her home

to his palace, which was set in the green hills above the Black Sea. He would keep her safe at the Moonlight Serai. He would never allow Bianca to be afraid again. "I love her, Darius," he said to his companion dog. "I will love her forever, no matter what her people or mine say. I can but pray she will feel the same. She is the other half of my soul. I know that now."

Chapter 7

"Praise blessed Maria!" Agata said as Bianca entered the house. "I am so relieved you have returned. Where were you in this storm?"

"Standing in the entry to one of the caves below, for the rain caught us unawares," Bianca answered her. "I thought it would never stop. Poor Prince Amir, for he has a farther distance to go before he reaches home, and the downpour has begun again."

Bianca did not see the prince for several days, for the rains continued. It was better that way, she decided. That brief, innocent kiss had set her senses reeling. She had wanted him to continue to kiss her, but praise Santa Anna, to whom she prayed daily, she had managed to retain her sense of propriety when she hadn't wanted to do so at all. Amir's mouth had been warm and his breath fragrant. She had never realized that a simple kiss could be so sweet, so tender, so tempting, but his kiss had been just that. It had offered her far more than she had the right to accept at the moment. Would that ever change?

Sebastiano's lips were cold, hard, his breath foul. Her husband's kiss demanded she surrender everything that she was, so he might possess it. In the brief and delicious touch of the prince's lips, there had been the mysterious promise of a shared ecstasy to come. Bianca wept silently into her pillow that night, and for the first time in her life felt desire for a man. If only her family could obtain the annulment they sought for her. If they did, she would be no man's chattel ever again.

She would accept Amir as her lover, for his every action in recent days had told her that he wanted her. Did he love her? How nice it would be if he did, but it didn't matter to her at all. She would gladly be his mistress, no matter what the world thought of her. But she would not have another husband, and no one would change her mind.

The next day, to her surprise and excitement, a messenger arrived from Florence with word from her family. The courier was not one of her family's servants but rather in the service of the Medici, as his proudly displayed badge revealed. He accepted a hot meal from Gemma in the kitchens, and then told her he was off for Pisa, for he carried messages for the Medici bank there from Lorenzo himself.

Bianca called Agata to her so she might share whatever news there was. Breaking the red wax seal with her mother's signet, the dome of San Marco, impressed into it, she opened the parchment and read aloud.

My dearest daughter, it began in Orianna's elegant and familiar hand. *The news is not what I had hoped to be able to send you after all this time, but all is not lost. The knowledge that you have left Sebastiano Rovere is now public, as is our quest for an annulment for you. Padre Bonamico has presented our request for your marriage's dissolution to the Holy See itself, traveling to Rome to do so. Your husband has appealed to his kinsman, Cardinal Rovere, to block any such action. Your grandfather in Venice has countered with his own pleas to the two cardinals from his own city. Regretfully, these matters take time, and the bribes both of our factions have paid so far to gain the Church's ear have been considerable. Unfortunately, more time is needed to gain a favorable result for our side. Lorenzo di Medici himself is sympathetic to your plight, and has offered his own courier to carry this message to you. But our family is not without its own resources, influence, and friends. Your husband carries on, as usual holding the orgies for which he has now become infamous, and appears less and less in the justice courts of the city. Honest folk have become distrusting of him. It is possible that his worsening and dissolute life will kill him sooner rather than later. Your father's business continues to thrive, as do your siblings. Francesca will be thirteen in the spring, and I have decided to allow her to accompany me to Mass then rather than wait until next year. Your grandfather wishes her to marry into a Venetian family, and so would have her join him and my stepmother after she turns thirteen so she may become used to Venetian ways, and to Venice itself. I wish you were here to see her, my darling Bianca. She misses you greatly. Your father and I miss you also, but take comfort in the fact that you are safe at Luce Stellare. God bless you until we meet again. Your loving mother, Orianna Pietro d'Angelo.*

Bianca laid the parchment aside with a sigh.

"Well," Agata said, "it is not what you hoped for, I know, but it could be worse."

Bianca laughed. "No, it is not what I hoped for, but at least now we have an idea of where things are at for us."

"We are stuck in the country, is where we are," Agata grumbled.

"I thought you were finding a bit of distraction with Ugo," Bianca teased her.

Agata colored. *"Signora!"* she said.

"I have eyes," Bianca told her.

"Filomena talks too much," Agata said.

"He is a nice fellow," Bianca told her servingwoman. "If you decided that you wanted a husband, you could not do as well in Florence. I understand that Ugo has his own cottage."

"With an old mother installed in it," Agata said sourly. "I don't believe he is a man for marriage at all."

"Ahh," Bianca said, "so there is the problem. Well, it will eventually solve itself, I am certain."

The prince came to the villa early the next afternoon, riding down the beach on a large gray stallion with a black mane and tail. The animal clambered up the steep path to be stabled out of the rain by Primo. Agata noted how Bianca lit up as the prince came into her little library, where a fire now burned to take the chill off the day.

"Amir!" she exclaimed as he was ushered into her presence. He was carrying something beneath his arm.

"I didn't know if you had a chessboard," he said as the box he carried was opened to reveal just that. There was also a small box that held two sets of pieces, one in white marble, the other in red marble.

"You don't know if I play," she said to him. In truth, she was a talented chess player.

"If you don't, I will teach you," he replied. "I have no

desire to travel into the city in such inclement weather, and I am bored alone with my servants. Are you not bored?"

She laughed. "Yes, I am," she admitted.

They played several games of chess that afternoon, but when he noticed that the light was beginning to fade, he arose. "I must go before I am unable to find my way back home and my horse and I end up in the sea," he told her. "I'll come back earlier tomorrow if the rains continue. If the weather clears, we'll walk together."

"Your mood is better for his visit," Agata noted with a smile. "He is a good man for all he is a foreigner. Gemma is disappointed she did not get to feed him."

"When he comes next, I will invite him to dine," Bianca replied. That night she fell asleep listening to the rain on the tiled roof beating against the shutters that had been pulled over her windows. Bianca was warm and cozy beneath her down coverlet. Jamila slept near her head, purring contentedly, lulling her mistress into a delicious dream state where she was free to be with her prince.

They began to ride together on the beach on sunny days and played chess on the days when the weather was inclement. The days grew shorter, the nights longer, and Bianca's seventeenth natal day came. The year she had turned fifteen had been the first she had ever been away from her family. She had been in her husband's house then. But last year and now this year she celebrated quietly at Luce Stellare. To her great surprise, Prince Amir brought her a gift.

"How did you know?" she asked him, eager to open the white silk bag he gave her. What was in it?

"A little bird mentioned it in passing," he replied with a smile. Her delight was so pleasing to see. "Open your gift, Bianca."

She did, pouring its contents into her palm. The rope of black pearls brought a gasp from her slender throat. She dropped the bag, letting the pearls extend to their length from her fingers. "Ohh, *signore*, they are beautiful!" she exclaimed. Then she sighed reluctantly. "But I cannot accept them, and you surely know the reason why," Bianca told him. Picking up the bag, she went to pour the pearls back into it, but he took the rope from her hands. Standing before her, he slipped them over her head.

"Let me see them displayed once, as they should be," he said to her. "I will defer to your honor, and keep them for the day you can accept them freely. I chose each pearl myself to be certain it was perfect and without blemish, as you are." He stepped back to look at the necklace, and considered how it would look against her unclad body.

As if she could hear his thoughts, Bianca blushed. His gaze was far too warm, and his dark blue eyes lingered on the pearls where they brushed the swell of her breasts. She lifted the jewels off, and gently poured them back into the white silk bag, which she then reluctantly handed to him. "I do thank you for the thought," Bianca told him. "I don't believe I ever had anything as lovely."

"Did not Rovere cover you in jewels?" Amir wanted to know.

Bianca laughed. "Other than a few large and ugly pieces, which I gladly left behind when I fled his house, no. He bought what was most expensive, not what was tasteful or beautiful. The jewelers all knew that. Anything delicately made, he passed over for large pieces that could be displayed to his advantage, not the wearer's."

At her invitation, Amir remained for the afternoon meal. Gemma served a lovely white fish broiled in butter and lemon, along with a dish of small pasta mixed with rice and flavored with olive oil and herbs. There were artichokes and a roasted capon that had been stuffed with sage and onion. There was bread, which they dipped in olive oil, and a delicious wine to drink. It was simple but surprisingly satisfactory. They were just finishing their meal when they heard the sound of horses' hooves outside.

Bianca grew pale and jumped to her feet, calling for Agata. Had he found her? She had to escape the villa. She would not allow Sebastiano to force her back to Florence as his wife. "Agata! Agata! Where are you?" She was becoming frantic with her fear.

Prince Amir saw the terror in her eyes, in her face. Jumping to his feet, he said, "I will protect you, Bianca! I will protect you!"

Agata ran into the *sala da pranzo*.

"Tell Primo to saddle my horse," Bianca cried. "I must get away! He cannot find me, Agata! He cannot! Hurry! Hurry!"

There came a loud knocking on the oak doors.

"See who is at the door," Prince Amir said sternly to Agata.

"No! No! I must escape! I must!" Bianca sobbed now, thoroughly frightened.

The knocking resounded again.

"*Go!*" The prince told Agata.

Pale herself, the servingwoman scurried off to do his bidding. Reaching the door, Agata pulled it open before her courage failed her. "*Signora!* Oh, *signora*! You have given us such a fright," she said to Orianna Pietro d'Angelo, who stood before her. "Come in! Come in! Mistress! Mistress! Come quickly! It is your mother!"

Bianca flew from the dining room, running straight into her mother's outstretched arms. *"Madre! Oh, Madre!"* And then she began to weep.

Orianna hugged her eldest daughter as the tears pricked the backs of her eyelids, but she would not let them fall. "Bianca, Bianca," she murmured into her child's dark hair. "I could not let another birthday pass without seeing you." She kissed the tears from her daughter's face. "I only wish I brought you better news."

"Have you eaten, *Signora*?" Agata asked and then answered her own question. "Of course you haven't. I'll have Gemma fix you something immediately."

"My men . . ." Orianna began.

"Primo or Ugo will have taken them to the kitchens. Their horses will be stabled, and they will sleep dry and warm in the barn, *signora*."

Bianca ushered her mother into the dining room

The prince came forward immediately to greet her. "Signora Pietro d'Angelo, I am Prince Amir ibn Jem." He politely seated her at Bianca's right hand. "I am your daughter's neighbor."

Orianna was rarely surprised, but Prince Amir's presence was totally unexpected. She sat down at the rectangular oak table. Surely Bianca hadn't taken a lover.

"We walk together, we ride, and occasionally he can even beat me at chess," Bianca said, smiling at the prince.

It was a warm smile that a woman gives to a man she is in love with, and Orianna heard in her daughter's voice something she had never before heard. *Madre di Dios!* Do not let her have acted foolishly. "Is that all you do together?" she heard herself asking.

Bianca looked puzzled, not quite comprehending her mother.

The prince, however, did. "You have raised your daughter to be a moral woman, *signora*," he said. "And I have no need to seduce her or bring shame to your name." He went to Bianca, who suddenly realized what her mother meant. Mortified, she wasn't certain what to do next. Amir took her hand up and kissed it. "Thank you for your hospitality, Bianca," he told her.

"Will you come tomorrow?" she asked, looking up at him.

"The day after, perhaps. You have your mother for company now, and I am certain she has much to tell you or she wouldn't have risked the journey," the prince replied. Then he looked directly at Orianna. "Can you be certain you were not followed? You have possibly endangered Bianca's safety by coming, *signora*."

"Rovere is in Rome," Orianna said. "My journey was planned in advance, and I did not depart from our palazzo, *signore*. I would never knowingly expose Bianca."

Amir nodded, and then, turning on his heel, left.

"You were rude to him," Bianca said quietly.

"Is he your lover?" Orianna asked bluntly.

"Of course not, *Madre*. I am a married woman, no matter the difficulties with Sebastiano. You did not raise me to be a loose woman," Bianca replied indignantly.

"Then why is he in your house and alone with you?" Orianna demanded to know.

"Because he is my friend," Bianca said. "It is my natal day, and he brought me a gift, which I, for the sake of my good name, was forced to refuse. I asked him to share my meal. I am never really alone with him. I am surrounded by my servants. There is nothing improper in our friendship, though I tell you I wish it were otherwise, *Madre*. He is kind, which the blessed Mother knows my husband has never been. He treats me with respect, which Sebastiano has never done, beginning with that travesty of a wedding night. I am a grown woman, *Madre*, not an innocent girl who is dazzled by a handsome man."

"He is very handsome," Orianna noted. "And proud too. However, you are correct in that he is respectful of you, Bianca. I will admit to being impressed by his care of your good name. Does he know the situation in which you find yourself?"

"Does he know I am a married woman and that I seek the dissolution of my marriage? Yes, *Madre*, he does," said Bianca.

Orianna nodded. "I will remain with you tomorrow, and then I must return to Florence. Your father did not want me to come and was fearful for us both, but I could bear our separation no longer. With Rovere in Rome, it was the perfect opportunity. My father sent half a dozen men from Venice to accompany me. I slipped through the church garden and met them outside of its gate. I will return the same way. My absence has been explained by saying I am making a retreat for a few days at a nearby convent."

"You said the news you brought was not good, *Madre*," Bianca reminded her mother. "What is it?"

Orianna sighed painfully. "The influence your grandfather has is limited to two elderly cardinals. Rovere, on the other hand, has his kinsman, and I am told that because of his predilection for debauchery, even in Rome, he has attracted the interest of several other high churchmen whose tastes are similar. The matter of your annulment has become a matter for study and further consideration."

"In other words, my husband has won," Bianca said.

Orianna said nothing. She could not deny it.

"I will die before I return to him," Bianca told her mother quietly.

"He will not care," her mother replied. "He is a gamesman, and his only interest is in winning. To have the most beautiful girl in Florence flee him six months after their marriage and demand an annulment was a serious blow to his pride. But to have the Church postpone her request for her freedom gives him the victory he needs to salvage his damaged reputation. And having that influence with the Church makes him more powerful in Florence. The di Medici are not pleased at all."

"But the di Medici cannot legally protect me from my husband," Bianca responded. "They must be careful of their own reputation, for we all know there are certain families who would topple them from their position of power and influence given the opportunity. There is nothing left for me now if I cannot be free of Sebastiano Rovere, *Madre*. I will remain here at Luce Stellare. Eventually it is to be hoped he will either die of his excesses or decide to let me go. If he should ever discover where I am hidden, I will find a way to kill myself, but I will not return to that man or his house ever again."

While she enjoyed her mother's company the following day, she actually wished Orianna gone so she might speak with Amir. But when Orianna did depart the following morning, Bianca felt an even deeper sadness, for she did not know if she would ever see her mother, or the rest of her family, again. Taking her horse, she guided it down the steep path to the beach and rode towards the prince's villa. She needed the comfort of Amir's presence and his strength.

To her surprise Darius came loping down the beach to greet her, his golden fur gleaming in the sunshine, the long, slender curl of his tail wagging as he reached her. Then she saw Amir on his own mount, waiting for her in the shadow of the caves. She urged her mare to their meeting, and almost leaping from the animal's back, flung herself at the prince in a display of utter desperation.

"What has happened, Bianca?" he asked as his arms closed about her. *Allah!* She had to be in great distress to behave so incautiously. Unable to help himself with her warm body pressing against him, he buried his face in her hair, which had come undone in her race to reach him. He breathed in the essence of her. *Sweet! Sweet! Allah!* He wanted her so much. If he had been another man, he could have easily taken advantage of her unhappiness, but he would not. "Tell me what is wrong, Bianca," he heard himself repeating. Then he set her back from him, looking into her tearstained face. "What has your mother told you?"

"Rovere has won," she began with a sob, but then recovered herself. "The Church in Rome has decided my request for an annulment from him is a matter for further study. It seems he and his kinsman, the cardinal, found among the church's holy men several with a similar nature to my husband. They, in turn, have used their influence to block that of my family. Even my princely Venetian grandfather's prestige is not enough to save me. Now Sebastiano will find me, and when he does he will kill me. He has that right as my husband, and none can gainsay him, Amir." She began to weep again.

"Come away with me!" he heard himself saying.

"What?" She had not heard him correctly.

"Come away with me," he repeated. "I will take you to my home on the Black Sea. He will never find you, and I will keep you safe forever, Bianca."

She closed her eyes briefly, imagining a life with this gentle, handsome man. It would be a good life, Bianca instinctively knew, and for the first time she was tempted beyond all reason. She was so tired of being afraid. Then she heard his voice.

"I love you," the prince said. "I have loved you from the moment I first saw you. I will always love you, beloved."

"I love you too," Bianca heard herself admitting, and she did. Then she drew in a long, deep breath. "But we are honorable people, Amir. I could never be truly happy knowing I had run away and shamed my family's name. I will not become your lover until I am free of Sebastiano Rovere. Religion and nationality mean little to me. I am a Florentine Christian woman, and you are an infidel Turk, but we love each other nonetheless. However, you cannot dishonor your name any more than I can mine." She felt suddenly stronger, and knew it was the knowledge of his love that had made her so.

"If Rovere finds you and comes to take you back, I will kill him myself," Amir told her. "Then you would be mine."

"They would arrest you," she said softly. He would kill for her. He loved her. No man had ever said such things to her. Bianca's heart raced with both fear and excitement.

"Not if they do not find his body," Amir replied. "Nor would they find us."

"We would have to wait several years for him to be declared dead if there was no body," Bianca countered. "I would be an old woman, and you would not want me then."

"I will always want you, beloved," he promised her.

He rode back with her to the villa, remaining to eat and play a few games of chess with her. By the time he departed, Bianca was feeling much better. If Sebastiano came, Amir would kill him. She believed it would happen and rested easier now. The rainy season came once again and all remained quiet at Luce Stellare. It was late winter before her fears were finally realized and Bianca was forced to face her husband for the first time in over two years.

He burst through the front door of the villa with a small party of men at dusk. His voice thundered through the small villa as he called her name, demanding her immediate attendance upon him. "Bianca! You will show yourself immediately, my disobedient wife. I have come to take you home, bitch!"

Bianca had heard the commotion as her doors were rent asunder. She had been in the little library by the fire sewing a silk shirt for the prince. Putting her work aside, she heard her husband's voice calling for her. She was not going to hide, she told herself. Amir would come, and Rovere would finally meet his fate. She rose, pale and frightened, but she was determined to stand up to him. He would be quite surprised.

Agata sidled into the room. Her face was pinched with fright. "I have sent Ugo for the prince. There are only four men with your husband."

"You and Gemma hide with the girls," Bianca said. "If you don't, I am afraid they will be raped, for he will set his men on my women, and I don't want that."

"I must stay with you, mistress," Agata said loyally.

"I will manage Rovere as best I can," Bianca told her servingwoman. "See to the other women for my sake, if not your own."

Reluctantly, Agata slipped away, and drawing herself up to her full height Bianca came forth from her library into the gracious entry of her home. "You are hardly welcome here, *signore*," she told him boldly. "My absence from your home these few years has surely made it clear to even you that I do not choose to cohabit with such a husband. You should not have interfered with the annulment I sought from you."

Madre di Dios, he had changed. The once-handsome face was now bloated and puffy, marred further by broken veins near and on his nose. His hair had thinned considerably.

He advanced on her menacingly. "You little bitch," he snarled at her. "How dare you make me the laughingstock of Florence by leaving me?" He was infuriated by her calm beauty. Even in a modest gown of dark green velvet, she enticed him, and it angered him. His hand flashed out to make hard contact with her pale cheek.

She was startled by the unexpected blow, but though her heart was hammering in her chest, Bianca held her ground. "How dare you treat your wife like a whore?" she countered. Her cheek was burning, and she knew it was scarlet with color now. A tiny frisson of fear began to bloom within her. Bianca thrust it back angrily. She was not going to allow this brute to terrorize her any longer.

"You are a whore," he shouted. "All women are whores, even those like you from respectable families." He turned to his men. "Find whoever else is in this house, and drive them out of it. Amuse yourselves with the women if you must. My wife and I have business to transact this night." He turned back to Bianca.

"Get out of my villa, and take these bandits you hired with you," Bianca said bravely. "There is nothing further we have to discuss, Sebastiano. I hate and despise you. Get out! Get out! Get out!" And she stamped her feet at him angrily. "Understand that I will never be your wife again, in any sense."

His face grew purple with his rage now. When she turned to leave him standing there, his fury broke. Stepping quickly forward, his fingers dug into her hair, causing the neat chignon she wore to come loose. Wrapping the long, dark ebony locks about his hand, he yanked her back and around so she was facing him once more. His breath, always unpleasant, was now absolutely rank as he screamed at her, "You are mine! Mine, bitch! Mine to do with as I please." His hand descended several times, beating her about the face and shoulders. "First I intend to punish your disobedience with my hands. Then I will spend some time fucking you into compliance with my wishes. Finally I will give you such a sound beating, there won't be a place on your silky white body that doesn't bear my mark. In the morning we will return to Florence, where my little donkey is eagerly waiting for you. I warned you long ago, Bianca, that you are my property, and mine to do with as I will. But before I kill you, *cara mia*, you will grovel at my feet and thank me for ending your torture. What say you to that, bitch?"

She looked up at him, one eye already swelling, her nose bloodied. "May you rot in hell of the French pox, my husband," she managed to say before striking out at him with her two fists. Her whole body was aching with his blows, but she would not give in to this wretched excuse for a human being. She clawed at him and spat at him. She covered him in the worst curses she could think of, seeing the brief surprise on his face. Then he laughed at her and began to beat her once more with his punishing hands while Bianca attempted to defend herself from his attack.

Suddenly, to her astonishment and relief, her five women servants rushed into the wide entry armed with brooms and pans. They first yanked Rovere away from Bianca and next began beating him with their household weapons as they shouted curses at him, pushing him roughly out the front door of the villa. There, Primo awaited to force the surprised man onto his horse, sending him away into the deepening night with a hard smack on the horse's plump flanks.

It had been done so quickly that Rovere could scarcely believe what had happened. Where were his men? What had happened to them? The cowards had probably fled. But without their wages? He would probably find them farther on down the road. The night was cold and damp. He was finally forced to stop in the open, for he could no longer see the road ahead of him. He huddled down in the dark, cursing his fate at a light rain began to fall. As soon as it became even vaguely possible to move on, he mounted his beast and got back onto the country road again.

His men were still nowhere to be found, and he was yet miles from the main road to Florence. He was hungry and he was thirsty, but having no choice rode slowly on. Every small wood he traversed, he did so nervously. And then suddenly ahead of him on the hilly road he saw a small party of riders. His men? No, there were at least a dozen of them. Well, they could have what little money he had on him just as long as he managed to gain the main road to Florence. As expected, the masked horsemen surrounded him.

"I am Sebastiano Rovere of Florence," he said boldly. "You can have what monies I carry, but allow me to pass so I may reach a respectable inn by tonight."

"Get off your horse," a deep voice ordered him.

"Do not be unreasonable," Rovere said. "The animal has little value, but I cannot walk to Florence." Then to his amazement he was yanked rudely from the beast's back.

"We do not want the beast or your money, Rovere," the deep voice said. "We seek your life in exchange for your many sins."

Sebastiano Rovere's mouth fell open with his surprise at the words uttered by the bandit. "Who are you?" he asked, now truly frightened. They were going to assassinate him. He should not have to die like this out on the open road.

"I will give you whatever you desire," he began, "if you will spare my life."

The party of masked bandits laughed heartily, and their spokesman said, "There is no amount of gold that could buy your life, Rovere. Your sins are too many and too great, I fear. No. Your time has come, and like your many victims, there will be no mercy shown to you."

"Gold! Women! Whatever you desire," Rovere babbled, and he peed himself in his deepening fear of his impending death.

Again the bandits laughed. "We are not barbarians, Rovere. Say whatever prayers you say so we may be finished with this and have justice done at last."

"At least let me know who you are," Rovere begged. "I want to know who delivers what you dare to call justice to a respected man of Florence."

"You are not respected, Rovere. You are feared by the weak and despised by your betters, of whom there are many. You have fallen too low to be saved now. Your evil has run its course, and it is time for you to meet your master, the devil."

Two men stood on either side of the unfortunate man. They held his arms tightly, preventing his struggles.

"I want to know who you are!" Sebastiano Rovere screamed as his executioner stepped forward.

"You have been tried by the good and found guilty of your sins," the deep-voiced man on the horse said. "You are sentenced to death. The weapon's tip has been poisoned, for although we know you are heartless, we have granted you the mercy you never gave to so many of your unfortunate victims."

"Nooo!" Rovere shrieked as he felt the dagger plunge deep into his chest. He screamed as it was twisted several times, and he felt the poison beginning to work as his lungs ceased to expand and he could no longer draw a breath. His executioner lowered the cloth that was shielding the face behind it.

"*You?*" he gasped, disbelieving with his last breath, and collapsed onto the road as he was released from the hold of the two men.

"Check to make certain he is dead," the leader ordered. "Cut his throat for good measure," he told the men who had been restraining the prisoner. "Cut off his cock and balls too. Stuff them in his mouth for whoever finds him to see. It is a fitting ending for a debaucher of women."

One of the men immediately complied. Rovere's blood pooled in the dirt of the narrow road, then began to congeal. His mouth bulged wide open as his genitals were pushed between his lips, which were even now turning blue.

His executioner turned away without a word, drawing the face covering up again.

"Leave his horse and his purse," the rider with the deep voice said. "Let whoever finds him know that the murder done was personal and not for gain." Then seeing all his companions mounted, he gave the signal and they rode away. Above the body of the dead man, carrion birds began arriving with noisy cries of anticipation in the gray skies above.

It was almost a month later when word reached Bianca that Sebastiano Rovere had been set upon and killed on the road as he returned to Florence. She was almost healed now from the beating he had administered before her female servants had driven him out of the villa. She had learned from Agata that they had quickly dispatched the four men-at-arms who had accompanied her deceased husband. Rufina and Pia, the two pretty housemaids, lured them with bared breasts and raised skirts while Filomena and Gemma had slit the throats of each man as he eagerly fell upon a girl.

"They would not allow me to help them with those men," Agata said, sounding relieved. "They said a city woman had too great a conscience, whereas a country woman did what must be done without regret."

"What happened to the bodies?" Bianca wanted to know.

"We put them in bags weighed down with stones. A cousin of Gemma's is the fisherman who supplies us with our fish. He took the bodies one by one out to sea and dumped them. They were scum hired by Rovere, and not his own men. They will not be missed by anyone," Agata assured Bianca.

They had been living in fear that Bianca's brutal husband would return with a stronger force to retrieve his wife and take his revenge on the women of the villa. Then had come word of his death. It had been a shock, for Bianca had never considered that her husband might be assassinated by an enemy, though such a thing was not uncommon in Florence. But as the shock quickly evaporated and relief flooded her, Bianca realized that she was at last free.

"Send Ugo to the prince with word that I must see him urgently," Bianca told Agata, and a smiling Agata hurried out to send the manservant on his way.

That fatal night that Rovere had arrived at Luce Stellare, Ugo had taken a horse and raced down the beach to the prince's villa to fetch him. When he had arrived he had learned that both the prince and his servant, Krikor, had gone to the city several days prior. He had quickly brought back word to Agata, and it was then the women had acted to drive Sebastiano Rovere from the house and rescue Bianca.

Afterwards Agata had told Bianca of the prince's absence so she might know he had not abandoned her in her hour of need. Amir had come immediately upon his return and, seeing her condition, had sworn in both Italian and Turkish, vowing to see Rovere dead the next time he came to the villa. Now, upon learning of her husband's death, Bianca wondered if her prince had not waited for Rovere's return to Luce Stellare but gone after her husband and killed him on the road.

She saw the gray stallion galloping down the beach from the terrace of the villa where she was standing watching for him. She waved to him, her heart beating rapidly as she considered what her new freedom meant for them.

Amir saw her on the terrace, and when she waved, his heart caught in his throat. She did not look frightened or unhappy. What was so urgent that she had sent Ugo for him? He urged his stallion up the path, and gaining the top he leapt off the animal to run to her side. "What is wrong, Bianca? Are you all right?" He looked anxiously at her.

"My husband is dead," Bianca told him.

"What?"

"Sebastiano Rovere is dead. I am free of him, Amir. Free!"

"How? When?" Allah, be praised! This was good news.

"The day my women drove him from the villa," Bianca said. "He was set upon as he traveled back to Florence. There is no doubt it was an assassination, Amir. Neither his horse nor his purse had been stolen." Bianca had not been told of the mutilation of her late husband.

"Do the authorities know who did it?" the prince inquired of her.

Bianca shook her head. "No one has admitted to it, nor was there any evidence that pointed to anyone. I do not believe anyone cared enough to pursue the matter, even his own sons. They took his body to the city and buried him. I still do not know how he found me in the first place, but it doesn't matter now."

"No," the prince said slowly. Then he pulled Bianca into his embrace. His hand caressed her face, cupping it tenderly as his mouth descended upon hers in a deep, hungry kiss. Raising his head, he looked into her eyes. "The only thing that matters now, beloved, is you and I." And then he began kissing her again.

Chapter 8

*H*er head was spinning with delight and excitement as his lips brushed, pressed, and coaxed her shy but eager responses. Bianca had never really been kissed until now. Her late husband had not been a man for romantic kissing. His rough kisses were meant to impress his ownership of her. She was discovering that kissing was a delicate art as she followed Amir's lead and returned the kisses.

When he ran the tip of his tongue along her moist lips, Bianca gasped with surprise. His tongue immediately took advantage of her open mouth, slipping inside to play with her tongue. The sensation was exquisite, and she eagerly engaged his tongue with hers. Tongue play with Rovere had been disgusting, for he used it as he did everything—to claim ownership. Amir, however, teased and played, their two tongues dancing joyously, his scented breath mingling with hers. She almost fainted with the sensation.

His arousal was instant. He quickly broke off the embrace in an effort to cool his own ardor. He did not want her first real experience with passion to be quick or rough, given all she had suffered at Rovere's hands, but he still held her close. The softness of her breasts against his chest was almost painful under the circumstances. But he would take her slowly this first time. And with care.

Then she surprised him by saying, "I know, I know, my beloved. You would treat me like a delicate flower, but I am not a delicate flower. I have waited my entire life for you, Amir. There is nothing you could do that would remind me of Sebastiano Rovere. I want you as badly as you desire me. Do you understand what I am saying, Amir?" Then she took him by the hand and led him into the villa, up the tiled staircase, and into her bedchamber. She shut the door behind them after they had entered the room.

"Bianca, beloved, you have never known the passion of one who truly loves you," he told her as she unlaced his shirt. He groaned as her warm hands slid over his warm, smooth chest. Her dark head dipped to kiss his nipples.

"I'm glad you did not bother to wear a tunic," she said to him, her hands going to his wide pantaloons and loosening them.

He laughed low. "Oh, my sweet Bianca, you have no idea the beast you are awakening in me this moment. It longs to devour you, my beloved."

She leaned forward and whispered hotly in his ear, "I want to see you naked, Amir, my love. I have waited so long, and feared I would wait forever. Now Sebastiano is dead, and I am free to do as I please. It would please me to see you naked, *signore*. It would please me very much, if the truth be told. Did you think because I am a respectable woman I could feel no desire? Feel no need for you?"

The truth was he had. Amir had assumed it would be up to him to stir desire in her, but now seeing that was not so, he was rather pleased. "I want to see you naked too," he growled, and his fingers reached around her and began unlacing her gown. He slowly drew the garment down to reveal her exquisite breasts beneath the sheer fabric of her chemise. Bending, he rubbed his face over the soft mounds of barely covered flesh. She shivered, her nipples puckering like flower buds. "I would worship at the shrine of your body, beloved," he told her passionately as they continued undressing each other until they both stood as the Creator had fashioned them.

He then knelt before her, pulling her body against his face. Her skin was satiny, warm, soft, and scented. His eyes closed, he rubbed his cheek against the tender flesh. The sensation was almost painfully exquisite. She was, he thought, utterly and completely flawless in every way. His desire to join their two bodies rose, but with supreme self-discipline he restrained it. It wasn't yet quite time.

Bianca almost swooned with the simple joy the touch of his cheek against her skin gave her. Her experiences with her husband had been horrific, but from the passion her parents seemed to have for each other, she knew Rovere's possession of her was not the way it should be. With Amir it was a far different thing. It was as she had always imagined in her girlish dreams. He stood slowly and carried her to the bed.

She could see the state of his arousal now, and smiled. "Do not wait," she said to him. "Afterwards there will be time for the rest of it. You want me now, and I would know the taste of true passion, not merely a possession by a man who believes he owns me." She lay back and opened her arms to him, smiling.

Amir could not deny her honest plea. He loved this beautiful woman, and she had admitted to loving him. "Let me have my way with you but a moment longer," he said. Then he covered her breasts with kisses, his lips slipping down her torso briefly. Bianca sighed with the delightful pleasure those sweet kisses offered. Finally, he covered her body with his. "I admit to being unable to wait any longer," he said, sliding between her welcoming thighs, guiding his cock to where it might enter her body.

Then he pushed himself slowly, slowly, slowly into her, for he knew that she had not been used for some time. She was, as he expected, very tight, but her sheath was slick with heated moisture and eager for him. The muscles of that tube squeezed him in an embrace. He groaned loudly with the incredible pleasure she gave him. He kissed her mouth fiercely, and she kissed him back as eagerly.

"*Fuck me!*" She surprised him, whispering urgently into his ear as he first pierced her, then sank deep inside her. "Do not treat me as if I would break. I am as hot for you as you are for me, my beloved prince. I will not shatter. Your honest passion is nothing at all like the brutal treatment I received at my husband's hands. Now make love to me as if you mean it! Show me the depth of your emotions—I beg you, Amir!"

He was burning up with his need. He began to use her hard, his cock flashing quickly back and forth within her welcoming body. He felt her sheath tightening and shattering about his cock, but he continued on, a thrust for each long night that he had been denied her passion, although he realized such a thing was really impossible. Still he drove himself in and out, in and out, in and out, seemingly unable to cease his action.

With the edge briefly taken off her own lust, Bianca wrapped her legs about him, encouraging him to greater and greater heights. She felt herself reaching for the heavens and wondered that she did not explode with her pleasure. She was higher than she had ever been. She soared among the stars. This was no passion forced from her by her brutal husband. This time her passion was freely given to the man she could not survive without. They were one! She cried his name over and over again until her throat was raw with the sound. "Oh Amir, my love, my love!"

He thrust and he thrust and he thrust into her softness, but then sensing her passion peaking a second time, he released his own joy, for he could not hold it back any longer. Burying his face in her long ebony hair, he cried her name once, *"Bianca!"* as he was drained of this first desperate need for her.

They lay still joined for some time, their combined breathing calming itself as they were restored to a state of peace. Finally he withdrew slowly and reluctantly from her wonderful body. Silently their hands found each other, fingers entwining as they stretched out next to each other. She nestled close to him, her head settling upon his shoulder. Reaching out with an arm, he pulled her as close as he might.

"I love you," he said quietly.

"I love you," she responded. "You are the only man I have ever or will ever love."

The admission filled him with untold happiness, for she had captured his heart and soul in her two small hands. His grandfather's harem was filled with women sent for the purpose of expressing loyalty. Most never shared the sultan's bed. When Mehmet wished to honor someone, he would usually give away these women, who, having been trained in the arts of passion while in the harem, were excellent examples of feminine perfection with a thorough knowledge of female skills.

This was how Amir had obtained the two women who were his wives. Gifts from his grandfather, both were good women rendered sterile before their arrival in order that Amir would father no children—particularly male children who might one day challenge the Ottoman's rule. There was little chance that Amir, son of Jem, son of Mehmet, would ever inherit the throne. And if by some quirk of kismet he did, then he would take fertile women to give him sons and daughters.

Both his wives were pretty, although neither could be called a beauty. Maysun was three years older than he was, and Shahdi was a year younger. He was fond of them, for together they kept his home a pleasant and orderly dwelling. He slept with them occasionally, and treated them well so that they were content in their lives. But love them? No. He did not love them. He had never loved them. He had never loved anyone until he had set eyes upon the woman who now cuddled next to him replete with passion.

They were now lovers and for the next month spent every waking and sleeping moment together. They were oblivious to anything but each other. Krikor, the prince's slave man, grumbled with the changes in his master's life. He did not like change, he said. Still, he could not help but chuckle now and again at Bianca and Amir. Agata and the other women servants of Luce Stellare smiled and sang at their work, very content to see their beautiful mistress and her beloved prince so happy. Bianca deserved some happiness, the women of the villa agreed. It was past time.

Then one day a messenger arrived bearing a message from the lawyer representing Sebastiano Rovere's estate. He wished to speak with the widow himself, and requested that she return to Florence. Bianca considered it, but then she sent back a message in her own hand telling the lawyer that if he wished to speak with her, he must come to Luce Stellare. She had no intention of leaving her home.

To her surprise, the lawyer came, and with him her two stepsons, Stefano and Alberto Rovere. Bianca was forced to house them, as her isolated home was nowhere near a village or an inn. "I don't want you here when they are here," she said to Amir. "If they see I have taken a lover, they will assume I left their father for you."

"Such a thing would not have been possible," the prince said to her. "How could we have met in the first place?" He didn't like the idea of leaving her alone with her late husband's sons or the lawyer.

"Common sense is not something the Roveres have. Now that he is dead, they will do what all families do. They will attempt to make him the victim of a bad wife in order to preserve some bit of respectability for him. They would not bother with me at all except that as his widow I have come into an inheritance," Bianca said.

"Will you accept it?" he asked her, both curious and jealous.

"No, Amir, of course not. I want only my dower portion back in full, with interest. I cannot continue to live on my father's generosity, Amir, nor do I want to, for it means I must obey my father once again. I will purchase the villa from him, and invest my monies with the di Medici bank. I would be independent. Lorenzo is not his late grandfather, Cosimo, but he will see that I am taken care of, I am certain," Bianca told her lover. "Once I counted him a friend. I hope that he still considers me such."

"I want you to marry me," the prince told her. "I want to take care of you, Bianca. I want to keep you safe from any harm."

"You already have two wives, Amir. And you cannot marry me," Bianca said quietly. "You are an infidel. I do not believe the sultan's grandson is about to convert to Christianity, is he?"

"No," he admitted with a sigh. "That in itself would be treasonous for me."

"Then we are at an impasse, *cara mia*. Yet I am perfectly content to remain your lover," she told him. "I have no obligations. My family sacrificed me to save themselves, and I am not likely to ever forget that. I love them, but I will not be ruled by them again."

He looked at her, surprised. "What has happened to you?" he asked her.

Bianca smiled. "Your love has made me strong, Amir. I do not want to be a frail female dependent on a father, or a husband. I can take care of myself. It pleases me to live in my own house. It pleases me to have Amir ibn Jem as my lover. I will be owned by no man ever again now that I know what real freedom is all about."

Astounded, he said, "And what happens when you are no longer pleased to have me as your lover, Bianca?"

Bianca saw the hurt in his eyes. She had been too candid with him. She had injured his pride. It was a mistake she would not make again. "Oh, my love," she said, throwing herself into his arms, "I shall never grow tired of your passion. More likely you will grow tired of me when I grow old and plump."

His arms tightened about her. He was just discovering what a clever woman she was. It was frankly quite a shock. He kissed the top of her ebony head. "I will go home, and leave you to manage your not-so-welcome guests," he told her. *And think on this sudden turn of events,* he said silently to himself. *I love her, but can I manage an independent woman?*

She heard the tightness in his voice. "Amir," she said, looking up at him now, "do not be angry with me, my love. Of all those I know, I thought you would understand better than any my need for true freedom."

He sighed. "I do," he admitted, reluctantly realizing that he actually did understand. "I have the same needs as well, beloved. That is why I reside here in the Republic of Florence instead of my own home on the Black Sea. Still, to hear you give voice to your desires surprises me. You have never before spoken of such things."

"I could not speak such thoughts before my husband's death," Bianca explained.

"No, you could not, could you?" he agreed. He tipped her face up to his, and gave her a quick kiss. "Send to me when your guests are gone, beloved."

"I will," she told him.

And then he was gone, calling for Krikor to join him.

Bianca watched him go, and then with a sigh turned to begin preparations for her guests. "Put the brothers in the guest chamber facing the sea, and the lawyer in the one facing the gardens," she told Filomena. "Cook simple meals," she instructed Gemma. "I don't want them settling in for a long stay. And serve passable but not the best wines. A day or two is all I can bear of such company."

"You should send to your father," Agata said.

"Why?" Bianca demanded.

"He can advise you. I do not think it is wise for you to speak with these people without someone there to see to your interests," Agata replied.

"I want nothing from Rovere but that which is mine," Bianca said. "I will not profit from his death, well deserved as it was."

"You deserve something for the time you spent with that demon and the misery he visited upon you," Agata said indignantly.

Bianca smiled, and patted her servingwoman's hand. "Whatever he has is cursed in my eyes. I would not bring his bad luck into my house," she explained, knowing that Agata would understand that.

"Ahhhh, yes!" her loyal servant responded, nodding. "Now I see, mistress. You are so very wise. Your mother would be pleased."

"I shall invest my dower portion with the di Medici bank," Bianca said. "Now let us prepare for our guests, for the sooner we can accommodate them, the sooner they will be gone."

The Rovere brothers and their lawyer came. All were dressed in black as a sign of their mourning. Bianca greeted them in a red gown trimmed in gold thread and tiny black jet beading.

"You do not mourn your husband, *signora?*" the lawyer, whose name was Renzo Guardini, asked her disapprovingly. He was a tall, thin man with a pinched face.

"I had not seen my husband in almost two years, Signore Guardini," Bianca replied. "Until he arrived at my villa shortly before his demise. In the brief time he was here and before he was driven off, he beat me severely while his men attempted to rape my women servants. I was seeking an annulment of our marriage, and he obviously did not approve. He was a monster. I am not a hypocrite to mourn a man I despised and whose debauchery was legend. I hope he is roasting in hell." She smiled. "Let us go to my library, which is a suitable place in which to conduct business," Bianca suggested, as she led them from the entry of the house where she had greeted them into the more comfortable surroundings. "There is a tray with glasses and wine, *signores*. Please help yourselves. My household staff is small and limited to women servants only, although I do have two men for the gardens and stables." She seated herself, and her guests did too after helping themselves to her wine.

"Your husband has left you a very rich woman," Signore Guardini began.

"I want nothing but my dower portion plus the interest it would have earned in a respectable bank from the time I was betrothed to him until his death," Bianca said.

"*Signora*, you do not understand," the lawyer said. "Sebastiano Rovere left his widow half of his fortune as well as his house and all of his slaves."

"Did he indeed?" Bianca was genuinely surprised, but then she saw her father's hand in that. Rovere had agreed because he wanted the most beautiful girl in Florence for his wife, and he didn't expect Bianca to outlive him.

"He did indeed," Guardini said sourly, his tone implying she didn't deserve it.

"I want only my dower portion plus interest," Bianca repeated. "I certainly don't want the house where I was so unhappy. I will free the poor slaves he held but for one."

She turned to Stefano Rovere. "Take Nudara, and sell her along with her damnable donkey to the highest bidder. Then give the monies you obtain to the Reverend Mother Baptista at the convent of Santa Maria del Fiore outside the city's gates."

"That slave girl is worth a fortune," Alberto Rovere protested, "and you would give that fortune to some shabby convent outside the city? I wonder if they would even take monies obtained from such a sale."

"As they are unlikely to know, and they are poor, I imagine they will be grateful for such an unexpected gift," Bianca said sweetly. "But should you dare to tell them the origins of their good fortune, Alberto, believe me when I promise you that you will suffer for your perfidy. My Agata will see that the evil eye is put on you. And I will curse you myself with a certain inability to perform. Some good should come from that vile bitch."

"There is a fortune to be made with the wench!" Alberto insisted. "If you could see how she takes that animal's doughy cock with little cries of pleasure, and then wiggles her plump ass, you would understand. The public would pay through the nose to see such a spectacle. Give her to me! I will give you half of all I earn with her, and you can give that to your favored convent. No one need know that we are the ones profiting."

Bianca looked at her stepson with distaste. *Madre di Dios!* He favored his father in his deviant tastes, which was unfortunate, but then with an unpleasant flash she remembered him on her wedding night. Catching herself, Bianca drew a deep breath. "Alberto, your brother will sell Nudara for me to the highest bidder with the monies to go to Santa Maria del Fiore. If, as you say, there is a great demand for this creature, then a publicly announced but private auction will bring out many bidders, and a great deal of gold."

He looked at her with Sebastiano's cold dark eyes. "I want Nudara, and if you do not give her to me, I will—"

"Will what, you pitiful little monster? You are about to make a great match, I am told. I wonder how they would feel knowing the kind of man they are entrusting with their virgin daughter. And you will know how to be certain she is a virgin, Alberto, won't you?" Bianca said softly, but her eyes were like blue ice. "Of course, if your dear father was blackmailing them as he did my father, your marriage may not take place at all. The girl is a very wealthy heiress—pretty, I am told, and a desirable match. I am astounded they would choose you for her husband."

"We are in love!" Alberto said.

"Then be satisfied that you and Stefano will split your father's considerable wealth instead of having to share it with me. There are things I know that your family would prefer not be revealed to the public eye. Do you understand me?"

He nodded but then said, "When did you become so hard, Bianca?"

She laughed. "I am not hard, Alberto, except where I must be. If I could survive your father's treatment of me, however, I can and will survive anything, including your attempts to force me to your will."

"This is not how things are done," the lawyer Guardini said, pursing his lips.

"Stefano, you are the eldest. What say you?" Bianca asked.

"I will see that your wishes are carried out, Bianca," he told her. He turned to the lawyer. "She is to have exactly what she asks for, her dower portion plus interest, and the monies from the sale of the slave will go to Santa Maria del Fiore. The other slaves held by my father will be freed, and given a year's wages as if they were free men."

"The di Medici bank will decide the interest owed," Bianca told them sweetly. Then she said, "Thank you, Stefano, for your generosity."

"I agree," Stefano said. "Brother?"

"I agree as well," Alberto replied, defeated.

"Then is our business done?" Bianca asked the lawyer.

"I must draw up the papers making these changes," Guardini said sourly.

"Please feel free to use the library. There is parchment in the drawer of the table you can use. And ink too. When you are done I will read it over, and if it suits me I will sign it. You will stay the night, of course, *signores*."

She could read; why was he not surprised? Guardini wondered. He had heard that Sebastiano Rovere's widow was a properly raised woman who was meek and obedient. This woman did not fit such a description at all. He had not heard until his client's death that his wife had left him. He was not a part of Rovere's circle of friends, and the truth was he hadn't wished to be. Rovere had wanted his own representation to be competent and dull. Renzo Guardini was just that, and content to be so.

Rovere's widow was like her father. He realized that, in spite of himself, he was admiring of her. He remembered the silk merchant seated in his chambers with Rovere, dictating the terms of the marriage contract. It was he who had insisted that if Rovere predeceased his daughter, half of his estate would go to the widow. Guardini had been shocked by such a request, and even more shocked that Rovere agreed to the terms. His client had just laughed and said, "If she can outlive me, she will have earned it." The silk merchant had nodded grimly.

Well, she had outlived him, but chose not to profit from her husband's death. He shook his head. Yet having met Bianca Pietro d'Angelo now, Guardini could not help but consider if she had a hand in her husband's death. She would not be the first woman to pay for the assassination of her spouse. But then where would she have gotten the monies for such a deed? She had been in hiding from Rovere, and her honest surprise at learning she had inherited half of his estate, an estate she would not accept, really ruled out any malice on her part. No. Rovere's wife had simply benefited from the man's ability to make enemies. And the belief that he could escape justice had been Rovere's downfall.

The lawyer set to work writing a document to be signed by Bianca and by Rovere's two sons, who were now each twice as rich as they had believed themselves to be. It took him some time, for he was not used to doing such work himself but rather assigning it to his notary, but by late afternoon he had written the document out four times. A copy for Bianca; one for each of her stepsons; and another for the court. The document stated that Bianca Pietro d'Angelo renounced the bequest made to her by her late husband, Sebastiano Rovere, with two exceptions. Her dower with interest calculated by the di Medici bank would be returned to her, not her father; and the slave woman known as Nudara would be sold, the profit from such sale to go to the convent of Santa Maria del Fiore.

"It's a simple enough document, but quite legal," Guardini said. "You are empowered to act for yourself as Rovere's widow. Sign here, *signora*."

Bianca signed the four documents, passing them next to Stefano, who then pushed the parchments to his younger brother. All three parties having signed, Guardini put his own signature and seal to the documents. Then he gave one to Bianca and one each to Stefano and Alberto Rovere. They then adjourned to the dining room for the meal, and afterwards were shown to their chambers by Filomena. The next morning the three men departed after being fed a simple breakfast of bread, cheese, and wine.

"Will you be returning to Florence now?" Stefano asked her as his horse was brought from the stable.

"No, Luce Stellare is my home now," she told him. "I am content."

"Your father will want to make another marriage for you, Bianca. I hope it will be a happier one."

"I want no more husbands," Bianca said quietly. "Tell me, Stefano, do you know how your father found me? Few knew where I was."

Stefano Rovere nodded. "Yes, I do, although I am ashamed to tell you," he said, looking embarrassed.

"But you will nonetheless," Bianca said.

He nodded again. "He kidnapped your brother Georgio, off the street one afternoon, brought him to the house, and showed him that damned donkey violating a whore. Your brother fainted with the shock of what he saw, for the whore screamed and screamed. When he was brought around to consciousness, my father threatened to put the donkey to Georgio unless he found out where you were hiding and told him. Of course the boy was terrified. He did my father's bidding. I know this because my father insisted I be in the chamber when the violence was done so your brother would not run. And afterwards I took Georgio home. I am sorry, Bianca, and I am very ashamed."

"You are forgiven, Stefano, for I know what a frightening man your father could be. He was not someone to pronounce idle threats. If he said it, he did it," Bianca told the young man. "I suffered at his hands enough to know that."

"Thank you," Stefano Rovere said, kissing both of Bianca's hands.

"We will not meet again," she told him.

"I understand," he said. Then he mounted his horse, joined his younger brother and their lawyer, and rode away.

She watched them go as relief swept over her. At last the Roveres were out of her life. She looked at Ugo, who stood waiting for the order he knew was coming. "Go to Prince Amir and tell him my guests have gone."

"At once, *signora*," the man said, bobbing his head at her and smiling.

Bianca laughed aloud, and twirled about. She was happy. She was happy! The darkness that had filled her life the past three years was finished. She was in love with a prince, and he with her. Her life was going to be perfect.

Amir came that evening, and their idyll continued as they spent the days walking, riding, and talking—and the nights in an ecstasy of endless passion. A look, and she was afire. A touch, and his desire flamed. Neither had ever imagined that a love like theirs could exist. They cherished each other, and the time they spent together.

Giovanni Pietro d'Angelo wrote to his daughter requesting that she return to Florence now that the danger was past for her. Bianca wrote him back that she preferred to live in the country. Master Pietro d'Angelo wrote again reminding his eldest daughter of her duty to him. Bianca wrote back that as a widow she was now free to make her own decisions, and she had made the choice to remain at Luce Stellare. Master Pietro d'Angelo pointed out to his daughter that he owned the villa in which she lived. Bianca replied that she would like to purchase the villa from him. He wrote that he would not sell it to her. She wrote that she would find another villa by the sea to buy.

Orianna Pietro d'Angelo arrived two weeks later. Mother and daughter greeted each other lovingly. Bianca invited her parent to join her on the terrace that overlooked the sea. Agata brought sweet wine and sugar wafers, then discreetly withdrew just far enough not to be seen, but close enough to hear the conversation.

One look at her daughter had told Orianna what she needed to know. Bianca had taken a lover. She was radiant with happiness. It would be the Turkish prince, of course. There was no one else nearby, and Bianca was too fastidious to take one of her male servants to her bed. Orianna had seen both Primo and Ugo. They were rough men of the earth, and hardly the type to sweep a girl like Bianca off her feet. No. It would be the prince.

"Your disobedience has distressed your father greatly," Orianna said, sipping at the sweet wine. It was quite good. She had never tasted anything like it before.

"My father must understand that I am now in charge of my own life, *Madre*," Bianca answered her parent. "I am a widow, not a virgin in need of protection."

"You must remarry, Bianca," Orianna said.

"Why? I did not find marriage to my liking at all, *Madre*."

"You didn't find Rovere to your liking," Orianna corrected her. "You are not unhappy with your lover, Bianca." She looked directly at her daughter as she spoke.

Bianca flushed, but then she said, "No, I am not unhappy with my lover, *Madre*. But he has no authority over me as a husband would have. We simply love each other, and share pleasure together."

"Is it the prince? Of course it would be. He is very handsome, and I suspect he was most persuasive," her mother said. "You are not as sophisticated as you think."

Bianca laughed. "Yes, Amir is handsome, and yes, he is persuasive, but would you be surprised to know that I am persuasive too, *Madre*?"

Now Orianna laughed. Suddenly they were no longer just mother and daughter, but two women together speaking of love. "Still," she said, "for propriety's sake you must remarry or enter a convent. You are not a courtesan, Bianca."

"I will not remarry, *Madre*. That is why I prefer to remain here in the country by the sea. Let any who remember me believe I was so badly damaged by my marriage that I have eschewed society altogether. Is it not better that way? I am not a woman for the convent either. You must speak of me in hushed tones when your friends ask."

"Do not be dramatic, Bianca. Marriage is the only option open to a woman of good family. You will not remarry in Florence. We will find you a husband elsewhere, and you will begin anew. Since you are a widow, your lack of virginity will not distress a second husband. The wealth you inherited from Rovere will make you most desirable."

"I took nothing from his estate but my dower plus interest. I have had the monies placed with the di Medici bank, *Madre*. I had Sebastiano's notorious slave woman sold, and the proceeds were given to your kinswoman at the convent that sheltered me those many weeks. I thought that only fair," Bianca told her mother.

"Bianca! You have been cheated!" Orianna gasped, horrified. "I know that your father saw to it that your husband's will gave you half of his estate should you survive him."

"It did indeed," Bianca said. "I did not want it, *Madre*. I wanted nothing that belonged to that man. When I fled I left behind the jewelry he had given me. It is cursed, *Madre*. All of it. Cursed! I could not have kept a bit of it in good conscience."

Orianna was pale with shock at her daughter's pronouncement. "You are a foolish, foolish girl," she told her daughter. "You would have been a very rich woman. We could have found you a great noble for a husband. Now"—she sighed— "I do not know."

"But I don't want another husband, *Madre*," Bianca said. "Why will you not understand that? I am happy now, and content. Am I not allowed to be so?"

"You don't want a husband now, Bianca, but what happens when your prince grows tired of you, or returns to his native land? What then, my daughter? Have you bothered to think that far ahead? No! You are just living in the moment, little *ingenua*!"

"The moment, *Madre*, is all any of us really has," Bianca replied. "I love Amir. I will never love another. If he leaves me, then I will be alone. But I will not love again."

Orianna sighed. "Those are the words of a woman in love

for the very first time, my daughter. You will love again. We all do."

"Did you, *Madre*?" Bianca asked softly.

Her mother flushed. "It is true," she admitted. "Your father was not my first love."

"You were a good daughter," Bianca said. "You did what you had to do, and you married the Florentine merchant who was willing to overlook the paucity of your dowry as the youngest child of a Venetian prince. Your parents saw that you came to know your husband before the marriage. My father is kind, and he understood your position. He respected you, and you gave him enough fondness to create a family, and the respect to which he was entitled. But you have never loved my father with the same passion that I love Amir, *Madre*, and I know you will not deny that, for you are too honest a woman."

"I see that I have underestimated you, Bianca," Orianna replied. "You are far more astute than I would have suspected until this moment. But the fact remains, Prince Amir is not a suitable husband for you, nor will he wed you. He is an infidel. He is tolerated in Florence because he is the sultan's grandson and an honest merchant. But if he were to violate the laws of the state he would be expelled and forbidden to return."

"Do you threaten Amir, *Madre*?" Bianca asked her mother. "You surely know he stands high in Lorenzo di Medici's favor."

"Even the di Medici are not foolish enough to defy the state or the Church. They keep their power by retaining the favor of the majority of Florentines. If they lose that favor, they lose their power, Bianca. Do you really believe they would favor a friendship over their own power? You are not that foolish."

"You would make me marry some stranger when I am in love with another man?" Bianca queried her mother. "Do you care nothing for my happiness? Was not my sacrifice for our family as Sebastiano Rovere's wife enough? Do you think I will ever forget my wedding night with that monster, or the nights of debauchery that followed as he introduced me into his perversions, or the beatings I received when I resisted? Now you would force me to wed another man who will have charge over my very life and death when I prefer to remain a free woman? I would die first, *Madre*! Do you understand me? I would prefer death. Force my hand in this matter and you will find yourself burying me in that great marble tomb that belongs to the Pietro d'Angelo family."

Orianna was shocked by her daughter's words. "Bianca! You cannot mean such a thing. Suicide is a sin in the eyes of the Church."

"What you propose when you suggest destroying my happiness is a greater sin in the eyes of God," Bianca shot back, angry now. "I would not care if Pope Alexander himself ordered it, I will not remarry, *Madre*."

It was at that very tense moment that Prince Amir arrived. He had not come by the beach this time but had ridden along the narrow path that served as a road to both villas and beyond. He saw Agata half hidden, listening to the conversation on the terrace, and moved quickly past her, for Bianca's raised voice was almost edged in hysteria. He wanted to learn who distressed her so and put an immediate stop to it. Brushing past the surprised Agata, he stepped out onto the terrace. "Beloved!"

She ran to him immediately, and his arms closed about her. Then his eyes met those of another woman, a woman he recognized at once as Orianna Pietro d'Angelo.

"Prince Amir," Orianna said.

"What have you said to upset Bianca?" He wanted to know.

"You are bold to interfere with a mother and her daughter, *signore*," Orianna replied. She reached for her goblet, only to find it empty.

"I love your daughter, *signora*," he said.

"I know you do, and she loves you, Prince Amir. But your liaison is unsuitable, as we both well know. Bianca is inexperienced, but in her heart she knows it too," Orianna told him. "She must remarry as soon after the mourning period as possible, for Rovere is over and done with. I have come with that end in mind, but my daughter will not listen. Perhaps if you explained to her the impossibility of your situation she would understand better, and do her duty by her family. My father is even now seeking a suitable match in Venice for Bianca. I had always meant for her to marry into Venice."

"But I wish to marry Bianca, *signora*. My lineage is more than suitable. My own mother was the daughter of an English merchant. It is from her I have inherited my talent for trade. I have made myself a wealthy man, *signora*."

"Impossible! You are an infidel!" Orianna said. "There is nothing that can overcome that fault but for a conversion to our Christian faith. I know you will not convert any more than I, or Bianca, would. Therefore, there is no hope for you, *signore*. I am sorry, but you certainly understand my family's viewpoint in this matter."

"I would take her back to Turkey. I will not ask that she renounce her own faith," he said. "She will live in my palace, the Moonlight Serai, in the hills above the Black Sea, and she will want for nothing. I shall never cease loving Bianca. You surely understand love, *signora*. Help us! Do not attempt to part us, I beg of you. But should you try to separate us, I will fight you with every resource that I have. I shall not allow anyone to take my beloved Bianca from me."

"*Madre di Dios!*" Orianna said. "You actually believe it is possible for such a marriage to take place or to succeed under any circumstances? *Never!* I will not allow it to happen. I will do whatever I must to prevent such a travesty. Love is not enough! It just isn't. You are a pair of romantic fools, but I will not allow Bianca to ruin her life. I protect what is mine! Be warned, *signore*, that I have my resources too. I will use them to prevent any marriage between you and my eldest daughter. If you truly love Bianca, then help her to accept the reality of this situation. Do not foolishly lead her on. She will never be yours, *signore*, but for this short sweet interlude that you have shared together."

Chapter 9

*B*oth Bianca and Amir were shocked by the vehemence in Orianna's voice, by her strong words. For a moment they remained silent, and then Bianca spoke.

"*Madre*, do you not want me to be happy?" Bianca asked her mother.

"You would not be happy as his wife," Orianna said. "Oh, at first, perhaps, but once you realized all you had given up and left behind, you would be miserable for everything you had lost and would now be unable to regain. And what of the other two wives he has? Oh yes, I know of them. I cannot allow you to make such a mistake, Bianca! I will do all in my power to prevent it!" Then, rising from her seat, she left them together on the terrace and stormed back into the villa, brushing past Agata who, seeing her coming, just managed to jump out of the way.

"I have never seen her like that," Bianca said, amazed.

"She is a woman who believes in what she says, and thinks she is protecting her child," Amir replied. "Did you not tell her that I had already asked you to marry me, and you had refused?"

"No," Bianca admitted. "The opportunity hadn't previously come up, but then it was suddenly there. Besides, if I returned with you to Turkey, why could we not go on as we are now, *amore mia*? I am content."

"We cannot go on as we are because you would live in my home. I would have you on an equal footing with my two wives, Bianca. As my lover you would not be equal in rank to them, and you must be. I cannot rid myself of either Maysun or Shahdi, for they were gifts from the sultan, who received them from political allies. He honored those allies by giving them to me, so I must keep them. They will be your companions, and though you will be my third wife you will remain first in my heart, a distinction they will understand. They know their places, and are content."

"Could we ride and walk together there as we do here?" she asked him.

"Yes, but not if we lived in the city. That is why I prefer the country, among other reasons. I like the freedom I have, and I know you will too. Yet you will be safe," he promised her. "Come with me, Bianca. Here, your family will not stop until they have separated us, and forced you into another marriage of their choosing. Your mother is a very strong woman, beloved. Stronger than many men. She truly believes what she has said to us. I see it in her eyes."

"But you have made a life here, Amir. You are favored by the di Medici, and other wealthy families. If you return to

Turkey you will be in danger from whoever succeeds your grandfather when he dies," Bianca said, concerned.

"Yes, I have a life here in Florence, but if I remain I cannot have you," he told her. "My grandfather will live for many more years. If we live peacefully and avoid his court, I will present no threat to his heirs or their heirs. The customs of the di Medici have made me a wealthy man, Bianca. I could live on that wealth, but I will not, for I am not a man to remain idle. I can conduct my trading business from Turkey if I set it up properly before we depart Florence. I have two assistants in my warehouse who could manage here without me, given the proper instruction."

"If they do not steal from you," Bianca remarked. "And they probably will."

He laughed. "They will steal a little," he said with a chuckle. "It is to be expected, and the cost of doing business, I fear. Let me prepare to return to Turkey with you, beloved. I can make you happy, and I will."

Bianca thought of her mother's words. If she left Florence with Amir she would never see her family again. Was she willing to give them up for this prince? She considered it, and realized she was. Her sisters would be married to men in faraway places. Her brothers would likely wed away but for Marco. Georgio already planned to go into the Church, and as a third son, Luca would be given to a foreign wife who could benefit their family from some distant place. Her parents would die eventually. Her family was already gone in her mind, she realized. "Yes, Amir," she said. "I will go with you. You are my home, my family now."

He drew her slowly into his arms, their eyes meeting in

perfect understanding. "I love you," he said, and kissed her a deep, lingering kiss.

Bianca relaxed into the embrace as the pressure of his lips on hers reaffirmed her decision. Their love was more than enough.

Watching them from her bedchamber window, Orianna felt a stab of envy. There was no mistaking the love her daughter and Prince Amir held for each other, but it simply couldn't be allowed to continue. Such a love between a good Christian woman and this infidel was wrong. She must get Bianca back to Florence, back to the safety of the family palazzo, where she might correct this mistake before it was compounded.

To Bianca's surprise, her mother departed the following day, taking her escort with her. "I will leave you both to contemplate the wisdom of your liaison," she told her daughter and Prince Amir. "You are a man of the world, *signore*. I can see you love my daughter, but you must know a union between two such different people cannot succeed. For both of your sakes I wish it were otherwise, but it is not. Accept this, and help Bianca to accept it so she may make another, happier union. This is her fate as my daughter. I swear to you that the man we choose this time will be of peerless reputation and kind. He will cherish and esteem the treasure that we entrust to him in Bianca. My child will tell you I am not a woman to make idle promises. I keep my word." Then she kissed Bianca on both cheeks and left.

They stood together watching as Orianna Pietro d'Angelo rode out of sight. Bianca shivered suddenly. "She will have her way unless we are quickly gone from here," she warned her lover. "I know my mother, Amir. She can be ruthless and without mercy when she is defied. She always meant me to have a Venetian marriage."

"Do not be afraid, beloved," he assured her. "I will begin making arrangements for our departure this very day. It will take time, however. I will not send you alone. We must go together. I need to settle my affairs in Florence, and advise my grandfather that I am coming home. The rest of it I will explain to him once we are there."

"I am suddenly afraid," Bianca said. "I have not been afraid since I escaped my late husband's palazzo. My mother could not have whoever it was she loved and left behind in Venice when she was married off to my father. Francesca once overheard my grandparents speaking of it when they visited, and she told me. My mother doesn't want me to have what she could not. She will do whatever she must to separate us, my love. Do not trust her or her words. Take me away quickly! Before she has time to act against us."

"As quickly as I can, Bianca! Now let us go for a ride and forget the unpleasantness your mother brought into our midst."

Bianca felt better when they returned. The air had been fresh and tangy from the sea, and her fears had evaporated in the warm sunshine. "What are you doing?" she asked Agata, finding her servingwoman busily packing her possessions when she walked into her bedchamber.

"Your mother told me to begin packing for our return to Florence," Agata said.

"I am not going to Florence," Bianca told the servant. "I am going to Turkey with Prince Amir. Will you come with me, or stay here?"

"As if I really have a choice," Agata said candidly. "If I stay, your mother will kill me for not stopping you and send me from the family's employ, so I must go with you."

"I will give you enough money to escape your servitude if you would prefer to remain," Bianca told the loyal Agata. "I do not want you unhappy, but I know my mother would blame you as if you could stop me."

"No, I will go with you willingly," Agata said. "You are a good mistress, and if it is fated for me to die unshriven in a foreign land, then so be it. We have seen no priest since we left Florence all those months ago, and I have almost forgotten my faith."

"You do not seem weighed down with your sins," Bianca teased, and Agata laughed. "Continue packing, for we are to make a journey no matter where we go."

Amir came to Bianca that night, climbing up to the little wrought-iron balcony outside her bedchamber window, entering her bed like a secret lover after removing his clothing. Naked, she wrapped herself around him, sighing as his hands caressed her from the nape of her neck to her shoulders and down her back. Their lips touched and the fires of their passion exploded. They reveled in the sensation of her breasts against his smooth, hard chest, her slightly rounded belly against his flat belly, her mons sensuously pressing against his mound.

They nibbled on each other. She on his earlobe, her little teeth biting down just enough to give the sensation of pain without hurt, her tongue sweeping around the curve of his ear's whorl while she murmured little endearments to him. He first nipped the nipples of her breasts, then fastened his mouth upon one, sucking it hard while his fingers played between her nether lips, teasing at the tiny nub of flesh that could set her afire, then pushing two fingers into her sheath, moving them back and forth until she cried his name.

He tucked her beneath him and entered her eagerly waiting body. She sighed with intense pleasure as his cock opened her to his passion, filling her with its length, its thickness. She wrapped herself about him, clutching him, her fingers digging into the flesh of his broad shoulders, scoring his back lightly with her nails as the intensity of their coupling increased her passion. She loved him. There was nothing else.

She was his! *His!* He had never in his life wanted and needed any woman until sweet Bianca. His own English captive mother had died when he was young. His father's women cared for him after that, but there was never again the love for him that his mother had lavished upon him. He was educated, fed, and clothed. Nothing more.

He had thought perhaps that one of the two maidens his grandfather had given him would love him, but neither did. They were grateful for his kindness and they were dutiful, but there was no passion, no burning need, no excitement. He was appreciative of their care of him when he was at home. But with Bianca, it was all different. There was a constant longing, a need that could be filled only by this beautiful woman. He would not let her go. She was his, and he was hers. Nothing was going to change how they felt.

Orianna Pietro d'Angelo, however, had different plans for her daughter Bianca. Her sudden arrival home but a few days after her departure was a great surprise to her household. They had expected her to be away for several weeks visiting Bianca. Her mood indicated she was not pleased. Both her servants and her children walked cautiously around the silk merchant's wife that day.

A servant had been dispatched immediately to fetch the master from his mistress's dwelling where he had been enjoying a leisurely afternoon away from his silk warehouses. His mistress was upset at his quick departure and cried, which annoyed him. He intended to be most put out on his arrival home, but one look at his wife's face told him the matter was very serious, else she would not be back so quickly. They spoke together in his library immediately.

"What is it?" he asked her, knowing Orianna needed little encouragement.

"Bianca is in love!" his wife began dramatically.

Was that all it was? The silk merchant decided that he was annoyed after all. "Is the man suitable? It will certainly solve the problem of what to do with her, *cara*."

"Do you consider an infidel suitable, *signore*?" she asked archly. "She has fallen in love with the Turkish sultan's grandson, and worse, he loves her."

"What?" He knew of the Turkish antiquities and rug merchant the *Arte di Calimala* claimed as their own member. "How did she meet him, Orianna?"

"His is the villa next to Luce Stellare," she explained. "But it does not matter how they met, Gio—they met. They are lovers in love! Such a thing cannot be allowed, husband. He is an infidel! He would leave Florence and take her to his home in Turkey, and she is eager to go with him. My father had planned an important marriage for Bianca before you forced her to wed Rovere," Orianna reminded her husband sharply.

"Would you have had Rovere see our son accused of a murder his own son probably did?" Giovanni Pietro d'Angelo demanded to know. Would Orianna never forget? It was water under the bridge now.

"My father has agreed to make another match in Venice for Bianca," his wife said.

"What of Francesca?"

"Francesca can come home to Florence, and we will seek a French marriage for her now. Our second daughter has my coloring, and is as great a beauty as Bianca is with her dark hair. What cannot be allowed is for Bianca to run off with this Turkish prince. You must go to Lorenzo di Medici. He can have the sultan request that his grandson return home. That will put an end to the matter, Gio. For God's own good mercy, you cannot allow Bianca to be stolen away."

"By the time the Medici sends to the sultan and gets an answer, Bianca and her prince could be gone," Giovanni pointed out to his wife. "If you have shown them your disapproval, and I am certain you have, they are even now preparing to flee."

"Let the di Medici imprison Prince Amir until he can be sent home," Orianna said. "Then we may forcibly fetch Bianca and bring her to her senses, Gio. Her marriage to Rovere was a horror, as we both know. Let her come home and see the benefits of a happy marriage between two good friends, Gio. In the meantime, my father will find her a husband of wealth and stature in Venice. I want our daughter happy."

She wanted Bianca happy, he thought. Yet she would plot to take their daughter away from the man she loved because he was an infidel. Giovanni Pietro d'Angelo did not discuss his religion with anyone, but having married a woman who did not love him, he thought perhaps the prince who loved Bianca, for all that he was an infidel, was a better match than some stranger of wealth and stature anywhere. But he knew better than to argue with Orianna in matters of their children.

She would not be denied that which she believed right, and Bianca's misalliance with Rovere had been allowed only to protect their oldest child, Marco.

"I will seek an audience with Lorenzo di Medici immediately, *cara*," he told her.

Orianna's shoulders relaxed, and she smiled at him. "Go back to your mistress now, Gio. I apologize for taking you away from her. I am sure you were relaxing from the cares of your business. Will you be home later?"

"But late," he said quietly as he arose to go. Orianna could be very understanding.

"Of course," and she smiled again. They were going to save Bianca from the biggest mistake of her life, and she felt reassured now. Orianna felt little guilt for the unhappiness she would cause her eldest daughter. It would be temporary. Bianca was like her mother—a practical woman. Once she accepted the fact that she had no other choice than to let her misery go, she would. As she had accepted the fact of her marriage to Sebastiano Rovere.

Giovanni Pietro d'Angelo, as he had promised his wife, sought an audience with Lorenzo di Medici. Although Florence was a republic, and had no noble lord ruling it, the head of the di Medici family had for some years been considered the most influential man in the city. The main government body was chosen regularly several times each year. Every male guild member who was thirty or older, free of debt, who had not served a recent term or was related to a man who was currently serving, was eligible for a two-month term in the Priori. Their names were drawn from bags kept at the church of San Croce. They served in the Signoria, which consisted of nine men. Six came from the major guilds, two from the minor guilds. The ninth man was called the *gonfaloniere*. It was he who was the temporary custodian and standard-bearer of the city's banner.

To make certain each of the major and minor guilds was properly represented when the names were drawn, only those eligible for that particular term were chosen to serve. Once elected for their two-month term, the members of the *Priori* moved to the Palazzo della Signoria to live. They were housed luxuriously, fed splendidly, and even entertained. Each man wore a bright scarlet coat with an ermine lining. The collar and cuffs of the coats were also ermine. The *gonfaloniere* had gold stars embroidered on his coat so he might be told apart on public occasions.

There were other councils as well, consisting of other citizens: a council of twelve citizens, and another of sixteen. They were called the Collegi. If necessary, other councils were elected for commerce, security, or war. There were various officials such as a chancellor and a chief justice.

When difficulty threatened the republic, the great bell in the campanile of the Palazzo della Signoria would be tolled to bring all the male citizens of the city over the age of fourteen into its piazza. Each section of the city gathered behind its banner to march together into the piazza. Once it was decided that at least two-thirds of the male population was there, it was considered a *parlamento*, which formed a *balia*, a committee to deal with whatever emergency had brought them into the public square.

Still, despite the pride the Florentines had in their system, there were always families like the di Medici who seemed more prominent than other wealthy families. Families that appeared to have more influence over the events of other men's lives. It was they that people like Giovanni Pietro d'Angelo, needing special or great favors, sought out in times of personal crisis. So it was that the silk merchant found himself being ushered into the presence of Lorenzo di Medici one afternoon, having begged an urgent audience several days earlier.

Lorenzo was probably the most charismatic di Medici ever born. Alone in a beautiful library, he was strumming on a lute, which, upon Giovanni's entrance, he handed to a hovering servant. He then dismissed the man with a graceful wave of his hand so he and his guest might have the privacy he knew Giovanni would want. He greeted the silk merchant warmly and invited him to sit. He himself poured the wine and handed Pietro d'Angelo an exquisite crystal goblet with a gold rim, which allowed the drinker to admire not just the taste but the lovely color of the vintage he offered.

He was surprised to see Giovanni Pietro d'Angelo coming to him. The silk merchant was a successful man. He was known to manage his own affairs with competence, and without the need or advice of others. "It must be very serious," he said to his guest, "for you to come to me, Gio. You look troubled. How is your beautiful wife? And your fine children? How may I serve you?"

"It is serious, my lord," the silk merchant said and then he took a deep swallow of wine before continuing. "What I need cannot be accomplished without your help. Whatever the cost of that help, I must have it."

Lorenzo di Medici nodded encouragingly and let his guest unburden himself.

"It is my eldest daughter, Bianca, my lord."

"A lovely girl," Lorenzo noted. "I remember Rovere displaying her at his more respectable dinner parties. And then she was not seen again. She had wit, Gio, and great charm. I was surprised when you married her to Sebastiano Rovere."

"I did not want to, my lord, but Rovere, to my shame, blackmailed me, and I had no other choice," Giovanni Pietro d'Angelo admitted.

"Tell me," di Medici said. "It will not go beyond this chamber."

The silk merchant reluctantly told the great man the tale of Stefano Rovere and his eldest son, Marco. He completed the story by saying, "I feared for my son, and I feared for our family's good name and fortune, *signore*. I knew not what else to do."

"Ahh, so that is how he obtained the fair Bianca," Lorenzo replied. "How dishonorable of him. The man was despicable, and the city better for his death. Do you perhaps know who killed him, Gio?"

The silk merchant looked horrified. "No, my lord, I do not!" he exclaimed.

"They did Florence a great service," Lorenzo di Medici said drily. "Gelding him and stuffing his cock and balls in his mouth were most fitting. But now let us get back to whatever problem it is you are having regarding Bianca, and we will see if we can help."

"*Signore*, you know the Turkish merchant Prince Amir ibn Jem?"

"A charming and intelligent man, and an honest, reputable merchant. Yes, I know him quite well, Gio. Why?"

"My late son-in-law would not allow us to see Bianca for some months after the wedding. Then finally one day my wife was permitted to enter his palazzo. She found our daughter abused, sick, and terrified of her husband. Rovere was in the courts that day. Orianna did not hesitate. She removed Bianca from her husband's home immediately and hid her in the convent of Santa Maria del Fiore until we were able to send her secretly to a small villa down by the sea that had been part of my mother's dowry. She has lived there ever since. Her neighbor is Prince Amir."

"They have become lovers," Lorenzo Medici said astutely.

"Yes, after Rovere's death but not before, my daughter swore to her mother. We wish to make a new marriage for Bianca, but she refuses to return to Florence or even discuss the matter. She would remain with the prince, and he would take her as a wife," the silk merchant said in a distraught voice. "Such a thing cannot be, my lord. It cannot!"

"No," Lorenzo di Medici agreed slowly, "it cannot. He is an infidel for all of his charm and good reputation among our community. But how do you expect me to help you with this problem, Giovanni Pietro d'Angelo?"

"Can you not send to his grandfather, the sultan, with all speed requesting that he recall Prince Amir to Turkey, my lord? If he were gone, my wife is certain we could bring Bianca to see reason," the silk merchant said. "She has no calling to the Church, and so she must be married again. Her grandfather in Venice is even now seeking a suitable match for her. That was where we intended marrying her before Rovere blackmailed us."

"I can send to the sultan with such a request, of course," the di Medici replied, "but it would be weeks before this matter could be settled and Prince Amir gone. In the meantime, he could get your daughter with child, and such a thing would make her unmarriageable, for no man of good family would accept her as his wife then."

"Then what are we to do, my lord?" the silk merchant asked despairingly. "What are we to do? I wish this man no harm, but he cannot have my daughter. My wife cannot eat or sleep for her distress in this matter."

"However," Lorenzo di Medici continued as if his guest had not even spoken, "we could secretly jail Prince Amir in the Palazzo della Signoria until his grandfather sends his Janissaries to escort him home. No one need know he is there. I will personally see that he is treated with all the respect due to his rank. Once he has disappeared, you can retrieve your daughter and make happier plans for her. Would that suit you, Giovanni Pietro d'Angelo?" Lorenzo di Medici smiled as he saw relief filling the silk merchant's face.

"My lord! It is a brilliant plan! How can I thank you?"

"It is actually a small thing for me, Gio," Lorenzo di Medici replied. "I know how to approach Sultan Mehmet, for my father's many years as a diplomat and my own small experience serving the republic taught me how to deal with great rulers. Make no mistake, Gio; Mehmet the Conqueror is a great ruler and an intelligent man for all he is an infidel. Sending Prince Amir away is a sacrifice on my part, for I have always enjoyed his company, and the treasures he has found for me over the past few years are unequaled. No other dealer in antiquities has ever been so successful. But while we can share our courtesans and whores with an infidel, we cannot give them or allow them to take our daughters. I have never known him to care enough about a woman to want her for a wife. He is unlikely to give Bianca up, and from what you have said, Bianca will not give him up willingly. She must be protected for her own sake. As for what you owe me . . ." He paused as if thinking. "There will come a day when I ask a favor of you,

Giovanni Pietro d'Angelo, and you will not refuse me, no matter the price."

Once Sebastiano Rovere had said almost the exact same words to him, and he had agreed for the sake of his family. But Lorenzo di Medici was not Rovere. He was a man of honor, more powerful, his family more dangerous, and the price would be correspondingly higher, it was true. But Bianca must be saved from her infidel lover before it was too late. "I agree," he said quietly. "I will not refuse the favor you require of me when you need it, my lord." He stood and held out his hand to Lorenzo.

The great man stood and accepted the silk merchant's hand as they shook in agreement. Then the two men sat again to drink their wine. When he had finally drained the goblet, Giovanni Pietro d'Angelo arose once more, thanking Lorenzo di Medici for his kindness. He returned home to tell his wife the matter would shortly be settled.

Orianna didn't ask him for any details. Sometimes it was better not to know. She knew what she needed to know. Prince Amir would be removed from Bianca's sphere. Orianna would shortly regain her eldest daughter's company. Then she would make a wonderful marriage for Bianca, and Bianca would be truly happy again.

But Bianca was happy as Amir made arrangements for them to leave the republic and sail to Turkey. He had already seen to a vessel to take them to Constantinople. He had just one more trip to Florence to put his warehouse into the hands of his two employees, who were being told he was seeking new antiquities for his business. As he had taken such trips twice before, they had no suspicion that anything was different. Later he would inform them that he did not mean to return.

"I wish you didn't have to go to the city," Bianca told him the morning of his departure. "Why can you not simply send a message to your men?"

"Because neither of them reads very well," he explained. "Actually only one of them can understand the bills of lading. They do better and are more reassured when their instructions are verbal, my love. They would consider it odd if I went off without speaking to them. Then they would gossip with others about it, and who knows what would be thought of my disappearance. So let me go and speak with them, Bianca. Krikor will come with me and I shall not linger. Two days at the most." He kissed her a lingering kiss, breaking away with a sigh. "Soon we shall be at my palace and you will be happy, beloved," he told her. Then he was gone.

Bianca was all packed and ready to depart. She waited two days, three days, and then a week went by. He had been delayed, of course, she thought, but he might have sent word to her. *How like a man*, she thought and she smiled. He probably expected with each new day that he would be leaving, and what a waste a messenger would be. But when the week ended and there was no sign of Prince Amir, Bianca took her horse and rode down the beach to the neighboring villa. When she arrived, she discovered to her shock that it was all closed up and deserted. As she walked around the outside of the house, she could see that heavy wooden shutters had been placed over the windows and the doors. She managed to peer through a crack in a kitchen window. Inside, the ovens and fireplace were cold, without fire. There was no sign of life whatsoever.

What had happened? Why was his home closed up when they had not gone yet? Frightened, Bianca returned to Luce

Stellare to see if her own servants knew anything. They didn't and were as surprised as she was, but that evening one of the young local menservants who enjoyed the housemaid Pia's company arrived at the kitchen door. They brought him to Bianca to tell his story.

"Three days after the master departed for the city," he began, "an official bearing the insignia of the di Medici family came to the villa. He paid us a full year's wages, instructed us to close the house immediately and return to our own village. He remained the night while we accomplished the necessary tasks and then left with us seeing the villa was secured. That is all that I know or can tell you. The only one of the servants not one of us was Krikor, and he had gone with Prince Amir, *madonna*."

"Thank you," Bianca told the servingman. "I see my family's hand in this," she told Agata. "They have somehow managed to involve the di Medici in all of this."

"Then you are lost," Agata replied.

"No! The vessel that was to take us to Turkey is due off our coast in just a few days' time. We are getting on that vessel, Agata. We will go to Turkey, and we will find our way to Prince Amir's palace, where we will await his arrival. He will come home eventually. I know he will! Lorenzo di Medici would not harm him, nor has my father the stomach for assassination."

"Travel alone? Without the prince? Are you mad?" Agata demanded to know. "We will be murdered, or taken into slavery without his protection."

"I shall tell the ship's captain that Prince Amir was suddenly called home, and took the overland route; that he has instructed the captain to deliver me off the coast nearest the Moonlight Serai because traveling by sea will be easier for me.

We will get to where we are going safely, Agata. I do not intend to allow my parents to make another marriage for me, no matter their well-meaning intentions."

"God and his blessed Mother help us," Agata said.

Bianca laughed. "I wish I could see my mother's face when she discovers that I am gone for all her manipulations."

But the next morning a troop of men-at-arms in the company of an official, all wearing the insignia of the di Medici, arrived at Luce Stellare.

"I have been instructed by my master, Lorenzo di Medici, to return you and your servant to your parents' palazzo in the city," the official told Bianca.

"I regret I cannot comply with such a request," Bianca told the official, but her heart was hammering against her ribs even as she spoke the bold words. "Neither my parents nor your master has any authority over me. Your men are free to water their animals, but then I would ask that you leave my house and my property immediately."

"*Signora*, I will not bandy words with you. I have my instructions. Whatever the legalities of this matter are, they are not my concern. I have been given my orders by my master himself, and I am not a man to fail in his assignment. I will give you one hour to prepare for the journey."

"You will leave immediately," Bianca told the pompous official bravely.

He sighed. "*Signora*, I beg you. Do not make this matter more difficult for yourself than it obviously already is. You will come with me in an hour, and if necessary you will be tied to your horse for the journey."

"*Signore!* Do not dare to threaten my mistress," said Agata, speaking up boldly.

"Woman, gather the servants who are part of this household and bring them to me immediately," the official told her.

Agata looked to Bianca, who nodded, realizing that those who had been so loyal to her should not be made to suffer with her. Agata hurried off, returning quickly with the four women servants and the two menservants.

"Is this all of them?" the official asked.

"Mine is a small household," Bianca told him.

He nodded, then spoke to them. "This house is to be closed up and secured immediately. You are to be paid for a full year's service now. Master Pietro d'Angelo thanks you for your good care of his daughter, and bids you all return home to your village. Any livestock here is yours with his permission. This lady will now be taken to Florence, and she will not return. Go now, and do as you have been bid."

"Filomena," Bianca called to her housekeeper, "take Jamila with you. She would not do well in the city."

"What of the dog, *signora*?" Primo asked her.

"The dog?" Bianca was confused.

"Darius, Prince Amir's hound. He showed up here a few days ago hungry. I combed out his fur, which was badly matted," her manservant said, "and we fed him."

Bianca felt a slight cramp in her heart. Both animals were to have gone with them. She turned to Agata and murmured something low. Her servingwoman nodded and ran off. "Will you keep the dog, Primo? You know he is a good hunter, and I do not think he would thrive within the city. He is not used to it. He needs to run."

Agata returned, and pushed something into Bianca's hand.

"Take this ring," Bianca said, giving Primo the bejeweled gold band that had been her wedding ring. It was the only piece of the jewelry her husband had given her that somehow was not left behind when she fled him. "It will keep the dog for years to come. Indeed, it will keep you and your family most comfortably."

He took the ring but told her, "I would keep the dog anyway, *signora*. He is a fine animal. One day the prince will return for him. I will keep him safe until then." Primo gave her a small bow. "May God protect you, *signora*." Then turning about, he left her.

"I will care for Jamila, *signora*. You need have no fear," Filomena said. There were tears in the housekeeper's eyes as she spoke.

Bianca removed the small jeweled crucifix she wore about her neck on a golden chain and gave it to Filomena. "To remember me by," she told her. Then she removed three rings from her fingers, giving the one with a small aquamarine to Gemma, her cook; and to each of the two little maidservants she gave a gold ring. They all began to weep.

Seeing that he would soon have a situation on his hands, the official barked sharply at the sobbing women servants. "Go about your business immediately! This house must be closed within the next hour or two. Hurry now!" He clapped his hands at them. Now he turned to Bianca and Agata. "*Signora*, you will have baggage that must be loaded. Your father was so kind as to send a cart and driver. My men will help load your belongings if your servingwoman will be so kind as to direct them. I assume you will ride your horse. Will your woman, or would she prefer to travel in the cart with the driver?"

"We will both ride our horses," Bianca said. Then turning, she left him to prepare for her journey. She didn't want to leave Luce Stellare but there was no way she could forestall this official mandate of the di Medici. Well, she would return to Florence but only because it was the last place she knew Amir to have been. She was going to find out what had happened to him. And she was going to make her parents wish they had never interfered with her life. "I did not run from Sebastiano Rovere," she said to Agata, "only to be forced into another arranged marriage for the benefit of everyone except me. I will find Amir, and I will go with him wherever he goes."

Chapter 10

*L*orenzo di Medici smiled at Amir ibn Jem as they sat together in a small chamber in the Palazzo della Signoria. "I trust you are finding your quarters comfortable," he said in a deceptively mild tone. He sipped at the wine in his goblet, noting that his guest did not. He could see his friend was not pleased at all by his imprisonment.

Amir laughed drily. "My apartment is better than a cell in the Bargello below," he answered his host. "The last thing I seem to remember was being at your dinner table, Lorenzo. It was an excellent meal, as I recall. Can you tell me now why I am here? I do thank you for seeing that Krikor was brought to me."

"I have written to your grandfather asking that he recall you, Amir," Lorenzo di Medici said quietly. "I regret having to do this, but your behavior of late has brought you to this state. Since it will be some weeks before I will receive a reply and you cannot be left to wander freely, I have seen to your incarceration during this interim. It is for your safety as much as anything else."

"My behavior? I only come to the city for the purpose of doing business, Lorenzo, and I rarely socialize with anyone whom I might have offended." Then the truth dawned on him. Amir gave his host a rueful smile. "This will be about my involvement with a certain lady, Lorenzo, will it not?"

His companion smiled and nodded. "How discreet of you not to mention her by name, my old friend. Yes, it is about the lady."

"Your walls have a tendency to absorb interesting bits of information, and then repeat them to any who would listen," the prince replied with a small smile. "However, my intentions towards the lady are honorable. I wish her to be my wife. I love her, and she loves me."

"Are you prepared to convert to the one truth faith, then, Amir?" Lorenzo di Medici asked, knowing the answer in advance. "You are an infidel, and as such will never be allowed to wed the lady in question. I'm sorry, but that is the truth of the matter, and surely you are sensible enough to understand that."

"I would allow her to keep her own religion, as my ancestor Sultan Orkhan allowed his Byzantine princess wife to keep hers," Amir said.

"The Greek church is a schism of the Holy Mother's Church, my good and dear friend," Lorenzo di Medici explained. "Here in the West, that princess was considered no more than your ancestor's concubine. If you wed your lady love, she would be considered as such, and her loving family would disown her. She could never again see them. She would be dead to them. Is that what you want for her?"

Amir was suddenly afraid for Bianca. "Where is she?" he demanded to know. "Is she all right? What has been done with her?"

"No harm has nor will come to her," the di Medici reassured his companion. "I have sent my own soldiers and a household official down to Luce Stellare to bring her back to her family here in Florence. The villa is to be shut up, the servants paid for a year and sent back to their own village. Her family will make her see the wisdom of their decisions. They will make another—a better—marriage for her. There is no harm done here. The lady was a widow, not a virgin. If there is no fruit of your entanglement, and that will be known quickly enough, then she will leave Florence sooner rather than later to become another man's wife. As for you, Amir, you will remain here in the Palazzo della Signoria awaiting the sultan's orders to return home to your own land." He drank deeply from his goblet, then continued.

"I regret having to do this, but I am told that shortly there would have been a vessel anchored off the coast opposite your own villa come to take you and the lady back to your own home there. You understand that we could not allow you to abscond with the daughter of a respected Florentine house. Such a scandal could have endangered the chances of the lady's other sisters marrying into the right families. So here you must remain, awaiting your grandfather's orders to return home. I hope he will not be too angry with you, but I have been given to understand you are one of his favorite grandsons, so perhaps this will not put you entirely out of his favor."

"A favor, Lorenzo," Amir said. "Will you allow my slave,

Krikor, to return to my villa to fetch my dog? I am particularly fond of that hound. I raised him from a puppy, and he came with me from Turkey. I should like to have him when I return home."

"Of course, of course," Lorenzo di Medici said, understanding. A man's favorite dog was a part of him. "The slave may come and go freely, even if you cannot. You may desire a courtesan to come and visit you. It is quite permissible. I am told you are most popular among these ladies. Warn Krikor, however, that he is not to attempt to contact the lady we have so carefully shielded from gossip this day, my friend. If he is caught he will be severely beaten. I cannot be defied in this matter."

"I understand," Amir said. "I value him too much in one piece to endanger him."

Lorenzo di Medici stood up. "Then I shall leave you," he said.

"What? You will not give me an opportunity to beat you in chess?" Amir asked.

Lorenzo di Medici chuckled. "Another time, old friend. I have sat as long as I can today. I have not yet ridden, and you know how much I enjoy both the exercise and the outdoors." He stood up and stretched his long limbs. "Perhaps one day you will ride within the piazza with me. I know you are an active man, and being cooped up here will eventually become frustrating for you."

"She can't be forced into another marriage," Amir called after his guest.

Lorenzo di Medici turned. "Eventually she will have no choice," he said. "You have met her mother, I know. Orianna will have her way sooner than later." Then he was gone, leaving Prince Amir ibn Jem to consider their conversation. Oh, Signora Pietro d'Angelo would try her best, but he did not believe she would overcome Bianca's determination.

Orianna Pietro d'Angelo was not getting her way in the matter of her eldest daughter. Upon her return, Bianca had refused to speak with her mother, despite the warm and loving welcome her family had given her. She would not eat unless the meal was brought to her chamber, and then she ate only what was necessary to sustain her, making a point of sending back her favorite dainty delicacies that were brought to tempt her. She began to lose weight—and she had never been a full-figured girl to begin with. Her lustrous, long dark hair became dull and lost its healthy sheen.

Orianna was at her wits' end. "Why do you refuse to understand that what has been done has been done for your own good?" she demanded of Bianca one day.

Bianca said nothing. Indeed, her eyes were not even focused on her mother.

Orianna shrieked with her frustration. "You are an ungrateful girl!"

Bianca shrugged, then turned and walked away from her mother. It was an act of defiance such as had never been seen in the Pietro d'Angelo household.

"I will send you to a cloistered nunnery until you come to your senses!" Orianna screamed. "I will give orders for you to be beaten daily, and fed on bread and water!"

Bianca turned. "Anywhere I do not have to listen to the sound of your harping voice, *signora*, will be paradise," she said. They were the first words she had spoken to her mother in the month since she had been brought home.

Orianna's mouth fell open with shock, and she collapsed against her servingwoman, Fabia, gasping.

"You are a wicked girl!" Fabia scolded Bianca.

"If I am, I have learned it at your mistress's hand," Bianca replied coldly.

Orianna made a noise that sounded very much like a squeak.

Bianca laughed and then said, "With your permission I will go and make my confession for these sins of disrespect to Father Bonamico."

Orianna could not speak but she nodded weakly. Perhaps the priest could talk some sense into her stubborn daughter.

Bianca called for Agata to join her, and the two women put on their hooded cloaks, left the palazzo, and walked across the piazza to Santa Anna Dolce. They found the elderly priest, and Bianca told him she would speak with him in the confessional while Agata waited for her.

"Forgive me, Father, for I have sinned," she began.

"Tell me the nature of your sins, my daughter," the priest answered her.

"I hate my mother," Bianca said, and heard a small gasp from the priest.

"She only wants what is best for you, my daughter," Father Bonamico replied.

"No, she wants me to live my life with a man I don't love, as she has had to do, and I don't want to follow in her footsteps, Father. I want to wed the man I love."

"I am told he is an infidel." The priest's voice was disapproving.

"Such things matter not to me," Bianca told her confessor. "I love him, and he loves me. Now he has disappeared, and they will not tell me where they have taken him, or if he is all right."

"Your immortal soul should concern you, my daughter," Father Bonamico scolded her gently. "Physical love is fleeting, a passing fancy. God's love will never fail you."

"Why can I not love God and Amir too, good Father?" she asked him.

"Physical love has but one purpose, my daughter. The procreation of children to sustain our faith. You cannot give this infidel children, for he would not allow them the one true faith. He is among the already damned, and doomed to suffer hellfire one day. No. Better you love only God, Bianca. And you can show that love by obeying your parents. They are mindful of the great sacrifice you were forced to make for your family's sake when they saw you wedded to Sebastiano Rovere. This time they will find you a good man who will truly care for and respect you."

"I will wed no man but the man I love," Bianca said. She arose from the narrow little bench in the confessional and drew back the heavy velvet curtain to step out.

"My daughter, I have not given you your penance," Father Bonamico said.

"I suffer each day I am apart from Amir," Bianca told him bitterly. "That is my penance, good Father. It is more painful than anything you could give me." Then she called softly to Agata and the two women left the church. She had always found comfort in the Church, but today she had not.

As they slowly walked across the broad piazza, a large, long-haired, golden hound loped up to block their way. Both women gasped with surprise, for there was no doubt it was Darius. The dog whined, pushing his long nose into Bianca's hand.

She knelt. "Darius! How did you get here?" Her other hand stroked him, and when it touched the dog's collar she realized there was a note beneath it. She slid the paper out, secreting it in the hidden pocket of her gown, then stood up. "Go back to your master, Darius," she ordered the dog, who then loped off into the little park on the edge of the piazza. She did not see where he went, but it didn't matter. "Let us hurry now so I may read the note," she said to Agata.

"Krikor was probably with the dog," Agata said in a low voice. "The prince would have come into the piazza and taken you away."

Gaining the palazzo, the two women hurried to Bianca's bedchamber. Agata locked the door behind them as her mistress drew the note from her pocket, opening it to read what was written inside.

Beloved, it began. *Do not fear for me. I am held captive in the Palazzo della Signoria, but well treated while they await an answer from my grandfather to recall me to Istanbul. Krikor is free to come and go, but our old friend Lorenzo has warned me if he is caught attempting to communicate with you he will be severely punished. I cannot allow it. Do not attempt to communicate with me. Soon I will be freed on the sultan's orders. Do not despair. I will find you, Bianca, wherever they take you. You are mine, and I, yours. This will be the only message I dare to send. Remember that I love you. I will always love you. Amir*

Bianca began to weep softly. "He is safe," she said. "I was so afraid that they had killed him, or were torturing him, but he is safe." She held the parchment to her breasts.

Agata waited a moment and then reached for the missive. "It must be burned so no one finds it," she said. "You want no one knowing he has reached out to you, mistress. They could be less forgiving of his behavior if they learned he had defied them."

"Let me read it over once more," Bianca said, and she did. Handing the parchment to Agata, she watched as her serving-woman refolded the note into a small rectangle before stuffing it in her pocket.

"I'll take it to the kitchens and burn it," Agata said. "The fires are hotter there."

"I am suddenly hungry," Bianca announced. "I want a bowl of pasta with olive oil and cheese."

Agata smiled. "I will tell the cook, who will be happy to know it," she said and then she hurried off to do her mistress's bidding. And while the cook crowed delightedly at the news that Bianca was hungry, Agata took advantage of his distraction to see the prince's note burned to ashes.

Bianca would still not talk to her mother, which distressed Orianna greatly. No one had ever treated her in such a hard fashion, and she was not used to it. It did not occur to the mother that the daughter was very much like her in her determination to have her own way. But Orianna was relieved that Bianca had begun to eat again. Her pale skin lost the sallow look it had developed. Her ebony hair grew shiny once more.

Seeing the improvement in his daughter's features, Giovanni Pietro d'Angelo decided that it would be better to send Bianca to her grandfather in Venice, where her younger sister Francesca currently resided with her mother's family. Perhaps if Bianca was away from her mother, her attitude would improve.

The silk merchant had never seen his strong-willed wife driven to her knees, but Bianca was doing just that. He was in a perverse sense admiring of his eldest daughter's resolve, although he would never make such an admission. She had recently taken to replying to almost everything Orianna said with the words "Amir will find me wherever you send me, and he will take me away." Those simple words had begun to get on Orianna's nerves, and her husband had almost laughed aloud the other evening when Bianca repeated them once again. Orianna had only been able to half muffle her shriek of frustration. She had shot her husband a furious look, seeing his struggle to contain his humor. He had been forced to reprimand their daughter. Bianca merely shrugged, giving him a half smile as if they were coconspirators.

"Why does she hate me and not you?" Orianna asked him afterwards. "It was your decision, not mine, that married her to Rovere. I protected her for as long as I could. And when I learned of the abuse she was suffering, I took her from Rovere's palazzo and hid her. It was I who begged my father to help us intercede in the matter of an annulment. Yet she hates me. *Me!*"

"You were her friend as well as her mother," Orianna's husband explained. "She knows you were the guiding force that took her from the man she loves. Do you not consider that a great betrayal, wife? Our daughter does."

"But, Gio, this prince is an infidel!" Orianna wailed.

"And the man you loved before you were wed to me was married to another, *cara mia*. That did not stop you from loving him, or trysting with him in defiance of your family. You have never ceased loving this man, although you were required to wed me, yet you have been an exemplary wife to me. So do not, I beg you, be surprised at our daughter's behavior over her prince. Like you, she will give her heart once, and she has done so."

"Would you allow this foreigner to carry her off?" Orianna demanded. Although she had always known her husband was aware of her youthful passion, he had never until this moment spoken of it. It made her uncomfortable to hear him voice her girlish indiscretions aloud, to understand that he knew her so very well when all she realized she knew of him was that he had been indulging her all these years.

"Prince Amir is an infidel," Giovanni Pietro d'Angelo said quietly. "Any serious or permanent liaison between him and Bianca is unthinkable. I do not disagree with you, Orianna, but I also believe that Bianca will recover more fully away from the mother she believes betrayed her. And she will have Francesca for company. Despite the four years difference in their ages, they always get on well. Her younger sister will divert her."

"They have not seen each other since Bianca married Rovere," Orianna pointed out. "Bianca is already eighteen, and Francesca thirteen. My father writes that he believes she will be ready for marriage in another year. He will choose the right man for her, you may be certain, for he adores her. Now, however, he will also have to seek a husband for Bianca. Still"—and Orianna laughed—"Papa does enjoy ruling his little world. Bianca will not be able to get around him easily. He did have five daughters himself."

"Then you agree that Bianca should go to Venice," the silk merchant said.

"Yes!" his wife replied. "The sooner, the better, for I will admit to you, husband, that my nerves are in shreds from dealing with her."

By chance, Agata spotted Krikor in the small market that catered to scent makers near the Ponte Vecchio. She made her way through the crowds until she was standing next to him.

"Do not turn your head, Krikor. It is Agata. Tell your master that the *signora* is being sent to her grandfather in Venice soon. He is Prince Alessandro Venier," Agata murmured in a low voice.

"Tell your mistress that a troop of the sultan's Janissaries arrived today. We leave for Istanbul tomorrow," Krikor replied, and then he moved away from her.

Agata made a small purchase of a carved ivory bottle filled with attar of roses, and then hurried home so she might report her news to Bianca.

"Perhaps he will take us on the road to Venice," Bianca said hopefully.

"No, that is unlikely," the practical Agata said. "The Janissaries will travel quickly with the prince, for they will want to bring him to the sultan as swiftly as possible. But perhaps he will find you in Venice. I told Krikor your grandfather's name, and he will tell the prince. He has promised that he would find you, mistress, and he will. Will you, however, want to go with him then?"

"Yes!" Bianca said. "I will never cease to love him. My heart is not a fickle one." And then she began to consider the road that Amir and his escort would traverse come the morrow. They would certainly begin by taking the Venice road, although they were unlikely to go to Venice. They would go early, of course, and if she was fortunate and quick enough, she might at least get to see him pass by.

She didn't tell Agata. Her servingwoman was loyal and loved her mistress, but she was likely to discourage such an adventure. Instead she sought out her younger brother Georgio. "I know you are responsible for Rovere finding me," she said without any preamble. "You owe me a debt for that, little brother."

"I had no choice in the matter," her sibling said, flushing with his guilty shame.

"I know the man who threatened you. You were right to be afraid of him, but that does not erase your debt to me," Bianca said in a hard voice.

"What do you want from me?" Georgio asked her.

"Two things. Your company early tomorrow, and your silence about it," Bianca said to him.

"Will it distress our mother?" the boy asked her.

"Only if she knows, but you will not tell her, Georgio, for if you do, I will revenge myself upon you in a manner you would not like," Bianca threatened.

"Oh, very well," the boy conceded. "Where do you want to go?"

"Before dawn to the gate leading to the Venice road," Bianca said. "There is something there I would see, and when I have I will return home."

"You swear it?" he asked her.

"You have my word, Brother," she said.

"And my silence?" he inquired.

"You will understand tomorrow," Bianca told him.

"And all debts between us are satisfied if I do this?" he said.

"Yes," she promised him.

"How early?" he wanted to know.

"Two hours before the dawn, for we must walk the city to reach there," Bianca replied. "I suspect the early streets could prove dangerous."

"They could, but if you dress discreetly we will not attract any attention," he told her. "Do you have a dark cloak with a hood, Sister?"

"I do, and I will wear it," Bianca said.

"Wear sturdy shoes, for the streets can be dirty and wet at an early hour," he advised his sister. "You'll destroy a pair of silk slippers if you wear such on your feet."

"I'll wear my boots," she replied.

"The trick to getting in and out of the house at that hour without attracting attention is to be quick, and to be stealthy. I'll meet you at the front door, Bianca."

"I'll be there before you, Georgio," she told him. "Do not be late."

He laughed. "Why didn't you ask Marco?" he wondered.

"The debt Marco owes me can never be repaid," Bianca replied to his query. "He has suffered over it, and I would not give him any more pain than he gives himself," she explained to her younger brother.

He nodded. "I'll see you in the morning," he said.

There! It was done. If she was fortunate, she would get a passing glimpse of Amir as he departed Florence. She needed to see that he was unharmed. She slept poorly, rising carefully and quietly so as not to disturb Agata, who lay upon her trundle snoring. She dressed quickly in a simple dark gown, and pulled on her boots. Then, gathering up her cloak, she slipped from the bedchamber. She had not bothered to undo her plait and brush her hair, for fear of awakening her servingwoman.

Bianca crept down the stairs of the house, careful to avoid the two steps that creaked when trod upon. She hurried to the front door to await her brother. There was a single lamp burning in the entry rotunda. Other than that the dark silence engulfed her. On a stool by the door, the doorkeeper slept heavily. She stepped back into the shadows as she heard a soft footfall on the stairs.

Georgio quickly came into view, and Bianca stepped forward. He said nothing, instead opening the door of the house just enough for them to slip through. The doorkeeper never even stirred. Bianca suspected her brother had drugged the unsuspecting servant, and found she was grateful. He took her hand and together they began walking. The streets were dark and Bianca realized that without her younger brother leading her she could never have found her way. Several times her foot struck some object and she stumbled, but Georgio kept her from falling. Twice she felt something—a rat she imagined, shuddering—run over her boot. The air for the most part was damp with a faint hint of rot. But the sky was growing lighter as they hurried along.

"We're almost there," Georgio said softly. "What do you want to do when we finally get there, Sister?"

"I would simply stand by the side of the road," Bianca said to him.

"Why?" he wanted to know.

"You will see," she said to him.

They reached the city gate to the Venice road. No one had gone through it yet, for the gatekeepers were just now removing the great bar that helped to keep the gate closed. They slowly opened the gate and a small line of traffic made up of vendors carrying fruit, vegetables, meat, poultry, and dairy products, along with flower sellers and others, began to slowly file into the city on their way to the various markets and other places of business.

Suddenly Bianca's ears caught the sound of many horses coming at a trot. She flung back her hood as the troop of Janissaries came into view. They were distinguished from other soldiers by their red and green garments, and the glossy brown horses they rode. From the pommels of their saddles hung metal-tipped whips that, when necessary, they used to disburse crowds. There was no need for that this morning. Because of the traffic coming from the opposite direction, they slowed their horses to a walk to avoid any accidents with the Florentine populace. Foreigners must be careful.

She saw him on his great gray stallion in the middle of the group. Her heart contracted with joy, for he looked healthy and well. Darius walked by his master's side. It was the dog who spotted Bianca, and barking, ran to her. Amir looked in the direction his hound had run. His deep blue eyes widened with a mixture of joy and pain.

Bianca put her fingers to her lips, kissed them, and flung her hand in his direction. His gloved hand reached up to catch her kiss, his fingers closing over it, then opening to press against his heart. Bianca's eyes filled with tears as she sent Darius back to his master.

Then she heard him call out, "I will find you, beloved!"

"*Amore mio!* I love you!" Bianca called back to him. Their eyes met briefly.

The troop of Janissaries suddenly moved on more quickly as the traffic lightened, allowing for their swifter passage. Bianca stood for a long moment watching them go. He still loved her. It was all that mattered to her. She could go to Venice knowing that by the time they found a suitable man to wed her, he would come for her. They would be together forever. Nothing would part them again.

"Let us go home now, Georgio," she said to her brother, who had silently and sympathetically watched all that had transpired with his sister.

"That was your prince," her sibling said.

"Yes," Bianca replied. "That was my prince."

"It will be full light when we get back home," Georgio said. "We had better go to Mass and pretend we only went out for that."

"Yes," she agreed. "Did you drug the doorkeeper?"

He nodded. "He has a weakness for sweet wine. I do it all the time when I want to get out and go whoring. Marco taught me that neat little trick and one day I will pass it on to Luca." He chuckled.

Bianca laughed. "Our poor mother," she said. "Here she believes she is in full charge of all of her children, and she actually has little authority at all."

"Please stop torturing her, Bianca," Georgio said. "She only does what she does because she loves her family."

"Did you know she was in love with an unsuitable man before she was wed to our father, little brother? I think she did not want me to have Amir because she could not have her true love," Bianca told her brother. "I believe even if he had not been an infidel she would have found some excuse to separate us."

"If that is so," Georgio remarked, "then perhaps you should be kinder to her, Sister. She has been a good wife to our father, and a good mother to her children. Yet she is unhappy, and still loves another man. I find that very sad, don't you?"

"You sound like a philosopher," Bianca teased, heeding the householder's warning and dodging the contents of a night jar that were being hurled from a window above. "Or perhaps even a priest."

"I am considering the priesthood," Georgio admitted to his eldest sister. "Marco is Father's heir, and he is a worthy one. Luca is a little roughneck savage, and I think he will become a soldier one day. I am a thinker, and I seem to feel the pain of others. I want to ease that pain. For instance, I did not know what it was you planned to do this morning, but I sensed that you very much needed to do it, which was why I agreed to accompany you. Not just because of the debt I owed you, Bianca, but because I can feel your unhappiness even when you smile these days. This prince you love may not be suitable in the eyes of our society, but I believe you will never be happy unless you are with him, Sister."

"Do not be a priest, Georgio," Bianca said. "Your heart is too good, and I do not believe that you can live with all the rules the Church sets forth. To dismiss a good man because he does not worship as we do does not seem right to me. Does it to you?"

"No," Georgio agreed, "it does not, Bianca. But could I not teach humanity kindness within the tradition of our faith?"

"They would try you for a heretic," Bianca said cynically.

They reached their own piazza just as dawn was breaking, and entered the church for the earliest Mass. Afterwards they walked back across the square to the palazzo and entered the house, smiling at the doorkeeper, who still looked sleepy but was awake.

"I did not see you go out, young master, *signora*," he said nervously.

"A bit too much of your sweet wine last night, Aldo," Georgio teased the doorkeeper. "We won't tell. My sister and I went to early Mass together. Father Silvio said Mass this morning. I think old Bonamico grows too old for such an early hour."

The doorkeeper chuckled.

"You do that too easily," Bianca said, smiling at her younger sibling, "but then our father says you are the one with the charm. Thank you, Georgio, for helping me." She felt better now than she had in weeks. Seeing Amir had given her new courage and strength now that they were preparing to send her to Venice. And Venice was closer to Istanbul than was Florence. Did her parents not realize they were helping her to rejoin her lover rather than keeping them apart?

She was measured for new clothing. The gowns and undergarments were fashioned and sewn. Everything was packed into her trunks along with her personal possessions. It was unlikely that when she left Palazzo Pietro d'Angelo this time she would ever return. Her family intended her for a new marriage in Venice. This time they expected her to remain where they sent her. Her new husband would be another older man. He would want children from her even if he already had them, if for no other reason than to prove he was still virile. She would live her life in a palazzo on a canal, traveling by her own personal gondola wherever she went. It might suit some women. It didn't suit her. Bianca wanted more than the security of a rich husband and a gondola.

"Like me," Orianna said to her eldest daughter, "you dislike being closed in as we are here in Florence. That is why you loved Luce Stellare so much. You liked the sea, and you liked the openness of it all. Venice is like that. It is an open city of blue water and blue skies. Except, of course, in the winter months when it is rainy, gray, and chill," she amended. "Still I know you will like it there," she continued. "And you will probably have Francesca for a lifelong companion. Your grandfather adores her, and I doubt I can make a marriage for her elsewhere because of that. I will have two daughters in Venice."

"For a time, perhaps," Bianca said. "But Amir will come for me, *Madre*, and when he does, I will go with him."

"Nonsense!" her mother responded. "You will marry into a fine, noble family and be happy, Bianca. Your prince is gone, and he will not return."

"I am not like you, *Madre*," Bianca said to her mother. "I will not spend my life longing for a man I cannot have while wed to another."

"You are impossible!" Orianna said, irritated. "I wish your grandfather good luck with you, Bianca. Be aware that he is not a gentle man. If you anger him he will not hesitate to whip you himself. Mayhap you need the stubbornness beaten out of you. I do not know what happened to the sweet and gentle girl you once were."

Bianca laughed, and the sound was a harsh one. "You forced me into marriage with Sebastiano Rovere, *Madre*. I would have died had I remained sweet and gentle. To survive that monster I learned to be hard and resourceful. But do not fear. I will go willingly to Venice if only to escape the confines of this city, and you, *Madre*."

"It cannot be soon enough for me," Orianna said angrily.

Giovanni Pietro d'Angelo had decided to have his two older sons, Marco and Georgio, escort their sister to Venice. He did not choose to leave his business, and besides, Marco needed to see the great commercial port that Venice was, for the bolts of silk that were his trade came through there. That was what had brought Giovanni Pietro to Venice all those years ago when he first saw the woman he would marry. His father had sent him for the same purpose, to learn all about the shipping trade.

They departed Florence on a winter's morning in a large caravan containing all of Bianca's worldly goods along with lavish gifts for Giovanni's father-in-law, who would now take charge of another of his daughters. They would travel through Bologna, and then across the small duchy of Ferrara before entering the territory belonging to Venice. Padua would be the last city they visited before reaching Venice itself. Because they were encumbered with a baggage train it would take a few weeks before they reached their final destination.

The weather was cold. And not all days were sunny. If there were no inns or religious houses in which to shelter, a group of pavilions was set up, each with a charcoal brazier for heat. They were uncomfortable at best, and freezing at worst. Bianca wondered whether her hands, her feet, and her face would ever be warm again. The wind from the north was biting most days no matter the direction in which they traveled. They rode huddled over their horses, shrinking deep into their fur-lined cloaks and attempting to avoid the damp cold that seemed inescapable.

Bianca eagerly looked forward to the two cities through which they would pass.

At least there they stayed in warm inns and ate hot food before they had to take up their journey once more in the winter weather. Perhaps if she had been nicer to her mother, Bianca considered at one point, her parents would have waited until spring for her to make this trip.

But then the land began to fall away, and the road they traveled was flat and there was water to be seen all about them as the coast with its many islands began to be revealed. In the distance they suddenly saw golden domes and towers springing up.

There was an almost magical and mystical look to it.

"Venice," said the local guide, who had joined them in Padua, pointing.

Chapter 11

Finally they could go no farther by land. They reached a place where there were barges waiting to be hired to take the baggage carts and the horses along with the men-at-arms who had traveled with them into the city. The three siblings and Agata were settled in a large gondola that would ferry them to their grandfather's palazzo.

"Prince Venier?" the gondolier said. "Yes! Yes! I know his palazzo." He pushed off from the quay. "Are you Veniers? Have you come from the estates on Kythira or Crete? Have you ever been to Venice before?" He was very curious.

"We are Prince Venier's grandchildren from Florence," Marco answered the gondolier. "I am called Marco, my brother is Georgio, and our sister is Bianca."

"Marco Venier! A famous name here in Venice, *signore*. Once there was even a Venier who was doge." The gondolier chattered on. "And it was a Marco who took the island of Kythira when Byzantium was taught its lesson in humility by the great Doge Dandolo. Of course it was only right that the Veniers take Kythira, for it is said to be the birthplace of the ancient goddess Venus, and the Veniers are direct descendants of Venus. That is why all its women are so beautiful, as your sister here. I have even caught a glimpse of the prince's other granddaughter, a glorious young maiden with red-blond hair, and a face to rival Helen of Troy!"

"Our little sister," Marco replied drily.

Bianca chuckled from her place between her two brothers. Francesca with a face to rival an ancient heroine? "She has obviously changed in the years since I've seen her," Bianca murmured, and her brothers snickered. "I recall a nosy urchin, nothing more."

The gondola glided swiftly over the water, entering a wide and busy waterway.

"The Grand Canal," the gondolier announced, a certain pride in his voice.

They were surrounded by boats of every kind everywhere, for Venice was a great port city. There were merchant vessels, boats carrying animals, boats carrying produce and other goods. Some sold their goods from their boats. Bianca gasped as a large warship called a galleass slid by them. Through the oar ports, she could actually see the several tiers of galley slaves who rowed the vessel. She shuddered. *What a terrible fate for a man to find himself in the galleys,* she thought. She noticed that her two brothers were oddly silent too. One of the dangers of traveling by sea for men was the possibility of being captured by pirates and sold into the galleys.

Now the canal was lined with great palazzos, and Bianca

waited for the gondolier to pull their vessel into one of the small stone quays, but he did not.

"Prince Venier does not own one of these palazzos?" Marco asked, curious.

"Oh no, *signore*," the gondolier replied. "Those palazzos are owned by the great merchants of the city. You will note that each has its own dockage. It is for their vessels so they may unload their cargo into the main floor of the palazzo. The families live above. Your grandfather's home is in a more private setting."

"You have a district for your nobility?" Marco inquired.

"Oh no, sir. Here in Venice the rich and the poor and those in between live next to one another. Like your Florence, Venice is a republic." Then the gondolier turned his attention to his vessel, steering it into a smaller canal. From their boat they could see houses, some large, some small, and here and there a palazzo. At the end of the canal their gondolier pulled into a small dock. As he did so, a liveried servant appeared to help the gondola's expected occupants out.

"Welcome! Welcome to Palazzo Venier," he greeted them, smiling broadly. "Your grandfather and your sister await you if you will follow me." He flipped the gondolier a large silver coin. "With the prince's thanks. The baggage train?"

"Not far behind," the gondolier replied as he pushed off. He would have lots of gossip now to share with the other gondoliers, and the city of Venice lived on gossip. Old Prince Venier was one of their most distinguished citizens. The arrival of three more of his grandchildren, the talk of a marriage he had overheard his passengers discussing—it was all too delicious, and might even earn him a cup of wine from one of the satin-garbed gossips in Piazza San Marco.

The liveried servant led them into the palazzo, but before Bianca might even look about her she found herself in a large airy salon in the presence of an elegant white-haired gentleman who looked very much like her mother.

"Welcome to Venice," he greeted them. "I am Alessandro Venier, your grandfather."

Bianca curtsied politely as her two brothers bowed to the prince.

"I am Marco," her elder sibling told their host.

"Named after the patron saint of our great city," their grandfather replied. "Your mother promised me when she left Venice with your father that she would name her firstborn son Marco. I am happy she kept her promise to me."

"This is Georgio, my next brother," Marco introduced the younger man.

"How old are you both?" their grandfather inquired.

"I am nineteen," Marco answered him, "and Georgio is sixteen, *signore*."

"You are neither of you yet married?" his grandfather wanted to know.

"No, *signore*," Marco said.

"Hmmm," his grandfather replied. "You are your father's heir?"

"Yes, *signore*, I am. I came to Venice so that Bianca might have a proper escort, and so I might learn a bit of the shipping trade here in your city," Marco explained. "Georgio and I will return with our hired soldiers to Florence shortly."

"I see," Alessandro Venier answered. He turned his head now, saying, "You will be Bianca, of course. Remove your hood so I may see you, granddaughter."

Bianca undid her cloak, letting Agata take it. Then she turned and looked at him.

A pity, the prince thought, that she was a brunette. Brunettes were so common. She had obviously inherited her Florentine father's coloring. Still, the skin was flawless, and the aquamarine eyes now engaging his quite boldly were spectacular. And since she was a widow, he would not have to worry about protecting her virtue. "You are different from your sister," he told her candidly.

"More so than you can imagine, *signore*," Bianca told him with the faintest of smiles. "I have been told you are to find another husband for me; however, I do not wish for another husband. I wish only to be reunited with the man I love."

"A child's wish," the prince said coldly. "Your mother has advised me that you are a difficult female. Understand that I will not tolerate any defiance from you. Your appearance in Florence may have been considered special, but your dark hair is a detriment here in Venice. I will nonetheless find you a suitable husband, and you will marry him without complaint, Bianca."

"May I see my sister now, *signore*?" Bianca asked him.

He almost chuckled. His granddaughter had his daughter's stubborn nature, and it took him back to the day when he had told her she would be marrying a Florentine merchant and not remain in Venice. She had wept and raged at him over it, but in the end she had gone meekly to the altar with Giovanni Pietro d'Angelo, as he had expected her to do. Bianca would do the same when he found the right match for her. "Of course you may see Francesca," he said to her. "She has been eagerly awaiting your arrival." He motioned to a servant with his hand. "Fetch my granddaughter," he said. Then turning back to his other guests, he asked them, "What think you of Venice?"

"Magnificent as our mother said it was," Marco quickly replied. "Today, of course, I shall remain with our family, but tomorrow, *signore*, I should like to visit my father's warehouses here, with your permission."

"You are all to call me *Nonno*," the prince said. "I am, after all, your grandfather."

"You are too elegant a gentleman to be called just *Nonno*," Georgio said. "I will call you *Nonno Magnifico*."

Alessandro Venier laughed heartily at this pronouncement. The boy had charm, and was amusing. If he continued to show humor, he would invite him to remain. He must write to Orianna and ask what plans they had for the boy.

A squeal of delight interrupted his train of thought. "*Bianca! Marco! Georgio!* You are here at last!" A young girl had run into the salon. She was tall and slender. At thirteen her breasts were budding as the material from her gown clinging to them attested.

"Francesca!" Bianca was amazed. Her little sister had indeed changed. The red-gold hair was luxurious. The green eyes sparkled. She hugged the girl warmly.

Their brothers looked surprised. This was Francesca? She had only been gone from Florence a little over a year, but the change was astounding. They greeted her with kisses and warm words.

"I have changed, haven't I?" Francesca said gleefully.

"Our gondolier said you have a face to rival Helen of Troy," Georgio told her.

"Who is she?" Francesca asked. "Do we know her?"

Her two brothers laughed at her ignorance.

"I can see your education has been neglected, *bambina*," Marco said.

"On the contrary," the prince interrupted. "Francesca has learned to dance all the newest dances. She can play her lute exquisitely and sing divinely. Her manners have become flawless. She has learned to supervise my kitchen and make the most wonderful scents from the flowers in my garden. She is perfectly educated."

"To be an ornament, but not a companion," Bianca noted.

"But the perfect wife is the most glorious ornament in her husband's house," the prince replied. "Francesca will soon have a husband to please and she will do it quite well, Bianca. Were you not an ornament in your late husband's house?"

"It is obvious that my mother said nothing to you of my marriage or the shameful way it was brought about," Bianca told him. "I will not discuss it here in the presence of innocent ears, but should you be curious, *Nonno*, you have but to ask me."

"Francesca, my precious, take your sister and her servant with you now. Help them get settled," Alessandro Venier said, dismissing his two granddaughters, which Bianca found slightly offensive. She was not some *verginale* like her sister. She had been a married woman, now a widow, and was entitled to more respect. Her grandfather was treating her like a child, and she wasn't. "I do not like him," she muttered under her breath. "He is too much like our *madre*."

When they had left the salon and were walking up a broad flight of marble stairs, Agata said, "Do not irritate your grandfather, mistress. You would do better to make him your friend and not your enemy."

"He does not treat me with the respect a woman of my age and experience is entitled to, Agata. He is old-fashioned and will be very angry when I refuse the man he thinks will make me a good husband. Better we not be friends."

"You don't want to marry again?" Francesca was puzzled. "Do you want to go into the Church now? You did not the last time I recall."

They had reached the top of the staircase, and followed the younger girl as she led them into a spacious apartment of several rooms.

"These are our rooms," Francesca said. "We each have our own bedchamber, and your Agata can either sleep on a trundle in your room or share a separate chamber with my Grazia. Now tell me why you don't want to marry again."

"It isn't that I don't want to wed again, but I want the choice to be mine. I have already made it, but our mother will not allow it," Bianca said to her sister.

"Why not? Isn't he rich enough?" Francesca asked, curious.

"He is a Turk," Bianca replied.

"An *infidel*?" Francesca's green eyes went wide with surprise.

"So he is called," Bianca said.

"Well, of course you can't marry an infidel, Bianca," her younger sister said. "Even I can understand that." Her tone was very assured.

"Why not?" her sister demanded.

"*Why not?* Bianca, if he is an infidel, he isn't a Christian. His ancestors probably killed our dear Lord! Infidels are terrible people. Everyone knows that," Francesca said with great conviction.

"Your knowledge, which is obviously based on ignorant prattle, is astounding," Bianca said sarcastically. "From where have you gained all of it?"

"Everyone knows infidels are wicked," Francesco persisted.

"Amir is the kindest and gentlest man I have ever known," Bianca told her sister. "I am so weary of being told that he is wicked because he is not a Christian. Are there wicked infidels? I'm sure there are. My late husband, may he burn in hell forever, was a wicked Christian. But there are good Christians and good infidels, Francesca. Do not judge a man by his religion. Judge him by his character, little sister."

"*Nonno* will find you a good husband," Francesca responded soothingly, as if she had heard nothing Bianca had just said. And she probably hadn't. She would grow up eventually. "Would you like to hear about the man I want to marry?" she asked her older sister, and then went on without waiting for an answer. "He is a prince," she said with a sigh. "His name is Enzo Ziani. He is so handsome, Bianca. He smiled at me when he came to visit *Nonno* last, and said I was a flower who would one day bloom magnificently." She sighed deeply. "He has been visiting a great deal lately. I believe he comes in hopes of seeing me." She giggled. "I love him already."

"How nice for you," Bianca said drily. Francesca wasn't going to understand her position. How could she? Her sister had been sheltered her entire life, and was now the obvious darling of their grandfather, with a Venetian prince for a suitor.

"Isn't it?" Francesca responded, not catching her sister's sarcasm.

Bianca settled quickly into her grandfather's house, and found it was as dull as her life in Florence had been. Her brothers remained for a little over a week but then were gone. They had strolled both the Piazzetta San Marco and the great piazza itself with their grandfather as he showed them off. Marco had made several business contacts, and would return to Venice on a regular basis for their father. Bianca, however, like most highborn women, was not allowed in public. The only women to be found on the piazzetta were courtesans and common whores.

Although she loved being on the water once again, it wasn't like her little villa. At least there she had been able to walk the beach freely, and ride in the hills about Luce Stellare. Her younger sister's whole life, it seemed, revolved around getting married and the object of her desire, Prince Enzo Ziani.

Bianca had been in Venice several weeks before she finally met him. And when she did, she realized immediately that her grandfather had not chosen this man for Francesca. Alessandro Venier had chosen Enzo Ziani for Bianca. Her little sister was not going to be pleased, but Bianca would let their grandfather take the brunt of Francesca's anger.

He was, of course, at thirty-three, much too old for Francesca but hardly too old for an eighteen-year-old widow. He was a widower, and had been married since he was seventeen to a wife who died during a tenth futile attempt to give her husband an heir. He had been without a wife for several years, but now his family was insisting that he remarry. His visits to their grandfather had been for the purpose of discussing a possible match between the houses of Venier and Ziani—the advantages and the dowry.

Her grandfather requested her presence one afternoon in his small private salon. She came to find him with a guest. Bianca curtsied politely, then waited to be invited to sit.

"Is she not lovely?" Alessandro Venier asked the man seated with him. "Her coloring is not Venetian, but have you ever seen eyes that color, Enzo?"

Bianca bit her tongue. Her grandfather spoke of her as if she were not there, and as if she were a fine thoroughbred animal. *Madre di Dios!* He was so old-fashioned and he had been given the power of life and death over her.

"No, I have not," Enzo Ziani said, rising, helping Bianca to a chair before reseating himself. He saw the anger that had flared up briefly in those wonderful eyes.

She thanked him with a faint nod of her head. At least he had manners, she thought. Francesca was going to be furious when she learned of her prince's visit.

"Bianca," Alessandro Venier said, "this is Prince Enzo Ziani. I have given him permission to call upon you."

"If you have, then you will have broken Francesca's innocent heart, *Nonno*," Bianca said bluntly. "My sister believes you have this prince in mind for her."

"She is much too young!" her grandfather snapped. "I shall not even begin to consider offers for her until next year."

"I am flattered to have attracted the little one's eye," the younger man said, "but she really is too young for marriage. The man who wins her heart will be fortunate."

"I will leave you and Enzo to become better acquainted," Bianca's grandfather said. Then he rose and left the room.

Bianca laughed. "He is hardly subtle, is he?" she said. "But as I do not wish to waste your time, *signore*, please understand that I have chosen not to remarry."

"Unless I am a certain Turkish prince," Enzo Ziani replied.

Bianca grew pale but then she said, "How could you possibly know something like that, *signore*? And how indecent of you to bring up such gossip to me."

"Your grandfather is an honest man, *signora*. He told me that your own mother had a stubborn nature too when it came to marriage. He wanted me to know the truth of your romantic nature because he said I should have to win your heart in order to win your hand," Enzo Ziani said. "Is that true?"

"My heart is already given, *signore*," Bianca answered him. "I will be candid with you, for I am not dishonest. After I was widowed, Prince Amir ibn Jem and I became lovers. I am told it is his faith that makes him unsuitable."

"But you do not care, do you? His unsuitability makes him even more desirable in your eyes," he said to her. "How charming you are."

"Do you think I am a child then to be so shallow?" Bianca asked, irritated.

"Ah, I have offended you," he replied, but he really didn't seem distressed by it.

"Yes, you have insulted me deeply," she told him. "You have loved and lost. Or perhaps you did not love your wife. Perhaps she was just a possession to be displayed on appropriate occasions and bear your children."

"Now you insult me," he said. He was finding himself fascinated by this beautiful woman who spoke to him so frankly. Most women had hardly anything to say of interest, except, of course, the more educated of the courtesans who were expected to be interesting if they were to be successful at their trade. A man's wife, or prospective wife, was supposed to be modest and retiring in everything except household matters and the raising of her children.

"Do I?" Bianca didn't look in the least sorry. "I suspect if you wish to make a connection with the house of Venier, you would do better to wait a year. My younger sister, Francesca, will be ready for marriage then. Her beauty, according to my grandfather, is more to Venetian tastes than mine is. Francesca considers you the ideal man and she is certainly the ideal woman for a traditional gentleman like you, *signore*. I am not. Would not a woman like my younger sister suit you better, *signore*?"

"I do not wish to wait another year," Enzo Ziani told Bianca as candidly as she had spoken to him. "My family is anxious for an heir, as I am the only son in our branch."

"Ahhh, you wish for excellent breeding stock, then," Bianca responded. "Best you wait for Francesca. We both come from the same mother and father, and *madre* is a fine breeder of brats. All of our mother's children have lived. Francesca is five years younger than I am, however. You will have more time to breed with her, *signore*, than with me."

He burst out laughing. "You are deliberately attempting to provoke me," he said.

"No, I am being honest with you," she said. "I am flattered that sight unseen you would even consider a marriage with me. I know that your family is an old and honorable one, or my grandfather would not even have considered you. But I am in love with Amir ibn Jem, and I will not stop loving him. He has promised to come for me, and he will, *signore*. How embarrassing to have your betrothed wife stolen by the sultan's grandson. There would be nothing you or Venice could do about it."

"Venice is a great republic," he countered.

"Yes, it is," Bianca agreed, "but they are just as afraid of the Ottoman sultan as is the rest of the world. Venice will make only a token outcry over my going. The sultan is very fond of his grandsons."

"If you believe your prince will come for you, then you are a fool. I do not believe you are a fool, Bianca. Your Ottoman prince has a harem full of beautiful women he has returned to, and in all likelihood has forgotten you already. You will come to realize that in time. I find you eminently suitable to be my wife, and I shall tell your grandfather so. We will celebrate our marriage in three months' time, in September, at summer's end."

"Tell *Nonno* what you will, *signore*. I will not agree, and cannot be made to do so. I will stand before the priest and deny your suit. Consider the laughter of all of Venice when I do, and the embarrassment it will bring to both of our families."

"You are a stubborn woman, Bianca," he told her, "but I will win you over. Now, come and kiss me."

"You have surely lost your mind to ask a woman who has so firmly rejected you to kiss you," Bianca said, jumping up from her chair so quickly it fell over with a clatter.

His response was to reach out and yank her into his lap and catch her chin between his thumb and forefinger, which allowed him access to her lips. His mouth closed over hers, kissing her a slow, deep kiss.

Bianca struggled so hard against him that his chair came out from under him and they both ended up on the floor of the salon in a tangle of her skirts. She shrieked angrily to find him laughing atop her. "Get off me, you monster! You brute!" She beat at him furiously with her fists.

"Why? I rather like having you beneath me. Now I will be able to dream of what is to come between us." He caught her hands and pinned her arms by her sides, his lips capturing hers again in a hot, passionate kiss. "*San Marco!* You are outrageously desirable!" he said upon finally releasing her.

Bianca didn't like the fact that she found his kisses exciting. Were respectable women supposed to enjoy being kissed by strangers? And the fact was that Enzo Ziani was indeed a stranger. He was not Amir, and his kisses, while provoking and appealing, were not Amir's. They did not leave her weak with a desperate longing. She yanked her head away, and gathering all of her strength pushed him off her so she might scramble to her feet. One of her silk slippers came off in the process, and he grabbed at her foot. She took great pleasure in kicking him away.

"You are a seducer of women, *signore*," Bianca told him angrily. "My grandfather shall learn of this atrocious behavior you have exhibited with me!" Then she stormed from the little salon, clutching her slipper in her hand.

Behind her Enzo Ziani still sat upon the floor, laughing. What a woman! And she was going to be his wife! He didn't give a damn about her Turk. He would make her forget all about that infidel prince when he made love to her. He jumped to his feet, smoothing out his fur-trimmed velvet robe. His cock was hard with the sudden need for her that had overcome him. Thank God his garment covered his lust.

Then suddenly the door to the salon opened, and Francesca came in. "Oh!" she said, feigning surprise. "I didn't know anyone was here, *signore*. How nice to see you. Did you come to see me?" And she smiled at him coyly.

Damn! he thought. Well, best to discourage her now

rather than have her mooning after him. "No, *bambina*," he told her. "I came to see Bianca. Has your grandfather not told you yet? I plan to marry your sister."

Francesca's face was suddenly frighteningly pale. Her green eyes grew wide with shock. "Marry *Bianca*? You are going to marry Bianca? She does not love you. She loves her infidel. Did my *nonno* tell you that? Or that he was her lover?"

"I know all of that. Bianca only thinks she loves this Turk, but she will come to love me, and even if she doesn't, we are a most suitable match," Enzo Ziani said to the beautiful young girl standing before him. "And your sister will do her duty by both of our families, *bambina*."

"You would be content to marry a woman who will never love you when you could have a woman who does love you?" Francesca demanded of him furiously. "And do not call me a baby! I am not a baby! I am a woman, *signore*." Then she flung herself at him, her arms going about his neck, her lips kissing him with a determined kiss. She released him as suddenly as she had entwined herself about him.

"Is that a baby's kiss?" Francesca asked him. "Is it?"

Enzo Ziani was astounded. He had never imagined a girl that young could have such passion in her. "It was not a baby's kiss, Francesca," he told her, "but you must not kiss me again. You are too young to be my wife, and your sister is not. Eventually there will be a fine young man chosen as your husband. Be patient. Now, if you promise to behave yourself, I will not tell your grandfather of this incident." He bowed to the young girl and quickly left the salon.

Francesca burst into tears. It wasn't fair that Bianca be married to the man that she, Francesca, loved. She wouldn't let it happen. It couldn't happen! Then she remembered that weeping would spoil her complexion and redden her eyes. Francesca brought her upset to an end. Then she went to find her sister.

"You are not going to marry Enzo Ziani!" she said, finding Bianca seated outside in their grandfather's small garden. "I forbid it! He is mine!"

"Who told you I would?" Bianca wanted to know.

"He did! You cannot have him, Bianca!" Francesca told her sister.

"You may have him, and gladly," Bianca said. "I have told him I will not wed him, and that he should wait for you."

"You told him that? Bianca, that is wonderful! Oh, you are the best sister in the world! I knew you could not be so cruel as to take the man I love from me."

"Now we must convince *Nonno* that you are the better bride," Bianca told her younger sister. "Your prince wants a wedding at summer's end."

"When is your prince coming?" Francesca wanted to know. "If he does not come and take you before then, they will force you to the altar."

"They can't," Bianca replied serenely.

"*Nonno* always gets what he wants," Francesca said. "Everyone wanted him to marry when his last wife died, but he said he had had enough of wives; he would be content with a mistress from then on. He has prevailed in that, and if your prince does not come to rescue you, he will prevail in this."

"Amir will come," Bianca said assuredly.

And indeed, Amir ibn Jem was preparing to go to Venice. He had been brought to his grandfather, Sultan Mehmet the Conqueror, upon his return home. The sultan had greeted him warmly.

"I never thought to see you again in this life, Amir. What exactly did you do that required I ask you to return from Florence? Certainly you didn't kill one of those fat and proud merchants?"

"Worse, Grandfather," Amir said. "I fell in love with a silk merchant's daughter and planned to bring her home."

"Ahhh," the sultan said. "Yes, if the silk merchant was influential—and he obviously was, since it was Lorenzo di Medici himself who requested your recall—that would present a problem. Ah, well, you will soon find another lovely woman to please you, and I am happy to have you back with me."

"But this is the one I want above all others," Amir told his grandfather. "I have fallen in love with her. I must have her!"

Sultan Mehmet looked at Amir. This was the one grandson who had never caused him a moment's concern, unlike Amir's father, Jem, who was forever quarreling with his brother, Bayezit, who had sired three sons on his wives. "How much trouble will it cause if you steal this woman?" the sultan asked.

"I don't know," Amir answered honestly. "She is one of four sisters. She has been widowed. I know her family has sent her to her maternal grandfather in Venice in hopes of finding a second husband for her. They would not allow her to see me when I was imprisoned, but when I departed Florence she managed to come and stand by the road. I swore I would find her, Grandfather. I do not doubt that her love for me has not wavered in the months we have been apart."

"What if, by the time you reach her, she has been remarried?" the sultan asked.

"I don't know, but I do know she will do everything she can to avoid any marriage to another man," Amir replied.

"So you mean to make her your third wife?"

"Yes. I took Maysun and Shahdi to my bed, and made them my wives at your request. They are good women, but I love neither. Taking Bianca as my wife will not lessen their position within my house. I know their fathers are not very important to you, but I will not shame their families or endanger the loyalty you have from those men," Amir told the sultan. "But I want Bianca for the wife of my heart."

"What if you have a son?" the sultan wanted to know. "I would be in no danger from such a child, but he would be considered a danger by my heir, or his heir."

"If Bianca were to give me a son, he would be taught loyalty to his sultan, but if I sensed danger to my family, I would remove them from your realm."

"You cannot go west again," the sultan told his grandson. "They would never accept an infidel with a Christian wife in the West."

"No, but I could go east or north or south if it were required of me," Amir said. "If the choice were mine, however, I should retire to the Moonlight Serai with Bianca, who shall be called Azura, and my other two wives. I will only journey to the city when my business demands it, or the sultan wishes my presence in his house. You know I am not a man for power, Grandfather. I hope I have not disappointed you too greatly by being more like my English mother's merchant forebears than my warlike Ottoman ancestors. I know my father is baffled to have sired such a son." He smiled at his grandfather.

The sultan nodded. "We get ahead of ourselves," he told the younger man. "I have many days ahead of me, Allah willing, and you do not have your woman back yet."

"With your permission, I will make plans to fetch her," the prince said.

"I know nothing about such a venture, Amir, nor do I want to know. If you are successful, Venice will complain, and perhaps even Florence. I would tell them with a clear conscience that I know nothing of what you planned," the sultan said with a chuckle, and he stroked the beard on his long face with a long hand. "They will not want her back once you have stolen her, even for all their protests."

"I understand, Grandfather," Amir responded with a smile.

"I am sorry to lose you in Florence. The information you were able to send me regarding the French, the Germans, and the rest of the western lords was very helpful. You were well liked, Lorenzo di Medici wrote me."

"The Florentines seem to be a clearinghouse for all the gossip in Europe. All the armies going back and forth seem to pass through the city. It is enormously prosperous, although probably second to Venice, since they have no port like the Venetians do."

"The Venetians have grown fat with their shipping. Much of Florence's goods go through Venice. The merchant families there are just as influential as the merchant families in Florence, if not more so," Sultan Mehmet observed. "I should really like to have Venice for myself, but it is better to let them have the illusion of being a republic. The doge does what I want, and so I must be satisfied with that."

"So you are still conquering," Amir said.

"There are places yet that can benefit from Ottoman rule," his grandfather responded with a smile.

The two men shared a meal together. Then Amir was shown to a bedchamber and invited to shelter for the night.

The next morning he departed his grandfather's palace, and taking a horse from the royal stables he rode to his own home known as the Moonlight Serai. He had sent Krikor ahead several days before to alert his two wives that he was coming. They greeted him warmly, exclaiming with delight at the gifts he had brought to them. He spent the night with them both.

Maysun was a tall, big-boned girl. She had dark brown hair and gray eyes. She had a sweet disposition, and was entirely content. His second wife, Shahdi, was more high-strung. A blond, brown-eyed Circassian, she had been disappointed to be given to an unimportant grandson of the sultan, although her family had been delighted. Still, as he was away much of the time, she had a freedom she might not have had with another man. Since she was a girl who had never been cloistered, this was a great relief to her.

After having spent the night with both of his wives, and having satisfied the two of them to their delight, Amir told them he would speak with them later in the day. Then he went to bathe. As much as he had enjoyed Italy, he realized he was very content to be in his own home once again. He was never more comfortable than when he was here. Breaking his fast with hard-boiled eggs, fresh apricots, warm bread, and yogurt, he smiled broadly when Krikor brought him a small cup of dark coffee.

"I'm going to go to Venice shortly to fetch Bianca," he told his servingman.

"Can you reach her before they marry her off again?" Krikor wondered aloud.

"She is mine," the prince said quietly.

Krikor said nothing. He had never seen his master so determined as he was in the matter of the beautiful Bianca. But then, she had been just as passionate. Surely they were meant to be together. "I will come with you, my lord. You cannot go without me."

"I should never go without you," Amir answered his faithful slave.

"When do we leave?" Krikor asked.

"Tomorrow. We sail from Istanbul to Venice, and back in one of my own ships. I don't want to have to worry about loyalties, for we must be quick. It is possible we may be pursued. I don't want Bianca in any danger."

"Knowing the name of her grandfather will aid us in reaching her more quickly," Krikor said.

"Send one of the eunuchs to bring my wives to me here and then go pack for us," the prince instructed. "We will travel lightly. And I will want Darius with us."

Krikor smiled, nodded, and went off to do his master's bidding.

Several moments later, Maysun and Shahdi came into the chamber where the prince had eaten his meal and was now enjoying his coffee.

"You sent for us, my lord," Maysun said. Both women bowed from the waist.

"Sit! Sit!" he invited them, and when they had made themselves comfortable he said, "I am going away again, but only for a short time. When I return I will bring with me another wife. Once she is with me, it is unlikely I will leave the Moonlight Serai again except at the sultan's command. I will expect you to welcome her into your midst, my ladies. I will want you to pack proper garments for her to wear on our journey, and clothing for her good servant. I must rely on you both in this."

"If you mean to remain at home, my lord, are not two wives enough for you?" Shahdi asked him, pouting. "Why must you bring a stranger into our midst?"

Maysun chuckled.

"What is it you find so amusing?" Shahdi demanded to know.

"This new wife is the woman of his heart, foolish one. Is that not so, my lord?" Maysun inquired of him, smiling.

Amir laughed. "She is, my wise Maysun. She is."

"Then go and fetch her, my lord, so you will know true happiness at last. She will be most welcome in our home, which will soon be her home," Maysun said. "If you love her, then we will too."

But Shahdi frowned unhappily. She had always hoped to win Amir's heart one day. Now, looking at him, she saw it would never be possible, and was sad. Maysun reached for her hand, for she knew her friend's hope. She had known it would never be.

Chapter 12

$\mathcal{E}$nzo Ziani began to court Bianca, despite the fact that she discouraged him at every turn. Francesca turned sulky to her grandfather's entire household, despite her sister's reassurance that she was not going to marry her suitor.

"If you are not going to marry him, then why do you encourage him?" Francesca demanded to know.

"I am not favoring him," Bianca protested. "*Nonno* brings me forcibly into the salon when Enzo Ziani arrives each afternoon. You see the footmen escorting me."

"I've seen him kissing you in the garden," Francesca accused.

"Then you have seen me struggling to avoid his kisses," Bianca countered.

"Has he touched your breasts? I will wager he has, you slut!" Francesca screamed jealously, for Bianca had beautiful breasts, and her own were smaller right now.

"How dare you question me like this!" Bianca fought back. "I do not want this man for a husband, but I cannot help it if our families think otherwise. He comes each day to win me over. I reject him each day when he comes. I do not know what more I can do to discourage him, Francesca. This situation is not my fault, and I wish you would stop blaming me for it. Blame our grandfather, who is a stubborn old man!"

"I hate you!" Francesca hissed and stalked off.

The betrothal between the house of Venier and the house of Ziani was announced to Venetian society with a grand banquet. It was considered a triumph for both families. Prince Enzo was handsome and well liked. The Florentine bride was beautiful. The wedding date was set for the twentieth day of September. The dressmaker came with her assistants to make the bride's wedding gown. They brought beautiful fabrics from which she might choose. They measured and twittered around her like a group of hungry sparrows in winter. She forestalled them as best she could, claiming the fabrics were not fine enough for her, insisting they send to Florence to her father for the cloth.

Bianca was furious with both her grandfather and Enzo Ziani, neither of whom seemed to comprehend that her refusal to even consider this marriage to Enzo Ziani was sincere. They treated her as if she were a child, unable to make her own decisions, and so they wisely made them for her. Then to have Francesca skulking about, sulking and muttering curses at her, was not particularly pleasant. Not that she blamed her younger sibling. After all, what was the poor girl to think under the circumstances?

"Oh, Agata," Bianca said one day to her faithful servingwoman. "What if they are right? What if Amir has forgotten me? What if I wait but in vain?"

"I believe your prince to be an honorable man," Agata said. "If he said he would return for you, then he will return, mistress. You must not lose hope or your faith in him. He will come."

"It had better be soon," Bianca said grimly. "We have been parted for months now, and it is already August." And then Bianca had an idea. It was a wonderful idea, but at the same time a terrible one. What if on the wedding day Francesca took her place at the altar next to Enzo Ziani? The bride would be heavily veiled, and they could dye her sister's hair dark. It would not be until Enzo Ziani raised that veil to kiss his bride that they would discover Francesca. But it would be too late then, for the marriage ceremony would have been performed and sanctified. Refusing the bride would cause a far larger scandal than accepting her. All Venice loved a good joke. They would laugh, but then they would consider how romantic it was, and the noble sacrifice Bianca had made for the little sister she loved. Everyone knew this marriage was not a love match. Now it would be, and Francesca would have her heart's desire. Ziani and her grandfather might fume privately, but Bianca would have more time to wait for Amir.

"That is a wicked, wicked idea," Agata said. "Your grandfather is correct in that she is too young."

"Would you have me forced to the altar instead? And then when Amir comes, I would have to run away, causing an even greater scandal?" Bianca asked. "So Francesca is wed a year before *Nonno* intended. Believe me, she is more than ready.

Many girls are wed at twelve. She is almost fourteen. She wants her prince and I want mine. The two families still get their way with this union, even if the bride is not who they intended her to be."

"All of Venice will indeed laugh at such a happening," Agata warned. "The two families will be made figures of fun, mistress."

"Only briefly, if they are clever and laugh with the rest of Venice. The story will be told that the younger sister wanted this handsome man, and so she cleverly stole him from beneath her elder's nose on the very day of the wedding. It will be considered a great love story, and if Enzo is wise he will tell the world how fortunate he is to have a bride who loves him rather than one who does not," Bianca said. "And then any scandal will die away, as it should when my disappearance becomes the next scandal."

"How will you account for your sister's not appearing for this wedding?" Agata wanted to know.

"Francesca has already proclaimed she will not go to see the man she loves wed to another," Bianca said.

"But will she go along with your little plot?" Agata wondered.

"I shall not know until I can speak with her," Bianca answered.

But Francesca wasn't of a mind to hear what her sister had to say. It was not until Agata had asked the younger girl's maidservant, Grazia, to intercede with her mistress that she would listen to what Bianca had to say.

"What is it you want of me?" she asked in a surly tone one morning when they had finished their meal. "Grazia says I should at least hear you out."

"Come, and walk with me," Bianca invited her sibling. "The garden is lovely."

"Well, you would know better than I, for you spend so much time in it with my prince," Francesca replied meanly.

Bianca did not bother to defend herself, instead leading her sibling outside where the chances of their being overheard if they spoke softly were far less than if they remained in the palazzo. When they reached the marble balustrade at the end of the garden, which overlooked a small canal, Bianca gazed about them carefully to be certain there was no one to hear her. Then she pulled her sister down onto a marble bench so they would be more comfortable.

"Do you wish to marry Enzo Ziani, Sister?" she asked Francesca.

"You know that I do!" the younger girl replied, her green eyes tearing up.

"Then you shall," Bianca said. "You will take my place on the wedding day next month. You will be heavily veiled, and we will dye your hair dark. When he raises your veil after the ceremony, it will be too late, for you will be his wife, Francesca."

"Oh, Bianca! Do you think such a ruse would be successful? Oh! If it were, I should be the happiest bride ever come to the altar," Francesca said, the angry and pinched look suddenly gone from her beautiful face, her plump lower lip quivering, for she was about to burst into tears of happiness.

"I believe it can be done if we are very careful, and very clever," Bianca said. "But that means you must continue to appear to hate me. You must declare over and over that you will not attend the wedding. I will prevail upon *Nonno* to allow you your way in this matter. I will tell him if I must accept this marriage, then I will not have the day spoiled by my sister's whining and weeping over a man she cannot have."

"You would really do this, Bianca? *Really? Truly?*"

"I do not want Enzo Ziani, Francesca. I remain in love with my infidel," Bianca said. "I will never love another man but Amir."

"*Nonno* and the Ziani family could order an annulment before the marriage is consummated," Francesca pointed out.

"They could, and it is a chance we must take, but I do not think they will. The mere fact that the brides were switched will be enough cause for scandal. Neither family will want to make the situation worse. Especially if you hint that Enzo took liberties with you before I came to Venice. Who can prove otherwise? And you need not say *what* liberties he took. After I have rejected Enzo Ziani so publicly, he could hardly annul a union with the sister who loves him enough to force him to the altar," Bianca explained.

Francesca's green eyes were shining with excitement. "This scheme is worthy of some of the tricks I played on our mother when I was a child," she giggled.

"It is better," Bianca replied. "I remember those tricks, Sister. This is a far more involved plot. Now, in order to play your part you must remain hateful and spiteful towards me for all to see. You cannot show your excitement at all. It will not be easy for you. But I will help you by beginning to show some small favor towards Enzo so he and *Nonno* think I am weakening in my resolve."

"I will hate that," Francesca admitted, "but yes, there can be no suspicions as to our plans, Bianca. Thank you! Thank you! You are the most clever sister any girl could have." Then she stood up, and her voice was raised so others might hear.

"Are you mad, Bianca? Forgive you for stealing the man I love? Never! Never!"

Bianca now stood. "But Francesca, it is not my decision. How many times must I tell you that, little sister?"

"Do not lie to me, you thieving slut!" Francesca almost screamed. "I have seen you shamelessly kissing him in this very garden!" She winked at Bianca. "And as for accompanying you when you make your stolen marriage to him, I will not! Nor will I attend such a travesty. You may all celebrate, but I will not!" Then the younger girl stormed back to the palazzo, where at least half a dozen servants had heard the outburst.

Agata hurried out to comfort her mistress. She found Bianca, her face in her hands, her shoulders shaking. "Oh, *signora*, do not weep," she cried out, rushing to comfort her.

Bianca uncovered her face to display a wide grin. She was laughing so hard that her shoulders shook, and was not crying at all. But she muffled her laughter so none would hear.

Agata clapped her hand over her own mouth as she sank down on the bench next to her mistress. "But I heard what that wicked girl said to you," she told Bianca. "Everyone in the palazzo and up and down the canal did."

"It was a ruse," Bianca explained. "Francesca is delighted with my scheme, but we cannot suddenly become reconciled publicly if we are to succeed, Agata. It must appear that we are still split apart because of this planned marriage."

"Ahh," the servingwoman said, understanding. "I see! I see!"

"Now escort your grieving mistress back into the palazzo. It is a hot day, and I must take a nap before I have to face my suitor this day," Bianca said.

Alessandro Venier had scolded his younger granddaughter over what became known as the incident in the garden. He had not heard Francesca's voice and words himself, but his servants had reported her outburst to him. He was astounded by both of his granddaughters. This particular generation seemed to have no respect for authority and tradition. All of his daughters, and he had had five of them by his four wives, had been biddable. Even Orianna, when faced with the reality of her situation, had done what she knew she must do without complaint.

But Francesca had been, until her sister's arrival, a delight. She had learned her lessons without complaint, attended Mass with him when he bothered to go, and been a delightful companion at the dinner table. She pleased him by playing her lute and singing to him in the evenings. She had been perfect in every way until now. But with Bianca's arrival, everything had changed. He hoped that with Bianca's new marriage, his dear little Francesca would return to her formerly charming and obedient self.

Francesca's infatuation with Enzo Ziani, while charming and amusing, had now become as tiresome as Bianca's insistence that she would not remarry. He could not believe his oldest granddaughter was so stupid as not to understand her situation, especially as she had no calling for the church. But if she was not stupid, then she was wretchedly stubborn. He wished Enzo Ziana good fortune with the wench. Despite Bianca's constant refusals to be courted properly, young Ziani wanted her anyway. Alessandro Venier shook his head wearily. He believed after four wives that he knew women reasonably well. A woman who constantly refused a man was not a woman he would have chosen to share his life or his bed.

But suddenly Bianca seemed a trifle more amenable to her suitor. Rather than having to send two sturdy footmen to fetch her, she came willingly when called to greet her visitor. She flirted slightly but not enough to give him great hope. Still, it was a pleasant change for Enzo not to have to do all the talking as they strolled in the garden. She wasn't even averse to sitting while he held her hand and recited florid love poems he had written to her, although Bianca found it difficult to restrain her laughter sometimes, especially when he compared her to a perfect summer's afternoon or a distant and elusive evening star sparkling just out of his mortal reach.

When he wanted a more intimate moment with Bianca it was difficult for her, but in order to continue the ruse that she was becoming more accepting of her fate she had to allow him certain liberties. His kisses were seductive, and frankly they made her head spin. Bianca was very confused by it. She had no feelings for Enzo Ziani at all. He aroused no lust in her and yet she found his kisses were quite exciting.

His hands knew just how to caress her so that she could not control the frisson of chill that raced down her spine when she allowed him to touch her. Bianca knew that she had to keep his kisses and his touches to a minimum. Enough so that he believed he was winning her over, but not so much that he would think her loose and untrustworthy. It was difficult. She had discovered to her surprise, or was it her shock, that a woman could respond to the lovemaking of an attractive man even if she wasn't in love with him. Did such emotions make her wanton? There was no one of whom she could ask the question.

But her small effort at appeasing Enzo's lustful appetites seemed to reassure him that once they were wed she would melt into his arms and he could fill her with passion.

"You are adorable!" he told her one afternoon. "I adore you, Bianca!"

"You are charming, I will admit," Bianca told him, "but you do not love me, Enzo. You want to marry me because our families believe it is the proper thing to do. And I certainly do not love you, *cara*."

"But you will love me!" he assured her. "Once we have married I will teach you to love me, Bianca, and you will."

"You are a dreamer, Enzo. You should marry a girl who loves you, and not a widow who longs for another man."

"I will make you forget this infidel, Bianca!" he swore.

"How young you sound," she said, laughing at him.

He laughed then also, realizing she was correct. He did sound like a boy. "I married Carolina when I was seventeen," he told her. "She was chosen specifically for me, a distant cousin brought from one of the islands for me. There was never anyone else, Bianca. I kept no mistress, for in the beginning we were both children playing at marriage. We could not get enough of each other. When she first told me she was with child, I was overjoyed. But then she lost the child. She lost them all. I could not betray her with another woman, for with each loss Carolina needed more and more reassurance that I continued to love her despite her failure to give my family an heir.

"I am a man, but the truth is my experience with women is not great. After my first wife died, I spent several years mourning her, for with her death came the realization that I had truly loved her. I believe I am coming to love you, Bianca. Who could not love your beauty and your sweetness?"

"Do not convince yourself that you love me, Enzo," Bianca told him. "I will take no responsibility for breaking your heart one day, *cara*, though I will do so."

But of course he did not listen to her. She was to be his wife, and this time, given her mother's record of successful births, he would have a wife who could bring his heir to a live birth. "My wedding clothes will match yours," he told her. "We will be the most beautiful couple in all of Venice."

And if the wedding gown being fashioned for her was any indication, Bianca thought she would certainly be a beautiful bride. It was being made of heavy cream-colored silk that had only recently arrived from the East at her father's Venetian warehouse. The bodice of the gown would be extremely close-fitting and embroidered with gold threads and small pearls. It would have a wide, square bodice, and the sleeves would be full and puffed and decorated with pearls and gold lace. The skirt would be full and divided to show a gold underskirt embroidered with diamonds and pearls in a seashell pattern. There would be several petticoats beneath. A cape of gold cloth would be attached to each shoulder by a large pearl clasp and would flow into a long train. On her head she would wear a high-crowned cap made of gold cloth with a heavy half-veil, which would hide her face until the ceremony was concluded.

Bianca stood silently as the gown was fitted to her form each day, and then refitted until it was finally finished. "The veiling is too sheer," she complained to the dressmaker. "I want a thicker veil for my cap."

"I will see what I can find, *signora*," the dressmaker said. "But do you not want your handsome bridegroom to be teased by a hint of your face beneath the veiling?"

"I am Florentine, not Venetian," Bianca said primly. "It does not matter that this is my second marriage. I will not flaunt myself before all of Venice on my wedding day until after the marriage is celebrated. In Florence, such a thin veiling would be considered immodest. My mother would be very upset with it. You are fortunate she is not here."

Agata and Francesca stifled their laughter. Both knew that Bianca told a bald-faced lie, but under the circumstances the dressmaker could not complain or deny her.

And when the woman and her assistants had departed, Agata locked the door of the bedchamber behind her. Then she and Bianca helped Francesca into the wedding gown to see what alterations would be needed, if any. But to their relief and the younger girl's delight the gown fit perfectly but for the bosom, which could be easily and quickly fixed.

Francesca preened before the long glass mirror in her sister's dressing room.

"It's a perfect gown," she said excitedly. "I shall be the envy of every girl in Venice for it, and for capturing Enzo Ziani as my husband."

"You are a very fortunate girl that your sister understands your passion for this young prince, and will help you attain your heart's desire," Agata said sternly. "Now let us get you out of this gown before you damage it."

"Then go and make a loud fuss above of how ugly I will look," Bianca teased.

"*Nonno* will be very angry when he discovers what we have done," Francesca said as she stepped out of the gown's skirts.

"Yes, he will," Bianca agreed, "but it will be too late then. Neither he nor the Ziani family will want to be more of a laughingstock than this trick will make them seem. They must laugh with the rest of Venice about it. And *Nonno* will have a difficult time of seeking another husband for me after this.

But, Francesca, are you certain this is what you want to do? Just because I don't want to marry Enzo Ziani doesn't mean you have to take my place at the altar."

"No," Francesca replied. "Enzo is the man I want, and now I shall have him. But, Bianca . . . what if your prince doesn't come for you? What will you do then?"

"He will come," Bianca said. But where was he? she wondered. Surely by now he had reached Istanbul and was already preparing his return. He had to be. It was less than a month until the wedding. She wanted to be gone before that day. She didn't want to put Francesca into the position of becoming a bride at such a young age. Francesca didn't understand that while marriage was of course the fate of every respectable girl, she had time before she must settle. Time in which to be courted by several suitable men. Time that Bianca hadn't had. But if Amir didn't come soon, Francesca would marry Enzo Ziani, and their grandfather would probably send Bianca back to Florence for playing such an incorrigible jest on two families.

The doge himself was coming to the ceremony. He had invited the families to have the ceremony performed in one of the chapels at San Marco's. It was an honor that could not be refused. Alessandro Venier purchased a new gondola, and commissioned two artists to decorate the vessel that would carry the bride to the ceremony and bring the newlywed pair back to his palazzo for a magnificent wedding feast. The gondola, while black, had a cabin that was gilded in gold and had stained-glass windows. The inside of the cabin was upholstered in velvet and silk brocade. On the wedding day it would be filled with flowers, along with the bridal couple.

"You had nothing like this at your first wedding," their grandfather said to Bianca.

"No, *Nonno*, I did not," Bianca agreed. "Nor was my gown as fine as the one being finished for me. I thank you for it."

"You will not be unhappy with Enzo Ziani, Bianca," Alessandro Venier said, speaking to her for the first time in kindly tones. "He is the perfect husband for you. I have had luck when choosing husbands for my daughters and granddaughters," he told her proudly. "Your own mother, though reluctant, has been happy with your father."

"Oh, she is, *Nonno*," Bianca agreed. *Of course she is*, the young woman thought. *He allows her to have her way in just about everything. But you will not get your way in this*, Madre. *I will have the man I love, even if you could not.*

August ended and the September days seemed to fly by. Suddenly it was the day before her wedding, and Amir had not come for her, nor had she heard any news of him at all. Bianca was struggling with herself not to panic. Francesca was almost sick with excitement, especially as she dared not show it to anyone. Even her own maidservant, Grazia, had not been included in Bianca's plot, for Grazia was one of the Venier servants. She had not come from Florence with Francesca. Her first loyalty was to her master, so Grazia could not know what would happen tomorrow, for fear she would expose their carefully laid plans.

"Go home and visit your sister's new baby," Francesca told her servant. "And you might as well remain for a day or two. I shall want no company tomorrow when my sister marries the man I love. I shall probably lie abed the whole day."

Grazia was delighted to accept her young mistress's offer. Francesca had not been good company ever since Bianca's betrothal had been announced. Tomorrow she would probably be a horror, weeping and bemoaning an unkind fate. Grazia was grateful to escape the scenes that were sure to follow over the next few hours and days. She was unaware that the plotters needed her out of the house so they might dye Francesca's glorious red-gold hair dark so the ruse would not be so easily discovered. The younger girl did resemble her older sibling enough that with dark hair she could easily fool even her family for a short time.

Bianca had given strict orders that no one but Agata was to serve her on her wedding day. When her grandfather tried to interfere, she pretended to have a tantrum so he would let her have her own way. Then together she and Agata dressed Francesca in Bianca's wedding finery. The younger girl was faint with her excitement.

"Are you certain you want to do this?" Bianca asked Francesca once again. "I can always simply refuse to dress and get in the gondola."

"No! No!" Francesca replied. "I want to marry Enzo!"

"So be it," Bianca said, drawing down the heavy half-veil that would shield her sister's features from early recognition.

Agata peeped out the window. "Your grandfather has just gotten into his gondola. He looks quite elegant today in his deep blue velvet robe. It is trimmed with gold and pearls like your gown. Ahh, here is the bridal gondola come up to the palazzo quay. 'Tis a good thing neither of you is sensitive to flowers, for I have never seen so many before."

Bianca hugged her sister gently. "Thank you for helping me," she said.

"Helping you?" Francesca laughed softly. "You are helping me, dear sister, and I shall be forever grateful."

"I will escort the bride downstairs," Agata said. "Stay hidden here, mistress, until I return, and the wedding party is gone." Then she opened the door to the apartment that the two sisters shared, and leading the bridal figure, she descended the stairs into the beautiful circular entrance hall. Agata was dabbing at her eyes with a scrap of linen, and the other servants who gathered to see the bride nodded to one another, touched by her devotion to her mistress. Agata, they knew, would be going to Enzo Ziani's palazzo in another day to serve her mistress in her newly wedded state.

Once the bride and her servant were outside the palazzo and on the quay, gloved and liveried footmen helped the bride into her flower-bedecked transport, spreading the skirts of her gown so they would not wrinkle. The big gondola pulled away from the quay, and led by her grandfather's vessel, glided down the small canal and into the Grand Canal. Francesca looked out the glass windows, enchanted by the beautiful sunny September morning, made even more beautiful by the colored glass. The cityscape on either side of the water appeared magical. Since her arrival in Venice a year and a half ago, she had hardly been out of her grandfather's palazzo and garden except for a few important and formal events at which Prince Alessandro wished to display his soon-to-be-marriageable granddaughter.

Francesca's heart was beating with excitement. In less than an hour she would be married to the man of her dreams. If he was disappointed at first, her love for him would erase that disappointment quickly enough; she was absolutely certain of it. She would be Enzo's wife, and she would devote herself to making him happy, bearing his children, and raising them beautifully, as her own mother had done. Bianca was a fool to throw away such a wonderful future by waiting for a man who would probably never return for her. Her older sister would probably be sent back to Florence to mitigate the brief scandal that would arise from this day's events. Heaven only knew what their mother would do to her. Francesca giggled, quite pleased with herself.

Suddenly outside there was shouting, and her gondola was bumped several times by another craft. Francesca peered through the windows to see what was happening. A number of large barges filled with cargo had cut off her vessel from her grandfather's gondola. And it seemed she was surrounded on all sides. *How inconvenient*, Francesca thought, irritated. She didn't want to be late for her wedding. And then the velvet curtain shielding the opening to the cabin was roughly pulled aside by a bald-headed, black-bearded man with one gold earring in his nose and another in his left ear. Reaching in, he caught her lace-gloved hand and yanked her forward.

Francesca screamed, pulling back. "What are you doing?" she demanded of him. "Let me go! Let me go!" She attempted to pull her hand from his, to no avail.

The villain ignored her demands and instead yanked harder, unseating Francesca, which caused her to lose her balance entirely. Pulling her from the cabin, her attacker tossed her over his broad shoulder as if she were a sack of meal. He leapt from the bridal gondola into a smaller gondola hidden between her vessel and the barges. To those watching, it was an amazing feat of balance. He could have just as easily fallen into the water with his burden, but the large man was light on his feet.

Roughly pushing his captive down into the boat, he pulled a dark cloth over her head. Francesca was still screaming for help that didn't come. The truth was her voice wasn't even heard over the shouting of the bargemen, Alessandro Venier's servants, and her own gondoliers, now splashing about in the waters of the canal where they had been tossed. What was happening to her? Who was this man dragging her from the wonderful life she had planned? Francesca began to cry. She was suddenly very frightened, finding it difficult to breathe, and her belly was roiling in her cramped, overheated position. Without warning, she fainted.

When she opened her eyes again she found herself suspended in the air between the little gondola below and a larger vessel above. Beneath her, she saw the oars of a galley. Francesca shrieked as her body, still sheathed in the wedding gown, swayed. She was being winched up, she realized, as a ship's rail appeared just beneath her. Several men ran to bring her on board, gently swinging her over the rail, lowering her to the deck, and unfastening her from the device that had held her. Freed, Francesca found her legs were somehow managing to keep her upright despite her terror.

"Beloved!" A tall, handsome man hurried forward. He was dressed in full white pants sashed in dark green and a white shirt open at the neckline, which displayed in part a bronzed chest. His face was clean-shaven but for a well-barbered dark goatee, and his eyes were a gorgeous shade of dark blue. "Did I not say I would come for you, Bianca?" He lifted the veil covering her face, looked at her, and stepped back in surprise. "Who in Allah's name are you?" he demanded. He whirled about, roaring, "You have taken the wrong woman, you fools!"

Francesca began to laugh as her fears evaporated with the knowledge of who this man must be. "No, no, *signore*, do not berate them. My sister and I exchanged places this morning, for I love Enzo Ziani and she insisted her prince would come."

Then without warning her belly rebelled and she vomited all over the toes of his dark boots.

"Who are you?" he asked her, signaling a seaman to clean the mess up with a bucket of seawater. "Let us walk the deck," he said to the bride, "and you will tell me."

"I am Francesca Pietro d'Angelo, *signore*, Bianca's younger sister. I have been living with my grandfather here in Venice since I turned twelve a year and a half ago. I was being prepared for a Venetian marriage. Then our parents sent Bianca here, and *Nonno* decided that Bianca was to wed my Enzo." Francesca went on to explain the whole plot to him.

Amir ibn Jem could not help but laugh when she had finished. His clever Bianca had been fortunate in having this younger sister who was willing, nay, eager to help her.

"Where is she now?" he asked Francesca.

"Hiding at *Nonno's* palazzo," the girl answered him. "If you wish to rescue her, you don't have a great deal of time, *signore*. And you must escape Venice as well, for they will know it is you who has taken her. She has insisted for months to any and all who would listen that you would not fail her. Where are we now?"

"Anchored in the middle of the lagoon between the island of San Giorgio Maggiore and the Lido," Amir replied. "How far is that from your grandfather's palazzo, Francesca?"

"The little canal to his palazzo is towards the end of the Grand Canal just past Santa Maria della Salute. I can show you, for you will have to get me back."

"I apologize for spoiling your wedding day," Amir said.

"It wasn't really mine," Francesca responded. "I will marry Enzo one day, but when I do he will know it is me, and that I love him. I was foolish to believe otherwise. I think everyone is correct. I am too young to marry right now. But had you not kidnapped me, *signore*, I should not have had the time to realize it. There is a great deal more to marriage than just a beautiful gown and a flower-bedecked gondola, I am told. But we must hurry now or you will lose the opportunity to regain your own love."

"I told my bargemen to keep everyone busy until my ship had a chance to make the open sea. They will do their best to delay the search for the stolen bride, but you are correct in that we must hurry," Amir told the young girl.

He gave orders in a language that Francesca didn't understand, and then she found herself being lowered once again into the small gondola. Amir swung himself down beside her, and then they were being poled away from the prince's ship. The gondolier rowed very quickly across the lagoon and into the Grand Canal. Francesca directed him to the little side canal where her grandfather's palazzo was located.

"The servants will all be busy preparing for the wedding feast, and drinking *Nonno*'s wine while he is not there to catch them," the girl told the prince. "If we are careful and quick we can slip into the house easily."

And they did, hurrying up the wide marble staircase and going down the hall to the apartment that the two sisters shared. Agata jumped with surprise when Francesca came into the room, but then seeing the familiar figure of Prince Amir she gave a little cry, which caused Bianca to come forth from her bedchamber.

Seeing her sister, she gasped with surprise, but then she saw Amir. Her aquamarine eyes widened, and then filled with tears. *"You came!"* she said, and the tears spilled down her pale cheeks.

He stepped forward, enfolding Bianca into his arms. "I came," he agreed. "Did I not promise you that I would?"

"It seems as if it has been forever," Bianca told him.

"We have not much time in which to make our escape, beloved," he told her.

"Agata, come and help me get the dark color out of my hair," Francesca said.

"Do not be long," the prince warned the servingwoman. Then, taking Bianca aside, he explained to her the farce that had transpired as he kidnapped the bride and had her brought to his ship.

Bianca found the whole thing very funny, and laughed as she had not in many months. But then realizing that they were still in danger, she stood up. "What shall I take?" she asked him.

"Nothing but Agata, if she would come," he said. "I have the proper garments for you both upon my ship, beloved. Your Venetian finery would not be at all suitable for the life you are to lead. Are you still certain you would come with me, Bianca?"

"Yes! And yes a thousand times, Amir ibn Jem, heart of my heart," she told him.

"Agata, come! We have to go now or we risk being caught."

Francesca's hair was now free of the dark dye, but wet. She ran to Bianca and hugged her hard. "Be happy, dearest sister!" Then she whispered, "He is quite outrageously handsome, Bianca. I don't blame you."

"I'm so sorry your wedding to Enzo was spoiled," Bianca told her younger sibling. "If you truly love him, Francesca, do not settle for another."

"I won't," Francesca replied. "But first I will make him jealous. Now go quickly before you get caught, and your prince imprisoned. The doge would love such a captive."

The two women and the prince left the apartment and hurried downstairs to flee the palazzo. Francesca had been correct. The servants had been so busy drinking their master's wine, and preparing for the wedding feast expected to commence shortly, that the fugitives had managed to come and depart without ever being seen. They entered the waiting gondola. Within a short time, they were rowed out of the Grand Canal and across the lagoon and hoisted up onto the deck of the galley. The gondolier, to their surprise, came too, for he was actually one of the prince's men. The little vessel floated off.

Bianca and Agata were escorted to a large cabin, where Amir left them to change into their Turkish garments while he gave orders for the ship to escape Venetian waters before the precious cargo it carried was discovered. The clothing, while totally different from what they had worn all their lives, was beautifully made. They each pulled on pantaloons, which they sashed at the waist, a modest long-sleeved shirt, a sleeveless vest, and comfortable slippers. There was a single sheer silk veil for head and face that they quickly realized was for the younger woman. The clothing was exquisitely made, of the finest materials. One set was the shade of a ripe melon, and Agata had immediately realized it was for her mistress, as it was decorated with small jewels and gold fringe. The other, which she now wore, was plain but actually a very pretty sea blue in color.

When the two women ventured back onto the main deck, suitably clothed in their new garb, it was to see the shining towers and domes of Venice fading into the distance, and the open sea stretching ahead of them. A new life awaited them, and Bianca looked happier and more at ease than her serving-woman thought she had in months. Agata did not know what awaited them beyond the sea ahead, but Bianca's joy was too potent to ignore. Whatever they faced, it would be good, the servingwoman decided.

Chapter 13

By midafternoon, all of Venice had heard the tale of how the Venier bride had been kidnapped on her wedding day and spirited away. It was suspected that she had been taken by some lawless Turk—a prince, it was said. Alessandro Venier's servants were quick to gossip, and they said the girl had been saying for months that her prince would come for her. And she had made no secret of not wanting to wed the charming Enzo Ziani, while her younger sister continued to proclaim her love for the man.

How delicious, the gossips in the Piazzetta and Piazza San Marco decreed as they strolled up and down in the presence of the city's best courtesans. The Ziani family was insulted by the bride's kidnapping, but they could hardly blame the old prince for what happened. Still, they wanted someone to blame. Instead of building such an extravagant gondola in which to transport the bride, could not Alessandro Venier have made better security arrangements for his granddaughter? Yet they had taken Bianca's words about her prince no more seriously than had her own family.

Alessandro Venier was himself shocked by what had happened. He decided to blame Francesca for the debacle. "You wished bad fortune upon your sister," he accused her, "and this is the result of your wickedness!"

"I did not want her to wed my Enzo, it is true," Francesca said, "but I would never wish bad fortune upon anyone, *Nonno*. This is your fault for insisting that Bianca wed a man she did not wish to marry. But you can redeem the Venier name by offering them me. I will be fourteen in less than seven months, and you said I should wed at fourteen."

Alessandro Venier looked sharply at his granddaughter. "What do you know of what happened, Francesca? How did this infidel manage to get word to Bianca? And where is her servingwoman? I would speak with her."

"I imagine Agata is with Bianca," Francesca said sweetly. "She is very devoted to my sister, *Nonno*."

"This kidnapping did not happen by chance! If the servant is with the mistress, then someone else in this house knew what was to transpire, and aided them," Alessandro Venier said furiously. "Was it you, Francesca?"

"*Nonno!* How could I have possibly contacted some infidel I have never laid eyes upon and concocted such an event as transpired today? I had nothing to do with it!"

Of course she hadn't, her grandfather thought. He was grasping at straws in an effort to salvage a bad situation. The truth was that even if they managed to regain custody of Bianca, the Ziani family would not have her now. By running off with her infidel, she had embarrassed them publicly. Even if Enzo Ziani were madly in love with her, he could not accept her back. Francesca interrupted his troubled thoughts with an even more troubling question.

"What will you tell my parents of this day?" she asked her grandfather.

"Go to your room," he said. What was he going to tell his daughter? That she had raised an impossible and disobedient child? The truth was that Bianca's first marriage was at the root of all this trouble today. If Orianna and her husband had not allowed themselves to be frightened by Sebastiano Rovere, God curse his soul, Bianca would have made a happy Venetian marriage and there would have been the end to it.

But they had practically forced the girl into the arms of that decadent monster, and now a second marriage had caused the foolish girl to rebel. This situation was not his fault, Alessandro Venier decided. It was the fault of Bianca's parents, and he intended to lay it at their door.

He would, of course, have to mend fences with the Zianis. Bianca's dowry was of necessity forfeited to them as a penalty. Then he dangled Francesca's larger dowry before them. He had added to his favorite granddaughter's dower portion himself. The family demurred. He pressed the issue. Enzo Ziani was publicly mourning his loss before all of Venice, drinking and whoring every night until he was the talk of the city.

"He is not of a mind now to wed again," the Ziani patriarch, Piero Ziani, told his old friend, Alessandro Venier. "The family wishes to allow him to indulge his grief and his embarrassment, but he must wed again soon. We need an heir. I will be frank with you, Alessandro. Francesca is beautiful and accomplished. But she is too young for my grandson, Enzo. Carolina was fourteen when she married him, and see how that turned out. No, we must seek an older woman, perhaps seventeen or eighteen, who will have a better chance of bearing a live child for us. Bianca was perfect. I regret what happened on what was to have been their wedding day."

"No more than I do, Piero," his companion said.

"Do you know for certain who took her?"

"It would appear that her kidnapper was Amir ibn Jem, the grandson of Sultan Mehmet. She knew him slightly, for he was her neighbor when she stayed at the Pietro d'Angelos' villa," Alessandro Venier said, telling but a half-truth.

"Enzo told me that he said he would come for her," Piero Ziani murmured.

"The words of a romantic fool. Who could believe such words but a romantic and even more foolish girl? And who would have thought he would actually come?"

Piero Ziani nodded in agreement. "Certainly he was just more than a neighbor to love her so," he said. "If it were not my family who has been embarrassed, or my grandson whose heart has been broken, I should be admiring of such a feat of daring. Enzo asked the doge to complain to the sultan and demand the girl back, but of course the doge said no. The scandal will die, and we cannot endanger our relations with someone as powerful as Sultan Mehmet over a stolen bride. Besides, no vows were spoken."

Alessandro Venier nodded in agreement, but in truth he was infuriated by the Ziani family's attitude. Then he realized that his friend was correct. In the grand scheme of things, Bianca was an unimportant girl. Venice was not going to war with a powerful trading partner over her. What was done was done. "If Enzo is not in any hurry to reconsider my granddaughter Francesca," he said to Piero Ziani, "remember that her mother birthed a healthy son nine months after her marriage. Marco is almost twenty now, Piero. Orianna wasn't much older than her daughter, Francesca. All my daughter's children have survived infancy and early childhood. Seven children. All healthy. All living."

"Let us see what happens in a month or two," Piero Ziani said.

Alessandro Venier had to be satisfied with that. He wrote to his daughter, Orianna, telling her everything that had transpired, cleverly shifting any blame for Bianca's escape onto Orianna's and Giovanni Pietro d'Angelo's shoulders. The Venier family had been made the laughingstock of Venice, and it was their fault. They should have kept Bianca in Florence until she had rid herself of her obsession for her infidel. And if she hadn't done so, then she should have been incarcerated in a cloistered convent where she would not bring shame upon their two families, as she had by running away. They must now consider her dead to them. Her name must never be spoken within the family ever again.

As for Francesca, he would do the best he could for her.

Reading her father's letter, Orianna was both furious and heartbroken by turns. To have been so defied by her own child angered her. To lose her eldest daughter brought her to tears. Still, her father was correct. Bianca's name must be forbidden to them. Her memory expunged. By choosing her infidel prince she had put herself beyond the pale of polite and respected society. Bianca was now dead to them all.

But sailing down the Adriatic coast, Bianca could think only of how happy she was once again. There being no real privacy upon the ship meant that any intimacies between her and Amir would have to be postponed for the interim, but she didn't care. They were together once again. A pavilion had been set up for the two women at the farthest end of the ship's stern. There were a silk couch and several leather and wooden chairs upon which to sit, and two small tables inlaid with tile. They spent most days here beneath a blue-and-gold-striped awning, which protected them from the direct rays of the sun. The ship's crew was not allowed near. Only Amir could join them.

The voyage they would make would give them time to grow used to several changes in their lives. Their clothing was but the start. Bianca would no longer wear the beautiful gowns she had grown up knowing, nor Agata her practical skirts. Turkish garb was, to their surprise, very modest. They wore pantaloons with a blouse and over it an embroidered sleeveless vest. A sash at the waist secured their garments. They were covered from neck to ankles. When they went up on the deck, each woman wore a pelisse with a hood that could be drawn up, and Bianca's face was veiled. But the biggest change of all was that Bianca would now be known by a different name.

"Bianca," Amir said, "means 'white' and is indicative of your old life in Florence and Venice. From this day forth, you will be known as Azura, for your beautiful eyes of aquamarine." Amir took her two hands in his and kissed them. "My beautiful Lady Azura," he murmured to her.

I am Azura now, she thought happily. *A new name. A new life.* It was good. To her surprise, she found it easy to slough off her old identity of Bianca. With it, she left behind all the darkness and misery of the past. But she did feel a certain sadness in leaving her family. Still, had they not as easily discarded her to Sebastiano Rovere in order to save her brother, Marco? Her only value to them had been how they might use her to help the family. Her happiness had meant little to them, but she had done the unthinkable. She had taken her own life in her two hands and made her own choice as to how she would live it. Gazing at Amir, she knew she had made the right decision.

Taking advantage of the autumn winds, their vessel raced down the Adriatic Sea towards the Mediterranean. They passed the islands of Corfu, Paxos, Cephalonia, and Zakynthos. Although his vessel was well armed, Amir found he was relieved to escape any attack by the very fierce local coastal pirates. An assault on his ship would have been beaten back, but he didn't want the two women aboard to suffer such a frightening event.

As they rounded the Peloponnese, he pointed out the island of Kythira, birthplace of Venus and ancestral home of the Venier family. The days were warm, although now and again they faced a rainy day. But then they were in the Aegean Sea, passing between Lemnos and Lesbos, cruising into the straits of the Dardanelles and finally the Sea of Marmara early on a misty morning. Slowly, as they reached the fabled city of Istanbul, the fog was burned away by a bright sun.

Azura had stood watching the city take shape before her. It was, she thought, even more beautiful than Venice. The city was constructed on seven hills upon a high, narrow spit of land between the Marmara and a bay known as the Golden Horn. As their ship grew closer, Azura could see the streets and buildings tumbling in disorderly fashion down the hills to the sea. They passed palaces and gardens built along the edge of the water.

"The Russians call this city Tsarigrad, which means

'Caesar's City,'" Amir told her. "The Northmen who come call it Mickle Garth, which means 'Mighty Town.'"

"It's amazing to behold, my lord," she told him. "Will we live here?"

"No. I will want my grandfather to know we have returned safely, but then we must make a three-day trip to my home. As I have told you, it is on the Black Sea. We will continue on this vessel, and while we are here you will remain aboard. It is unlikely the sultan will want to see you, beloved. If asked, he must appear ignorant of your and my actions. Venice is an important trading partner for us."

"Men!" Agata snorted when he had gone. "I will wager the doge sent no one after you, mistress. Christian and infidel will cry religion when it suits them to do so, but neither will permit any interference between them with regards to their trade."

Azura laughed. "You are correct," she agreed, but as she spoke she was watching Amir as he left the ship and mounted a great white stallion that had been brought for him to ride from the docks to his grandfather's palace. A coal black man, bare-chested and garbed in cloth-of-gold pantaloons, held the beast, which was beautifully caparisoned in a fine red leather saddle and a bridle of silver. There were six Janissaries who surrounded her prince as soon as he was mounted, and they rode off.

Azura watched him go, thinking that in three more days they would be at the palazzo she would now call home. No, not palazzo. Serai. The Moonlight Serai. Amir had been teaching her Turkish, and although she had never before spoken any language but her own, she found she was picking it up surprisingly easily. It would allow her to speak with his other two wives, which was important to making friendships with them.

Agata was not having as easy a time, however. "It twists my tongue," she complained, but she nonetheless struggled on, discovering to her surprise that she understood more of the language when it was spoken than she herself could speak. That, she realized, could prove useful to her and to her mistress. If the new household into which they were being fitted thought she could not understand them, Agata could learn more information that might help them. She explained this to her mistress.

"That is very clever, Agata," Azura told her. "Amir tells me that his two wives are ready and eager to welcome me, but I am no fool. I cannot be certain of that until I know them. Their servants will talk in front of you, and you will be able to keep me informed. I shall be the third wife, Amir says, but first in his heart."

"These infidels are permitted four wives, I have learned," Agata said. "I do not deny he loves you, mistress, but you will have to work hard to keep his favor."

Azura nodded. "I know," she said. "I have said nothing before, but I knew this before I decided to come with him, Agata. I knew back at Luce Stellare that if I followed him, I would have to share him with the others. But I have loved him almost from the first moment we met. I should rather have part of him than none of him."

"You are a rare woman indeed, mistress," Agata said sincerely.

"Or a fool," Azura said with a wry smile. "Still, I am happier with him than I have ever been with another."

Yes, she was, but these past weeks at sea, bereft of his passion, a passion she had been denied for so long now, had been difficult. Why was it that people believed women could not have the same longings as men? She ached all over from the lack of his touch, and the few kisses that they had managed to steal since they had been reunited had made her need only worsen. And now she must share his passion with two other women! Yet even such thoughts could not disturb the newly named Azura's happiness. She had made her choice and there was no going back.

Sultan Mehmet greeted his grandson warmly. "From your smile I am led to believe you have attained your heart's desire, Amir," he said.

"I have," the prince answered, bowing low before his grandfather and ruler.

"And how much trouble did you cause in Venice to attain it?" the sultan asked.

"Has their representative complained?" Amir countered.

"No," the sultan answered. He signaled a slave to bring refreshments, indicating that he wished his grandson to remain for a time.

"Let me tell you a tale of adventure," Amir said, and when his grandfather nodded, he began. "Once there was a prince so desperately in love with a beautiful lady that he would do whatever he had to do to make the lady his own." Amir then went on to tell the sultan of how, unbeknownst to the prince, his lady love and her sister had switched places on her fateful wedding day. He related the comedy of how the wrong girl had therefore been kidnapped and brought to the prince's vessel. How upon discovering the ruse, the prince had had to return the wrong maiden and fetch his lady. How they had then escaped Venice, undoubtedly leaving behind chaos and scandal for the two families involved. He used no names, so even the attending slaves, who got caught up in the story, could not possibly claim that the prince in the tale was Amir.

Sultan Mehmet roared with laughter as he considered Amir's eagerness to be reunited with his lover, only to discover it was her younger sister. He was admiring that the girl had kept her wits about her despite her fright, and helped Amir straighten out the whole situation. "So in Venice no one knows it was the younger girl who would have wed the man she loved, and not his lady love? An adroit plot, my boy. You have claimed a clever woman for yourself. I can only hope she will get on with Maysun and Shahdi. Nothing is worse for a man than a quarrelsome harem."

"My wives are pleasant and easygoing women," Amir said. "They will welcome Azura into our home."

"You have named her Azura?" the sultan asked.

"For her eyes, Grandfather. Her eyes are the most amazing shade of aquamarine," Amir explained.

The sultan smiled a slight smile. His grandson was indeed a man in love. It was fortunate for them both that he had not inherited his father's disobedient nature. Mehmet knew he could thank the English *kadin* who had been his son, Jem's, favorite for that.

She was a wise girl that they had named Zayna, meaning "beauty," who had quickly learned the ways of the harem. She had carefully protected her only son, teaching him utmost obedience to the sultan. By the time she died, when Amir was yet a boy, he had learned his lessons well. Amir was the only one among his male sons and grandsons that the great sultan trusted not to betray him.

The sultan's own sons were always quarreling. His eldest

son Bayezit's sons were as ambitious as their father, each having different mothers aspiring to see their own son rule one day. But Jem's only son had wisely taken himself from the midst of it all once he was old enough to make such a decision. He had become a merchant prince living in Florence, sending back bits and pieces of information and gossip to his grandfather from time to time.

He had disappointed his own father in doing so. Now Amir was back within the bounds of Mehmet's empire. Would he really be content to be a country gentleman with his women, his dogs, and his horses? But then he would also have his three trading vessels, and his interest in them had always been very strong.

"My lord grandfather."

The sultan's thoughts were interrupted. He focused his dark eyes upon Amir.

"My lord, I would ask a boon of you. I would have Azura come to the Moonlight Serai as my legal wife. Will you represent her before your personal imam so this may be done today?"

"Of course!" the sultan said enthusiastically. "You do this lady great honor, Amir." Then he called for his imam to come to them. A scribe joined them in order to write up the papers that would make the woman known as Azura legally married to the Ottoman prince known as Amir ibn Jem. Under the law, it was not been necessary for Azura to be present at such an event. When it was done, the imam prayed for the health of the sultan and his empire before Amir departed back to his ship carrying the legal parchments declaring Azura to be his wife.

He found her and Agata in the large cabin of the vessel

eating their main meal of the day. While Azura bemoaned the lack of that wonderful Florentine invention, the fork, she seemed content enough to use her fingers now, picking up small pieces of roasted lamb with two fingers and scooping the saffroned rice up with three in a spoonlike motion. He joined them, seating himself cross-legged at the head of the small table.

"You found your grandfather well, my lord?" she asked him politely as she ceased eating herself and prepared him a plate of food with Agata's help.

"Very well, and pleased enough with me to have his own imam and scribe see to the legalities of our union, beloved. You are now officially my wife," he told her.

"Do I not get to come to my own wedding?" Azura asked him, sounding slightly annoyed. "Remember that you swore I should not have to give up my own faith, Amir."

"You do not," he said.

"Then we must have a priest of my faith bless this union," she told him.

"You will not find a priest in all of the empire who would bless such a union, beloved," he told her honestly. "You must be content to know that within the laws of my grandfather's empire you are now considered my legal wife, Azura." He drew the parchment he had carried from the palace out of his robes. Unrolling it, he held it out to her. "There is the sultan's signature on this document. He acted for you as your parental guardian. He did you a great honor."

The old Bianca rose briefly, but she forced her away, allowing the woman she now was, and must be, to speak for her. She had chosen this life freely. She had gladly walked away from everything she had been born into so she might be with this man. "Was it a nice wedding?" she asked him mischievously. If she was already damned to a fiery hell for this marriage, her words were not going to make it any worse for her with God.

"It was simple and quick," he said, reaching out to grasp her hand and squeeze it. He was not a fool. He knew how much this acceptance cost her, but that she was willing to endure it only proved her great love for him. He kissed the hand in his.

"Shall I leave you, mistress?" Agata asked. The serving-woman could feel the tears pricking at her own eyelids. The love between these two people was overwhelming.

"No." The prince answered for them both. "I had best go topside and give orders for our departure." He scrambled to his feet and left them.

"How very much he loves you," Agata said.

"I know," Azura responded. "I know."

Their ship sailed from its dock on the Golden Horn and made its way through the narrow straits of the Bosphorus. On either side of them, beautiful green hills edged the water. Finally they exited the straits into the Black Sea. Their route kept them within sight of the shoreline, for this sea could be fickle. The storms that came up quickly were apt to be very dangerous and deadly. Then, on the third morning, Agata awakened Azura excitedly. "Come! Come and see," she said to her mistress. "We have anchored, and Moonlight Serai is within sight! It is like a pristine white jewel in the green hills, mistress! It is beautiful. In all of Florence or Venice, I have never seen anything so beautiful!"

Azura arose from her bed and came to look. "Oh, how lovely!" she exclaimed, gazing out at the small palace that would soon be her home. It was set upon a high cliff above the sea. There would be outbuildings, of course, and gardens, for Amir loved gardens. She didn't think any place that he called home would be without gardens. She was eager to see all of it. "Let us quickly dress," she said to Agata.

The cabin door opened and Amir came in. "Ahh," he said, pleased, "you are awake and can view your new home, beloved."

"When may we go ashore?" she asked him excitedly.

"Shortly," he told her. "I must go and see that the messenger I sent from Istanbul arrived safely and that all is in readiness for you."

"A messenger?" Azura said, curious.

"A pigeon," he told her. "It is how I communicate with my grandfather or my women when necessary, or my captains communicate with me when their vessels arrive in port after a voyage. It is very convenient."

"Oh, look!" Agata cried. "A flag has just been raised from the rooftop of the Serai, my lord. It is green and has a crescent moon upon it."

"We are being welcomed," Amir said with a smile. "Obviously my message was received by my head eunuch, Diya al Din. He manages my household as a majordomo would serve a noble house in Venice or Florence. The eunuch serving as guardian of my harem is called Ali Farid."

"Have you other women in your harem besides your first two wives?" Agata inquired of the prince boldly. It was a query she knew her mistress wanted to ask but would not. Agata also understood that once they left this vessel her ability to ask such candid questions would be severely curtailed.

Amir looked amused by the question. "I have no need for

a harem filled with quarreling women," he told them both. "There are none I need or wish to impress. The only other females in my household are servingwomen. Perhaps your mistress has not told you, Agata, but my first two wives were taken at my lord grandfather, the sultan's, request to honor the political allies from whose families these women came. Their positions are to be respected, but it is your mistress who has my whole heart.

"Now do not dare to question me again, woman. Though you are not a slave, you are a servant in my household and subject to the same rules and customs as all the others who serve me. Such boldness will disturb the eunuchs. Do you understand me?" He looked directly at her, his blue eyes grave.

"Yes, my lord prince," Agata replied, bowing from the waist as her mistress had recently taught her was the polite action to go with any response to him, be it yes or no. "Forgive my boldness. It will not happen again."

His mouth twitched but he managed not to laugh. This sort of adjustment was going to be very difficult for the outspoken Florentine woman, but Amir knew she would try hard for the sake of her mistress.

"If we have been welcomed, my dear lord, then are we free to go ashore?" Azura asked him, smiling. "I will admit I am eager to take a bath, for certainly I am rank after our many days at sea."

"Get dressed and put on your pelisses," he told them as he left them. "I will go now and make certain the boat is ready to take us ashore."

Shortly after he had gone, the two women, cloaked and veiled, joined him upon the deck. They were settled into a boat, which was then lowered from the vessel into the choppy sea. Despite the sunlight dancing upon the water, Azura could comprehend how the Black Sea had gained its name. She had never before seen waters so dark and forbidding. She thought of the bright blue and blue-green waters of the Adriatic, the Mediterranean, and the Aegean seas through which they had traveled. Even the little sea of Marmara had a far friendlier look than these waters. Both women were relieved to have their transport rowed quickly to the rocky shore, where a party of people awaited their arrival.

"My lord prince, welcome home!" A tall, thin black man stepped forward, bowing.

"Thank you, Diya al Din," Amir said. "The lady with me is my new wife, Azura, and her servant, who is called Agata. Know that Azura has my full love and trust, old friend. I have waited long to find and claim her."

"I am happy to hear it, my lord prince," Diya al Din said. Then he turned to Azura, and bowing, bade her welcome to the Moonlight Serai.

A litter had been brought down from the little palace, for the climb up was considered too strenuous for a woman. Both Azura and Agata were ensconced and carried up by the four bearers, who didn't seem in the least winded. They went at a trot through a magnificent garden now giving way to autumn, then into the palace itself. When they finally set the litter back down, its curtains were drawn open by a light-skinned eunuch, who helped them out. They found themselves facing another tall, coal black man. This eunuch, however, was larger boned than the elegant Diya al Din.

"I am Ali Farid, master of the prince's harem." He introduced himself in a high-pitched voice. "I welcome the lady

Azura to the Moonlight Serai. Be advised that you will answer to me in all that you do, and your servingwoman as well. I will not allow disobedience among the women for whom I am responsible. As my master's third wife, you are the least among them. Now follow me, and I will take you to your quarters."

Agata looked as if she were going to explode like a Chinese firework, but a warning look from her mistress aided her in keeping silent.

Ali Farid led them from the hallway where the litter had been set down and through a set of large double doors opening into a large tiled room empty of furniture.

"Here we allow the local women to come so they may display their goods for your inspection. You may purchase what pleases you," he said, explaining the purpose of the chamber. "I will pay for your purchases." Turning right, he led them through a smaller paneled door into a little anteroom, and then through another paneled door into a square salon. It was furnished with low tables, lamps, and a rainbow of multicolored pillows. At the salon's far end was a wall of lead-paned windows. Beyond it, a wonderful garden looked out onto the sea.

"I have never before seen such a marvelous display of windows!" Azura said aloud. "It is beautiful, Ali Farid, as is this entire chamber."

"Yes, it is," he agreed, pleased by the compliment. It seemed as if the prince's third wife was an amenable woman. "This corridor," he said, pointing to his left, "leads to the harem baths. Perhaps the lady Azura and her servant would enjoy a bath shortly," he said, sniffing delicately.

"Indeed, yes!" Azura told him, and she laughed. "Even I

find the scent lingering about me rank after all those days at sea, Ali Farid."

"If I have offended, I beg the lady Azura's pardon," the head harem eunuch said.

"Nay, I fear 'tis I who have offended," Azura told him.

He nodded slightly and then pointed to an open arch leading to another corridor. "The bedchambers for the ladies of the house are there. There are three on one side of the hallway, and one on the other. Each of the three smaller chambers has a separate chamber for a servant." He led them to the far end of the row, ushering the two women into the little suite. "Here are your rooms," he told Azura. "I will send a eunuch to serve you, my lady, and he will escort you to the baths." Then, with a little bow, he left them.

"Well!" Agata said. "I am not certain I like this Ali Farid."

"He serves Amir well, and that is all that matters," Azura said. "We have entered a different world. You knew it would not be as our old world was. Watch, listen, and learn. Did you see the other two wives as we came? It is almost as if this harem is deserted but for us. I didn't even see other servants."

"They are here, you can be assured, my lady, and have already peeped at you from wherever they have hidden themselves," Agata replied. Then she walked into the bedchamber. "*Madre di Dios!* This chamber is hardly a fit place to entertain the prince, my lady. There is no real bed either."

Azura followed her servingwoman and looked about her. The chamber was not large, but neither was it small. Its walls were half-whitewashed and half-tiled in beautiful turquoise blue tiles. The bed, a thick mattress that sat upon a low dais, would hardly fit two. There was a single painted chest for her possessions, of which she now had few; a small seating area of pillows; a low table of ebony; and several lamps, one hanging, the others set upon the table. "I must assume that this is all that I am expected to have," Azura said. "The prince's apartments will be larger. I suspect it will be where we have our private moments, Agata."

"It is indeed sparse, my lady Azura, but like all new beginnings it requires a personal touch," a voice said, and an elderly brown man stepped into the chamber. "I am Nadim, sent by the officious Ali Farid to serve you as your personal eunuch, my lady Azura. I am not important or influential, but then a third wife is not considered so either. I suspect, however, having seen you, that the peerless Ali Farid has erred in his judgment this time. It will take him a while to realize it, but by then I hope to be invaluable to you so he will not be able to dismiss me. I will serve you loyally, my lady Azura."

She laughed, and even Agata, who had understood the eunuch's words, smiled. She liked this man already, and knew he would indeed serve her well.

"I am told you badly need the baths, my lady. I will escort you now if you are ready," the eunuch said. "I have already alerted the bath slaves."

They followed him from Azura's new quarters to the baths, but when Nadim followed them into the antechamber of the baths, Agata bridled.

"You cannot come in here!" she scolded him, struggling the find the proper words in this new language.

"It is my duty," he said slowly so she would understand. "I am a eunuch, and have no lust for the female body."

Azura quickly spoke in their own native Florentine cant. "I know it is very different for us, but he is correct. And the bath women do what needs to be done, Agata. Nadim will just help me to undress and fetch fresh garments. You need have no shame."

"Well, mistress, if he doesn't mind, I'll just wait until he leaves to disrobe," Agata said nervously.

"My servingwoman is not yet comfortable with eunuchs in the bath," Azura told Nadim as she allowed him to help her undress.

He nodded, understanding. "It is different for women who come from the West," he said. "Will you object if I burn these garments? I do not believe they can be washed clean after so many weeks of wear. What else have you?"

"There were two changes of clothing for both of us aboard our ship," Azura told him. "These garments were the better of the two, I fear."

"I will see you have fresh clothing when you have bathed. And I will see that you are given a complete new wardrobe as quickly as it can be sewn, my lady. I do not intend to have either of those two complacent females who claim the titles of first and second wives outshine you. They are not worthy of Prince Amir. You, I can see, are." He looked her naked body over with a surprisingly sharp eye. "Yes, you are truly beautiful."

Then, with a little bow, he hurried off carrying her old clothing.

"Well!" Agata huffed. "He is very bold for an old slave man."

"No," Azura said slowly. "He will prove to be of great value to me in this new world once I can be assured of his loyalty."

"How can you know if he is your creature or not?" Agata wondered as she stripped her own dirty clothing off.

"I am not certain yet," Azura told her, "but I will know."

The head bath attendant hurried over to them now, smiling broadly. "Welcome, welcome, my lady Azura. Gracious, we have a great deal of work to make you presentable for the prince. We have already received word that he will want you in his bed tonight. I can tell you"—and she lowered her voice—"there were certain noses in this household very much out of joint when that news was bandied about."

"I very much appreciate your help," Azura said politely, already suspecting that this woman was very important within the harem hierarchy. Amir had informed her that good manners within the harem, even towards the lowliest, were very much valued. She let the woman lead her off while Agata, now as naked as her mistress, followed.

"I am Halah," the bath mistress said. "First you must be rinsed. Step into this marble shell," she instructed Azura. Then she clapped her hands and two women began to pour warm water over the new wife. Once rinsed, she was brought to another shell where the two, wielding large soapy sponges, washed her once, rinsed her, and then washed her a second time. But after the second soaping, Halah came with what looked like a long, thin blade, and carefully went over each inch of Azura's skin. The young woman was astounded to see the soapy water filled with dirt with each pass of the blade. She was rinsed again. A third soaping and rinsing followed. Then they washed her ebony hair.

While Halah personally served Azura, the other two bath women helped Agata, teaching her how to properly bathe. "I do not think I have ever been so clean in all of my lifetime," Agata said in the new language, and the two bath women smiled and nodded in agreement, leading Agata to a warm pool, where she joined Azura to soak for a time in the perfumed waters. Slave women brushed their hair dry while they rested.

"We will do this daily," Azura told her servant. "This is something I should like to share with my mother and sisters."

"The priests would denounce it as a vanity of the flesh," Agata said.

Azura laughed. "You are probably correct," she said.

They were taken from the pool before any part of them had time to wrinkle. The nails on their fingers and toes were pared and their mons plucked. Agata was led away and found Nadim awaiting her with fresh garments. She blushed but the eunuch ignored her other than to hand her each piece of clothing as it was needed. In the meanwhile, Azura was led to a marble bench where a down mattress had been laid out for her to lie upon. Lotion was spread over her body in sections as the strong yet gentle hands of a young eunuch massaged her until she was almost asleep. She was content and relaxed.

Nadim was awaiting her with fresh garments. "This is called a kaftan," he told Azura. "You will find it very comfortable to wear and sleep in. I have sent your Agata to the kitchen to fetch the light meal I ordered for you earlier. She told me that neither of you has eaten this day." He slipped the kaftan over her head, drawing it down carefully.

"You have beautiful hair," he observed. "It is like the blackest silk."

"In my home city dark hair as mine is considered ordinary. It is the maidens with the golden and red hair who are praised," Azura told Nadim.

"And yet you are extraordinarily beautiful," the eunuch said.

"The prince tells me that the women of the harem spy on one another, and use the eunuchs to bring them information," Azura said to him. "Will you spy on me?"

"No," he told her without hesitation. "The fact that the prince has called for you to come to his bed tonight, ignoring tradition that requires his wives be brought to serve his needs in the order of their importance, tells me that you will eventually hold all the power in this harem. Ali Farid does not realize that yet, else he should not have sent me to you. I served your prince's mother until her death. Before she died she asked Prince Amir to keep me in his household always. He has, but because my history has been forgotten by the self-important, I have been only tolerated, and given the least important tasks to do.

"When the prince was home last and told us that a new wife would soon join the harem, I went to him secretly and begged to be appointed her eunuch. The prince remembered my long and faithful service to his mother then and brought me to Ali Farid, telling him I would be the eunuch to serve his new wife. Since I am considered unimportant, it was thought the new wife would also be unimportant. But this is not so, my lady Azura, is it? I suspect that you have the prince's heart. Once they become aware of it, the lady Maysun and the lady Shahdi will accept that you are the first lady of this harem. Until then they will seek to undermine you, for that is the way of the harem, and you should know it."

"The prince said they would welcome me," Azura told Nadim.

"Of course they will, for they have no other choice," the eunuch said. "But the prince does not live within the walls of his harem. The women do. If you will protect me from Ali

Farid, my lady Azura, I will protect you from the others. My best interests are served by my loyalty to you, and you alone."

"It is said that the Florentines are devious in their politics," Azura said to him, "but the intricacies of the harem are even more guileful, I see. I will take you at your word, Nadim, and I will place my trust in you. But if you betray me, be warned that my revenge will be swift and final."

"I am warned, my lady Azura, but you will have no need to lose your faith in me, for as I served Prince Amir's mother faithfully, so will I serve you," Nadim told her.

Chapter 14

They returned to her little apartment, where Agata was already waiting with a tray of food for them both. They sat upon pillows before the little table and ate. There was fresh warm bread, yogurt, a honeycomb, a bunch of green grapes, and hot mint tea. Nadim and Agata served Azura first, and when she had eaten her fill they finished the bounty that remained. Then the two women lay down to rest while Nadim sat cross-legged outside of his lady's quarters. He could hear the hum of voices coming from the salon at the end of the corridor. He concentrated hard in the silence and was able to make out the conversation going on.

"She is beautiful," the first wife, Maysun, said. She did not sound happy.

"Far too beautiful," the second wife, Shahdi, agreed.

"There is nothing we can do about it." Maysun spoke

again. "Perhaps she will become arrogant and difficult with his favor."

"It is to be hoped," Shahdi said. "Remember, we promised we would welcome her. I would not break our promise to the prince."

"We will welcome her given the opportunity, but first Ali Farid insisted we remain in our quarters. We could not meet her in the baths, and now that old eunuch who has been assigned to her guards her while she sleeps," Maysun replied.

"The eunuch is an old fool. He will not be of much use to her," Shahdi said, sounding very pleased.

Nadim grinned to himself in hearing her. *Stupid peasant. Daughter of a tribal chief, and so unimportant that the sultan passed you on to a grandson. What do you possibly know, kept here in a country harem?*

"The old eunuch once served our prince's mother," Maysun told her companion.

"A woman long dead and long forgotten. Wife to a rebellious prince who will mcct an unfortunate end one of these days," Shahdi said. "Praise Allah our prince is a more prudent man."

"What if she has a child?" Maysun asked.

"Surely she has been rendered sterile, even as we are," Shahdi replied. "The sultan wants no more rival claimants to his throne. That is why we were made sterile before we were given to our prince."

"This Azura is a foreigner," Maysun pointed out. "She is not a slave, and not of our world until now. He loves her, and if he loves her he will want a child of her."

"Is there no way we can render her as we are?" Shahdi

wondered. "Perhaps we should consult Ali Farid in this matter. There must be some poison we could introduce into her food or clothing that would make it impossible for her to bear our prince a child. At least then we should be as equals."

"Do nothing until I have thought long and hard on it," Maysun told her companion. "One child would not be so terrible, and it could just as easily be a daughter as a son. It might be nice for us to have a child to raise."

"You are too softhearted," Shahdi scolded.

"And you too quick to act," Maysun replied.

"Until we meet her we can't really know anything," Shahdi said.

"Perhaps when she has rested the old eunuch will bring her forth to meet us," Maysun said. "I think we should now go to the bath mistress, and see what she and her attendants have to say about this new wife our prince has taken."

Nadim heard the women getting up. He wasn't certain they wouldn't first return to their own little apartments, so he lowered his head and feigned sleep as he sat. But they did not come, going instead directly to the baths. He was pleased with what he had heard. Now he would be certain to personally prepare or oversee everything that his lady ate. He would have to warn her servingwoman not to accept any food gifts. Poisoned candy paste and fruit were favorite weapons among the harem women.

When Azura awoke she was briefly confused as to where she was, but then she remembered. She could not recall ever feeling so relaxed or so clean. And she was hungry. "Agata!" she called, and her servant came. "I am famished. Where is Nadim? He will know what to do about my hunger."

"I am here, my lady Azura," the old eunuch said. "Your

companion wives will eat shortly. Would you join them or remain here in private?"

"I think, as we are now a family, that I would do best to meet these women," she answered him.

"A wise decision," he told her. "They are curious, and a little afraid of your coming. The bath women have sung your praises. I would tell you if you do not know that the lady Maysun and the lady Shahdi are childless. They are not able to bear children. You, I believe, are. Do you wish to give your husband a child? Or would you like me to prepare you a daily draught that will prevent a child from being conceived?"

Azura's eyes widened with surprise. "No! No!" she cried softly. "I would give Amir a child of our love."

"Then say nothing of your heart's desire to either of the other wives. And take no food from their hand," Nadim warned her. "The harem of a prince can become a house of jealousy, especially if a favored woman can give her husband what others cannot. Do you understand what it is I am saying to you?"

Azura nodded.

"It seems to be the same the world over," Agata said in her native tongue. "In Florence poison is also a favorite weapon for women."

"What is it that your woman says?" the eunuch asked Azura.

"That poison is a woman's means even in our homeland. Her name is Agata, and she can speak a little of this new language, but it is difficult for her. It was not for me, although I know I will need to be corrected, and you must do it so I learn to speak properly," Azura told him. "If you remember to talk slowly when you address Agata, she will learn eventually."

"She already understands more than she lets on," the eunuch said with a small smile. "It is clever of her to feign ignorance. She will hear much that way that will be of use to you, my lady Azura."

"How can you be so certain of what you say?" Azura asked him.

"I watched her in the baths following the instructions of the attendants quite well while she stumbled over her own speech, making them laugh," he answered. "She will have to improve her skills with our language, and I will have to learn yours. Agata and I must work together to keep you safe and happy," Nadim told Azura.

"We will teach each other," Agata said, surprising the eunuch, but he chuckled.

"We will do well together, you and I," he told the serving-woman.

She nodded in agreement.

"Now come, my lady Azura, and I will bring you to the salon, where your companions now await you," Nadim told her.

The two women followed the eunuch from Azura's small apartment down the corridor and into the salon. The sun was already setting in the hills behind the Moonlight Serai. It dappled the dark waters of the sea before the palace. Maysun and Shahdi were seated, awaiting Azura's arrival.

"My ladies, I present to you your prince's new wife, the lady Azura," Nadim said.

The younger woman bowed from the waist. "I greet you, my lady Maysun, my lady Shahdi," she said in careful Turkish.

"Join us," Maysun invited. The bath women were right. Azura's skin was flawless. "We welcome you to your new home, Lady Azura."

"Yes, welcome," Shahdi echoed, not sounding as if she was entirely sincere.

"You have traveled a long distance to reach us. Our husband was most anxious to find and retrieve you," Maysun said. She looked to the hovering attendants, and nodded.

Almost immediately they disappeared, then reappeared several moments later with bowls and platters that were set upon the table around which the three women were seated. There was a roasted shank of lamb carved into small slices set upon a platter, bowls of saffron rice, yogurt, bread, and a large plate of fresh fruits.

Nadim watched as Maysun and Shahdi helped themselves, noting whether they favored one side of a bowl or platter. They did not. Nonetheless he personally picked the lamb slices for Azura, which he laid upon a piece of flat bread with some yogurt. He dipped his fingers into the bowl of rice, tasted it, and nodded to her.

"Your eunuch is overcautious," Maysun said.

"Indeed," Shahdi snorted. "This is not Istanbul."

Azura waved Nadim away with a little shake of her head, silently admonishing him. "He is kind, and takes his position most seriously," she said in a soft voice. "I find I am already grateful for his gentle care of me. This world of yours is new to me. I do not mean to offend, but I suspect women's behavior is much the same in Florence where I was born as it is here at the Moonlight Serai." She gave them a little smile.

"We are not a large household. The crime of poisoning could hardly go unchallenged here as it might in a great harem," Maysun said sharply. "Your eunuch is foolish to believe we would harm you. Both Shahdi and I were *given* women. You are a *chosen* woman. We have both known that eventually our husband would fall in love. I hope for all our sakes that we can get on, Azura."

"As do I," came the reply. "I am told you both come from cultures where a man is allowed, if he chooses, to have four wives. You certainly know that the world from which I come grants a man but one wife. Jealousy is an emotion that comes easily to women. Knowing that Amir can take favors from any of us must nonetheless be as difficult for you both as it will be for me. There was a brief time when he was mine alone," Azura said to them candidly. "Still, I was raised in a home with several sisters. I am used to the company of women, and am generally peaceable. But understand that if I am attacked, I will retaliate in kind. It is in my nature."

Shahdi laughed aloud. "You are very outspoken," she noted. "I may come to like you when I know you, Azura." *How clever she is,* Shahdi thought. *And strong. We will have a difficult time ridding ourselves of her, should we decide to do so.*

Maysun smiled. She took her position as Amir's first wife most seriously, but she was at heart a kind woman. "Tell us how you met Amir ibn Jem," she said.

So while they ate Azura told them a little bit of her life as Bianca Pietro d'Angelo, of her unfortunate marriage, and how she had come to meet the prince. They were fascinated by her recitation, and laughed to learn the part that the great hound, Darius, had played in bringing the two lovers together. Neither of them had ever bothered themselves with the dog. In the worlds from which they had come, dogs were not pets but used for hunting, herding, and guarding the villages. When the meal had been cleared away, they sat with small porcelain cups of mint tea exchanging histories.

Azura learned that Maysun was the younger sister of a

fierce Georgian warrior who, in admiring the great Ottoman Mehmet, who became known as the Conqueror, had offered his services, along with those of the warriors who followed him, to the sultan. Mehmet had graciously accepted the Georgian warlord's fealty, taking his sister into his own harem as a token of loyalty. That she was of little interest to the sultan did not distress her brother. She had been given and accepted as a token and pledge. Nothing more. Maysun had no illusions and understood her place in the world.

"I saw the Conqueror only once," Maysun told her companions, "when I was presented to him. After that I was absorbed into his large harem, an unimportant girl among many such as myself. I was very fortunate to be given to Amir ibn Jem. I know I am pretty, but I am no beauty to capture a man's heart as you are," Maysun concluded.

"My tale is not quite as hers," Shahdi said. "I am a Circassian. Our women are considered to be beauties in this part of the world. My father sold me when I was ten to one of our great slave merchants who decided I had promise. I was trained and then purchased by a warlord who was also pledging his fealty to the sultan. I was included in a great train of gifts and slaves this man sent to the Conqueror as a token of his good faith. Like Maysun, I ended up unnoticed until I was picked to be given to our prince.

"So many women are given to the sultan for his pleasure, but only a mere few ever are taken to his bed, and of those, fewer still manage to gain his personal favor, some briefly, but others longer. Being sent to the sultan's harem usually means a lonely life unless you are fortunate enough to be given away to another that the sultan wishes to honor, as we were given to our husband," Shahdi explained.

"What do the women of the harem do?" Azura asked her, curious.

"They spend their days beautifying themselves in the hopes that the sultan will notice them. Some, wiser than the others, find tasks to make them useful to the powers that rule the harem. Their lives are more interesting and fulfilling," Shahdi replied.

"There is so much about your world that I do not know," Azura said slowly. She loved Amir, but now she wondered if that would be enough.

"You have but to ask us if you are confused," Maysun said sweetly.

They had been kind enough, Azura thought afterwards as she prepared for bed. The kaftan had been taken from her and a gossamer-thin silk chemise with a high rounded neck and long full sleeves was given to her to sleep in. She was about to lie down when Nadim stepped aside to allow Ali Farid into the little chamber.

"The prince wishes your presence, Azura," he said. "Remove your sleeping garment, and come with me."

She looked to Nadim. He shook his head, and quickly drawing off her silk garment, handed it to Agata to store away. Undoing her single plait, he ran a brush through her long ebony hair. It shone in the lamplight as it fell in rippled waves down her back to the base of her spine. The faint fragrance of night-blooming moonflowers touched his nostrils. It was the perfect fragrance for her.

Ali Farid looked Azura over with a critical eye, then nodded. "You are a beautiful woman. No wonder our prince fell in love with you." Then he turned and hurried out.

Azura stood frozen, but then Nadim gave her a little push.

"Walk slowly, and with your head up," he murmured. "There is no one to see you, my lady Azura. This is our way."

Following his direction she walked out of her little apartment. Ali Farid led her from the harem wing down a softly lit corridor through a pair of great bronze doors.

They were in an antechamber. He pointed to a carved wooden door. "Your lord and master awaits you, lady. When he has taken his pleasure of you, you are to return to your own bed unless he invites you to remain. You will find Nadim waiting outside of these doors to lead you back." Then he turned about and left her.

Azura knocked at the carved door, opened it, and walked into Amir's bedchamber. She wanted to run to the bed and cover herself, but there was simply no avoiding her nudity. She glided across the floor as he watched her. He wanted to grin, for he could see her distress. She had given up much for him, not really knowing the world she was about to enter, and he could not bear for her to be unhappy now.

"Usually when called to her husband's bed, a wife crawls across the floor and up into the bed," he teased her as she slipped in next to him. He too was naked.

"That's almost as awful as it is ridiculous," Azura told him. Then without waiting another minute she kissed him full on the lips, pushing him back amid the pillows.

His strong arms wrapped about her, pulling her atop him. His hand smoothed down her graceful back and over her sweetly rounded buttocks. "I can see you have missed me, beloved," he said, laughing softly. She was so different from the other two, allowing her passion to bloom before his eyes while the others always remained restrained beneath him. It was he who had awakened her to love. It was she who had awakened him.

"That whole voyage was made worse by the beautiful landscapes we sailed past, the moonlit nights, and our inability to be together. I can see that you missed me as well, my husband," Azura told him, kissing him again. She sat up, straddling him boldly.

Reaching up, he captured a lock of her hair, bringing it to his lips to kiss. Her fragrance assailed him, but as much as he would have enjoyed taking her then and there, he wasn't going to do so. When they had first become lovers, in that brief, sweet time at Luce Stellare, he had been gentle with her, loving her in a way that would not frighten her. Now, however, she was his wife. Now she would learn that the man she was wed to was filled with great passion and lust for her.

He gazed up at her, smiling. She was so very beautiful. Her round breasts enchanted him. He leaned forward so he might kiss their dainty nipples, drawing her down just slightly in order to bury his face in the sweet valley between those breasts and inhale the fragrance of her skin. He had been hard before she even entered his bedchamber. Just thinking about Azura aroused him. No woman had ever affected him in the way that she did. No woman had ever had his love until Azura.

She pulled away again so she was just above him. The palms of her small hands glossed over his smooth bare chest, making little circles of movement. His skin was beautifully soft, but his body was also hard and sculpted beneath her touch. He lay perfectly still, enjoying her attentions. Her shapely thighs held him as if he were her mount.

His hand reached out to brush over her plump mons. Two

fingers pushed past her nether lips and beneath her, past her love jewel, gliding slowly into her wet sheath. He smiled a slow smile, seeing her eyes widen in surprise. "I want you to ride my fingers," he said softly as he sensuously stroked the hot hidden flesh that closed around those invasive digits. "Ride until I tell you to cease, Azura. This is but the first of the pleasures we shall share this evening, beloved." His dark blue eyes glittered wickedly.

At first she could not move. Her very breath seemed caught in her throat. He had never made such a request of her, touched her in such a voluptuous manner so that her body felt as if it would shatter with a word, a single touch. However, she had never before clambered atop him in so bold a fashion. The sensation of those two fingers inside of her was acute and very exciting. She obeyed his command without another word.

Azura felt deliciously wicked as she began to move her body just slightly so that the fingers now buried deep inside her began to mimic her rhythm, stroking her, fanning the flames of her increasing desire. Her eyes closed, and with each subtle movement she made, her need increased. She moved faster, faster, faster until suddenly she felt the walls of her sheath convulsing around his fingers. She shuddered with release, and felt her cheeks grow hot with the realization of what had just transpired. *"Oh! Oh! Oh!"* Azura gasped as another and final tremor wracked her.

Amir's fingers slid from her body. He pulled her down, rolling her onto her back.

"A sweet beginning, beloved," he murmured in her ear, kissing it, his breath hot, nibbling on the fleshy little lobe. "You are a most obedient wife, Azura," he teased.

She opened her aquamarine eyes and looked up at him.

"You treated me with more delicacy in my villa by the sea," Azura said to him.

"You were a properly raised Florentine woman, a young widow, with only a cruel and crude knowledge of passion. I think I would have frightened you to death had I been as bold then as I will be now," Amir told her.

"Now that I am the infidel's wife," she said softly.

"Yes, you are my wife, beloved. Mine! I will open those beautiful jeweled eyes of yours to the many sweet ways that lovemaking can be pursued," he told her.

She smiled up at him and said simply, "I adore you, Amir. Teach me to please you, and please me as you will. I have no fear of your love, for I know you will never hurt me. I trust in you, my love, so much so that I am willing to share you with your other wives."

"Never bring them into this chamber when we are together, Azura," he said gently. "I will always hold them in my esteem, but it is you that I will forever love."

Then he kissed her, his lips proving as they moved over hers the truth of the words that he had just spoken. Everything about her excited him. Her exotic scent, her silken hair, the very warmth of her sweet nature, her growing wisdom, her kind heart.

They could not seem to cease from caressing each other. He cupped her breasts in his two hands. She stroked his cock with teasing fingers. Their bodies twined and untwined, learning and relearning. Their tongues tasted each other's flesh, licking, nipping, their soft moans of longing echoing in the air. The time and the distance that had separated them had only increased the passion they felt for each other.

Finally Azura took his handsome face between her two

hands, scattering little kisses across his eyelids, the bridge of his long nose, and across his thin but sensuous mouth. "Am I shameless that I can wait no longer?" she asked him.

In answer he covered her with his body, sliding into her welcoming sheath. "Am I?" he countered, smiling. "I have waited too long for you to return to me, beloved." Then he began to move on her, slowly pressing forward, slowly withdrawing, over and over and over again until she wrapped her limbs about his torso. Her nails raking down his long back, she hissed one word at him.

"Faster!"

With a growl of delight he complied, his cock flashing back and forth with increasing rapidity.

Azura's eyes closed as she began to drown in pleasure. She reveled in the sensation of his thickness, his length, the fire he was arousing within her very soul. His body felt so solid beneath her hands, beneath her legs as they squeezed him. She could not remember being filled with such deeply felt gratification. It had always been wonderful with him, but suddenly it was beyond that. Her head was spinning with such intense feelings she wasn't certain she could survive it.

"Amir! Ohh, Amir!" she cried out as the sensation of being swept up into the heavens overcame her.

He groaned deeply. He couldn't seem to get enough of her. He thrust harder and deeper until his swollen manhood cried its surrender, exploding, his heated juices filling her hidden garden, overflowing onto the bedding beneath them. He could scarcely catch his breath. He was suddenly both exhausted and filled with contentment. When her legs fell away from his torso, he wrapped his arms about her, drawing her so close she protested, but only faintly. Then they both fell into a deep sleep.

Towards the dawn, Ali Farid came to find Nadim seated cross-legged outside the prince's bedchamber door. "Why have you not escorted your mistress back to her own bedchamber?" he demanded of the old eunuch.

"They are not yet ready to be separated," Nadim told the head harem eunuch.

"He has never lingered so long with the other two," Ali Farid said, puzzled. "In fact he has taken his pleasure quickly, and then dismissed them."

"He does not love the other two," Nadim replied. "He does love my mistress, the lady Azura. She has his heart."

Ali Farid nodded slowly. The old eunuch could be correct, and if he was, no matter that Maysun and Shahdi were the first and second wives. It would be Azura, the third wife, who would hold the power in the harem. He would watch and think on this new information. "Continue to wait," he said to Nadim.

When the sunlight finally filled the room outside the prince's bedchamber, the door opened. Nadim was instantly upon his feet, surprisingly agile for his age. He draped a soft cotton kaftan over Azura, and wordlessly led her from her husband's quarters to the harem bath, where she was bathed, and then to her own small bedchamber where she lay down and slept for several hours. When she awoke there was a meal awaiting her.

The harem quarters were quiet. She called for Agata, and together they went out into the gardens. There they found Maysun and Shahdi carefully pruning some rosebushes. The two other wives greeted Azura with cheerful smiles, and Maysun suggested that they walk together, handing her shears to an attending gardener.

"You pleased him well last night," she told Azura. "We heard him singing this morning. It is rare that he sings." The truth was that they had never heard him sing.

Azura blushed. Having her intimate moments with Amir discussed so openly by another woman was a new experience. She wasn't certain it was something she would become used to, and she was not certain what to say in return. The other two wives took her silence as modesty, and were well pleased by it.

"You have made him happy again, which means all here at the Moonlight Serai can be happy," Shahdi added. Secretly she was a little annoyed, for she had believed their husband was content before Azura came. Now it would appear he had not been. Why could she and Maysun not be enough for an unimportant prince who avoided both battle and the responsibilities of his great family?

"I am glad, then," Azura replied, finally realizing that the two older wives appreciated her demure manner.

"You have not been trained in the way of harem women," Maysun said. "I have heard that proper women from the West come to their husband's beds as virgins, but know nothing of how to make love. They rely on their men to teach them these things. You had a husband once, didn't you?"

"Yes, a cruel man," Azura said. "His manners with me were depraved and corrupt. When my mother learned of it she stole me from him, hid me away, and my family attempted to have the union dissolved. It was then I met Prince Amir. We became friends, but not lovers, as I was a married woman even if I did not live with my husband. Eventually my husband found me. He beat me, but the women who served me drove him from my house. He was returning to Florence to get aid in his attempt to bring me back when he was murdered upon the road."

"By robbers?" Shahdi asked. "Or enemies? Or was it your family?"

"It was not a robbery, for his jewelry remained upon his person, and his full purse was still on his belt," Azura said. "No one has ever found out who killed him. His reputation was such that no one, even his grown sons, cared. They were glad he was dead. He was an evil man, and had no real friends."

"Being a virtual innocent then was quite permissible," Maysun said, "but now we share a husband. We would be remiss if we did not school you in harem ways. Amir loves you, but as with all men, love is not enough. We will teach you how to entertain him like a good Turkish wife. He must not get bored, and seek a larger harem."

"You mean a fourth wife?" Azura asked.

"It isn't just another wife we must all consider," Maysun said.

"He could add other women, such as concubines, to this harem," Shahdi explained. "He wouldn't have to give them the status of wife as he has given the three of us, but he may have other women. You must learn how to keep him happy, Azura, for all of us."

Agata snorted at this, and spoke in their native Florentine dialect. "They would put a great deal of responsibility upon you," she grumbled. "I do not know if I would trust these two. What is it they wish to teach you? Will it be proper behavior, or will it shock the prince, causing you a loss of his favor?"

"I think I can trust Nadim to guide me," Azura replied. "I believe these two mean well. They have no illusions about Amir's love for them or his love for me."

"What is it your woman says?" Maysun asked.

"This new language is difficult for her," Azura explained. "She wanted to know exactly what it was you were saying to me. She has been with me for many years, and did not have to follow me here, for my younger sister would have taken her into her service in Venice. But she came, and like a mother is protective of me."

"Ahh," Maysun said, smiling and reaching out to pat Agata's arm reassuringly. "You need not worry, faithful one," she said. "We mean your lady no harm."

Agata nodded enthusiastically, smiling back. "I understand now, lady," she told the first wife in halting Turkish. "Thank you! Thank you!"

It was a very credible performance, Azura thought. As far as Maysun and Shahdi were concerned, Agata was a devoted retainer, even if she was not too clever.

"In a few days' time when you have settled yourself," Maysun said, "we will begin to teach you the many ways in which a woman can pleasure and please a man."

"I will be happy to have my ignorance corrected and hope to be a good student of your wisdom," Azura assured the first wife.

Over the next few days Maysun became more reassured by the respectful attitude exhibited by the new third wife. Bianca was a kind woman at heart. Shahdi, however, remained wary and suspicious. She had secretly hoped one day to win Amir's heart, and especially now that he seemed to be home for good. Azura's arrival had given her pause for thought. Shahdi wondered if she could win Amir away from the lovely Azura, or if he might come to share his heart with her as well. She must rethink her strategy.

Both women might privately resent the fact that their shared husband called Azura to his bed each night, but her manner was so sweet, and the truth was that Amir was the master of the house. They had no choice in the matter at all. But Azura was sensitive to the two other women who had struggled against their own jealousies and fears to welcome her. She could see that Shahdi in particular was having a difficult time despite the gentle Maysun's efforts to keep her calm.

"You cannot keep calling only me to your bed, my love," she chided him several nights later as they lay together recovering from an enthusiastic bout of passion.

"Yes, I can," he said. "I respect their position in my life, but you are the woman I love and adore, beloved."

"You are behaving like a child with a new toy," she replied, scolding him further. "All women need tenderness. They have made your home a pleasant place to live. And before I came into your life they gave you their bodies to slake your lusts. You cannot simply ignore them now. If not for their sakes, then for mine, take them to your bed as well, my dearest husband. If you do not, they will one day resent you. They have no children upon which to lavish their love and attentions, Amir. They never will. Be kind to Maysun and Shahdi, for they have been good wives to you."

"I have spent more time in your world than my own these last few years," he said. "My own mother was English, and my father's favorite. I have come to see that there is as much wisdom in having one wife as in having three," Amir admitted. "Yet you, beloved, raised in your strict society, have a more open heart than I do. When your moon link breaks I will entertain the other two. I promise." He caressed her face with a gentle hand. "Will you give me a child, beloved?" the prince asked her.

"If God wills it I will most gladly," Azura answered him.

"A daughter," he told her. "Do not give me a son."

"All men want sons," she said, surprised.

"Not I," he told her. "I would have a daughter as beautiful as her mother."

Azura could not help but repeat his odd request to Maysun and Shahdi. "Why would he not want a son?" she asked them.

"Ahh," Maysun replied, "if he were anyone but the sultan's grandson he would want a son, but the blood running through his veins is ambitious and warlike. The Ottoman rulers always fight for their throne. Our own sultan has two sons who quarrel over which of them will inherit. Our husband's father, Prince Jem, is a skilled warrior who leads his own men into battle. His half brother, Bayezit, however, is wiser. He delegates only the best generals to lead his troops.

"Prince Bayezit already has several sons, of whom one, Selim, is also among his grandfather's favorites, as is our husband. Our prince believes his uncle Bayezit will inherit Sultan Mehmet's throne. When that happens, he could follow a family tradition and slay all other male claimants to the throne but his own offspring; sometimes even a troublesome son is strangled. This is why Amir ibn Jem wants no sons. A princess of the royal house has value to the sultan. Another prince is but a rival for the throne."

"Then Amir could be killed when the old sultan dies," Azura said fearfully.

"Our husband is safer than most princes," Maysun replied. "He has never shown any ambitions. His uncle is also fond of his brother. Our lord husband is cleverer than most. If he thought he was in danger, he would flee."

"Then I shall pray for a daughter," Azura said.

"What kind of a world is this we are now in?" Agata grumbled in her own tongue.

"It is no better or worse than the worlds we have known in Florence and Venice, where poisoning and assassinations are almost an art," Azura answered her.

"But to murder your male relations when you gain a throne is barbaric," the servingwoman responded.

"I think it is probably very efficient," Azura said slowly, thinking about it. "You don't want to waste all your time and resources quarreling and fighting with your relations over your throne. A ruler wants to rule, and for his people's sake he must. Removing the troublemakers is probably best, although I would at least give them a chance before I did." She chuckled. "We must both pray if God gives me a child that it be a little princess, and not a troublesome prince."

Chapter 15

*F*earful for her mistress's safety, Agata consulted Nadim. "If my lady has a son they both stand in danger," she fretted, having now learned that often the wives of unwanted princes were also disposed of by a new sultan. "Only God can predict the child's sex. Better there be no child then."

"Your mistress is young yet," Nadim said. "There is time for a child when she can feel safer. If she birthed a son and there was danger, the prince would not leave them behind. Still we can prevent any conception temporarily, Agata. Is that what you wish?"

"In Florence there was a woman who made a potion to do just that. My aunt, Fabia, sought just such a nostrum for my mistress's mother when she wished to rest between the births of her seven children."

"Yes, there are such things available here as well," Nadim said. "Would you have me find such elixir for our lady?"

"Oh, Nadim," Agata replied, worrying aloud. "Do we dare to interfere with God's will if we do this? And yet I fear for my mistress."

"There is no harm in protecting her for the interim, Agata," the old eunuch said, soothing the servingwoman.

"It will not render her sterile like the others, will it?" Agata asked.

"Maysun and Shahdi were made sterile by a physician in the sultan's house," Nadim explained. "Our potion will simply prevent a child temporarily."

"Then we must do it," Agata replied.

"First you must make certain she is not already with child. The prince has used Azura most regularly and enthusiastically since she arrived," the eunuch pointed out.

"Her moon link broke this morning," Agata said.

"It was on time?" he asked.

"Exactly. She will bleed for four days. No more," Agata told him.

"Then tomorrow you will begin giving her a *strengthening* drink," Nadim said. "I will gather the ingredients myself and mix it for you before she awakens."

Agata nodded her agreement.

For the first time in many months her mistress was happy. She was wed to the man she loved, and if she had lost her family by this action she had gained a new one. Used to the company of other women, Azura was comfortable with Maysun and Shahdi. The three women had settled into a reasonably easeful relationship. Maysun actually seemed content with the situation. Shahdi waited and watched for what she hoped would eventually be her turn.

While the first two wives knew that Amir loved Azura

above all others, her presence had brought him home again. He had not been able to take them to Florence, for two women, each called wife, would not have been tolerated, even if he was a foreigner. After several years of being alone for most of the year, Maysun and Shahdi were content to have him back, to have his attentions if only for a few days a month. There was always the chance that Amir would get a child on Azura. Then the first two would share him until well after the child was born.

Amir found himself pleased at how well his household had settled itself with the addition of Azura to his harem. He hunted. He rode and oftentimes he took Azura with him, which at first surprised Maysun and Shahdi. While they had both been raised in a tribal atmosphere, it was the rare woman who rode a horse. Women walked or rode in carts. They watched from a terrace now as Azura and Amir, accompanied by Darius, raced along the sandy edge of the stony beach below their small palace. Their enjoyment of the scene was suddenly interrupted by Diya al Din.

"Are they on the beach?" he asked, looking down to see for himself. "You!" He reached out to grasp at a servant's arm. "Go down and tell the master he must come at once. A messenger has just come from Istanbul. Hurry! Run!" Turning, he said to the two women, "Go back to the harem, ladies."

"What messenger?" Maysun asked him.

"This is not your concern, woman," the head eunuch said.

"Do not be so pompous, Diya al Din," Shahdi told him. "If it has to do with our husband, then it is most certainly our concern."

"I do not know what the missive he carries says, but he

wears the badge of our great lord and master, Sultan Mehmet," the head eunuch responded. "The sultan is old. Who knows what it is about, but until the prince comes we must wait for answers, and pray there are no Janissaries behind this messenger."

"Better we pray the sultan's gardeners are not behind the messenger," Maysun said nervously.

"Allah forfend!" Shahdi cried, frightened, for she knew, as did everyone, that the men who so lovingly tended the sultan's gardens were also his personal executioners.

"There is no need to fret," Diya al Din said, with more conviction than he felt.

"Where is this messenger?" Maysun asked.

"I have put him in the prince's antechamber," Diya al Din told her.

"There is a spy hole into that chamber," Shahdi murmured. She caught Maysun's hand. "Let us go now so we may watch and listen."

"I will come with you," Diya al Din said. "I was not aware there was a spy hole there, ladies. How did you know it?"

Shahdi smiled mischievously, but did not answer him.

The three hurried to the prince's apartments and secreted themselves so they might listen. They could see the messenger pacing back and forth as he waited for Prince Amir. When the recipient of the message entered the chamber, the messenger bowed and slipped down upon one knee, holding out the rolled parchment to Amir. He took it, opened it, read it, and then said, "How long did it take you to come from Istanbul?"

"Two days, Highness. I rode hard," was the reply.

"Do you know if the sultan still lives?" Amir asked.

The messenger shook his head. "He was not in Istanbul,

Highness, but had crossed over to Bursa and begun his spring campaign."

"Then who sent you?" Amir wanted to know.

"I do not know, Highness. I was simply dispatched from the palace," was the reply.

"This is not good. Not good at all," Diya al Din murmured softly.

"*Hush!*" Maysun hissed at the eunuch.

Realizing that the messenger was just that, and knew nothing more, the prince sent him to the kitchens to be fed. There was no reply necessary to the information he had just received. "Go and eat. Rest the night before returning to Istanbul," he told the man.

The messenger arose, bowed, and went off. Amir read once again the parchment he had received. Azura slipped from an alcove where she had been standing and went to her husband. She looked up at him questioningly, a gentle hand on his arm.

"Go and find the others," he instructed her, "and tell Diya al Din to gather the household. I will speak with them all."

While he spoke, those hidden at the spy hole hurried off to be where they should be. Azura came into the harem and called to her two companions. "I know no more than you do," she said. "Come, and let us learn what the message brought to our husband said."

"What message?" Shahdi asked innocently.

Azura laughed. "Do not dissemble with me, Shahdi. I found that spy hole weeks ago. Florentine homes tend to have them, and I recognized the difference in the texture of the wall," she told them. "And I heard you. Even using his softest voice, Diya al Din is recognizable. How did you know the spy hole was there?"

Maysun chuckled at the chagrined look on Shahdi's face, but said nothing.

"There was nothing to do all those years our husband was away. I know this little palace inside and out. Probably better than anyone," Shahdi admitted.

Together the three women joined their husband and the gathered household in the salon used for visitors.

"I have received a message from Istanbul," Amir began. "The sultan had only just begun his spring campaign when he took seriously ill. I cannot tell you if he yet lives, or has passed into the next life. My uncle, Prince Bayezit, was with him. I expect we will hear something further in the coming days."

A low moaning arose from the house slaves, and even the two chief eunuchs looked distressed by what they had just heard.

"There is nothing to fear," Prince Amir assured them. "Go now about your duties. Diya al Din, see that a watch is set on the road both day and night. I want no more surprise visitors." He turned to his women. "Come," he said and left the room, returning with them to the harem quarters, where he sat down in the women's dayroom, inviting them to join him. He would elucidate further in private with them.

Maysun told the slaves to bring mint tea and sweet cakes. When they had, she dismissed them, asking Agata to make certain they went. Shahdi took Amir's small turban from his head while Azura settled the pillows about and around him. The refreshments came and finally Amir spoke to them.

"If he dies there will be a struggle for the succession," he told them. "My uncle will win, for while my father is the better tactician, the Janissaries are on my uncle's side. He knows how to delegate authority far better than my father, who is too modern a man and looks to the West. My uncle, while forward-thinking, is a traditionalist. The Janissaries prefer tradition, like campaigning in the spring."

"You will have to tread lightly," Maysun warned.

"What if your uncle sends his gardeners to you?" Shahdi asked.

"I do not believe he will, since I have no intention of supporting my father," Amir replied. "Bayezit is a fair man and he knows me well."

"He has three living sons," Maysun reminded Amir.

"From three different mothers, and of the three only my cousin Selim is suited to rule. Ahmed enjoys life too much, and Korkut is a scholar."

"Selim is the youngest," Shahdi noted.

"If my grandfather has died, it is my uncle who will rule. His sons will have to wait their turn," Amir said, "and Selim will be vigilant, I am certain."

"You are the eldest of Mehmet's grandsons," Maysun pointed out.

"And the least interested in either ruling or fighting, as is well known by all," he told her. "I am not considered fit to rule. My mother learned the way of the harem quickly, and knew how to help a son survive. All who are important are aware that Prince Jem's son is a disappointment to him, giving his unquestioned loyalty to the sultan first, and preferring to dabble in carpets and antiquities, not warfare and power. I have been called the un-Ottoman," he said with a small smile.

It was then that Azura spoke up. "You cannot know what your uncle will do, my lord, no matter his past friendship with you. You must be on your guard, at least for the interim. We need to plan an escape should we have no other choice."

They looked at her, surprised.

"Do you understand the situation, then, Azura?" Shahdi asked her.

"I am Florentine," Azura answered her. "Deception is in our blood where matters of survival or profit are concerned. I understand very well what is happening. I did not defy my family to become Amir's wife only to lose him." She turned to him. "We must prepare for whatever is to happen, my lord."

"The Moonlight Serai is not a castle. It is a pleasure palace, and as such it provides us no real defenses, as a castle might," he explained to her.

"Then we should go," Azura said.

"No," he responded. "To flee would be to proclaim I was guilty of some crime. I will not do that. I will trust in my uncle's goodwill. Someone in my grandfather's palace sent to warn me of the changes that might take place. I will remain and show my loyalty to the new sultan, whoever he may be— if indeed my grandfather is dead."

Still, he made certain that Diya al Din posted slaves on the hills to give them advance warning of any visitors.

They heard nothing for the next few weeks. Spring moved into early summer.

Finally, late one June morning, the watchers on the hills surrounding the Moonlight Serai began signaling from one to another and finally to the little palace itself that a large party of riders was approaching. Amir sent word to his wives, and then they waited—Amir in his own quarters, the three women in theirs.

"It will be the Janissaries," Maysun said, and Shahdi nodded.

"Why are you so afraid of these Janissaries?" Azura asked. "You speak of them as if they were the devil's own soldiers."

"They are!" Shahdi replied.

"The Janissaries are the young sons of Christians taken in war," Maysun explained. "They are then cosseted and cared for with great kindness, converted to Islam, and finally trained in the fiercest warfare and taught total loyalty to the sultan. Whomever the Janissaries follow will be sultan. If truth be told, the Conqueror preferred Jem among his sons because of his warlike proclivities, despite the fact that the prince was always rebelling against his father. But the Janissaries lean towards Bayezit, for he embodies the old traditions of the Ottomans. It is likely the Janissaries approaching this palace have been sent by Bayezit to either ascertain our husband's position in the succession or kill us all."

For this she had fled Florence, fled Venice, given up her family? To die at the hands of strangers in some stupid war over a succession? Azura felt fear filling her. Angrily she forced it back down. "We are not going to die," she said.

"No," Shahdi replied. "With luck, after we are all raped, we'll be given to some officer or sold to add coinage to the Janissaries' already fat coffers."

Maysun gave a little sob.

"Stop it, both of you!" Azura said. "No one is going to die today. What a pair of silly ewe sheep you two are. I am going to the spy hole in our husband's apartment to learn what is happening. Don't tell Ali Farid if you can find him. I expect he has hidden himself away by now. Agata, come with me!"

The two women hurried from the harem apartments, making their way quickly to Prince Amir's quarters. The corridors of the little palace were empty and quiet, for all but the bravest among the slaves would have hidden themselves by now. Quietly Azura and Agata secreted themselves within the narrow confines of the spy hole. Amir was pacing his antechamber with slow, measured steps. He was dressed soberly in a dark blue silk robe trimmed with silver embroidery. His head was covered by a small matching turban. Azura worried that he might look too regal.

They heard the sound of booted feet in the corridor. Agata reached out to clutch at her mistress's sleeve. Azura stared intently through the spy hole, her eyes meeting those of Amir. He knew she was there. The large double doors to the prince's apartment were flung open by two frightened slaves who nonetheless had remained. Diya al Din was with them. He was ashen in color but he too had stayed.

"My lord prince," the head eunuch spoke. "You have visitors."

A Janissary captain stepped forward. He bowed respectfully. "Prince Amir, I am Captain Mahmud, sent by your uncle, Sultan Bayezit," he began.

"Is my grandfather dead?" Amir asked the captain.

"The Conqueror died on the fourth of May at the hour of afternoon prayer," Captain Mahmud said.

Amir briefly closed his eyes, his lips moving in a silent prayer. When he opened his eyes again he looked directly at the Janissary. "How may I serve the sultan?" he asked the man before him.

"I have no instructions other than to deliver my message to you, Highness," was the reply. Captain Mahmud understood the delicate position of this Ottoman prince.

The prince turned briefly to Diya al Din. "See that the

captain's men are well fed, and their horses taken care of," Amir instructed the head of his household staff.

The eunuch bowed. "At once, my prince," he replied.

Amir now turned his attention back to the Janissary. "I am grateful that my uncle thought to send me word," he said.

Captain Mahmud's lips twitched with amusement but he answered politely, "And I am grateful for your hospitality, as my men will be. We will, however, begin our return to the capital as soon as they have eaten and the horses have been taken care of by your slaves."

"My wives will be relieved," Amir responded with a grin. "The approach of your troop frightened them."

"I hope the children were not afraid," Captain Mahmud said.

"There are no children," Amir replied. "But come and join me in some refreshment." He clapped his hands, and to his relief his slaves hurried in with sweet, cold fruit sherbets and a light meal of roasted chicken, saffron rice, and warm flat bread with a dish of yogurt mixed with dill and cucumbers for dipping.

The two men sat companionably upon the cushions about a small ebony-and-ivory-inlaid table.

"Women with children tend to give all their attention to their offspring," Captain Mahmud noted. "Women without children give all their attention to their lord and master. That is a good thing, eh, Highness?" And he chuckled.

Amir nodded. "I must admit my wives spoil me terribly, and I feel no lack at being childless," he said. Then he leaned forward, dipping a piece of bread in the sauce, putting it in his mouth, and chewing it thoughtfully. "Tell me what is happening, Captain. I cannot believe my father has taken my uncle's decision either lightly or easily."

Captain Mahmud put a piece of chicken in his mouth and scooped up some rice. "No," he said, then swallowed. "Your uncle managed to reach Istanbul first, where we had already taken control of the city for him."

"My grandfather's Grand Vizier favored my father," Amir remarked.

"We executed him before the new sultan arrived in the city, and also intercepted and executed his emissaries to Prince Jem," Captain Mahmud said.

All but one, Amir thought, realizing now who had sent the messenger to him warning him of the changes to come. "And my father?" he asked.

"Is rousing the Turcoman tribes to fight for supremacy in this quarrel," the Janissary captain said. "I must admit to admiring Prince Jem's fiery spirit, Highness, but he will not prevail."

"No," Amir said, "he will not. Does my uncle wish me to return to Istanbul with you?"

"No, no, that is not necessary, Highness. You are content here in your little palace, and the sultan knows he has your complete and total loyalty," Captain Mahmud replied, smiling toothily.

"Indeed, the sultan does have my complete loyalty," Amir responded.

"Then there is nothing more to say," Captain Mahmud answered.

As he had ceased eating, a slave brought a bowl of rose water and a linen napkin for his hands. The Janissary washed the grease and other food residue from his fingers, and dried them. Amir did the same. Then both men rose as Diya al Din came to tell his master that the Janissary troop had been fed and their mounts cared for, and were now ready to depart.

"Let me escort you to your horse," Amir said. "Please convey to my uncle, the sultan, my grateful thanks for sending me word of what is transpiring. He has honored my house." The prince bowed to Captain Mahmud, who bowed in return before mounting his animal. Amir stood politely as the Janissary troop, in their distinctive red and green uniforms upon their brown horses, wheeled about and galloped off. "Make certain they go," the prince instructed his head eunuch. "Send to the watchers on the hillsides to be certain. Tell them they are to remain at their posts until I instruct them otherwise."

"At once, Highness," Diya al Din said.

"Then gather the slaves so I may tell them what they should know," Amir told the eunuch before returning back into his home and going to the harem quarters, where his women awaited him anxiously.

Azura came immediately to him, and his arms wrapped about her briefly. "I listened," she said.

"I know," he answered, then drew her down onto the cushions with the others. "Sultan Mehmet is no more," he told them. "My uncle has seized the throne, and is now Sultan Bayezit. My father is already fighting him, but I believe we are safe. My uncle knows I will not join my father. I have no soldiers or adherents to trouble the sultan. There are no heirs of my body. I am no threat to Bayezit."

"Then why did he find it necessary to send a full troop of Janissaries to tell you of your grandfather's passing?" the suspicious Shahdi wanted to know.

"My uncle was displaying his newfound power," Amir

replied with a chuckle. "He knows my home is not defendable. He was showing me his authority over us."

"Are the Janissaries really gone?" Azura asked.

"I believe so, but the watchers on our hills will tell us if they have not returned. From now on I shall keep a watch so that we will not be taken unawares."

"What will happen if your father does not cease his strife?" Maysun wanted to know. "Will the sultan punish us?"

"My uncle is a patient man, more like his grandfather Sultan Murad," Amir answered his first wife. He could see his women were frightened by this new turn of events, and it disturbed him that they should be so. "The sultan will find a way to quiet my father's ambitions," he assured them.

But Prince Jem was a determined man. Where Bayezit was more serious, patient, and contemplative, his brother was a more romantic figure, a brilliant soldier, and oddly an extremely talented poet. Bayezit held to the great traditions of the Ottoman, which was why the Janissaries favored him so greatly. Jem, however, looked to Western Europe and change. The Janissaries did not want change.

Jem raised a force of Turcoman warriors and captured the city of Bursa, declaring himself sultan. He reigned supreme for almost three weeks. He offered to split the empire with Bayezit. Jem would rule in Asia and Bayezit in Europe. The sultan in Istanbul instead appointed the great Janissary hero, Gedik Ahmed Pasha, to lead his troops against Prince Jem. Bayezit was the first of the Ottoman sultans not to lead his own soldiers, but to instead send a competent commander. Twice, Jem was defeated, but Gedik Pasha could not capture him, and Jem was finally driven into exile.

But even in exile, he agitated resentments against his

brother. Amir's trading vessels brought him word of his father's travels as he escaped. Jem moved through Jerusalem to Cairo, where he sought sanctuary with the Mamluk sultan, Kait Bey. He made a holy pilgrimage to Mecca and Medina, then returned to Ottoman territory to once more attempt to wrest the throne from his brother. This time, however, his army deserted him before the gates of the city of Angora. Jem fled south to the Cilicia and the Mediterranean.

Still, the sultan tried to appease his brother, offering him a generous income. "The empire is a bride that cannot be shared between two rivals," he told Jem. Bayezit was saddened when his sibling, refusing to understand, sought refuge with the Knights Hospitaliers on the island of Rhodes. Of course he was received with honor, the Christians delighted to have the sultan's brother in their midst to use as a pawn. The sultan then signed a treaty with the order's Grand Master paying the knights forty-five thousand pieces of gold each year Prince Jem remained in their care.

Word of all of this filtered back to Prince Amir in bits and pieces. It came via his own trading ship captains, who were instructed to learn all they could of Prince Jem's activities. Amir did not intend being taken unawares if he could avoid it. He was not of a mind to suffer for his father's rebellions. His uncle was being very patient, but eventually the sultan would lose his patience. He had done everything to pacify his brother, but Jem refused to be mollified.

But to Amir's relief, his uncle did not seem to consider his nephew culpable for his father's actions. Captain Mahmud's Janissary troop had gone back to Istanbul. Life at the Moonlight Serai took on a regular and almost placid pace. The prince's trading vessels came and went regularly. The seasons came and went. Azura often thought how surprised her mother would be to learn of the quiet life her daughter now lived. She wondered if Francesca had managed to capture Enzo's heart; how her younger sisters were growing up. Did they ever think of her? Or was Orianna so angered at having been foiled in her plans for the daughter she had named Bianca that her name was never spoken in the palazzo of the Pietro d'Angelos?

And then one day she was surprised in a way she had not expected. Her husband came to her after speaking with one of his vessel captains. He carried a sealed letter, which he handed to her. Azura took it from him, a questioning look upon her face.

"What is this?" she asked him.

"Someone has written to you," he answered. "It was given to one of my captains in Bursa, beloved. Open it."

Azura broke the wax seal and unfolded the parchment. Her eyes widened at the familiar hand. "It is from my brother Marco," she told him as she quickly scanned the missive. "He would come and see me, Amir."

She saw the prince's face tighten with suppressed anger, and quickly said, "I do not need to see him, Amir. We will ignore this." She slowly folded the parchment.

"I wonder what he was doing in Bursa," she said, almost to herself.

"The Silk Road comes to an end in Bursa. He was undoubtedly there on your father's business," Amir told her.

"But how did he know how to find me?" Azura wondered.

"He undoubtedly learned of my ships, and sought out any of my captains in that port," the prince reasoned. "That was very clever of him."

"I never thought Marco particularly clever," Azura said drily.

"Do you want to see him?" Amir asked her.

"I do," she admitted, "but if it disturbs you, I will not. Perhaps it is better to let sleeping dogs lie, my lord."

"No!" he replied, swallowing his pride and his anger that Azura's family was again attempting to interfere in their lives. "Your family is curious, and will once more attempt to lure you back to them. Let him come! I will not release you, beloved. I will not!"

Now Azura laughed, and slid her arms about his neck, her body pressing against his. "I don't want to go back, Amir, my dearest love. I am simply curious about why Marco has chosen this moment to contact me, although he is undoubtedly curious about this life I live with you. I held him responsible for my marriage to Rovere. I believe he wants to see if I am happy with you. If you would have him come, then let it be according to your word. I am content to abide by it." She kissed him a long, sweet kiss.

Wrapping his arms about her, he enjoyed the kiss. How long had they been together now? Almost three years, and he was as happy now as the day he had brought her to the Moonlight Serai. No, happier, he reconsidered. "He may come, but he must sleep on the ship that brings him. I'll tell my captain." He kissed her a long, hard kiss.

How vulnerable he is, Azura suddenly thought, *enjoying his possession.* "Of course, my dearest lord."

"He will not meet the others," Amir said.

"Certainly not!" Azura responded, shocked. She had come to have certain Turkish sensibilities. A man's harem was sacrosanct.

"And you will visit with each other in the salon used for visitors," Amir told her.

"Perhaps the garden as well," she suggested.

"If your companion wives do not wish to walk," he added.

"You are most generous, my lord," she said.

"You are making fun of me," he accused her.

"This is my older brother who wishes to visit, Amir, not a former suitor," she replied, laughing softly.

"Any other man who attempted to visit you who is not my uncle or my father would find himself with his throat slit," the prince told her seriously.

"Then I shall certainly tell Marco not to reveal the location of my home to anyone else, my lord," she said. "I should not want the blood of innocents on my hands."

"Azura, this is serious," he said. "It is unusual for the family of a woman such as yourself to come visiting under such circumstances. I don't want to allow your brother here, but I can see it means a great deal to you. I will always strive to please you, beloved." He sighed. "You know how much I love you."

"Loving me does not mean just possessing me, Amir," she said, gently chiding him. "You must trust me, for I would never betray you in any way. I have an opportunity to do what so many women who are brought to the empire do not. I can tell my family I am well, and gloriously happy with you. Happier than I have ever been in all of my life. Being your wife suits me even if I must share you with Maysun and Shahdi. That is what I would tell my brother so he may tell our family. Let there be no doubts about how I feel. I love you, my lord Amir. Only death will part us."

"I am a jealous fool," he declared.

"You are," she agreed, "and I am flattered by it, but I shall see Marco and reassure him of my happiness. Whether he agrees with me or not, he will tell our family what I have said."

Marco Pietro d'Angelo was brought across the Sea of Marmara and through the Strait of the Bosphorus into the Black Sea. When the ship anchored just off the north coast he could just see the white marble of the palace on the green hills above. He was rowed ashore, and met by a tall, handsome, fair-skinned man with deep blue eyes and dark hair who didn't look foreign at all.

"I am Amir ibn Jem," the prince said, introducing himself. "Welcome to my home."

Marco bowed in spite of himself. The man before him had presence and dignity. "I am Marco Pietro d'Angelo, Bianca's older brother," he responded. "I must assume you have brought me here so I may see my sister."

"Come!" the prince said, not bothering to answer his visitor's question. "We must climb this hill to get to the palace where your sister awaits you."

The prince climbed easily and quickly, but Marco, not used to physical exercise, was slower. By the time they reached the top of the hill he was puffing and out of breath.

Amir smiled wickedly to himself. Azura's brother would have to climb that hill each time he came to see her. He would be quickly gone. "Your sister awaits you in the garden, Marco Pietro d'Angelo," the prince told his winded guest. Then he pointed.

Marco looked in the direction the prince pointed. He saw a veiled female figure dressed in a violet silk robe standing quietly. "Bianca?" He walked forward, and when he reached her Marco recognized his sister's beautiful eyes above the sheer veil.

Azura lowered the delicate silk covering her face. "Marco," she said, smiling at him. Then, leaning forward, she kissed him on both cheeks and, taking his hand, invited him to sit with her. "Why have you come?" she asked him. "You have distressed my husband by your actions."

"Your husband? You are married?" He looked surprised.

"Under the laws of this land, yes, I am Prince Amir's third wife," Azura said quietly. "Did you believe I had been kid-napped and forced into carnal slavery?" She laughed. "I'm sure Mother spread such a rumor, for to admit that her daughter loved an infidel would have been beyond her."

"They said you screamed and struggled when you were taken from your bridal vessel," Marco told her. "It created a great to-do in Venice, and a scandal when the doge refused to intervene with the sultan."

"It was not me who was taken from that flower-bedecked gondola," Azura said. "It was Francesca. She was in love with Enzo, and I knew Amir was coming for me. So we conspired to switch places that day." She then went on to explain to her brother how when Amir discovered that the veiled bride was not Bianca he had with Francesca's aid returned to their grand-father's palazzo so they might again switch places. "Did Fran-cesca finally capture Enzo's heart?" Azura asked her brother.

"No. He was married three months later to an Orsini. A widow who had produced two sons for her late husband," Marco told her.

"Ahh, poor Francesca," Azura said sympathetically. "Is she married yet? I'm sure another husband was found for her."

"Grandfather sent her back to Florence. He said he was too old to have to contend with young marriageable girls any longer. He claimed that both you and Francesca have disgraced the Venier name. Mother was furious, as you can imagine."

"Yes, I can indeed imagine," Azura said. "Are the others well? And our father?"

"All thrive," Marco told her.

"I am glad," Azura said. Then she arose. "You may come and see me again tomorrow, Marco. And you will tell me then why you have sought me out." Turning, she left him standing surprised by her departure.

A slave was at his elbow. "I am to escort you down to the beach, sir," he said to Marco. "You will be taken back to the vessel, and my master says you are to return tomorrow at this same hour." He led the guest from the prince's garden and back down the steep incline to the shore, where a small boat was already waiting to return Marco to the anchored ship.

Marco Pietro d'Angelo was disappointed. There were so many questions he had for Bianca, but she had controlled the conversation. Still, he had been told he might return. He would ask his questions then, and this time he would get his answers.

Chapter 16

Azura watched him go from a window in the harem. He had grown into a man in the almost four years since she had seen him. Yet he seemed a stranger to her in many ways. She had seen the many questions in his eyes. She would have to answer them if he was to depart satisfied. Amir's arms went about her, and she leaned back against him.

"You are sad," he said.

"Yes, oddly I am," Azura admitted, "but not by the life I lead. Rather by the knowledge that my family has not yet come to terms with my decisions." She told him what her brother had told her. "I can but imagine how angry my mother was to have her plans for me thwarted, but to have her second daughter sent home in disgrace must have been terrible for her. It will reflect upon my two other younger sisters, I fear. I wish I didn't know. I wish Marco had not come."

"He does not have to come back," Amir said.

"Yes, he does, for I cannot send him away without giving him the answers to all his questions, my love. I must shut that door firmly and forever this time," Azura said with a sigh.

He knew she was right, but it pained him to see the distress that her brother's coming had caused her. Tomorrow after they had spoken he would speak with Marco Pietro d'Angelo himself. Then he would send him on his way with instructions never to return. He didn't want Azura upset like this ever again.

The following day Marco came once more to visit with his sister. This time the slave escorting him led him into the charming little palace, taking him to a small salon. He was invited to seat himself amid the cushions set about a low table. A sweet drink and a plate of honeyed confections were brought to him. As anxious as he was to see Bianca again, he found himself easily settled amid the strange seating. He found the fruit drink he was sipping delicious, and the crisp little cakes, which he couldn't resist popping into his mouth one after the other, irresistible.

His sister entered the salon smiling. She was unveiled, and wore a rich robe of crimson brocade silk trimmed with gold and black embroidery. Her beautiful dark hair was loose and uncovered. "Marco, welcome," she said gracefully, seating herself across from him, taking the small goblet of sherbet from the attending slave.

"You are different today," he noted. "You do not greet me veiled."

"We are indoors. I have no need to go veiled in my own home," she explained. "I see our servants have made you comfortable, and that you still possess a prodigious sweet tooth, big brother."

"Your home," he said softly, almost questioningly.

"Yes, Marco, my home," Azura repeated. "This little palazzo is called the Moonlight Serai. 'Serai' is the word for palazzo here. I live with my husband, Prince Amir, and his other two wives, Maysun and Shahdi. We are happy together."

"Did you know of the others before you came?" he asked her.

She nodded. "Yes, I did, but it made no difference to me, Marco. I love Amir, and loving him was all that mattered to me. Not family. Not faith. *Only him.*"

"Has he bewitched you, then?" her brother wondered.

"Do not be foolish, Marco," Azura said with a laugh. "Have you never really been in love that you would ask such a thing of me? But of course men rarely admit to tender emotions, lest they be thought of as weak."

"I do not understand what you mean by this all-consuming love," he admitted. "I have a good wife. I have a child. I care for them, but there are other things in life to which I must attend. I do not have time for this love as you describe it." He did look genuinely perplexed by her words, and by her attitude.

"Why did you seek me out then, Marco?" his sister asked him candidly.

"I would take you back home if you would go," he said.

"Oh, Brother, how naive you are," Azura told him. "I don't want to go back, but even if I did, there would be no way for me to return other than to a convent where I would be reviled by the good nuns for my wicked and lewd behavior, and expected to spend the rest of my days in the deepest of repentance for my sins. I have many sins, Marco, but loving Amir cannot be counted among them.

"I do not wish to send you away today without you under-standing that the choices I made were mine. I made them freely. I have no regrets about what I did. None! And it is re-ally very simple. We are two people who fell in love, who wanted to be together despite all the obstacles others placed in our path to prevent our union. But we overcame every-thing. I am his wife, and I am happier than I have ever been in all my life."

"Do you not miss your old life at all?" he asked her.

She laughed. "My old life and my new life are quite simi-lar, Brother. In Florence or even Venice a married woman is cloistered in her home to protect her. She rarely leaves her home. In Turkey a married woman is also cloistered in her home to protect her, and she rarely leaves her home. I direct my slaves in their duties, although I share that chore with my sister wives. I would have done virtually the same thing in Florence or Venice. If I have a child, I will raise it here as I would elsewhere. When the child is grown I will seek a good marriage for it. When I die I will be buried. As you can see, there is little to no difference in my life here or there, Marco."

"You have no family here," he pointed out harshly.

"Our mother plans for great marriages for her remaining daughters, Brother. We both know that means the others will leave Florence when they wed. The daughter of a wealthy Flor-entine merchant is a prize highly sought after, especially by the nobility, who are always in need of funds. Our mother will find the best titles for my sisters, you may be certain. And once wed and gone, they will be as I am. Their husbands, their children, and those kinsmen around them become their family.

"How much time do you have for our parents now that

you are wed, Brother? The fact that you toil with our father in his silk trade is the only reason that you see him on a daily basis. Do you see our two brothers, Georgio and Luca? Or our sisters? Or our mother often now, Marco? I suspect you do not. Why should it be different for me? Go home. If you would please tell our parents that I am happy, I shall be content. Live your life for yourself and your family, not for others, Marco."

"As you so selfishly have?" he demanded angrily of her.

Azura laughed, not in the least disturbed by his tone. "Yes!" she told him. "As I have. I will not apologize for what I have done to anyone."

"Your name is forbidden to be spoken in our parents' house," he told her.

She laughed again, but this time there was a bitter edge to her laughter. "Yes, I expect my name is forbidden, but is it so because of what I did or because I was successful in defying our mother? But no matter. Bianca Pietro d'Angelo does not live in the Moonlight. Prince Amir's third wife is called Azura for her beautiful eyes."

His face crumpled. "I will always hold myself responsible for what you have done, what you have suffered," he told her. "Had Stefano and I not disposed of that poor woman's body in the Arno, Rovere could not have blackmailed Father into giving you to him as a bride. You would have been spared his cruelty and brutality, Bianca. You would have made a good marriage and been happy."

Now she understood! He had not sought her out because their parents had sent him. Their parents comprehended that her decision to go with Amir had been irrevocable. It was poor Marco who didn't understand. He believed her forced first marriage had caused her to take the wrong path in life.

Reaching across the table, Azura took his hand into hers and looked directly into his troubled brown eyes.

"Listen to me, Marco," she began. "Yes, my marriage to Rovere was a nightmare, but because it was, I was able to recognize real and true love when I found it. I would not have otherwise. I would have gone through life a frightened but dutiful wife to a man I felt little for, even as our mother has. I know you don't really understand what I mean by the love I have described to you, but you need feel no guilt for the path I chose to take, Brother. I should thank you, Marco, and I do. It is true that I once held you responsible for my misery as Rovere's wife, but I no longer do. The unhappiness he caused me was his sin, not yours or mine. But without a knowledge of good and evil, I would not have found my own happiness, big brother." She squeezed the hand she held and smiled into his familiar and troubled face. How much like a younger version of their father he had become, she thought fondly.

"Now I want you to go home and be happy and content yourself," she continued. "Become a prosperous silk merchant following in our father's footsteps. Respect and care kindly for your wife and children. Gain proper prestige with an envied mistress. Serve the state as often as they will have you. Be charitable, remembering your many blessings. And when you happen to think of me, Marco, know that I am happy and content as the wife of my dearest infidel. I would have it no other way, nor should you. If you still perceive that you have sinned against me, Brother, I freely offer you my full forgiveness."

His eyes were filled with tears, which he quickly wiped away with the back of his hand. "Bianca . . ." he said, and then to her great surprise he broke down sobbing.

She moved quickly around the table to enfold him in her embrace as he wept.

"Dearest brother," she said, "you must not grieve for me any longer. Please, oh please, tell me that you understand, Marco. It pains me to think you will go and not comprehend. What can I do to make you see?"

He had shocked himself with the emotions that had overcome him so suddenly. He had not cried since he was a small boy. Men did not weep like maidens or old women. And then, as the sound of her gentle voice calmed him, he came to realize that she had truly forgiven him, if indeed she had once held him responsible for her unhappiness. Her warm embrace soothed him. He gathered himself once again, easing himself from her arms. "I understand, Bianca," he told her. "How can I not when I see you filled with such happiness and peace?"

She smiled at him, her delicate fingers brushing away the evidence of his sorrow. "I am glad then, and I can send you home without the burden of your unnecessary guilt, Marco. Give my love to Francesca, and tell her of my happiness. I will pray that she finds hers. And the others too."

"You still pray to our God?" He had thought she would be forbidden to do so and be forced to pray to the deity of the infidels.

"Of course I pray to God," she said, almost laughing. "Amir promised I should not be forced to give up my faith. I have no priest, it is true, but I know God hears my prayers even without one."

He nodded, then said, "I did not ask you before, Bianca, but do you have any children? I would tell our father, who will gladly receive news of you, even if others will not." They both knew he referred to their mother.

"No, but I hope to one day. Maysun and Shahdi are sterile, for it is not wise for Ottoman princes to have too many children, especially sons. Sons pose a danger to the sultan, to his heir, and to their family."

"So that is why Prince Amir lived in Florence," Marco said, fascinated.

"He told me when you are the sultan's grandson, it is better to be a merchant than a warrior. His father even now quarrels with his brother, Sultan Bayezit."

"Does that not put you in danger?" Marco asked, concerned.

"No," Azura told him. "Amir has always been loyal to the sultan, whoever he may be. He does not involve himself in politics. His uncle knows he will not rebel, even for his father's sake. We are told that the prince, Jem, now resides on the island of Rhodes under the protection of the Knights Hospitaliers."

"I know little of politics except when it should affect the silk trade," Marco told her. "I came to Bursa because it is there that the Silk Road ends, and I wished to speak with some of that city's merchants. I have found a new source of particularly fine silk and silk brocade that will please our father greatly. The robe you wear is exquisite. With material like that, the Pietro d'Angelos could corner the trade in silk."

She laughed. "You are Father's true son, Marco. I know he is proud of you."

"He does not say it if he is," Marco grumbled, helping himself now to one of the small honeyed nut confections that was still left upon the plate.

They spent another hour or so in comfortable brotherly-sisterly companionship. The concerns between them were now settled. Azura knew she must be the one to end the afternoon. Finally she forced herself to rise, and he rose too.

"You must go, Marco," she told him. "I am glad you came. It is unlikely we will see each other again in this life, Brother."

"I know," he admitted, "but I am relieved to see how happy you are, Bianca, and I am grateful for your forgiveness."

The two siblings embraced, and then Azura escorted him from the salon, surprised to see Amir awaiting them outside.

"My lord?" she said.

"I will escort your brother back to the beach, beloved," he told her.

She gave a little nod of her head. "You are most gracious, my lord." Then she turned to her brother a final time. "Farewell, Marco. Remember my words, and go with God in your travels." Then kissing him on both cheeks, she turned and hurried off down a corridor and out of his sight.

"Come!" Amir said to his guest.

"I am grateful that you allowed me to see Bianca," Marco said as they exited the little palace and began the climb down the steep path to the shoreline. "She has put my mind at ease, and forgiven me for past wrongs."

"I am glad, but you cannot come again," Amir told him. "It was not easy for Azura to leave all that was familiar to her, but she did it for my sake. I can but hope a woman will one day love you that much, Marco Pietro d'Angelo."

"It was difficult for me as well," Marco told his companion, refusing to be bullied even a little by this prince. "She is my sister, the closest to me in age of all our siblings. I should not upset her willingly. If it be your will, my lord, that we not see each other again, then I accept it. My sister has already told me most firmly the same thing," he concluded with a small smile.

Amir barked a sharp laugh. "Did she? Did she indeed? Ah, what a wonderful female creature she is." His handsome face relaxed now as the threat of Azura's family began to fade away.

They reached the beach, where a little boat was waiting to take the young silk merchant back to the anchored vessel.

"The captain has been given orders to set sail immediately," the prince told his guest. "His destination is Istanbul. You will find a ship there to take you home." He held out his hand to Marco. "I greeted you in peace, brother of my wife. I now bid you farewell. Go in peace and with my friendship."

Marco took the prince's hand and shook it. "Thank you, my lord," he told him. "I can see that you have treated my sister well. I cannot deny her love for you. I offer you my friendship, *signore*." Then he waded out to the small craft, and climbed into it. He turned with a smile and gave Amir a friendly wave. Then Marco Pietro d'Angelo faced the sea again.

The prince watched as the little boat was swiftly rowed out to the large ship. By the time the prince had climbed back up to the palace gardens his vessel was already under way, sailing from the small cove that served the Moonlight Serai and headed for the Bosphorus. He reentered his home and went directly to the harem. There he found Azura as he had expected he would, standing by a window watching too.

Hearing his entry, she turned, smiling. "He did not come for my family's sake. He came for his own. I have relieved his poor burdened conscience," and she went on to explain her conversation that afternoon with her brother.

"Are you saddened to see him go knowing you are unlikely to meet again?" he asked her.

"No. My life is here with you," Azura told him, smiling to herself as she spoke. Men! Why was it that they always seemed to need reassurance from those they loved or cared for? she wondered. Then she looked into his deep blue eyes and said, "I want a child, Amir. A child of our love for each other. Maysun and Shahdi would like me to have a child too, for the harem is lonely without the laughter of children."

"You know the dangers, beloved," he reminded her. "My uncle could at any time turn on me because of my father. Remember that he has three living sons of his own. If our child were a male, it could present a danger to us all, but to you in particular. Besides, there has been no sign of a child in all the time we have been together."

"Because Nadim mixes a potion each morning that Agata presents to me as a strengthening drink. I am not supposed to know it is to prevent conception. There is no harm in it, so I drink it down quite dutifully," Azura told him with a small laugh.

"I should have them both beaten!" Amir exclaimed, feigning anger.

She laughed again. "They protect us by their actions," she told him.

"A child," he said slowly. "I had not thought to have a child, especially when you did not seem to prove fertile. A daughter who favored her mother would be a joy. Still, it is a serious chance that you contemplate, beloved."

Amir knew his uncle well. Bayezit was a patient man, but he was also unafraid to act in his best interests, as his race to reach Istanbul when Sultan Mehmet died had proved. He had been at a farther distance than his brother, and yet he had gotten to the capital first, where he had promised the Janissaries what they wanted and paid the right bribes so that his brother had no chance at all of gaining the throne. Bayezit would not hesitate to have an infant slain if he felt the child was a future danger to his throne. And how would Azura feel having her newborn torn from her arms and smothered? Could he subject her to that?

Still, if they dared it, a child would bring their house such joy. And it could as easily be a daughter as a son. A daughter who one day could be used to the sultan's best advantage in an important marriage alliance. An Ottoman princess would please his uncle. Of all Amir's cousins, he suspected that the youngest of the sultan's sons, Selim, would be the one to father a large family. Ahmed, despite Bayezit's favor, preferred gambling, drinking forbidden wines, and pretty page boys. Korkut was a serious scholar interested only in his studies. But Selim was much like Bayezit himself. Selim would take the throne one day, outsmarting his brothers as his father had, and it would be Selim's family that would prevail.

"I do not know if I can put us in such jeopardy, beloved," Amir considered. "The sultan has been favorable towards me, but there are those who have his ear, who would just as soon see my father and me dead. My uncle's three *kadins* are ambitious women, especially Ahmed's mother, Besma. It is rumored she managed the death of Bayezit's eldest son, the offspring of another *kadin*, to further her own son's chances at the succession. How would you feel if after you gave birth your son was taken immediately from you to be killed?"

Azura gasped, horrified. "They would not do that!"

He said nothing, and his silence gave confirmation to his words.

"Would they?" she whispered.

"I cannot bear to see you unhappy, beloved," Amir told her. "If you want a child, I will give you one, but understand the risks involved if I do and you bear me a son."

"If we had a son, why would the sultan have to know?" Azura asked. "We do not live in Istanbul. How would he even learn that we had a family?"

Amir laughed. "If I did not inform him of a child's arrival, it would appear treasonous on my part. You are thinking like a Florentine."

"I am a Florentine," she said.

"No," he told her. "You are my beloved, my wife, and everything that came before us is irrelevant. I will not share you with your history except where I am involved. I am a jealous man where my wife is concerned."

She kissed his mouth sweetly. "You must learn to share me, for I want a child, Amir. I will take the chance that your uncle will be merciful to us if I have a son, but I will have a daughter so we need not fret about it."

"You have shown no signs of a child yet," he said. "How can you be certain that you will have one now that you have decided you want one?"

"I have told you that I only need to stop drinking the strengthening drink that Nadim mixes and Agata feeds me each morning. They think I do not know," Azura explained to him. "My mother drank a similar liquid when she did not wish to have more babies. It is possible to control these things."

She had mentioned this to him before, he now recalled,

but he had been so concerned with other matters it had slipped entirely from his mind. Once again he didn't know if he should be angry or not. He realized that his slaves were indeed attempting to safeguard him and his wives as well as their household. "Stop drinking the potion," he said to her. "I will speak with Nadim and with Ali Farid. We will take our chances and have a child, beloved." As he said it he wondered if he was being wise. Women were known to die in childbirth. He didn't want to lose her, but he also wanted to make her happy. He caught her hand and kissed it before placing it over his heart for a moment. Then he released it with a smile.

"Now I will be content," Azura promised him. "And Maysun and Shahdi will be as well, for this child will belong to all of us, my love."

"Come to me tonight," he said, and she smiled into his eyes.

"As my lord commands," she purred, giving him a quick kiss.

He grinned mischievously at her and chuckled. "How amenable you are, beloved, when you gain your own way with me."

"All women are easy to live with when they are happy," she replied.

Agata no longer brought her the strengthening drink in the mornings, and they all began to watch her carefully. Still, despite the passion shared between Amir and Azura, there was no quick sign of a child. Azura found herself disappointed, but Nadim and Agata comforted her, assuring the third wife that the conception of a child was God's will and not man's. It had only been a little over a month since the decision had been made.

Then late one morning Captain Mahmud and a small troop of Janissaries arrived at the Moonlight Serai. They had orders requesting that Prince Amir return to Istanbul, for his uncle, the sultan, wished to speak with him.

Azura was suspicious. "What does he want? Why could he not simply send a message to you? Why must he see you?"

Maysun and Shahdi, being better-versed in the politics of the Ottoman Empire, were even more concerned, although they kept their fears to themselves. They did not wish to distress Azura when she was attempting to breed. But what if Amir was being summoned only to be met by the sultan's gardeners, his executioners? What if Prince Jem's behavior had finally brought his brother's patience to the breaking point, and his only son was to suffer the punishment of death for it?

"He is the sultan, and he has requested my presence," Amir said. "I must go."

"A request is written on a parchment and delivered by a single messenger. This is a demand with a troop of Janissaries sent to fetch you," Azura replied.

"Nonetheless, I must go," Amir said quietly, and kissing each of his wives in turn, he left them, going with Captain Mahmud and his troop of Janissary horsemen. The truth was, he had no idea why his uncle would send for him unless it had something to do with his rebellious father. To his relief he was taken to Sultan Bayezit immediately upon his arrival. Entering the august presence, he bowed low with each step he took forward.

Bayezit watched his nephew come towards him making the proper obeisance as he came. He smiled faintly to himself. Amir was a careful man, he thought. "Come, Nephew, and sit by my side so we may talk," he invited the prince.

Amir did as he was bid, kissing his uncle's hand respectfully, his eyes darting quickly around the room for any sign of gardeners. There were none. "Thank you, my lord," he said. "I am happy to see you looking so well."

"Unlike your troublesome father, Nephew, you are loyal. Because of your faithfulness I am sending you to Rhodes with the payment for your father's keep. I want you to speak with Jem personally. Try to convince him to cease his resistance to me, and make his peace. I would happily welcome him back to govern one of my provinces, whichever one he chooses. I will give you a province and its income too if you succeed."

"I will gladly go to Rhodes for love of you, Uncle, but I wish no part in the government, and my ships bring me enough income that I neither need nor want any government allowance. Give these honors to your sons. I am content."

The sultan stared at his nephew, then finally said, "You are unique among the males of our line, Amir, for you are, or you seem, content simply to be."

"I have seen what ambition does, my lord," Amir answered his uncle. "I have my own wealth, three wives, a home I love. I want for nothing. Perhaps I am simply lazy, for being sultan is a great deal of work."

"You have no children, then?" the sultan asked.

"None," the prince answered. "I should have told you if I did, my lord."

Bayezit nodded slowly. "Your fidelity is impressive, Amir ibn Jem," his uncle told him. "My father always said that you were trustworthy. Go to Rhodes for me. I will not hold you responsible if you cannot bring your father to reason, but you must try for my sake and for my brother's sake."

"I will do my best for you, my lord uncle," Amir told him. "When do you propose I leave? And I assume I will have Janissaries with me to guard the gold?"

"You will leave in a month's time, and ride overland down to the Mediterranean coast. From there you will embark for Rhodes. The gold will await you at your destination and be loaded aboard the vessel taking you to Rhodes. Captain Mahmud will meet you first at Bursa and go with you. There is no need for a troop of his Janissaries, for they would only attract attention. I would have you be discreet, Nephew," the sultan told Amir. "You can get yourself to Bursa?"

"I can," Amir said. "Would you like me to use one of my own ships to transport the gold, my lord? I should gladly give you the loan of one."

"I would! You are generous, Nephew," the sultan said.

"Nay, my lord, I am a practical man," Amir told him. "Load the gold in Bursa. Captain Mahmud and I will sail from there rather than riding overland. It will be safer."

"If you think that is best, Nephew," the sultan said to him, "then do it. I will see that the treasury sends the gold to Bursa."

"If you have no further need for me, then, my lord, I will return home to inform my wives that you have entrusted me with a mission. They need know nothing more, but I would not have them worry," Amir said.

His uncle nodded, and waved him away. The prince hurried from the sultan's presence and three days later returned home to his overjoyed women, who had been genuinely frightened. They were full of questions as to why Bayezit had called upon Amir, and when they learned he was to go to Rhodes, his wives were none too pleased.

"You will be gone for several months," Maysun complained. "If you are charged by the sultan with trying to bring your father to reason, you must remain long enough with Prince Jem so that you can be said to have tried, but not so long that suspicions are cast upon you and it is suggested that you are plotting with your father. I do not like this. I do not like it at all. Why can the sultan not be satisfied that you are not your father, or your father's man? This task your uncle sends you to do for him appears to be a trial of sorts. You are being tested once again, although you have done nothing to warrant it."

"And it is a fool's errand," Shahdi chimed in. "Your father cannot be moved, and everyone in the world knows it. Someone who has influence with the sultan is playing a wicked game. Who is your enemy, my lord? Do you even know?"

"This is a woman's trick," Azura said quietly, and they turned, surprised once again by her grasp of Ottoman politics. "Amir has done nothing that would, that could, that should arouse anyone's suspicions as to his loyalty to the throne, to his uncle, the sultan. But a woman, ambitious for her son, would be distrustful of him.

"He is the Conqueror's oldest male grandchild. His has a legitimate claim to the Ottoman throne one day. Yet he eschews politics, will not accept a position governing for the sultan, does not lend his sword to the continuing conquest of the empire. He lives quietly, amassing wealth, and without children who could be used against him. Why does he do this? What motives are behind this behavior? Does he hope one day to seize the throne when Bayezit's three living sons are involved in a fight for it?

"A man like that is indeed to be looked upon with suspicion by certain folk. You must test him constantly. Force him to reveal his true motives," Azura said. "And when you have done so, then you must destroy him and wipe all evidence of him from the face of the earth, and from the minds of the people. In that way you protect your own interests, and those of your son. Who among the sultan's *kadins* would have that kind of influence with him, and would do such a thing?"

"Besma," Amir said without hesitation. "She is Ahmed's mother. She is believed to have seen to the murder of my uncle's eldest son by another of his wives. Now it is her son who is the eldest. She is determined that he follow in his father's footsteps."

"She is determined that her son rule," Shahdi said drily. "She would murder the sultan if she believed she could accomplish it and put her boy on the throne. I wouldn't be in the least surprised if Azura wasn't correct about the bitch."

"We must protect our husband from this plot," Maysun said.

"There is no plot that I can see," Amir said. "You are allowing your imaginations to run away with you. Sending me personally to deliver the first payment for my father's upkeep to the Grand Master of the Knights Hospitaliers in Rhodes is my uncle's way of showing courtesy to these men. It is an elegant gesture and will not go unnoticed. Remember that the reputation of the Ottoman in the Christian world is that of a barbarian. My uncle would have us more than just feared. He wants the respect of others, and good manners will go a long way to helping erase the notion that we are savages. That I will also attempt to turn my father from his path of destruction will not be considered unusual for a loyal servant of Sultan Bayezit."

"I still think you are being tested," Maysun insisted, and Shahdi nodded in agreement but kept silent.

"When will you go, my lord? Tell us of your plans," Azura said, attempting to turn the others away from their concern. She was not certain that they were not correct, but she could see that Amir did not wish to believe it. He was an honest man of ethics, preferring to believe that those he dealt with were also. He was wrong, of course, and they would have to protect him. Azura had listened carefully at her father's table when he discussed his business with her mother. Human nature was not always as straightforward as Amir himself was. But if there was a plot, there was little any of them could do except hope the prince's honest behavior proved his detractor wrong.

He told them he would send for one of his own vessels and sail to Bursa. Once the gold was loaded aboard and Captain Mahmud joined them, they would depart for Rhodes. Krikor, his personal servant, would travel with him. The women spent the next few weeks preparing Amir's wardrobe. He must look every inch the Ottoman prince he was to both honor the sultan and impress the Knights Hospitaliers, most of whom were nobles from their own lands.

While treating Maysun and Shahdi as kindly as he always had, Amir wanted to spend as much time with Azura as he could. Her very presence in his life each day gave him a peace and strength he had never known. He had not loved any woman until her. The knowledge that they would be separated for many long weeks actually gave him physical pain. He would have taken her with him if he could have, but he realized the seriousness of this mission that he had been entrusted with by his uncle.

Arriving at a great Christian stronghold with a woman would have but given truth to all the evil thought of his world. Not that the Knights Hospitaliers did not have their own mistresses installed on the island to see to their needs and keep them company. He would put aside his own wants in favor of his uncle's when he traveled to Rhodes for the sultan; but while he remained at the Moonlight Serai he would enjoy the company and the favor of his beautiful Florentine wife.

He loved it best when they lay together alone and naked. The chamber in which he slept was a simple room, square in shape, with a few simple pieces of furniture. The bed they shared was a thick mattress covered in black silk set upon a low raised platform of ebony. Seeing her creamy flesh upon the dark fabric and her long, soft black hair almost obscured upon the cloth kindled his desires. Had she been anyone other than who she was, the tenderness with which she loved him would have left him helpless. Instead it gave him a strength such as he had never known.

They kissed slowly at first, lips firm yet soft, enjoying the sensation of a gentle beginning that more often than not grew into fiery passion as lips moved from mouths to pulses beneath the skin of a throat, to a wrist, to the shadowed valley between her breasts or above his beating heart. Hands caressed heated flesh, teasing at nipples, stroking a belly, fondling a buttock. Her fingers cupped the cool pouch that contained the jewels of his sex, cuddling them in her warm palm until he whimpered with his growing need.

Her mouth suckled upon his throbbing cock as he had long ago taught her to do. Her tongue licked the great length of him until he thought he might burst with his need to possess her. His fingers explored between her nether lips, brushing against the moist flesh, finding and playing with the sensitive gem of her womanhood until she cried out with the pleasure he gave her. They had learned to prolong the culmination of their union because both Amir and Azura had quickly discovered that enough was never enough for either of them. Their passion for each other seemed to grow greater with the passing of time rather than fade with familiarity.

Now on this night before his departure she lay beneath him gasping with delight as he pushed slowly into her tight sheath. "Oh yes, my love!" Azura cried, encouraging him onward. "Yes!" She wrapped herself about him tightly. He filled her, and she struggled to implant every bit of this memory deep in her consciousness for those months ahead when she would be without him.

"I want to go deeper," he growled softly in her ear. "Unlock your limbs and let me guide us, beloved."

She complied, and when she had, he gently pushed her legs as far back over her shoulders as he could, then drove himself into her eager body. Azura gasped as he began a fierce rhythm, moving himself deeper and harder with each ferocious thrust of his loins. She was quickly overwhelmed with her need, and cried out with pleasure, but he did not cease moving faster and faster and faster upon her. A second wave began to arise within her. He sensed it, and slowed himself to a stop, the better to prolong their passion. Azura felt his lust pulsing strongly and tightened her sheath about him.

"Witch!" he groaned as he once again began to pump himself within her.

They had never before attained quite the perfection they did this night. Azura screamed softly as his juices exploded, flooding her with his loving tribute. She didn't know whether she was conscious or unconscious. She soared. She flew. He groaned and shuddered in her arms, burying his face in her perfumed hair as her legs fell to the mattress weakly and she wept with the joy that they had just shared. He kissed the tears from her cheeks.

Chapter 17

When he had caught his breath once more, he wrapped her in his arms and slept. There were no words necessary between them now. She awoke several hours later and returned to her own bedchamber, but she did not sleep again, arising even before Agata, hurrying to the baths and then dressing herself quickly so she might be able to see him depart. When she returned to her chamber to dress, both Nadim and Agata were awaiting her with her garments. They had chosen one of her favorite colors. Peach.

On the portico of the little palace Prince Amir bade his three wives farewell. Maysun demanded that Krikor make certain his master was kept warm on the sea voyage. Shahdi advised him to be cautious dealing with his father and the Knights Hospitaliers. Azura, however, kissed him tenderly as she gazed into his eyes and said, "Come back to me safely, my dearest lord. Each day we are parted will be like a hundred years for me."

"Each night I am without you will seem like a thousand years," he murmured in return. "I love you, beloved. Remember that you have my heart in your keeping." He kissed her gently. Then he turned abruptly and, with Krikor at his heels, departed.

Standing together, the three women watched as the two men descended to the beach, where a small boat stood ready to take them out to the anchored vessel in their cove. They saw Amir reach the ship with Krikor and go aboard. They heard the drum of the slave master who kept time for the galley slaves start to beat, and saw the oars of the prince's transport begin their rhythmic movement as it pulled away and out of the little harbor. Then, as if some silent signal had been given, Prince Amir's three wives began to weep, but just as suddenly broke into laughter at their common behavior.

"What a fine trio we are." Maysun said with a chuckle. "If we were the sultan's wives we would have to contend with his always being away conquering some place or other."

"That is why it is better to have a merchant for a husband, and not a sultan," Shahdi added.

"Some merchants travel all the time," Azura said. "I'm glad Amir does not, but I will miss him. He told me he will be gone for several months."

"We will survive," Maysun said in practical tones. "We did when he was living in Florence for those few years."

"Just where is this island of Rhodes?" Shahdi asked. Both she and Maysun had little formal education.

Azura, however, did have education, and she asked Ali

Farid to find them a map so she might show her companions where their husband was now going.

The prince's ship moved quickly from the Black Sea into the Bosphorus, then into the little Sea of Marmara, reaching Bursa in just a few days' time. Captain Mahmud was awaiting Prince Amir. The sultan's treasury had delivered the forty-five thousand pieces of gold. It was counted out before Amir by a treasury official in a small dockside shed, and then the bags were loaded upon his vessel for transport to Rhodes.

They set sail immediately, passing through the Dardanelles and into the Aegean Sea, keeping within sight of the coast at all times. They sailed past the islands of Lesbos, Khios, Samos, and Kos. Amir was surprised that his ship traveled without an escort, but Captain Mahmud said that it was thought an armed escort would have drawn unwanted attention to the ship. It was believed that a ship belonging to Prince Amir's merchant fleet coming out of Istanbul would not attract much attention. After all, it was the ships returning from the east that carried the richest goods, not those headed east. Of course, a sharper eye might have noticed the ship riding low with its heavy cargo, but they were not troubled with pirates, for which Amir was grateful.

Shaped like the head of some ancient Spartan spear, the island came into their view at last. It was mountainous terrain, the heights covered in pine and cypress forests.

The lowlands had enough flat land, where vineyards, orchards, and groves of olives were grown. The island's coast was rocky and difficult, but the harbor at Rhodes, its main city, was deep and navigable.

Over the centuries the island had been occupied and claimed by many cultures. Byzantium claimed it after the First Crusade, but its tenure came to an end almost two hundred years ago, when the Knights Hospitaliers claimed it for themselves, building a more modern city in the European style and surrounding it with strong walls. No one had been able to breach those walls, not even Prince Amir's grandfather Mehmet the Conqueror. This was the sanctuary the sultan's brother, Prince Jem, had chosen. Their ship anchored in the harbor.

"I will go ashore, and formally announce your arrival to the Grand Master of the order," Captain Mahmud said. "Do you speak French, Highness?"

Amir nodded. "I can communicate with the Grand Master in several languages," he replied. "Say I would like to come ashore today after our time at sea. He will assume I have a delicate constitution."

Captain Mahmud chuckled. "They are ferocious fighters and fierce sailors, this particular band of knights," he remarked. "Yes, better to let them think you weak, Highness. 'Tis a clever ploy."

"See if they will allow you to speak with my father, and tell him I am here. He will understand why, and be annoyed," Amir told the Janissary.

"When did you last see your father, Highness, if I may be so bold?" the captain asked.

Amir snorted. "I have not seen him since I was ten," he replied almost bitterly.

"I last saw my father when I was six and the sultan's forces came from the sea to attack my village. They killed him and those who opposed them, carrying off the women and children. I was chosen to be sent to the Prince's School to be educated and eventually become part of the Janissary corps," Captain Mahmud responded. "A father sires you, but life shapes your character, and kismet brings you your good fortune."

"I cannot disagree," Amir said. The Janissary captain's story was not an unusual one. Many of the children taken, educated, and trained became valued civil servants for the sultan's government. Though many were nothing more than simple soldiers, others used their education to advance themselves, gaining both wealth and rank.

Captain Mahmud went ashore, returning a few hours later. The Grand Master, he said, looked forward to welcoming Prince Amir, who was invited to stay at the great stone castle that was the headquarters of the order. "I saw your father, Highness," the captain reported. "He was surprised that you were here but will be happy to receive you."

Amir chuckled. "Yes, I will wager he is indeed surprised that I am here. Well, let us go. Krikor! Is my finery suitable enough to impress?" the prince asked his servant.

"You will bring honor to your uncle, my lord," Krikor answered his master. He had dressed his master this morning in white and gold.

They were rowed ashore, where a small honor guard of horsemen met them, escorting them to the castle. There Prince Amir met the man who was temporarily serving as Grand Master of the Hospitaliers, Henri-François Plessis D'Aubusson. The two men greeted each other cordially.

"We are most honored to receive the sultan's nephew into our midst," the Grand Master said, bowing. He was a man of medium height with dun-colored hair and eyes. He wore a bright crimson tabard emblazoned with a white cross as an outer garment.

"My master, Sultan Bayezit, is grateful for the generosity you have shown towards his brother, Prince Jem. My uncle wishes there to be only peace between them. The stipend is being off-loaded from my ship now. When you are ready Captain Mahmud will count the coins before you so you may see there is a full measure as promised."

The Grand Master was impressed. This young prince had great elegance and his manners were without fault. He was curious, however, and could not refrain from gaining an answer to something that he found odd. "Why are your eyes blue?" he said, and was then slightly amused to see Prince Amir's dignity shaken before he recovered himself.

"My mother had blue eyes," he answered the Grand Master. "She was English."

"Ah, of course," the Grand Master replied. "You will take a meal with me, I hope, Highness. But now you will want to see your father. I will take you to him myself. When you return home to Istanbul you will be able to tell Sultan Bayezit that his brother is being housed as befits his position."

Amir could not help but laugh aloud. Then he said to his startled companion, "My uncle has a forgiving nature where his brother is concerned, my lord. But eventually I suspect my father's behavior will try the sultan's patience beyond its limits. This sultan values loyalty above all else. Continued defiance on my father's part is foolish. We both know he cannot hope to prevail. Nor would Christendom protect Prince Jem did they not think to gain an advantage over the sultan by doing so. There is no advantage to be had, for while he loves his brother, Sultan Bayezit loves his realm more, which he should. The sultan is the father over all his people, my lord. A good father will not betray his children, although the child may betray the father."

The Grand Master nodded. Prince Amir had spoken candidly. "I will remember your words, Highness," he told the younger man. Then he brought him without further discussion to the vast apartments where Prince Jem had installed his miniature Oriental court. "I do not intrude upon your father unless invited," he said quietly.

Amir nodded and as the Grand Master turned to depart, the prince said to the two enormous black slaves guarding the doors, "I am your master's son. Open the doors for me." Then he passed through them when they did.

A black eunuch hurried forward as he entered the antechamber. "Prince Amir," he said. "Your father is awaiting you. Come this way."

Amir followed the eunuch and was led into a beautiful presence chamber, where his father sat ensconced upon a velvet-cushioned gilt throne. Beneath Amir's feet was a magnificent wool carpet of reds and blues. Footed bronze lamps burning scented oils lit the chamber. Seated upon multicolored silk cushions around the throne were half a dozen richly dressed and lightly veiled women.

Amir smiled, amused. "'Tis most impressive, Father," he said, greeting the man who had sired him—a man he barely knew but by reputation and had not seen in years.

"You look like your mother," Prince Jem acknowledged. "You may come closer."

Amir moved forward. He looked at this man and decided he would not like him. He wished he could be anywhere other than the castle of the Grand Master of Rhodes. He wanted to be home at the Moonlight Serai. Home with Azura. How long before he would see her again? He would not be able to reason with his father. His father wanted to be sultan yet had not the strength nor the resources to gain that office. He had believed that because Mehmet favored him he would easily gain the throne. *I am wasting my time here,* Amir thought, and was irritated, but he would spend the next month trying to bring Prince Jem back into the sultan's good graces. Time lost that could be spent with Azura. *Beloved!* he called out to her with his longing heart.

And Azura as she walked in the early autumn garden placed her hand on her belly. The winds had already begun to blow from the northwest as the days grew shorter. She was with child at long last. She wanted to tell Amir, wanted to share her happiness with him. Maysun had advised against it, however, and Shahdi had agreed. Both of Amir's first two wives were overjoyed that Azura was to bear a child. This babe would be raised by them too, and their empty hearts would soon be filled.

"There is no way we can be certain a message sent to Prince Amir would reach him," Maysun told Azura. "No one outside of our home must know you are with child, Azura. It is just too dangerous, given our belief that the *kadin* Besma plots against our husband. If the child you carry is a son, the danger increases for all of us, but we all agreed it was worth the risk. We will cross that bridge when we must and not before. And there is always the possibility that you will birth a daughter. A daughter will not cause any distress among the sultan's harem. An Ottoman princess is an asset."

"So I have been told on several occasions," Azura said

with a small smile. "But I cannot help but wish Amir knew of our good fortune."

"We cannot take the chance." Shahdi echoed Maysun's caution.

Amir's family did, however, receive two messages from him over the next few months. The first came to tell them that he had arrived safely. The second in deepest midwinter arrived filled with his frustration at attempting to deal with his strong-willed father, who refused to accept the reality of his situation. The message also contained the promise to return home soon. He would come back, he wrote, in the spring.

In his absence, Azura's companions took excellent care of the expectant mother. They catered to her odd appetites. She longed for sugared violets. They found them. They rubbed her feet and legs, which were prone to cramping on the damp winter days. And they sat together sewing tiny garments for the expected child. Even Shahdi had softened in her attitude towards Azura. She embroidered the infant's gowns with a creative, skilled hand.

The one appetite, however, they could not compensate, was Azura's need for Amir. It seemed some nights she desired him more than she ever had when he lay in her arms. It surprised her just how great her lustful needs for him were even as she lay awake staring at her big belly. Some nights she would bite into her pillows to keep from screaming. Azura had no idea if this was normal. She couldn't ask Maysun or Shahdi, since neither had ever had a child. It was not something that she and her mother had ever discussed, as that would not have been seemly; and Agata certainly had no knowledge of such things. So she kept her longings to herself, and prayed for her husband to hurry home before she dissolved into flames with her need for him.

He was coming even as she hoped for it. The stipend was long since delivered. His months with his father had proved fruitless, even as everyone had known they would. Amir bade Prince Jem and the Grand Master farewell, sailing from the island of Rhodes on an early March morning. Reaching Istanbul, he went immediately to the palace to report to the sultan, who was even now preparing to send out his armies on campaign.

Bayezit was impatient with the preparations, and had little time for Amir, already knowing he could not have possibly succeeded. He had sent his nephew on this fool's errand at the nagging of his *kadin* Besma, who saw plots against her son everywhere. Now irritated for having given in to her, and silently shamed that he had wasted Amir's time, he greeted the prince shortly. "Is the news good?" he demanded.

Amir bowed. "The news is what you expected, Uncle. Your brother cannot be swayed from his course. He will probably die trying to unthrone you."

"Stubborn fool," the sultan muttered. "He is well treated?"

"He has set himself up lavishly in a wing of the Grand Master's castle. He practices warfare with the knights daily to keep his skills honed. I believe they plan to move him to France or Italy eventually, Uncle," Amir said. "He refuses to believe their concern for him is actually for themselves. He believes what they believe. That he is a weapon to be used against you eventually."

"What would you do if you were in my position?" Bayezit asked his nephew.

"Allah forbid I should ever be in your position, Uncle!" Amir said wholeheartedly. "But were I? You have said yourself that the empire is a bride that cannot be shared between two husbands. And a wild dog that cannot be tamed must be killed. There is no other way around it. I'm sorry."

"He is your father," Bayezit said quietly.

"You have been more father to me than Jem ibn Mehmet," Amir said honestly. "He may have sired me, but the few memories I have of him all involved my mother weeping her broken heart out. Never once do I recall him throwing a ball to me, or showing me how to use a scimitar. You and my grandfather were the men who influenced my life, Uncle. Prince Jem is a stranger to me, and even more so now that I have spent so many of the last weeks with him. Do not break your heart over him, for he is not worth your patience or kindness, Uncle."

The sultan nodded, considering that his nephew was a pragmatic and honest man. "You have done me a great service, Amir," he said. "Now go home, Nephew. You will always have my trust."

Amir bowed, and hurried from his uncle's presence.

The *kadin* Besma had heard everything between the two men, as she had hidden herself behind a tapestry in the sultan's privy chamber when one of her spies brought word that Amir was back. She didn't trust Amir ibn Jem. She could not believe that he was that noble. He was the eldest of the Conqueror's grandsons. She was sure he was but biding his time. He might be loyal to Bayezit if such a thing as true loyalty existed. But it was unlikely he would support any of Bayezit's sons when this sultan could no longer rule. No! He would seize the throne for himself unless she could prevent it. It was her son, Ahmed, who must be the next sultan.

She had already seen Bayezit's first son, Mustafa, removed to make way for her own boy. Of Ahmed's two half brothers, only Selim, the younger, worried her. Korkut was too involved in his studies. He could not bring the Janissaries to heel, which a future sultan must do even as Bayezit had. But Selim was another matter, and he was extremely well guarded by his overprotective mother and aunt as well as the Agha Kislar, Hadji Bey. Still, there would be time for Selim's demise. First she must see to the execution of Prince Amir, lest her own precious boy be threatened by this likable and capable man.

Threatening his cousin was not a priority for Amir ibn Jem. It never had been, and it never would be. He wanted to get home as quickly as he could. He and Krikor decided to ride the several days' distance from the capital to the Moonlight Serai. They both agreed that they had had enough of ships for the interim. They had been away for seven and a half long months. Spring had reached the Black Sea. The hills were already green with new growth and dotted with early flowers.

His arrival surprised them all, for he had sent no messenger ahead. He greeted Diya al Din and Ali Farid and hurried into the harem. With cries of delight Maysun and Shahdi ran to greet him. He hugged them both, but his eyes were searching the chamber for Azura. Agata had run to fetch her mistress, who was napping. Now Azura came from her bedchamber into the dayroom.

He looked at her, shock etched upon his handsome face. "What has happened to you?" he demanded to know, hurrying to her side. Then he turned to the others. "Why did you not send to me that my beloved was ill?"

"*Ill?* She is not ill," Maysun said, and all the women began to laugh. If he had ever before seen a woman heavy with her unborn child it was so long ago that the recollection had faded away from his own memory.

"If she is not ill, then why is she so swollen with evil humors?" Amir insisted upon knowing. His look was one of great concern as he wrapped his arms about Azura.

"She is swollen because she is close to having your child, my lord," Maysun told him. "But of course you would not know what the sight of a woman with child is, for you were not raised in your grandfather's harem. Only after your mother died were you brought to the Prince's School to be educated. You have had no experience with a woman carrying a child, my lord. Azura will deliver her babe in just a few weeks' time."

"Welcome home, my dearest lord," Azura said to him, smiling. "I hope you are pleased by what you have found."

"*A child!*" His voice was both reverent and surprised.

"We have kept Azura's condition a secret," Maysun went on.

Amir nodded. "Yes, 'twas wise. While I yet stand in my uncle's favor, news such as this could bring us difficulties." Then he turned his attention to Azura. "You are well, beloved? I have no knowledge of these things." He looked to Maysun. "Can you deliver this child, and keep Azura safe too?" he asked her.

"There is no need to worry, my lord. Women have been having babies since time began," Maysun said, but the truth was she had never delivered a child.

"I will deliver my mistress's child, my lord," Agata said. "I helped my sister when my lady's mother birthed five of her children. I know what must be done."

"We will send for a physician from Istanbul," the prince decided.

"No, we will not," Azura contradicted him. "Agata knows what must be done, and so do I. No one is to know of this child's existence until after it is born. My baby must at least have a chance at life." Her lip trembled as she said it. Once the danger of birthing a son had not seemed so serious, but with each kick the infant in her belly gave her to remind her of its existence, she realized the peril they both faced should that child be a male. A male whose claim to the Ottoman throne was as legitimate as that of any of the claimants. She rested her dark head against his shoulder. "I am glad you are home, Amir."

He called her to his bed that night, and marveled at the great change in the beautiful body he had loved previously. He positioned her between his legs, and let his hands roam over her large round belly. He could actually see the faint outline of his child. He put a hand over it, and it kicked out at him. Startled, he pulled his hand back, but then they both laughed. He was amazed that her beautiful round breasts were now twice their usual size, the nipples prominent and ready for suckling. And all this had happened in the time he was away. He was astounded, for to him it was a sudden change.

Maysun had explained to him how they might copulate without injuring the infant. Azura was more than eager, and wept with her delight to feel his hard length filling her once again. Gently he brought them both to perfect fulfillment twice, scolding her when she begged for more. If truth be told, he wanted more too, but he feared harming the child.

"At least you had the diversion of other women in your travels," she complained at him when he told her enough. "I have had to spend long nights aching for you, my lord. Do not deny me, for I burn for you."

"I have had no woman since the night I left you," he told her.

"Not one?" She sounded very pleased.

"Not one, you greedy houri," he swore. "If your belly were not in our way, I should take you to my couch for the next month, and never let you off your back."

Azura sighed with contentment. "I am happy then, my lord, that you have suffered too. But carrying your child has not been easy. I shall be glad to birth it."

"You do not say *he* or *she*," he remarked.

"I dare not," Azura told him. "I will not even consider a name."

"Mehmet for a boy in honor of my grandfather," he told her.

"Do not even think it, my lord!" she begged him. "I want this child, but I live in fear of a son and pray for a daughter." Her eyes filled with tears. "In my own need and selfishness I have taken such a terrible chance in having this child," she admitted.

He held her close now. "It will be all right, beloved," he promised her, knowing even as he said the words that he could not really promise her anything at all. His only hope if this child was a male lay in his uncle's generosity towards him. The sultan would have to be notified immediately when the birth occurred no matter the child's gender.

The days grew warmer and longer, and then fourteen days into May Azura's child decided it was time to be born. The waters protecting the child spilled from her, but it was not until several hours later that the pains began. They were ready in the harem with the birthing chair. Beneath it there were clean linen cloths spread. The hours moved slowly, but despite the increasing severity of the pains, the child would not come easily. Night came. Azura screamed with each new pain. Her ebony hair was lank and wet, her body covered in sweat. Finally, in the hour before midnight, the baby's head crowned. Then its delicate shoulders came forth, and finally, pushing with a strength she didn't think she had left, Azura birthed her child.

Crouched beneath the birthing chair, Agata caught the baby as it finally came forth. "It is a girl!" she cried. "It is a girl!"

They were the last words Azura heard, for she fainted with her final efforts. Maysun and Shahdi took the infant, who was squalling now, from Agata. Azura would need attending to, for she was bleeding heavily. Stopping the bleeding was paramount, and praying vocally to the Holy Mother and Santa Anna, Agata managed to stem the flow. Azura was weakened by the great loss of blood, and nothing would do but that Amir send to Istanbul for a physician. Krikor was dispatched immediately, carrying a message for the sultan as well as a request for a physician of his choosing.

Bayezit was surprised to receive his nephew's communiqué, but equally relieved that the child born was a female. Killing an infant was not in his nature. He wisely kept the news of Amir's daughter from his *kadin* Besma. He also instructed a competent physician to see that his nephew's third wife did not give birth again. He could be generous, but he could not speak for whichever of his sons succeeded him.

They put the baby to Azura's breast, and weak as she was, she fed her daughter, though it weakened her further. The physician demanded a wet nurse be found, but Azura insisted upon feeding her infant at least once daily so that her own milk would not dry up.

She would feed her child when she was well again, she told

him. The physician smiled. He would tell the sultan of this brave young woman who was such a good mother. Indeed, the infant had three mothers, for the prince's two other wives doted upon the baby.

"Atiya is her name," Azura finally told Amir. "Maysun says it means '*gift*,' and our daughter is a great gift to this house."

Amir agreed, and then showed her the gold rattle that the sultan had sent to their daughter. "He is pleased with an Ottoman princess, and says he will choose a distinguished husband for her one day." He looked down at his daughter as she nursed at her mother's plump white breast. Atiya had a tuft of black hair. He touched it, smiling as it curled about his finger. "She is so delicate," he said softly.

"She will not break," Azura told him, smiling.

The baby was healthy, and Azura slowly over the next few months regained her strength. The baby thrived and seemed to grow more each day. The soft dark hair with which she had been born fell out, leaving her as bald as a melon for a few weeks, but then the infant's hair grew back as thick and dark as her parents' hair. Her blue eyes were not the aquamarine color of her mother's but neither were they the deep blue of her father's.

Rather Atiya had clear bright blue eyes that showed curiosity about everything.

The baby quickly came to recognize the faces of those around her, smiling winningly at Maysun and Shahdi, who constantly argued over who would carry Atiya about her world on a particular day. She cooed and Azura could have sworn that she flirted with all the men in her life. Her father. Nadim. Ali Farid and Diya al Din. She had the three eunuchs in particular wrapped about her tiny finger. She went through a period where she was demanding of her mother, but Azura quickly put an end to that, lest the child become spoiled. In personality Atiya reminded her mother of her own mother.

The baby was six months old when Amir and Diya al Din both sensed the little palace was being watched. Azura rode out with her husband. He put her off for several days until she grew suspicious and demanded to know why. He told her.

"Who would watch the Moonlight Serai?" Azura asked him. "Should we be afraid? Are we safe, my lord?"

"I do not know, but I intend seeking the answers to all your questions, beloved," he told her. "I must be patient, however, lest I frighten our watcher off. I want answers as much as you do. I do not believe it is Tartars or other raiders. More likely someone from Istanbul reporting to the sultan's minions."

"But your uncle trusts you," Azura replied.

"He does, but there are those among his people who cannot believe an Ottoman prince lives who is without ambition for the throne," Amir answered her. "My father's continued behavior does not help me."

"The others do not know, do they?" she said.

"No, and you must say nothing. You know how easily Maysun and Shahdi can be made fearful."

"Are we truly safe in your uncle's realm?" Azura asked.

"I had thought we would be, and as long as my grandfather lived, I believe we were. The sultan's heart is good towards me. He does not hold me responsible for my father's misdeeds, but eventually his patience will be frayed. He has three *kadins*, and they are concerned with any who might threaten their own sons."

"A *kadin* is the title given to the mother of the sultan's

sons. Is that correct?" Azura queried him. "Their position must give them a certain power."

Amir nodded. "Yes, it does. Family is all-important to the Ottomans. All of their children are welcomed into this world, and cherished, but particularly sons. And when a sultan dies, his successor's mother gains the stature of becoming Sultan Valideh. It is she who controls the harem along with the official known as the Agha Kislar," he explained.

"How many *kadins* does your uncle have?" Azura asked.

"Three," Amir told her, "and one of those three is a very dangerous woman. Her name is Besma. It is said that she engineered the death of my cousin Mustafa, who was my uncle's eldest-born, the son of his *kadin* Kiusem. Nothing could be proved against Besma, however, and her son, Ahmed, my uncle's second-born son, became the oldest. She is a very jealous woman, and too often my uncle gives in to her simply so she will cease her nagging. Fortunately his Agha Kislar, Hadji Bey, does not like *kadin* Besma. He favors the younger of Kiusem's sons, Selim, and so his master's difficult *kadin* is usually prevented these days from her mischief."

"Yet she murdered a prince," Azura noted.

"Never proved," Amir reiterated. "When I learn who watches, we will know more," he promised her.

But the watcher was clever. He obviously suspected he had been discovered.

Before Amir might ride out and surprise him, the watcher disappeared. Still curious, Amir considered going to Istanbul, but realized his appearance uninvited in the capital might offend his uncle. Instead he sent a message to the Agha Kislar with his own trusted Diya al Din. The head eunuch of the prince's household had been trained with Hadji Bey.

Hadji Bey was surprised to see his old companion. It had been years since the two had met, for Diya al Din had served Prince Amir's mother first. The prince's eunuch waited for two days before the great Agha Kislar was able to see him, but Hadji Bey welcomed him warmly, expressing his regret that his old friend had been forced to wait.

Diya al Din waved the Agha Kislar's concerns aside. "There is no emergency," he said. "It was pleasant to wait, and be waited upon. I cannot recall the last time I was free of my duties as head eunuch of Prince Amir's household."

"Sit, sit," the Agha invited.

Immediately slaves brought hot mint tea and small sweet pastries for the two men. For a brief time they sat together enjoying the refreshments.

"Now tell me why you have come," Hadji Bey finally asked his guest. "You say it is no emergency, yet I suspect it may be important, else Prince Amir would not have sent you to me. How may I serve him?"

"Someone has been watching the Moonlight Serai," Diya al Din said. "When my master sought to learn the identity of the watcher, he had fled. Do you know of this?"

"No," the Agha Kislar said, "I do not, but *kadin* Besma has of late begun to lobby once again with the sultan over Prince Amir's presence so close to Istanbul." He clapped his hands together, and instantly a slave was by his side, leaning down to receive the Agha's whispered instructions. The slave ran off, and Hadji Bey said, "We will shortly know if that troublesome woman is involved. I spend more of my time these days preventing her mischief than I should have to," he grumbled. "If she is responsible for this, she has kept it secret, for I have several spies in her household and have heard nothing.

Now, tell me of your prince's child. Is it indeed a girl, or was that simply a ruse to keep the infant safe for the time being?"

"No, no!" Diya al Din exclaimed. " 'Tis a little princess in truth. They have named her Atiya. She has dark hair like her parents, and fine bright blue eyes. Her mother is very beautiful, and the baby promises to be too."

"She is doted upon?" Hadji Bey said with a smile.

Diya al Din chortled. "Oh yes!" he replied. "The prince's first two wives are sterile, and you can imagine their delight over Princess Atiya. They have already made a true demanding little Ottoman of her. The lady Azura has scolded them about it, but then the baby will do something outrageous and they all laugh over her antics. As for my master, he is like all fathers of daughters. Besotted."

The Agha Kislar listened, a smile upon his dark face, but he was gauging the truth of Diya al Din's words. This eunuch was no less loyal to his own master than the Agha was to the sultan, but the more he listened, the more Hadji Bey was convinced that his guest spoke the truth. Prince Amir's child was indeed a female. Not that he would not make absolutely certain eventually with his own spies. There would be time enough for that.

The Agha's slave returned and murmured in his master's ear before moving from the small comfortable chamber where the two eunuchs sat companionably.

"It is as I suspected," Hadji Bey said, his tone edged with anger. "*Kadin* Besma spies upon Prince Amir's household, though she could actually learn little if nothing from a distance. Is it possible there is a spy among your slaves? A new purchase, perhaps? Allah forgive me, but if there were a way of ridding my master of that damned woman, I would take it."

"The household I manage is small," Diya al Din said. "I have brought no new slaves into it for years. Still, I will investigate when I return and will report to you."

"Then the stupid woman wastes her time," the Agha Kislar said. "But why she would do so is of more concern to me. It will take some careful investigation on my part, and that will take time. Return to Prince Amir, and tell him what I have told you, Diya al Din. Your master has a friend in me. Should *kadin* Besma be plotting any mischief against him I will learn of it, and do my best to prevent it."

"I am grateful for your friendship," Diya al Din said, and he was. He left Istanbul and returned to the Moonlight Serai. He did not like harem politics. They were always dangerous. Praise Allah the women of his household were sensible females.

Chapter 18

The mother of Sultan Bayezit's eldest living son, Ahmed, was a jealous woman. She had borne one son, and doted upon him to the exclusion of everything else. She was very beautiful, and she was fascinating. She had lover's skills unlike any other of the sultan's *kadins*. Bayezit was both repelled and fascinated by her, which was why she remained in his favor. He knew she was involved somehow in the death of his son Mustafa, but as no proof had been forthcoming he had no excuse to either accuse her or punish her, much to the sorrow of his other *kadins*, who must now fear for their sons.

The woman he loved best of his *kadins*, Mustafa's mother, Kiusem, had been devastated by the loss of her child, but she had also given the sultan a second child, his youngest son, a boy named Selim. Besma was forever telling the sultan of Selim's alleged faults and weaknesses while crying the accomplishments of her own offspring. Besma meant for Ahmed to follow his father on the throne. She planned to one day be Sultan Valideh, and rule through the son who ruled the empire. She would allow nothing to stand in her way, but for all her power she had made equally powerful enemies.

The return to Turkey of Prince Amir had not pleased her at all. Like Bayezit's three surviving sons, this prince had a legitimate claim to the Ottoman throne, and he was a man. When she dared to question Bayezit about it after a particularly satisfying evening in his bed, he had told her that his nephew had been expelled from Florence.

"For what reason?" She pursued the matter intently. "What did he do that they would ask you to remove him? He cannot be very wise to have offended so greatly. He obviously grows more like his traitorous father every day. What a pity, for I know he was of great use to you there. But of course, like your brother, he thought only of himself, and not of his duty to his sultan," Besma said. She would not allow another rival to threaten Ahmed.

"I believe it had to do with a lady," the sultan had told her, beginning to be irritated by her shrill tone. "He became too involved with a woman from an important family, and they objected."

"The Florentines are as debauched as Romans," Besma responded, parroting what she had heard from harem gossip. "I do not believe your nephew was banished for his involvement with a woman. I think he is in league with the di Medici family, and means to have your throne with their aid. If not now, one day in the future. He plans to supplant your sons, my lord. We are all in danger from this prince. He is worse than his father, for he pretends loyalty and friendship. At least

Prince Jem is honest in his desire to be sultan," the *kadin* Besma said.

Her words disturbed Bayezit, but try as he might he could find no fault with his nephew. The sultan had given Amir the opportunity to throw in with his father by sending him to Rhodes, but Amir had shown not the slightest disloyalty. Captain Mahmud had reported his nephew's every move. The sultan even had several spies in his brother's house, thanks to his Agha Kislar. They had confirmed Amir's strict allegiance to the sultan alone and his anger that his father could not be made to see reason. Bayezit was absolutely convinced that his nephew was faithful.

"Amir has no desire to rule," he told his *kadin*. "Of that I am certain."

"How certain will you be when he slays your sons, my lord? You must act now to prevent such a tragedy, such a miscarriage of justice," the *kadin* Besma insisted.

"Woman! You are a viper at my breast," the sultan accused her. "I will hear no more of this foolishness you prattle. The day is coming when I will have you sewn into a silk bag weighed down with stones, and order it sent to the bottom of the sea!" And he sent her from his bed. Her amorous skills were not worth listening to the constant stream of vitriol that poured forth from her mouth. He was no fool, and understood that her interest in Amir was not for him. It was for her son, Ahmed, whom she hoped would succeed him. She would do whatever she had to do to keep the path to his throne clear for her child.

After his eldest son's untimely death, he thought Ahmed might one day be worthy, but Besma had spoiled his second son for such responsibility by indulging him in numerous vices that left him self-indulgent and lacking in self-discipline. His third son, Korkut, offspring of *kadin* Safiye, was a serious scholar and not the least bit interested in ruling. He was a young man who was monastic in all things, living simply and always surrounded by books. It was Bayezit's youngest son, Selim, for whom the sultan had high hopes. Even now the boy governed the province delegated to him with a sure hand, and scrupulous attention to the law, which pleased Bayezit most of all.

He knew that eventually Besma would seek to remove Selim, as she was rumored to have removed his brother. For now, however, she had fixated all her attention upon his brother Jem's son. He was sultan, and yet he was helpless to curtail her ambition. Short of having her strangled and sewn into a silk sack to be dropped into the Bosphorus, as he had previously threatened her, he must rely upon his Agha Kislar to keep Besma in check and Prince Amir safe. A snort of laughter escaped him. The world believed him to be all-powerful, invincible. Any man who truly believed he was such was a fool, and deserved whatever he got from life, Bayezit thought wryly.

The visit paid to Hadji Bey by Diya al Din, and the subsequent information he had received from the spies he had in *kadin* Besma's household, had alerted the Agha Kislar to the need to protect Prince Amir and his household. It would not be easy, for women like Besma, who believed they were protecting their children, were like wild beasts. The Agha knew what needed to be done. First, however, he must convince the sultan that it was the best course to take. Prince Amir must leave Turkey again, and this time he could not return. His exile must be permanent. But where was he to go? That would be the largest problem they had to face. Could he remain within the sultan's purview? Or would he have to return to Western Europe?

I must investigate further and think on it, the Agha said to himself. The problem with Western Europe was that Amir could not take all three of his wives with him. And if he went alone, or took the wife of his heart that Diya al Din had spoken of, what would happen to the other two? Their families would eventually learn of it, and be insulted. They might join forces with the sultan's enemies. And while not in love with his first and second wives, Prince Amir was fond of them. An equitable man, he would not cast them off or leave them again.

Florence, Rome, and Venice were all out of the question. France was no better. And beyond France? England. But the English were engaged in a civil war among their kings right now. It was hardly a safe place for an Ottoman prince with three wives. It was also unlikely that the English would allow such a guest to take up permanent residence in their realm, even if the sultan paid for his nephew's refuge and peace.

Was there a place within his master's realm for an Ottoman prince with a direct and strong claim to the throne? Some unimportant and distant location where they might secrete and settle Prince Amir and his family in safety? Some area that would not draw *kadin* Besma's notice? What nameless and obscure locale was available to them for a man who had no desire to rule but simply wished to live quietly with his wives and child? And then it came to him.

El Dinut! A small fiefdom on the North African coast whose current ruler, the dey, had actually been a friend and companion of the Conqueror himself. Loyal to Bayezit, he would, if asked by the sultan, give discreet sanctuary to Prince Amir and his family. It was unlikely that *kadin* Besma would ever know what had happened to the prince once he was gone, and they would see that something else took her attention, thus diverting her from further mischief.

Yes! El Dinut was certainly the answer to their problems. Its climate was agreeable and Prince Amir would be able to conduct his small trading venture from one of its easily accessible harbors. There would, of course, have to be a slight change in Prince Amir's identity for extra security. His title would no longer be used. He would become simply Amir ibn Mehmet, a well-to-do merchant.

Hadji Bey spoke with the sultan, outlining his plan. The sultan approved, and gave his Agha Kislar permission to write to the dey of El Dinut in the sultan's name. The letter was sent by a single messenger who traveled quickly, returning two months later with the dey's answer. Haroun al Hakim, dey of El Dinut, would welcome Prince Amir gladly, he wrote. He remembered his old friend Sultan Mehmet speaking fondly of this particular grandson. And he would see that the presence of Prince Amir and his family was kept discreet. Hadji Bey shared this news with the sultan, who now reluctantly agreed it was time for his nephew to go.

Kadin Besma had continued to lobby her lord about his nephew despite his refusal to pay attention to her concerns. She had even involved the other *kadins*, who might dislike her (and they did) but also considered another male heir one too many. While the other *kadins* did not really believe that Amir constituted a threat, there was always his father, Prince Jem, hovering like a bad smell in the background. An undercurrent of turmoil ran through the sultan's harem, and Bayezit did not like it. If removing his nephew was what it would take to bring peace and order back to his household, he would do it.

Besma, however, had her own plans. It never occurred to her that there might be a way of removing Prince Amir other than violence. As one of the sultan's favorites, she had amassed a great deal of her own wealth over the years. Now she planned to use some of that gold to solve the problem of Amir. The eunuch who served her personally, Taweel, was utterly devoted to her. Unusually tall, thin, and black as night in color, Taweel was Besma's link to the world outside of the harem. He could come and go without question and with impunity, even if she could not. He was her eyes and ears.

Now, upon her order, he set out into the city to seek a man who was known by only the single name Sami. The name meant "all knowing." It was said of Sami that whatever you wanted, desired, or needed, he knew where to find it, and for a price would obtain it for you. Besma wanted a troop of ruthless and murderous Tartars who would sweep down upon the Moonlight Serai, murdering its inhabitants and destroying the little palace. They would be well paid, half in advance, half upon the satisfactory completion of their task. They were free to carry off the women in the Moonlight Serai and take slaves, but the lord of the palace was to be slain without mercy.

"For proof of his death my mistress would have the gold signet ring he always wears on his right hand," Taweel told Sami. "And the finger upon which he wears it as well. The ring could be stolen, but the finger will be the actual evidence that the task has been completed to my mistress's satisfaction."

The broker of all things possible considered the tall eunuch's request, and then he said, "And am I apt to face a troop of Janissaries come to peel the skin from my bones if I find what it is you seek?" Sami demanded. "I know from whom you come, Taweel, and whom you serve. This is a dangerous business you propose."

"But you will do it," Taweel said, smiling, and his large white teeth were fearsome in his black face. "The commission you collect will be a fat one, my greedy friend."

"It will be very costly," Sami replied. "*Very, very costly.*"

"She will pay," Taweel responded. "Now find her the Tartars she wants, and send to me when you have them so I may personally come to give them their instructions." The eunuch handed Sami a small bag of gold coins, which the purveyor of all things mentally weighed in his palm. "A small retainer for your services," Taweel said, and then returned to the palace to report to his mistress the success of his mission.

"He will be discreet?" Besma asked her servant.

"His life and his livelihood both depend upon his discretion," Taweel assured her. "But if you so desire, I can slit his throat once the mission had been accomplished, lady."

"It is to be considered," Besma responded. "And we might recoup some of my gold too. But then I might need him again one day, so perhaps I will let him live."

Hadji Bey did not yet know of Besma's intentions towards Prince Amir, for she had shared her thoughts only with her minion. The Agha had taken it upon himself to make a rare and secret visit outside of the palace, leaving quietly in the dark of night when even the most curious eyes and ears slept. He traveled in the company of only one man, Captain Mahmud, whom he knew the prince had come to trust. They traveled quickly.

Their arrival at the Moonlight Serai was greeted with great surprise by Diya al Din, who practically fell over his own silk slippers when a slave came to tell him of the Agha Kislar's presence in the house. "My lord Agha!" he greeted his guest, and he bowed respectfully to the great man.

"I have come to speak privily with your master," Hadji Bey said.

Diya al Din hesitated a moment. He didn't know whether he should run and fetch the prince immediately or settle his two guests in the salon first. Finally he decided on the latter. "Come," he told them, leading them into the charming light-filled chamber with its view of the gardens beyond the windows. "Let me make you comfortable before I go to fetch my lord Amir." He signaled slaves to come with fruit sherbets and sweet cakes and a bowl of pistachio nuts even as he settled them. The Agha Kislar looked weary to Diya al Din's sharp eye. How quickly had they traveled?

Satisfied that the guests were comfortable, Diya al Din ran for his master. He found him in his own small privy chamber planning the next year's voyages of his three ships.

"My lord, my lord! The sultan's great Agha Kislar has just arrived to speak with you!" the eunuch burst out, unable to keep the excitement from his own voice.

Amir jumped up. "Hadji Bey himself? Allah! What has happened? Where have you put him? Quickly! Quickly! Take me to him!" He swiftly followed Diya al Din to the salon where his guests waited. Seeing Captain Mahmud with the Agha, the prince's eyes grew wary. "What has happened?" he asked them. "No, my lord Agha, do not get up. Stay seated and be comfortable." He joined them. "Tell me my uncle is well."

"The sultan is healthy and well," the Agha responded,

impressed that the prince's first concern had been for Bayezit. "I apologize for startling you, but I could not send a message ahead of my coming, for this trip has been made in the utmost secrecy from all but my master. You and your family are in grave danger, my lord prince. It is the sultan's wish that you be relocated in secret from your home here to El Dinut, where its dey has agreed to welcome and shelter you."

"Why are we in danger, and why is that danger so great that we must leave in a clandestine manner?" Amir wanted to know.

"There are those who have the sultan's ear who do not trust in your goodwill, my lord. They would have your uncle dispose of you and your family in a more traditional manner," Hadji Bey said quietly.

A small wry smile touch Amir's lips. "Kill me, in other words," he said.

The Agha Kislar nodded in the affirmative.

"But I have done nothing to cause anyone to be suspicious of me," Amir pointed out. "I have served my uncle with honor, and all I wish is to live peaceably."

"Your uncle knows that, my lord. The suspicions are not his, but others continue to carp on your near presence. You know that the sultan prefers settling these family matters in a pacific manner. The dey of El Dinut is an old friend of your grandfather's. He is ready to welcome you and your family to his small kingdom. Captain Mahmud and a troop of his Janissaries will be stationed in El Dinut at the invitation of the dey. It is on the sea, and you will simply be another merchant to the citizens of El Dinut. To forgo any curiosity, you will not use your title. You will be known simply as Amir ibn Mehmet, a wealthy merchant who has settled himself in El Dinut."

"This is not a request, Hadji Bey, is it?" the prince said.

"No, my lord, it is not," the Agha Kislar replied with a sigh. Then he added, "There are many advantages to making this great change in your life. You are able to take your whole family with you, and all of your possessions, your slaves, your animals. But most important of all, you will be as far away as you were when you lived in Florence."

"In other words, once I am out of sight you will be able to divert those who are fearful and irritated by my near presence from causing my uncle any embarrassment by creating an unseemly carnage. Such an unfortunate event could be made public, thereby tarnishing his reputation as a just ruler," Amir said shrewdly.

The Agha nodded. "Indeed, my lord, indeed," he said with a faint smile. "But, of course, your exodus must be quick and discreet. Your whereabouts must be kept secret from all but a few. Are your own ships available to transport you?"

"It can be arranged," Amir said. "I am only just now setting the voyage schedule for the year ahead. It is a long and difficult journey you are asking me to make with three women, and a child barely out of infancy."

"Would you rather see your women murdered, or carried off into slavery? And what of your daughter? She is an Ottoman princess even if she never knows it," Hadji Bey said. "Does she not deserve to be raised by her mother in a safe place?"

Amir felt a flash of anger, but he restrained himself from any outburst. It was not the fault of the Agha Kislar that they must leave the Moonlight Serai. Hadji Bey had not said it, but Amir knew without being told it was his uncle's *kadin* Besma who was responsible for all of this trouble. It was the Agha's duty to make certain the sultan's household ran smoothly, and that his *kadins* brought Bayezit pleasure. Besma's ambition for her only son was well known.

Amir had never before cared one way or another for power other than the power over his own life. Today, however, he wished he had the authority to make Besma disappear. The woman was a thorn in everyone's slipper. Her madness and her ambition were beyond impossible. That she had the ability to wreak such havoc with his own life and the lives of his small family infuriated the prince. However, as he was not a man for murder himself, he knew he must accept his uncle's will in this matter as the best solution.

He held no animosity for his cousin Ahmed. Ahmed would never rule, no matter what his mother thought. She had ruined him in her efforts to bind him to her by indulging his vices instead of teaching him to control them. Ahmed preferred forbidden wines and sating his lustful nature to the possibility that he would one day rule his father's and his grandfather's expanding empire. He had no interest in governance, as the province he was charged with ruling showed by its disorder.

And yet his ambitious mother could not see it. What Besma saw was Ahmed as the next sultan, and herself ruling through him. And to foster her ambition, Amir and his family must now flee to the tiny fiefdom of El Dinut. He must uproot himself and leave the home he loved to protect them all. Amir ibn Jem was not happy, but he also knew that he really had no choice.

"How much time do we have?" he asked the Agha.

"I would send your women away as quickly as possible," Hadji Bey said. "While we were traveling to reach you, Captain Mahmud told me of a rumor that reached his ear just before we departed Istanbul." He looked to the Janissary.

"The corps has spies everywhere, as you know, my lord," Captain Mahmud began. "Recently one of them, knowing my friendship with you, came to tell me that a man in the city who is known as a broker of all things—his name is Sami—has sent out a call for a troop of Tartars. *Kadin* Besma's personal eunuch, Taweel, was seen coming from Sami's place of business just before that request was circulated. I feel those Tartars are meant to attack the Moonlight Serai. You have no defenses for this palace, my lord. You are vulnerable to such an attack."

Amir could no longer control his irritation. "You are the most powerful man in the palace, Hadji Bey," he said angrily. "Can you do nothing to stop this damned woman? My wife is only just now recovered from childbirth after almost eight months, and Atiya is not even a year old. Now I must expose them to the rigors of a long journey! Certainly my uncle knows how duplicitous this *kadin* is."

"She *pleases* him in his bed in a way no other woman does," Hadji Bey said candidly. "He believes he needs her, and depends upon me to control her. Short of cutting out her tongue or slitting her throat . . ." The Agha shrugged. "Your uncle's responsibilities are great, my lord prince. He must have what pleases him, and it is my duty to see that he does." Then he reminded Amir, "And it is your duty to obey the sultan's commands."

"I know, I know," Amir responded. "I am grateful he has even considered making provision for me, and I will obey. Have I not always done my duty by the sultan, Hadji Bey? I am his most loyal servant."

"You have, my lord, you have," the Agha replied. "And now that we have settled this matter, I would see your daughter so I may tell the sultan of her when I return."

"Krikor," the prince called to his faithful slave, who stood quietly on one side of the salon. "Tell Ali Farid that I wish the lady Azura to bring our daughter here so the Agha Kislar may see her."

"At once, my lord!"

Several minutes later Azura came into the chamber carrying her child. She was dressed in a lavender silk kaftan trimmed in gold and silver threads. A sheer pale pink silk covered her dark hair, and she was veiled. The baby was dressed in a soft pink robe. She was rosy cheeked, her bright blue eyes looking around her. The young mother bowed to her husband, and to Hadji Bey.

"This is my third wife, Azura," the prince said, "and our daughter, Atiya."

Hadji Bey reached out to loosen the veil covering Azura's face. His fingers, she noted, were long and elegant. He looked at her admiringly with the distinct eye of a connoisseur, then refastened the veil. "Her eyes are extraordinary," he said. "She is beautiful enough for your uncle's harem." Then he fingered one of Atiya's loose raven curls. "The child is a mixture of you both," he noted. "She has your stubborn chin, my lord, but her mother's sweet mouth. I shall tell the sultan that Atiya is a true Ottoman princess."

"Return to the harem, beloved," Amir murmured to Azura. "I will come later, and tell you everything that has happened this day."

With a polite nod of her head, Azura left the men. There had been a third man in the salon. He wore the uniform of the

Janissaries. He had taken a quick look when Hadji Bey had unveiled her, but then as quickly averted his eyes politely. She wondered who he was, but Amir would tell her later. Maysun and Shahdi were waiting excitedly for her.

"What does the great Hadji Bey want of our husband?" Maysun asked.

"I don't know," Azura replied. "He said he would come later and tell us."

"They will remain the night," Shahdi said. "It is much too late in the day now for them to return to Istanbul. Amir will entertain them."

"With what?" Maysun demanded to know. "We have no dancing girls."

"Food and drink, of course," Shahdi responded. "They will talk, like all men do, and probably gamble together."

"A poor welcome for the sultan's Agha Kislar," Maysun said. "If only we had known he was coming. I wonder why he did not send ahead."

Azura handed Atiya off to Agata. "We can wonder all we want," she said. "We will know nothing until Amir comes."

He came long after the sun had set that day, but the three women waited, for a visit from the sultan's Agha Kislar was a rare—indeed, an almost unheard-of—event. He looked tired, and he looked worried. They settled him comfortably in the single cushioned chair that was meant only for him, and seated themselves around him on low stools. Amir looked at them and sighed deeply. "We must leave the Moonlight Serai almost immediately," he began, and the three women gasped in shock.

Amir held up his hand to stem the flow of their questions temporarily. Then he went on to tell them everything the Agha Kislar had told him. He told them what he believed with regard to the sultan's *kadin* Besma. Then he concluded, "We have no choice. To remain at the Moonlight Serai invites danger at the least, death more likely. I will not give the lives of my family merely to quell the madness of one woman's ambition for her son. We must go, but at least my uncle has provided a safe haven for us."

"But we have always lived here," Maysun said.

"From the time your grandfather gave us to you," Shahdi added.

"Where is El Dinut?" Azura wanted to know.

Amir smiled. His first two wives could not see beyond today. Azura, praise Allah, had wisdom. "El Dinut is on the Mediterranean Sea. It is a long journey from the Moonlight Serai," he replied. "We will have to travel by ship."

Azura nodded. "Will it take us as long as it took when you and I came from Venice?" she asked him.

"A little longer, beloved. El Dinut is nearer the Italian states and France," he explained. "I want the women to go first, within the next few days."

"Yes, Maysun and Shahdi must go first," Azura agreed. "I want them to take Atiya with them." She spoke as if the others were not even in the room. "I will remain to see that the household is packed up, and then come with you, my lord."

"You must go with the others," he told her.

"No," Azura responded. "I will not leave until you leave. I did not give up my people to be without you, Amir."

"Besma's Tartars could come, and I would be slain," he said.

"If that happens, if there is no hope, then I will die with you, my lord, but I will not leave you," Azura replied quietly, adding, "Nor will I become slave to some Tartar."

He wanted to argue with her, but he saw the determination in her beautiful eyes. Those wonderful eyes that had first attracted him to her. She was brave enough to stand by his side, and while his every instinct was to force her to go, he would not. "Very well," he said. "We will depart together, but the others must go ahead of us with Atiya."

"Will Agata come with us?" Maysun asked.

"Yes," Azura answered her. "The voyage will be long and dull. And it may be difficult at times. She will be of more use to you than your pretty little handmaidens, especially with Atiya. And when you reach El Dinut she will be of great value to you as you settle yourselves in this new place. I am certain the dey will host you until we are able to find ourselves a new home in which to live."

Shahdi began to cry. "I do not want to leave here," she said. "We are happy here."

"We will be happy wherever we are because we will be together," Maysun said, for she could be a practical woman. "We will begin packing up our possessions in the morning. If we must go, then the sooner, the better! I have no wish to find myself standing over some Tartar's cooking fire or in his bed. Do you, Shahdi?"

The second wife looked horrified at such a suggestion. While both women had been born into seminomadic cultures, ending up in an Ottoman prince's household had been a marvelous fate for them. They had lived in luxury for enough time that they did not want to return to anything like their previous life. "No!" Shahdi said emphatically in reply to her fellow wife's query. "No!" she repeated.

Before the Agha Kislar departed the following morning, he promised Prince Amir, "I will do my best to stop *kadin*

Besma from sending her Tartars, but do not depend upon it. She is a resourceful female. She will use poison, a single assassin, whatever means she can find to gain her objective until I may turn her attention in another direction. Do not delay, my lord prince, but know you go with your uncle's blessings."

"Such knowledge is comforting under the circumstances," Amir replied drily.

The Agha Kislar laughed aloud at the prince's sarcasm but said nothing further. There was nothing left to say. There were times when he blessed his absence of lust and this was one of them. That the whims of one woman could be responsible for the disruption of an entire family struck him as ridiculous. Nonetheless, the sultan believed he needed this particular *kadin*, and the sultan's wishes must be considered. Hadji Bey returned to Istanbul determined to foil *kadin* Besma.

At the Moonlight Serai the entire populace of the little palace was now told of the evacuation to come. Messengers were dispatched overland to Istanbul to the captains of Prince Amir's three vessels now docked in the port. The first of the ships sailed immediately, anchoring two days later in the cove below their master's home. Its large cargo hold was immediately loaded with household goods and the personal possessions of the first two wives and the baby.

Agata came to bid her mistress farewell. She was not pleased by this sudden change in their lives. "I do not want to leave you," she said. "Who will take care of you if I am not here, mistress?"

"I need you to look after Atiya," Azura told her. "God forbid anything should happen to me; who would tell Atiya of her heritage? Maysun and Shahdi love my daughter, I know, but it is you, Agata, that I entrust with her life. The prince and

I will not be far behind you, I promise. There is only a little left to do." She wrapped her arms around her faithful servant and hugged her. "Go with God, Agata."

"I will not fail you, mistress," Agata promised, brushing away the tears that had suddenly overcome her and begun to slip down her worn cheeks.

"I know you won't," Azura said, patting the woman on her arm. "Go now!" She watched sadly as Agata departed the harem. This would be the first time in all of her life that she had been without Agata's companionship and care. Earlier, Azura had bidden her child farewell, nursing her a final time, drinking in her infant beauty, before kissing the sleepy baby and turning her over to the slave woman who would now be responsible for Atiya's nourishment.

One of their own household now, the slave woman had recently weaned her own child. She was healthy and grateful to be taken from the prince's farm fields into his household staff along with her child, also a little girl, who would serve as a playmate for Atiya. And she was grateful to Agata, who had discovered her and suggested her to the beautiful third wife, who everyone knew was the prince's true love.

Now Azura watched as Agata joined Maysun, Shahdi, and the rest of the women servants trekking down to the beach, where they were ferried out to the large vessel at anchor awaiting them. The second of the prince's ships was now also anchored in the cove and had been being filled all day with the rest of Prince Amir's possessions and with the slaves. The third ship was due on the morrow. It would carry the prince and Azura, along with his horses. Azura's cat had been sent with Agata, for Atiya enjoyed its antics. Darius, the prince's favorite hound, would travel with his master.

She watched from the empty harem as the first two vessels finally weighed anchor and departed. They were now alone but for Diya al Din and half a dozen male slaves who cared for the horses. They ate a cold meal that the cook had left them the night before. Afterwards, Azura walked through the little palace thinking how sad and lonely it now was without the inhabitants who gave it life. Even in her husband's bed with Amir next to her, the night seemed extra dark and silent.

Azura hardly slept. Every sound was cause for suspicion. Dawn brought little relief from the fear that had suddenly crept into her. She sensed something she could not quite put her finger upon, but it was not good. The skies above were gray with the threat of rain. Amir had the horses in the stable led down to the beach to await his third ship. The sea was oddly calm, and they could see their ship's sails on the horizon as the vessel came nearer and nearer.

"I think it better that we wait on the beach," the prince told her as he draped a long dark cloak over her shoulders.

Azura felt a pang of sadness. It was time to bid good-bye to the Moonlight Serai. A home she had come to love. A place where she had been happy, where her only child had been born. She sighed deeply. It was surprisingly painful. She had not ever felt such an emotion, not even upon leaving her childhood palazzo in Florence.

It was at that moment that Diya al Din hurried into the chamber. "My lord, there is a large party of horsemen on the hills above the palace. We must leave quickly, my lord!" His face was pale with his fear.

"Come!" Amir said, leading both his wife and his servant from the chamber. They hurried into the gardens and taking the path from its far end moved quickly down the steep route to the beach below. There they found the two barges from the prince's ship already loading the horses for transport out to the vessel that had just arrived in their little harbor. The blindfolded animals were being led quickly onto the flat carriers, which were then rowed out to the waiting ship. A door in the vessel's side was opened, a ramp pushed forth, and each horse was led into the cargo hold, where stalls had been built especially for the beasts and their grooms.

It but remained for a boat to come ashore to pick up the prince, his wife, and Diya al Din. His chief household eunuch suddenly gasped, growing almost gray, and pointing to the horsemen upon them. The prince pushed Azura to Diya al Din and drew his scimitar. "Get her to the boat!" he shouted. "Carry her through the water if you must!"

"I'm not leaving you, Amir!" Azura cried, shoving the eunuch away.

It was too late. The horsemen surrounded them. Fierce Tartars with dark eyes and long moustaches. Their horses danced about the three. But then their leader, a young man, burst out laughing, realizing that they believed him to be the enemy. "Amir! Do you not recognize me? I am your cousin Selim," he called out, jumping down from his stallion.

The prince felt the tension in his shoulders ease. He had not seen Selim since he was ten. The young man clearly was several years older now. Was he fifteen? Sixteen? Seventeen? He looked well-grown. "I thought you were governing your province, cousin. And where did you get your Tartars? Surely they are not the ones hired by *kadin* Besma to kill me and my family."

"No, no," Selim replied. "The bitch's Tartars are just now descending upon your home. They will be very disappointed to find it emptied of chattel, livestock, and goods, for I'm certain they were promised all they could loot in addition to the monies that have been paid them for this foul deed. As soon as you are safely aboard your vessel, we will go up and engage them. Now give me your gold signet ring. Besma wants it as proof you have been slain, and if my men are to collect the other half of her bounty, we will need it. She did ask for your finger, so we shall have to find one upon which to put your ring, lest any suspicions remain in her dark heart."

Amir burst out laughing. "You mean to steal her gold from her, Selim? You will slay her hired men and substitute your own for her assassins with the purveyor of all things, Sami? And how in the name of Allah and the seven djinns did you learn of what was to transpire here? No! Do not tell me. I think I know, but better you not confirm it." He pulled the gold signet ring from his finger and tossed it to his cousin. "Here, and with my blessing," he said. "Of course it will be difficult to find a finger as elegant as mine," he teased the younger prince, "but if it means she believes me dead, so much the better. But poor Ahmed will never rule, no matter her efforts."

Selim's gray eyes met his cousin's deep blue ones. He nodded, saying softly, "No, he will not, cousin." Prince Selim then held out his hand to Prince Amir to shake. The two men embraced. "Allah keep you safe, cousin," Selim said.

"And you also, cousin," Amir replied. "Whenever you have need of my loyalty, it is yours to command, Selim."

"I will remember that," the younger man said. "Now go quickly!"

The little boat transporting them out to Amir's ship was awaiting him. Diya al Din and Azura were already in it. He waded out and climbed aboard, turning to give a final wave to Prince Selim. His cousin acknowledged the salute from his saddle, and then, turning, raced up the hillside with his own Tartars. Almost immediately they could hear the shouts of battle beginning as the sultan's son and his men met the assassins of *kadin* Besma, who found themselves outnumbered but were deterred from flight.

Aboard the larger ship at last, Azura stood by the rail as it set sail. Her eyes went to the Moonlight Serai, shining and white in the sunlight, cradled by the soft green hills that surrounded it. She felt Amir's arm go about her shoulders as the sadness threatened to overwhelm her. She could see the small figures of the Tartars battling through their gardens, flames rising from the empty barn that had once housed their horses. "I do not know this Besma," Azura said, "but I think for the first time in my life I hate someone."

"She is not worthy of your scorn," Amir told Azura. "And all of her efforts are for naught, beloved. We are together, and we are capable of making a new life in El Dinut for ourselves and for our family. I believe our destiny is to live into old age, happy together. We will see our daughter grow to womanhood, marry, and give us grandchildren. These things will never be Besma's, but they will be ours."

"I pray for it, Amir," she responded, but her heart was still sad to see the place that had once been their home being destroyed. Would it ever again be someone's home?

"I am an expert reader of kismet, beloved," he told her. "It shall be as I say. Do you trust and believe in me, my love?" He looked down into her beautiful face, her marvelous aquamarine eyes shining with their unshed tears. Allah! How he loved her.

"I have left everything that I knew and held dear once before for you, Amir," Azura told him, smiling up at him. He was a man grown, and yet he still needed her reassurance, and she gladly gave it to him. "I love you, my infidel prince. I once again gladly follow you because you have never promised me anything that you did not give me. I trust you, Amir. So we will live happily together into our dotage with our grandchildren about us. We are fortunate, my dear lord, when so many are not."

Above them the sails creaked as the wind started to fill them. The vessel began to move slowly from the Moonlight cove and out into the open sea. Azura, once known as Bianca, felt the swells rise gently beneath the ship's prow. It was a new day. A new adventure. Ahead lay El Dinut and their new life. Nothing else mattered. They had allowed no one to part them. No one ever would. They were together. *Always and forevermore!*

And Afterwards

*I*n the year 1512, Selim, son of Bayezit and his favored *kadin* Kiusem, succeeded to the Ottoman throne. He had been recalled to Istanbul by his father months before when Besma's ambition for her son had driven her too far. She had been caught attempting to murder Selim and his now large family. Bayezit had strangled her himself in a blind rage and then suffered what was probably a small stroke.

With his mother's death, Prince Ahmed fled his younger brother, going to Adrianople, where he boldly declared himself sultan. A civil war broke out, but though it took two years' time, Prince Selim was in the end victorious. To his small credit, Ahmed died fighting in that last battle. Prince Korkut remained loyal to his father and his younger sibling, governing the Macedonian provinces.

Bayezit, now sixty-five and in worsening health, decided to resign the sultanate, naming Selim as his heir. The new sultan's uncle, Prince Jem, was now dead. He had died in Naples of poison. It was rumored that the Borgia pope had seen to Jem's demise at the request of Sultan Bayezit, whose patience had run out prior to his retirement. As for Jem's only son, Prince Amir, he had long ago disappeared from his home on the Black Sea along with his entire family. Where they were, or if they even lived, was unknown. Bayezit died shortly after his son's reign began. Selim was free to rule without interference of any kind, as he and his sons were the only male heirs to the throne now.

In the house of Giovanni Pietro d'Angelo, his wife, Orianna, had come to regret that she had not understood her eldest daughter's great love for the Turkish sultan's grandson. She missed Bianca and the warm friendship that they had once shared. Although Marco had made the effort to find and see his sister, bringing them word that she was happy and safe with her infidel, it brought no peace to Orianna.

And Bianca would never know that it was her own mother who had freed her from her first marriage by consorting with the family of the vengeful apothecary whose innocent niece had died at Rovere's debauched hands. It had been Orianna who had insisted to them that she deliver the fatal blow to their mutual enemy. It was Orianna who had plunged the poisoned dagger into the chest of Sebastiano Rovere, killing him and freeing Bianca from his evil possession.

Of course, upon her return to Florence she had gone immediately to Santa Anna and confessed her sin to Father Bonamico. The priest was shocked and briefly rendered speechless when the unrepentant Orianna said to him, "I will do whatever I must to protect my family, good Father. Even if it will endanger my immortal soul." Bound by the oath of the confessional, Bonamico could not expose her. Orianna had relieved her own small guilt at taking a human life by putting it on the elderly priest's shoulders.

He hardly knew what penance to give her because he did understand her motive and secretly agreed with it. Realizing that, he knew he would have to give himself a severe penance as well. "Donate one hundred gold florins to Santa Maria del Fiore," he finally said. "And you will continue to do so each year on this date until your death, my daughter. I will pray for your soul and that you are not again driven to such an extreme."

"Will you not pray for Rovere's soul too?" she wickedly asked him.

"Even his two sons did not pay for Masses," the priest said drily.

The silk merchant's wife had then departed the confessional. She and Giovanni had three other daughters to match. She would be more careful the next time. She would not make the same mistakes with Francesca, or Luciana, or Giulia as had been made with Bianca. Wherever her eldest daughter was, Orianna hoped she was happy. She would have been glad to know that in a place called El Dinut, Bianca, now called Azura, was indeed very happy with her prince and their daughter. The kismet that Amir had promised Azura was even now fulfilling itself.

About the Author

Bertrice Small is a *New York Times* bestselling author and the recipient of numerous awards. In keeping with her profession, she lives in the oldest English-speaking town in the state of New York, founded in 1640. Her light-filled studio includes the paintings of her favorite cover artist, Elaine Duillo, and a large library. Because she believes in happy endings, Bertrice Small has been married to the same man, her hero, George, for forty-eight years. They have a son, Thomas, and four wonderful grandchildren. Longtime readers will be happy to know that Finnegan, the long-haired bad black kitty, and Sylvester, the black-and-white tuxedo cat who is the official family bed cat, are thriving.